"WHAT A[...]

"Kissing you," Nicholas said, stating the obvious, bringing his mouth down on hers once again, unable to stop from tasting her, unable to stop himself from groaning aloud from the pleasure of it.

Still kissing her, for God knew nothing now could make him stop, he led her to her opened cell door, backing into the room and kicking the door closed with his booted foot. Am I mad? he thought as he brought one hand to cover her breast. "Don't think of anyone else, Claire, only me," he whispered harshly against one ear.

"No," she said and pressed her lips against his, not caring what was happening, only that it felt good, so good. I will not think about what he is doing to me, that it is stupid and probably wrong, she thought, closing her eyes. I don't care, I don't care, she thought as she pulled him toward her, even closer. None of this matters. It might not even be really happening. . . .

MEMORIES OF YOU
by Jane Goodger

A TOPAZ BOOK

TOPAZ
Published by the Penguin Group
Penguin Books USA Inc., 375 Hudson Street,
New York, New York 10014, U.S.A.
Penguin Books Ltd, 27 Wrights Lane,
London W8 5TZ, England
Penguin Books Australia Ltd, Ringwood,
Victoria, Australia
Penguin Books Canada Ltd, 10 Alcorn Avenue,
Toronto, Ontario, Canada M4V 3B2
Penguin Books (N.Z.) Ltd, 182–190 Wairau Road,
Auckland 10, New Zealand

Penguin Books Ltd, Registered Offices:
Harmondsworth, Middlesex, England

First published by Topaz, an imprint of Dutton Signet,
a division of Penguin Books USA Inc.

First Printing, February, 1997
10 9 8 7 6 5 4 3 2

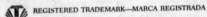 REGISTERED TRADEMARK—MARCA REGISTRADA

Printed in Canada

PUBLISHER'S NOTE
This is a work of fiction. Names, characters, places, and incidents either are
the product of the author's imagination or are used fictitiously, and any resemblance to actual persons, living or dead, events, or locales is entirely
coincidental.

patients. "Yeah. I noticed, too. But I didn't want to say anything because it seems too . . . spooky. Watch this."

Donna, a huge woman cursed with a bulldog face but who had the biggest of hearts, gently moved the woman onto her back. The patient's heart rate increased slightly. Across the hall, the man's heart responded in kind, the monotonous beep of the heart monitor picking up a beat. Within a minute, she turned back toward him, let out a soft sigh, outstretching her hand. Then she was still. The man's hand twitched.

The two had been brought in together, both suffering from severe head injuries. The prognosis for them was also similar—and unfavorable, or so the doctors said. But Janice and Donna agreed that they were dealing with an unusual case. They had heard about the patients' arrival. When the man and woman had been brought in, they had both become so agitated when they were separated, the doctors had been forced to keep them in close proximity. They had even debated for a short time whether to put them in the same room—something that was against regulation.

Perhaps the strangest thing of all was that as far as anyone knew, the woman and the man did not know each other. They had met for the first time before boarding the helicopter, and according to an officer who'd been there, they had barely exchanged a word. How then had they forged this unbreakable bond? It was downright creepy, Janice thought. Donna, the romantic of the two, thought they surely must be in love, though she couldn't explain how or why.

"They're perfect for each other." Donna sighed.

Indeed they were. The woman, First Lieutenant Claire Dumont, was a fair-haired beauty, and the man, Captain Coleman Brennan, big and beefy, with short-cropped sandy hair and a face that looked as though it had been carved with a loving hand. Both had taken on the fragile pale beauty of coma patients.

"You're impossible," Janice said, smiling at her friend. Still, she had to agree with Donna. She had a feeling that if they had been placed in the same bed, the two would have curled up together, content to sleep forever in each other's arms.

Chapter One

The Blackhawk helicopter's rotors kicked up a blur of sand as it landed with a soft thump near Seoul, South Korea. The helo and its crew of four had just returned from a routine border patrol near the demilitarized zone, one of the constant stream of patrols that had been monitoring North Korea's activities for years.

Claire Dumont, helicopter crew chief and an army first lieutenant, hopped down from the machine and pulled off the helmet that never failed to give her a raging headache, despite its light weight. The biting air gave her head immediate relief as she ruffled her short hair distractedly. Oblivious to the admiring looks from the ground crew, she headed toward the Humvees parked on a sand-covered road waiting to transport the crew to their barracks.

As usual, First Lieutenant Claire Dumont was oblivious to just about anything that didn't come with bullets or fly in the air. The men, and they were all men in her crew, joked that her heart was made of gunmetal and the rest of her of impenetrable armor. The daughter of a four-star general, the sister of a major and a captain, Claire had always known she would be a soldier. When she was six years old, she had pleaded with her father to allow her to attend an all-male military school in her home state of Virginia. Of course, she had not, for as much as her father thought her interest in things military amusing, he was an old-fashioned sort who believed women had no business wearing a uniform. Not that he would ever come right out and say such a thing to his spitfire daughter. Claire often wondered if he had lived how he would have felt about her flying what was considered borderline combat duty.

Two years earlier, the happiest day of her life, the day she graduated from West Point Academy, became her saddest. Her entire family and twelve others were killed when a small plane crashed in dense woods in New Jersey. They had been on their way to see her graduate third in her class. With their deaths came a burning desire to make her father proud, even though he would not be alive to see it. She pictured him in heaven looking down at her and being begrudgingly proud. Her mother would simply worry about her daughter and her brothers would be rooting her on. It was that image that comforted her when she felt consumed with grief.

With no family and few friends, Claire threw herself into her career. When she was off duty, she studied books on strategic warfare and on the inner workings of the Pentagon. Her hair was cropped short, and more than once clerks at the commissary had called her sir. She never minded. She took it as a compliment.

The thing of it was, she was a beautiful woman, with brilliant blue eyes and softly curling blond hair. And had she bothered to put on a bit of makeup or a flattering dress, she would have been model-pretty. But she might have been a nun for all the interest she outwardly showed in the opposite sex. Claire had decided long ago that in order to make it in a man's military, she must as much as possible act like a man. If she felt attracted to a particular male, she would make sure she kept as far away from him as possible. Claire Dumont had a goal, and falling in love would only distract her. She wanted to be the youngest female general in the history of the Army. A first lieutenant at just twenty-two, she was well on her way.

In the six months she had been stationed in South Korea, she had become something of a legend among the men. One by one they had made an attempt to crack her resistance. Claire simply was not interested. Sometimes late at night as she lay flat on her back, her arms outstretched as if punctuating her aloneness, she wondered if there was something wrong with her. No man had turned her head, at least not far enough for her to give up on her goal. Did there exist a man she could love, who would become her world? She was beginning to think not, and was also beginning to think it was not such a bad thing. Having no ties could only help her remain focused. And your heart didn't break if it wasn't tied to another person. Maybe her heart had shattered so badly when her family died, there was nothing left.

Instead of gracefully accepting rejection, some of the men around her blamed Claire, joking that she was either frigid or preferred other women. Claire knew what they said, but she didn't care. Let them waste their time pursuing women, she'd be spending her time studying military strategy and advancing her career. She was completely and totally happy. That's what she told herself at least once a day and sometimes she actually believed it.

Claire walked across the cold concrete already thinking about the next day's mission. Another captain was expected to join the crew so he could log in the required flight hours, and that always made her nervous. It always seemed that when she had finally gotten comfortable with the men she worked with, there was a change.

"Hey, Dumont, we're headin' for the 'O' for some brews. Coming?" Claire turned to Major Rodney Vera, a painfully thin man with a hound-dog face. The crew always included her, and she almost always declined. Not only did Claire guard her heart against love, but also against friendship, though she would have stubbornly argued she was guarding her career. Seeing her hesitation, Vera said, "Just one. We'll make sure you're tucked in with your rifle by twenty-one hundred."

"Can't," she said with real regret. "I've got to study these new maps. And if I don't do it now, I won't do it, and we'll end up in the demilitarized zone." They both knew how unlikely such an event was, but Vera good-naturedly accepted her decline, and lumbered off to a Humvee full of beer-thirsty men. Claire glanced down at her watch. Sixteen hundred. Damn. It was going to be a long night.

Blood. There was always so much blood. And endless screams.

Capt. Coleman Brennan pressed the heels of his hands against his eyelids trying to push away the feeling of helplessness that overwhelmed him after one of his dreams. Always his dreams were variations of the same theme: violence, blood, and terror-filled screams. But perhaps the worst was the feeling that he could not stop something beyond terrible from happening. He sat up in bed, allowing a sharply cold breeze from his window, open a crack, to dry the sweat covering his body. He glanced out the window, grimacing when he saw the dim glow on the eastern horizon. No sense in trying to get back to sleep now.

Ever since Coleman could remember, he had been plagued with these violent dreams. As a young boy he had been afraid to go to sleep, and so had tried in

vain to remain awake. As a last resort, his mother
had a mild sleeping pill prescribed for her son, whose
haunted eyes wrenched her heart each time she told
him it was time for bed. His doctors said he would
outgrow the nightmares, most children did. Coleman
never did. To allay his parents' fears, he began lying,
telling them the dreams had disappeared. But if anything, the older he got, the more graphic, the more
debilitating the nightmares became. The sense that he
needed to stop something from happening only
increased.

He lay back on his pillow, hands tucked behind his
head, and stared at the acoustic tiles above him. He
refused to let the darkness that touched his soul show.
No one, not his friends, his family, not any of a number of women, knew that something black and evil
lived inside him. All his life he sought to ignore this
corruptness that he believed was an innate part of his
soul. And so he had always tried to do what was right.
Every decision he made was well thought-out, even
those made quickly. He was known to be fair-minded,
if a bit unbending. He loved God and country and so
he made a good soldier, intelligent and loyal. The
dreams came anyway.

Coleman heaved himself out of bed, immediately
throwing himself to the icy tiled floor for fifty pushups,
sweating out the demons that possessed him. Two
hundred stomach crunches, a five-mile run, and Coleman Brennan had pushed aside the darkness that enveloped him each night. He refused to let it rule him.
Indeed, it was such a part of his life he might be
alarmed to sleep the night through in peace.

Claire relaxed by the helicopter and waited for the
crew. She sat on her helmet, elbows on knees, and
watched the approach of the rest of the four-man
crew. Her eyes sought out the new captain and found
him lagging behind chatting with Major Vera. She

couldn't see much of him under his helmet but that he was tall.

"Christ, Lieutenant, do you always have to be first on scene?" asked Capt. Morty Jeffreys, the copilot.

Claire smiled sheepishly. "I thought I was late today," she said honestly in her soft Southern lilt.

"Hell, you might think this was your first flight, not your hundredth. You're making us all look like slackers," Jeffreys complained good-naturedly.

"It doesn't take much to make you guys look like slackers," Claire shot back, grinning. Her eyes went to the new captain. He was smiling at their friendly banter. Claire gave him a casual salute then shot out her hand in greeting.

"Lieutenant Dumont."

"Captain Brennan. Pleased to meet you." Coleman nearly gasped aloud. That touch of hands acted like a switch in his head and gruesome images of blood and sounds of screams engulfed him. No one noticed when his skin turned ashen, or that he dropped her hand too quickly. He was filled with an inexplicable despair. And something else, something absurdly like . . . joy. As quickly as they had come, the images were gone, leaving Coleman reeling.

Coleman turned away, praying no one had noticed his strange reaction to Lieutenant Dumont. His demons had never visited him while he was awake before, and he felt paralyzed by the realization they could invade his waking moments. Why now? If not for his iron control, a control he refused to lose, he would have sunk to the helo pad and cried like a child. He clenched his jaw. He could not lose it here, not in front of the crew, right before a flight. His military career meant everything to him and the horror of being discharged with a Section 8 was a nightmare he refused to accept. I am not insane, he thought fiercely.

He let his gaze travel to Lieutenant Dumont, steeling himself against the visions he feared would besiege him once again. But all he saw was a strikingly beautiful woman deep in conversation with Major Vera. He felt a nudge to his arm.

Captain Jeffreys gave him a knowing grin. "Told ya. All work and no play."

Cole shot the smaller man a crooked grin and shrugged. But his eyes stole over to Claire, who was shoving her helmet on over her leather skullcap with a comical grimace on her face. Jesus, man, get a goddamn grip, he told himself when he realized his heart had picked up a beat. He didn't need or want a relationship now, and certainly not with one of his crew mates.

Within minutes, the crew had left their guts on the ground as the helicopter swiftly rose into a cloudless sky. Coleman and Claire listened to the cockpit chatter in silence. Although they were both hooked up to a shared radio frequency, not a word was exchanged. Cole sat across from Claire and was making a concerted effort to keep his eyes anywhere but on the woman who had evoked such an odd and violent mix of pain and euphoria.

Twenty uneventful minutes into the flight, a teeth-smashing explosion threw them out of their seats. Suddenly the helicopter went into a hellish spin. Claire and Coleman scrambled back into their seats, their hands grasping blindly for support, fear-filled eyes darting around the cabin.

"We're hit, we're hit," came Vera's frantic voice.

Hit? Claire thought crazily. Hit by what? Despite her training, despite the fact she was a soldier working in one of the most dangerous areas of the world, the thought of being hit by enemy fire was absurd. Vera and Jeffreys struggled to keep the helo up, but the explosion had apparently damaged the rear rotors.

"We're going down," Vera said in a voice so calm it was chilling. "May Day! May Day!" The craft tilted violently and Vera cursed as he struggled to maintain some control. The crew was strangely silent, as if accepting their fates, and Claire wanted to shout at someone to do something. Her hands clutched her seat until it cut painfully into the flesh, even through her gloves. Blue sky and brown earth swirled around them as the craft whirled out of control, rushing to the ground at an alarming rate. Claire was seized with a deep panic.

"I don't want to die," a voice inside her screamed. "I don't want to die."

Seconds before the inevitable bone-crunching impact, Claire felt a tug at her hand. She looked down and watched with detachment as Captain Brennan removed her glove. Taking her hand in his warm one, he entwined his fingers through hers, gripping her hand tightly in his. Just before their world went black, Claire looked up into Coleman Brennan's gray eyes then down at her hand, which tingled with a strange electricity. She had never felt so at peace in her life. She couldn't hear the roar of the churning engines or the sounds of desperation from the cockpit. She closed her eyes, lay her head back, and squeezed his hand in hers.

When the helicopter finally crashed, Claire felt one moment of unimaginable pain and fear before she was sucked into a calming blackness.

Chapter Two

"Wake up, dang it!"

Claire shook her head, not wanting her deep sleep to be disrupted. But when she felt a boot dig painfully into her side, she sat up ready to give hell to whoever was being so rude. She wasn't a green recruit anymore and would not be treated like one.

"Who the hell do you . . ." Her voice trailed off as she looked into a filthy face. The man, with a squashed nose, piggy brown eyes, and a dirty, salt-and-pepper beard, peered down at her with disgust. Claire suddenly remembered the crash and looked about her for the rest of the crew, for the wreckage of the helicopter. But what she saw was so unlike what she thought she should, she clamped her mouth shut. She expected to be lying amid the wreckage of the helo. She expected to be hurt, but felt no pain. She expected to be anywhere but lying on this cold, snow-covered ground in the middle of a dense forest.

"Get up, boy. You're holdin' us up and we sure ain't waitin'," the man said.

Claire dragged her gaze back to the man who was shouting at her. He sure wasn't part of any Uncle Sam's Army she'd ever seen and he wasn't North Korean either. He was an American, and from his thick southern accent, he was, like her, a Southerner.

"Where's the crew? Where's the wreckage," Claire asked, rubbing her head in confusion. Her hand stopped and her stomach gave an odd twist when she realized both her skull cap and helmet were gone.

"Boy, I don't have time for coddling. Get your arse in gear, grab your rifle, and git going." The man grabbed the collar of her shirt and heaved her up until she stood unsteadily. He shoved her hard toward where a group of men walked ahead of them, picking their way through thick woods choking with brambles.

Claire was about to angrily announce she was not a boy when she glanced down with puzzlement at the weapon she was holding. It weighed a ton and looked like an antique. A rifle musket, she thought, studying the weapon. She remembered seeing similar ones in her grandfather's collection. Her hand automatically went to her right side. Where was her nine-millimeter sidearm? What the *hell* was going on?

"You ain't refusing to come are you, son?" the man asked with menace. "You know what we do to deserters, don't you?"

Get a grip, Claire, she told herself. Something was very, very wrong here. Think, girl, think. She began walking in the direction the man had shoved her, more to give herself time to figure out what was happening than to obey his command. She glanced down at her attire and panic gripped her. She was no longer wearing her flight suit, and though she could tell it was some sort of uniform, it was nothing she had ever seen before. Her boots, uncomfortable things, were too large for her feet and were made of stiff brown leather instead of the shiny black she had been wearing during the crash. Why would someone have dressed her this way?

"Little pissant all right?" a man wearing lieutenant's bars asked the dirty man.

"Yeah," came the disinterested reply.

"You're not part of this unit, boy. You a deserter?" the lieutenant asked as he fell in step with her. He was no older than she was, Claire thought, but his face was lined from weariness, purple-stained beneath his eyes. He was nearly as dirty as the first man, but neater, and his eyes were kinder.

Claire swallowed, knowing instinctively that she should not tell the man she was a woman. Her hand went up to feel her short locks in a nervous gesture. "I lost my unit, sir. I would never desert." He seemed satisfied, but Claire was becoming more and more alarmed. The landscape, the trees, even the sky looked familiar to her. She knew she was on United States soil. But *I should not be here,* she thought wildly.

You are not where you are supposed to be!

Claire could feel herself beginning to hyperventilate, and forced herself to remain calm. Surely there must be an explanation. Perhaps she was dreaming. Or maybe she had had amnesia and had just woken up in the middle of some crazy war game in which everyone carried antique weapons and wore scruffy uniforms. No. Nothing made sense.

"Sir. I got a knock on the head. I'm a bit confused. I can't remember anything," Claire said hesitantly. "Where are we?" Did she really want to know?

"About thirty miles north of Winchester."

"As in *Virginia*?" Claire tried to stamp out her growing panic, but her heart raced wildly in her breast and a cold sweat broke out, making her shiver uncontrollably.

Lieutenant Jason Leighton gave a hard look. "That's right. Yankees are building up their forces and we're going to head them off. We're joining up with Early's troops if we can get by that damned Sheridan in Winchester." He spit as if even saying the Yankee general's name had somehow contaminated his mouth.

Claire bit back a laugh. "You did say 'Yankees,'

right? I did hear you correctly. Is this some sort of joke. Some sort of war game?"

Lieutenant Leighton stopped impatiently. "Just what is your problem, Private?"

Claire stiffened. "Well, for one thing I'm a lieutenant, sir."

The man was clearly amused. "Well, now. Somehow you got yourself into the wrong uniform, soldier. I don't see any stripes on those puny shoulders."

Claire moved the material on her shoulder, her eyes widening as they took in the empty spot on the grungy uniform. Seeing that plain material frightened her more than ever.

"Is this some sort of a joke? Because if it is, it's not funny anymore," she said quietly. She shook her head. "This isn't right. This is all wrong."

"Well, you got that right, boy," Lieutenant Leighton said bitterly.

For the first time Claire studied the man's uniform. Although it was filthy, she could see it was gray with gold braiding. The men around her wore similar uniforms. Their hats were a hodgepodge of styles, but the most common style was horribly familiar. Claire's stomach churned. It is not possible, she thought. Someone is playing an elaborate joke on me. Her intellect immediately dismissed that notion. I was in a helicopter crash and must be unconscious, she thought, trying to maintain some composure. This is a dream. A nightmare.

"Sir. One more question." Claire took a deep and steadying breath. "What year is it, sir?" Oh, please God, say 1996. Say 1996.

The lieutenant spared the youthful soldier beside him an odd, penetrating look. "Eighteen sixty-five. What year did you think it was?"

Claire felt her entire body clench. Impossible. Of course it was impossible. And so there was nothing to worry about. Claire felt herself ridiculously close to laughing at the lieutenant who looked at her so seriously. People did not go back in time, at least not in the real world.

The melting snow seeping into her worn boots might feel real, the stench of unwashed male bodies might smell real, the sour taste in her mouth might even taste real. But it wasn't. It could not be.

She knew she had been in a helicopter crash in South Korea. Was she dead? Was this some awful purgatory. Or hell? That almost made more sense, she thought with growing alarm. But surely nothing she had ever done deserved ending up in hell, she rationalized.

"What the hell's wrong with you, soldier?" the lieutenant said, losing his patience.

Claire jerked back from her thoughts to look again at the young officer walking beside her. "Nothing, sir. I'm just a bit muddled. My head's clearing up now." She kept her voice low and gruff, hoping she could maintain her disguise at least until she managed to escape the regiment.

Eighteen sixty-five. As Claire trudged along, trying to keep her distance from the other soldiers, she tried to recall everything she could from her military history classes and her own reading. Born in Virginia, she had grown up around the Civil War's battlefields and probably knew more about the war than most. Snow on the ground meant it had to be January or February, still a few months before the fall of Richmond. She knew the Confederacy was at its weakest point, knew that Lee's hold on Richmond was eroding. And she knew that thousands of men would die in battles in the next few months. If she was really in Virginia and the year was truly 1865, Claire was in the deepest trouble she had ever been in. The only comfort she could find was that it was all too impossible to be true.

The men were strangely silent as they struggled through the forest. Above their heads, the sky was brilliant blue, but the sun was making a weak effort to send its warmth down to the forest floor. Gloveless and hatless, her feet soaking wet, Claire was colder than she had ever been in her life. Her cheeks were numb, her ears burning hot from the sharp air, and she found herself biting her bottom lip to stop the tears that threatened.

She walked silently, praying no one would ask too many questions or look at her too closely. She walked until her body was numb, until her mind was blessedly blank.

That night, the men who had tents huddled in them, and those without shivered, exposed on the frozen ground. A scout had spotted a small Yankee camp five miles away, and the order came down, accompanied by groans from the weary men, that no fires would be allowed that night. Claire watched as men cleared away the snow from the ground and then covered themselves with brush and leaves in an effort to keep warm. She followed suit, her hands red and raw and so cold she could not feel them as her fingers scraped away the snow. As twilight softened the day and cast the forest in a rosy hue, men came around to the troops handing out pieces of bread. Claire felt she was starving, but she nibbled slowly on her ration, closing her eyes and pretending it was a Big Mac.

Sitting cross-legged, Claire felt something jabbing into her thigh and, curious, dug her hand into her pocket to investigate. Letting out a small gasp, Claire brought out a worn piece of paper wrapped about a locket. Putting the paper aside, she studied the beautiful silver locket she held in her grubby hand. Looking about to make sure no one saw the piece, she moved her thumb over the latch, popping the locket open. It was a picture of a family, a mother, father, and three children, all dressed rather darkly and staring solemnly at the camera. Claire didn't know much about society in the 1860s, but the family appeared well-to-do. The intricate locket alone would have told her that.

Claire studied each face, her eyes straining in the diminishing light, somehow entranced by their faces. Who are they? she wondered. And whose uniform am I wearing? Her eyes moved from the mother and father to the three teenaged children, two boys and a girl, all with hair so blond it appeared almost white in the picture. Much like her own hair, she thought, and then became very still. The girl, her hand resting on her brother's shoulder, wearing a high-necked dress with a lace collar, held just a hint of a smile on her lips. Claire's hand began to shake as she stared at the girl.

It was like looking into a mirror.

Claire closed her eyes, willing the girl's face to change. Her heart beat painfully in her chest as she opened her eyes to look once again at the photograph, clear and crisp, without any blurriness to play tricks on her tortured mind. A coincidence, she thought, that the girl would look so much like her. Or maybe my mind is playing tricks. Maybe this is just part of this nightmare. Then she remembered the paper the locket was wrapped in. It was a letter.

My dear Maryellen,

I have just now received your letter. Thank God you are alive, your uncle and I were beside ourselves with worry. My dear, dear niece, my fear for you knows no bounds and I can only think that your tremendous grief has led you down this ill-chosen path. I pray daily that you are not killed, that you are not found out. You cannot know how dangerous it would be for a young girl to be discovered among the ranks of the Confederacy. I beg of you to come home, to forget the vengeance in your heart. Your mother, God blessed her soul, died of a broken heart when your dear brother was killed

and I fear she suffers still in heaven knowing what
you have done. Please come home.

Your loving Aunt,
Georgette.

Claire slowly folded the letter along the well-worn
creases, her brow furrowed in thought. It was obvious
she was wearing this girl's uniform, Maryellen something, and she wondered where she was. A horrid
thought suddenly occurred to Claire and she fought
back a violent shiver that shook her body. What if she
were not only in this girl's uniform, but also in her
body. What if she had somehow been transported
into . . . No. Uh, uh. No sireebob. It looked like her
own body, it sure felt like her own body. Impossible
that she had not only gone back in time but also into
an exact double. As impossible as all this was, Claire
thought, once again waging a battle with panic.

She closed the locket and carefully slipped it back
into her pocket, somehow comforted to have its slight
weight there. She rubbed her hand over the material,
touching the locket through her pants. No. Not her
pants, Maryellen's. Then where the hell was Maryellen? Claire's eyes suddenly got wide. Don't think
about it, she thought frantically. Don't you dare think
that you're in somebody's *dead* body. That would be
just too gross. Claire put her hands on both sides of
her head to stop her thoughts. I'll go crazy if I keep
thinking, she thought. Maybe I already am crazy.

More mentally and physically exhausted than she
had ever been, Claire lay down, oblivious now to the
hard, cold ground, and fell asleep, one hand resting
on the locket. She fell into a sweet dream that had
her smiling in her sleep. In her dream it was warm
and sunny and she was a young girl. She wore a long
white dress with a pink sash and sat on a porch sipping
a lemonade. Her feet were bare and dirty and felt

good on the gritty wood step. A young man, who she knew was her brother in the dream, but was not her brother, handed her a dish of ice cream. "Here you go, Maryellen, put a little meat on those skinny little bones of yours 'else you won't get no beaux."

Claire woke abruptly in the middle of the night, shattering the well-being the dream had given her. The dream, as pleasant as it had been, had shaken her. She could explain why the boy had called her Maryellen in the dream. That letter and locket had bothered her, not to mention everything else that had happened in the last twenty-four hours. No, it wasn't what happened in the dream that was so disturbing, it was the dream itself. For she knew with a certainty she could not explain, that it had not been a dream. It had been a memory. And that memory had not been hers, but Maryellen's. Staring up at the still-dark sky, Claire could almost feel this other girl. "You in there, Maryellen?" She felt silly for saying it at first. And then terribly, terribly afraid.

Claire awoke before the sun rose with a fierce need to relieve herself. She almost groaned aloud when she realized she was still in the middle of the cold forest wearing her ragged Confederate uniform. Punching the ground with frustration, she was nearly overwhelmed with a feeling of hopelessness until she felt the locket pressing against her leg. She closed her eyes and took a long and fortifying breath. Don't panic, she told herself, slipping her hand into her pocket and wrapping her hand around the locket.

She looked about her, carefully trying to find a spot where she could pee and would not be observed, more for safety than for modesty. She stood, eyes adjusting to the darkness, and made her way around the men's sleeping forms, praying no one observed her. A holly bush gave her the most protection and she quickly saw to her needs, grimacing at the lack of toilet paper. Yuck, she thought, as she pulled up her pants.

Escape.

Now was the time, she realized suddenly. She turned to go deeper into the woods when she spotted the shadowy form of a lookout. Her eyes scanned the forest, trying to pick out other sentries, trying to determine if there was enough distance between the men for her to slip through unnoticed. Claire sat back on her haunches and studied her options, noting wind direction and marking her best path. She did not want to think about what would happen were she caught. She knew deserters were hung or shot at worst and imprisoned at best. But prison would be nothing compared to staying with these men and facing combat. It was unthinkable to Claire to take up arms against fellow Americans.

Claire eased forward, her hands buried up to her wrists in snow. She smiled, knowing that the same snow that made her so cold, would also muffle her escape. She took careful steps, keeping her body as close to the ground as possible, her eyes glued to the lookout who rolled and lit a cigarette as she watched him. Claire's heart beat wildly in her breast, but she felt a kick of adrenaline stamp out her fear.

"Where you goin', Private?" The question, asked so casually, held a frightening amount of menace. Claire stood slowly and turned to see Lieutenant Leighton leaning up against a tree, a pistol pointed toward her heart. Oh shit.

"I was testing the sentry's readiness, sir," Claire ad-libbed impressively.

"That right? Very commendable of you. See, I thought you might be thinking of leaving our little party." He put the pistol back in his holster. Lieutenant Leighton looked at Claire with a touch of compassion, but also one of hard resignation. For if he had caught the soldier deserting, he would have prosecuted, he would have been present at his execution if that were the sentence.

"What's your name, Private?"

"C-Carl Dumont, sir."

"Private Carl Dumont, next time, I'm not askin' questions. Next time, I'm just hauling you in and chargin' you with desertion. You understand, Private?"

Claire flushed beneath his stern gaze. "Yes sir." She wanted to shout at him that she was not a part of his unit, she wanted nothing to do with killing Americans. But she could just stand there, shamefaced. Even though desertion was exactly what she had technically been contemplating, being a good soldier was so ingrained in her that having a superior chastise her was demoralizing. It mattered not that this was not truly happening. As the eastern sky lightened, Claire once again felt tears threatening. Another day here.

The soldiers walked for endless miles, stopping only once during the day for a meal of cold beans and moldy bread. Claire suspected then that the bread she had eaten the night before had been equally moldy, but it had been too dark to see the fouled parts. Claire had never been so exhausted in her life. This forced march made any exercise in officer's training school a lark. Her feet were swollen in her boots, her shoulder ached from the heavy rifle strapped there.

It was late afternoon, the sun sending long shadows on the well-trodden snow, when the regiment stopped at the edge of the forest before a field apparently part of a farm. The men hunkered down in a hollow, their eyes intent on the field in front of them. Claire found herself wedged between two scruffy men, both old enough to be her father. One got up on his knees, intending to relieve himself then and there. His friend threw him a look of disgust, but the other man just cackled. "When you gotta go, you gotta go. I won't get none on you." Claire wrinkled her nose in disgust, careful to keep her eyes averted from the steaming yellow stream that created a puddle not a foot away from her hand.

When Claire felt a warm splatter on the side of her face, her first thought was that the disgusting creature had peed on her. To her horror, she realized that blood, not urine, soaked her face. The man's head had quite literally exploded from his shoulders. Claire stared helplessly at the jerking mangled body next to her and let out a little mewling sound of terror.

"Get down," the man next to her shouted while roughly pressing her head into the reddened snow. "Shit. Stupid cuss. I knewed he was gonna get it one of these days. Stupid cuss. Jesus Christ. Jesus, there's nothin' left to him. Head blown clear off. Shit."

Claire wanted to scream at the man to shut up, but a part of her knew that in his own coarse way, he was as horrified by the man's death as she was. She began shaking uncontrollably as all around her guns exploded. Smoke soon obscured her vision as she lay there paralyzed, unable to move, unable to load her rifle. She could barely see across the field, where the Yankees had built a small bunker. We're shooting at Americans, she thought wildly. We're shooting at our own.

The battle was blessedly brief, nothing more than a skirmish, really. Once the officers determined the Yankee superior force, they withdrew, hoping to call more regiments to the area to assist them. It was unlikely, for the nearest troops were just north of Winchester, several miles away. And they were busy with their own fighting in their attempts to reach Richmond to lend a hand defending their capital.

Twelve of their men had died, six were wounded. As far as anyone could determine, not a single Union life was lost. No one appeared overly concerned about the loss of life, no one seemed even to think about it. What had been a horror to Claire was nothing more than a little scuffle to them, and it hit her suddenly the horrors these men had seen in four long years of war.

Disheartened, hungry, and tired, Claire walked with the troops, sharing their frustration. She was very much aware how quickly she had become wrapped up in the fighting, how quickly she began to relate to the men. How quickly she had, in her mind, become a Confederate. I'm an American, she told herself. I was born in 1973. I am a member of the U.S. Army.

Then why am I wearing a Confederate uniform and fighting Yankees?

It had only been two days since she had woken up confused and disoriented on the forest floor. But already she was beginning to forget that she had an entire other life. The one she was in now was too real. The blood, still on her face, coming off now in brown flakes, was real, too. Wounded men's groans, the wagon stacked with the dead, a horse's soft nicker, the sickening smell of blood mingling with dung—she could not make this up even had she tried.

For four more days they marched, enjoying a warm surge of air that turned the ground to mud. But on the fifth night it grew sharply colder and a fine icy mist began to fall. By morning, the trees were bent under the weight of a thick coating of ice, branches drooping, creating silver-laden weeping willows. Their blankets and clothes, even their hair were coated with ice. Forgotten was the breezy warmth of the day before as the men gathered up their gear silently, eyes filled with dead resignation.

Claire awoke to find that during the night someone had stolen the socks from her already-ravaged feet. Grimacing, she tugged her boots over her frozen feet feeling a rage build against the son of a bitch who had taken her socks. It was the last straw. Claire sat there, her buttocks growing wet, her clothes soaked through, and refused to move. Enough was enough. Okay, God, she thought, joke's over. If I'm dead, then kill me. But just get me the hell out of here, get me home. She had tried to take the events in stride, pushing away the panic that threatened to send her running, screaming, through the forest. She closed her eyes and willed herself to disappear. She still felt the damp earth seeping into the seat of her pants. Clenching her eyes, she concentrated harder, her hand straying unconsciously to the locket. Disappear. Disappear. Claire became very still, her breathing shallow, her mind blessedly blank. I did it, she thought with wonder. I've disappeared.

A hard knock on the back of her head brought her back and it took all of Claire's willpower not to crumple up into a ball and cry. I want to go home, she thought pathetically. I hate it here.

"Git going, Private." It was the sergeant who first found her. "Lieutenant Leighton says we'll see action today. Feels it in his bones. His bones ain't never wrong."

The mortar shell hit a small group of men who had just dived into a trench dug into the hillside and the air was suddenly filled with their agonized screams. Dig in! came the command. And so everyone dug. Claire's hands were raw from digging into the near-frozen earth with a tiny shovel someone had thrown her way. She dug until her back ached and her thighs felt like jelly. Gratefully, she sank into the trench and watched as the Yankees made their way closer and closer to the spot where the Confederates hid. Her rifle was cocked and ready, although Claire told herself she would not use it. She fought the urge to send a warning shot to the Yankees, her mind protesting killing Americans. But she knew that had she done anything to help the enemy, she would be shot on sight. And she did not want to die. She felt none of the excitement she thought she would feel when confronted with combat. She felt only cold, stark terror.

A constant stream of Confederate bullets was sent the Yankees' way until it seemed the sky was black with raining lead. When the Yankees began a hasty retreat, Claire joined the triumphant men as they ran down the hill, whooping a victory cry. They ran past the injured and dying Yankees, past trenches cut into the ground from some forgotten battle. Claire tripped and fell countless times, but kept running with the tide of soldiers around her. She ran toward the retreating Yankees until her lungs ached and her legs, already weary from the endless marches, were ready to cave in under her.

And then it changed. Confederates began falling around her. The whoops turned into shouts of surprise as a surge of blue uniforms moved toward them. So many Yankees streamed through the woods, their ranks appeared endless. Confused and startled to be suddenly confronted and vastly outnumbered, the men began retreating toward the nearest trenches, while all around them soldiers fell crying out in agony. Claire stood against the flow for a few long seconds, staring with disbelief at the huge number of Yankees headed their way. And then, along with everyone else, she began running, diving to the ground only when she heard the telltale scream of a mortar falling to the ground. Tree limbs crashed to the ground as the shells obliterated the forest.

Claire heaved herself up, clutching her rifle by reflex as she took a few desperate steps before throwing herself to the ground again. Around her were dead and dying soldiers from both sides, some turning their heads, eyes bleak and filled with death, as she struggled to her feet once again.

As she took her first step, something tugged at her left foot. She pulled but was caught on something. Frantically she turned to look behind her to see how far away the Yankees were. Then she looked down. Her ankle was grasped in the bloodied hands of a badly wounded Yankee. With an animal sound she heaved her foot, almost demented in her attempt to wrench her ankle free from the silent soldier. "Let go!" she screamed over and over. "Let go!" But the dying soldier's eyes were glazed over, even though he appeared to be looking into her soul. Almost crazed in terror as she saw the approaching Yankees, she pointed her rifle at the soldier's chest and fired. The soldier jerked and died, allowing her to pull free.

Panting and letting out inhuman sounds, Claire ran toward the retreating troops. She was a just a body, mechanical and unfeeling, as she ran across a field and into a forest. She ran even when her body was nearly collapsing from exhaustion, an awkward gait, her arms limp by her sides, her rifle dragging on the ground. When Claire finally stopped running, the world was silent. Even the birds were still. She dropped to her knees, gasping for breath, finally becoming aware of herself. She was alone.

Chapter Three

February 20, 1865

Two soldiers huddled alongside a poor excuse of a road attempting to eat their noontime meal in the middle of a cold, steady downpour. The road, no more than two ruts with an uneven mound of grass separating them, seemed to fade into the forest, its path obliterated by the rain. Their horses stood nearby, heads sunk low as if driven down by the storm.

Major Nicholas Brooks threw away his soggy lunch with disgust. Water filled his tin with sharp pinging sounds as he let nature wash his plate. It seemed Major Nicholas Brooks was disgusted with a great many things this day: the cold rain, himself, the endless War Between the States. And most of all, he was disgusted by the young lieutenant whose job it was to escort him to his new assignment. Nicholas realized he might be allowing his feelings of distaste for his new assignment to transfer to the man who brought the orders with him. Nevertheless, he found himself staring darkly at the young man sitting across the muddied road from him huddling against the torrent. The man was everything Nicholas held in contempt, a man who used the considerable influence of his privileged birth to avoid fighting for his country except in a very token way.

A West Point graduate, Nicholas lived and breathed the military. He loved its regimentation, the camaraderie, its purpose. He hated war as much as the next man, hated its waste. But goddammit, when your country needed you, you fought for her with your last breath. You did your duty, you prepared yourself to die while praying that you did not. You cried when you saw your flag standing tall while the smoke of battle obscured all else, and you cried when you saw it lying in tatters on the ground.

That's why he had difficulty knowing that he fought against some of his own fellow West Pointers. Taught to love country above all else, he was baffled to learn that many of his classmates fought for the South. To Nicholas, the war had never been an issue of North versus South or slavery versus freedom. The war had to do with keeping his country together, of maintaining the Union above all else. It was that simple.

And now, he could no longer do his part. He was a fighting man, a leader, well loved by his regiment because he knew how to bring them into a battle, knew when to pull back, knew how to rally his men to a fervor when all seemed lost. He knew his latest assignment, to head a prison camp in Maryland, was the way the army said thank you. Scores of officers had joined the Veterans' Reserve Corps, as Nicholas had, after becoming wounded. It was a way of staying in uniform, and as distasteful as it was to him it was a way of contributing to the war and keeping tabs on his regiment. He could almost hear his commanding officers commiserating over his military future. He knew he was lucky to still be in uniform. But God, how it hurt! To know your men were dying out there, while sitting behind a desk signing papers.

Nicholas stood quickly, picking up his tin and flinging the water out of it. He ignored the sharp pain in his leg and the dizziness he felt as he sloshed toward his horse. Weakness! Nicholas had never felt weak in his life. He had always been a big man, muscular and tall, with a hard leanness that was evident even when he sat seemingly relaxed, and Nicholas was sickened to realize he was not the man he once was. And never would be. His life as he knew it ended with the explosion of a Rebel mortar. Lucky to be alive, the doctor had told him. Lucky to keep your leg that was nearly torn in two at the knee. Those two nightmarish months spent in an army hospital left him feeling wasted and weak . . . and worthless.

Brooks spit as he neared his mount, wishing he could expel the bile that rose to his throat when he thought about his men, out there fighting while he was here thirty miles from the nearest battlefield. He heaved himself onto the horse and waited patiently for the lieutenant to hoist himself from the rock where he sat. His leg felt as if it were newly wounded, his head, where a piece of shrapnel would remain until the day he died, was beginning to throb as well.

Shit, he thought, closing his eyes against the pain. Not again.

Mounting his horse, the young lieutenant eyed his scowling superior warily before saying, "One more day's travel, sir, and we'll be at the camp." Lieutenant Phillips' heart hammered hard against his chest when the major turned his granite eyes his way.

Major Brooks's lips quirked slightly at the fear he saw in the lieutenant's eyes. Then he silently chastised himself. He prided himself on being a fair man. A good leader was always willing to give his men the benefit of the doubt, something he had failed to do with this lieutenant.

As he kicked his mount forward, he offered, "If I were you, Lieutenant, I wouldn't be in such a godawful hurry to get there."

They rode on in silence, each huddled against the

rain that fell relentlessly throughout the day. Both
men suffered, for the wetness made their thighs and
crotches raw from rubbing on the soaked wool of their
winter uniforms, and the cold made their hands ache
as they held the reins. Their stiff leather gloves were
saturated and did little to warm their hands. The
drumming of the rain against their hats was a monotonous thing, the horses' hooves slurping into the mud,
soporific. Used to being outdoors, the major was less
affected by the weather, but he was not immune, especially after his weeks in the hospital.

"We've got to get out of this goddamn rain," he
muttered. The lieutenant, raising his head as if awakened by the unusual sound of the major's voice,
grunted in response.

"When we stop, sir, I'll look for some kind of shelter. There must be something around here that will
shield us from this rain." Lieutenant Phillips hoped
the two would run across a farmer or at least a deserted hunting shack, but they were surrounded by
nothing but endless woods.

They stopped for the night after eyeing a promising
jumble of boulders a few hundred feet into the forest.
Dismounting, Phillips volunteered to explore the rocks
to see if they offered any shelter. Another fitful night
spent sleeping in the cold rain would not do either
man any good. Grabbing his musket rifle, he walked
toward the rocks, his footsteps almost silent on the
waterlogged leaves. The closer he got to the rocks,
the more promising they looked. One large flat rock
appeared to lie on top of another, jutting out far
enough to create a sort of roof.

Twenty feet from the rocks, Phillips stopped dead,
the hairs on the back of his neck tingling, his heart
beating hard against his chest. Someone was under
that ledge. Through the gloom of rain and oncoming
dusk, he saw the outline of a person, a man with well-
worn boots and muddied pants. The rest was in a

shadow. Phillips turned his head to see if he could get the major's attention, but Brooks was nowhere in sight. If he yelled, he'd be warning whoever lay under the rock as well as Major Brooks. Raising his rifle, he pulled back the hammer slowly, praying the telltale click would not signal the man under the rock. But the hammer click might as well have been a cannon sounding in the silent forest, especially to the soldier sleeping beneath the rock. Suddenly the boots disappeared as the man drew into a crouch, to remain hidden in the shadows. Phillips' hands, numbed from the cold, felt slippery on his rifle as he trained it where he guessed the other man to be.

"I won't shoot if you don't." The voice, Southern and boyish, came from beneath the ledge.

Oh, shit, Phillips thought, a Rebel, a goddamned Rebel. He had thought perhaps the man was a Union deserter. He had never expected to find a Reb so close to Maryland. What the hell was a Johnnie Reb doing this far north? He was not about to ask, not with his heart in his throat and his slick hands beginning to shake. Kill or be killed. How many times had that been drummed into his head? He sure didn't want to die, he thought, his brown eyes straining to see into the shadows. He'd have to kill, he thought as he quickly knelt to one knee and guided the rifle's sight. He squeezed the trigger the way he'd been taught, knowing that if he did not, the soldier beneath the rocks would. His eyes registered surprise when all he heard was an empty click as his rifle jammed, and opened wider still when he heard the loud report of a rifle being fired a moment later.

Phillips dropped his rifle and looked down at his gut, already red from the Reb's bullet. Over the roaring in his ears, he heard, "I told you not to shoot. Why'd you have to go and shoot. Oh, God. Oh, God."

Phillips clutched his gut as the pain began to register in his mind. Blood seeped in rivers over his hand and down the front of his shirt, spreading quickly into his wet uniform. He looked stunned at the steam rising from his wound before falling forward, holding himself up with one arm held out straight. Looking up through pain-dazed eyes, he saw the soldier emerge quickly from the rocks and run toward him. He's come to finish me off, he thought dazedly. To his surprise, the soldier took him by his shoulders and helped him lie down.

Claire, hunkered down and holding her rifle at the ready, had prayed the Union soldier would not shoot. But when she saw his finger squeeze the trigger, self-preservation had kicked in. Seeing the soldier fall, blood spreading quickly in the rain, Claire ran forward filled with sickening regret.

"I'm sorry, soldier. I told you not to shoot." Phillips groaned as a horrible burning pain washed over him.

"It hurts," he said, looking up at Claire. Through the haze, Phillips realized how odd it was for this Reb to be bent over him with apparent concern. Why wasn't he running away? Why wasn't he finishing him off? Instead, he was opening his shirt up, saying words of comfort. He heard the soldier gasp when he saw his wound. God, his gut burned, burned.

I'm dying, Phillips thought calmly, closing his eyes against the incessant rain. The soldier's voice sounded as though it were coming from a great distance as he lied and told him he'd be okay. That Southern voice making the words sound even sweeter. He felt a hand wrap around his own and thought he heard the soldier praying. Praying for his soul. And he died.

"Don't move, Reb." Major Nicholas Brooks trained his rifle at the back of the young man who hovered over the body of the lieutenant and watched as the soldier tensed.

"Stand. Slowly, hands raised." Claire, her gut clenching almost painfully, followed his orders. "Turn around."

When the soldier finally turned to face the voice that had been commanding him, Major Brooks let out an oath. The soldier standing before him, shivering as much from fear as the cold rain, could not have been more than sixteen. Dirty and bedraggled, he looked at Nicholas with the eyes of a combat veteran. His light blue eyes held no fear, no pain, just a hard awful acceptance. They've resorted to sending out babies, Nicholas thought with disgust, taking in the boy's slight frame. And starving them as well.

"Anyone else with you, boy?" Nicholas demanded loudly over the hiss of the rain as he walked toward the Reb. When he got no response, he cuffed Claire on the side of her head.

"Speak up, Private. Are you alone?"

Claire, her eyes lighting with anger at the rough treatment, said, "Yes, sir."

"You'd better be telling me the truth," Nicholas ground out with menace. "So, you're a deserter," he said, not bothering to hide his disgust.

Nicholas watched as the boy's fists, still held high in the air, clenched with anger. "No, sir!"

She had not deserted on purpose, and although she had thought to escape the Confederate regiment, the accusation from this officer angered her.

"Then you're dumber than I thought. You're lost. Very lost."

Claire's cheeks flushed with shame, giving Nicholas his answer. Claire studied the man before her with an odd detachment. He was tall, taller than most men she had encountered here thus far, and he looked tired. Mean and tired and somehow familiar, although she knew that was impossible. Dark smudges under gray eyes marred what could have been a handsome face. Nicholas scanned the woods, taking in Claire's rifle still lying beneath the rock outcropping. Phillips had been ambushed, that seemed certain, for he'd only heard a single shot. A rather cowardly way to fight, he thought, giving Claire a scathing look.

Trembling hands still raised, the young soldier was silent. No, the Reb was more than silent, Nicholas thought, giving the boy a hard look. He was complacent, accepting that he might die here in these thin woods so far from home. And, in fact, Claire truly did not care what happened to her now and the look she returned almost chilled Nicholas's soul. My God, he thought, it's almost as if the boy is willing me to kill him, almost as if it's what he wants.

With a hard, clipped voice, Nicholas said, "You are a prisoner of war of the Union Army. You're in luck, Private, I was on my way to Fort Wilkins. That's where you're going." He saw fear for the first time in the boy's eyes.

Claire had heard of the notorious Yankee prison camp from fellow soldiers as they huddled around the fire. It was a place, they had said, where Rebs went to die. Although Claire knew no Union camp compared to the horror of Andersonville, she was frightened just the same. Nicholas realized his prisoner was more afraid of Fort Wilkins than of dying, and he wondered what would make this soldier fear living more than dying. Goddamn this war, Nicholas thought, but as young as he was, this boy was still a soldier who had ambushed a man under his command.

Pushing the butt of his rifle into the small of Claire's back, Nicholas marched her back to the horses. Grabbing Phillips' mount, he led her back to where the lieutenant lay, pale and lifeless on the forest floor. The blood, thinned by the endless rain, glowed scarlet against Phillips' dark uniform. Next to him, the boy began shaking as he looked at the dead man. Nicholas watched as the soldier squeezed his eyes shut against the image and clenched his fists. When he opened those eyes, they had changed, as if someone had painted them with something dull, something that took away all light.

Over the past hellish days, Claire had become more and more adept at making herself disappear, making her mind blessedly blank. She had frightened herself by remaining in her "trance" for several hours, "awakening" in the dark when the last thing she remembered was daylight. But it was better than what she was living through, it was better than the torturous thoughts that plagued her, that had her convinced she was insane.

All night Claire walked silently behind the horse, her eyes avoiding the dead man's head that bobbed up and down in the rhythm of the horse's gait. You killed him. You killed him. The cruel thoughts raged over and over in her head. That's two you've killed. Two men. Oh, God, why is this happening to me? I want to go home now, okay? she pleaded. I want to go home.

Nicholas rode relentlessly, ignoring his leg, ignoring the dull but persistent ache in his head. Sometime around midnight, the rain blessedly stopped, leaving behind chilled, damp air that was almost as bad as the rain. They stopped for just two hours, Nicholas slumping against the tree, letting the Reb lie where he stopped, still tied to the mount that held the man he had killed. Claire slept almost immediately, giving Nicholas a chance to study the woman he believed to be a boy.

The uniform was obviously too big for the boy, he thought, seeing the length of rope tied around his waist that kept his too-long pants up. The gray uniform, while filthy, was in surprisingly good condition, making Nicholas wonder if the boy had stolen it. The boots, however, were a different story. What was left of them were far too big for his feet, that was immediately apparent. He wore no socks and probably suffered from foot rot. If there was one thing every soldier learned, it was to keep your socks on. Apparently no one had bothered to teach the boy that. Dirty hair was plastered to his head and looked as though it had not seen soap in weeks. He was pathetic and tragic at the same time. This boy had no business in a uniform, no business having the eyes of an old man, no business killing a good man.

The major allowed himself to drift off as he sat against a thick oak, one hand resting on his rifle should his prisoner awaken and try something stupid.

When the sun came up, creating a world that sparkled brilliantly from the rain that still clung to the trees, the two had been on the road for several hours.

When they began seeing signs of civilization and traffic on the road, which had become smooth and well traveled, Nicholas knew they had almost reached their destination. Moving away from a small town, no more than a dozen buildings cramped together along a slow-moving, muddy river, the land became more and more sparse. Coming off a rise, Nicholas spotted Fort Wilkins for the first time. It looked nothing like what his imagination had conjured, for it looked . . . almost welcoming.

Two rows of five barracks, long and narrow wooden buildings, were divided by a wide road. Smoke came from chimneys at each end of the barracks rising lazily in the still, cold air. At one end of the camp were several buildings Nicholas assumed were guards' quarters, storage, a small hospital, and the camp commandant's office. Prisoners milled about, a few guards lazily holding their rifles and leaning against the barracks' walls stood watch. The ground was muddied and well trampled, and Nicholas noted the area inside the camp was oddly devoid of vegetation. It was as if someone had waved a deadly wand and killed anything green, anything that dared grow in such a place.

*   *   *

Lieutenant Nelson Cunningham wiped his hands on his trousers as he watched the approach of his new commanding officer. A goddamn hero, he thought with disgust, that's just what we need around here. He tugged on his uniform in a vain attempt to pull out the wrinkles, and stroked his black mustache with a thumb and forefinger. Cunningham's black eyes followed Nicholas's progress as his hands continued their inventory by smoothing his long black hair, slicked back from a receding hairline.

The letter he had received about Major Nicholas Brooks had given little information about the new commandant other than to say he was a hero of the Union, having been badly injured six months before in the Shenandoah Valley. A man of honor, the letter had called him, but aren't we all, Cunningham thought with an ugly smile on his thin lips.

When the door opened, Cunningham walked over, his hand extended. "Welcome to Fort Wilkins, Major. Lieutenant Cunningham at your service."

Nicholas gave the man a curt nod. "Lieutenant."

Nicholas eyed the agreeable-looking officer in front of him. Cunningham's thin face was smooth and neatly shaved except for a mustache that Nicholas thought was overly bushy.

"You must be tired, sir. I'll show you your quarters," Cunningham said, giving him a smile that Nicholas thought was overly friendly.

"I take it you are the camp commissary," Nicholas said, and seeing the man's nod, he continued. "I'd like to see all records just so I can familiarize myself with the routine here."

Cunningham stiffened. He had not expected an officer close to retiring and taking a position in a war soon to end to be so diligent in his duties. "Today, sir?" Cunningham asked, not bothering to hide his surprise at the major's request. "I assure you, Major, they are in order."

Nicholas raised an eyebrow at the man. "I'm sure they are, Lieutenant. As I said, I want to familiarize myself with the routine. One of my duties, in addition to making sure none of these Rebs escape, is to make sure these prisoners are being fairly treated. You have a cemetery outside that shows there has been a poor history here."

The lieutenant's eyes shifted away from the intense look the new camp commandant threw his way. He had been at the camp under the former commandant and had found nothing objectionable about his methods of keeping the prisoners under control—keep them weak and sick and you keep them in Fort Wilkins.

"Things have much improved, sir. I'll have the records to you first thing in the morning. More pressing is the prisoner release in two days. Five hundred men going, and about three hundred more coming in the next day. We get all the goddamn overflow from Delaware."

Nicholas jerked a nod. "As I said, Lieutenant, I'd like to look at the records now." He gave a tense, polite smile, but one that seemed to cover his growing annoyance.

Cunningham gave Nicholas a hard look. "Yessir. How far back do you want the records?"

"Six months should do."

"Yessir." Cunningham turned to go, a hunted look in his eyes. He had not thought to cover his tracks. He had not thought it would be necessary. The books would show the major nothing out of the ordinary. But if he were to look further, if he were to match the actual goods received with the paperwork, Cunningham would be discovered. He prayed the major would be satisfied with only the books. For months he had been in cahoots with several contractors. The government paid for good quality meat, flour, rice, and beans. But the contractors did not always supply what was listed on the purchase order and they and Cunningham had made a tidy little profit thanks to the U.S. government. No other commandant had bothered to check whether ten pounds or one hundred pounds of pork were delivered. Hopefully, Major Brooks would not either.

Nicholas was weary to his bones and eager to get to his quarters for a good night's sleep. His eyes were bleary from trying to decipher the near-illegible scrawl of Lieutenant Cunningham. Everything appeared to be in order, but he was uneasy about the man's reaction when he'd asked for the records. For all his neat appearance and military bearing, Nicholas found he did not trust Cunningham. He was about to leave his office, convinced that any business would be better put off for the morrow, when Sergeant Stanley Grenier knocked on his door. Grenier, while not a military man, was so damned likable Nicholas could not seem to bother with the man's lack of regimentation.

"Enter."

Entering was the last thing Sergeant Grenier wanted to do. Major Brooks's scowling countenance was not easy to take during mundane business. And the news he was about to impart was anything but mundane. He managed to walk toward the major, who still sat at his desk, hunched over a pile of papers.

"We've got us a small problem, sir." Nicholas looked up at the man, who fairly squirmed under his gaze.

"Yes?" Nicholas prompted when it became clear the man was loath to tell him what the problem might be.

"It's one of the prisoners, sir. The lad you brought in yourself. You see, sir, he's a she. It's a woman, I mean she's a woman."

Chapter Four

Nicholas sat back, a stunned and disbelieving look on his face. The boy he'd taken in, who had walked silently behind that horse for miles, who had killed a man? That boy was a woman? No. It was not possible. Women were soft, they wore dresses. They cried. Women did not go about filthy with short-cropped hair toting rifles. Women did not soldier.

"You must be mistaken, Sergeant."

"I wish I was sir. But one of the other prisoners recognized her as someone from home. He was concerned for her safety, afraid of what would happen should she remain with the other men."

Nicholas looked at the top of his desk as if it would offer up some answer. When he lifted his gaze to the sergeant, he saw the man flinch. He'd had that effect on men before, Nicholas knew, and realized he must be angrier than he'd thought. Angry with himself for not seeing through that woman's disguise and with her for trying such a fool trick. What sort of woman would become a soldier? It was simply beyond anything Nicholas could imagine. In his world—God, in anyone's world—women simply did not do such things!

"Where is she?" he spit out, stressing the word "she."

Sergeant Grenier left the room and momentarily returned with the young "boy" who had killed Lieutenant Phillips and whom Nicholas had taken prisoner. She looked up at him through greasy strands of dirty blond hair, fear finally showing in those damned soulless eyes. Her hands were clasped in front of her and he could see that she trembled. Bootless, she appeared smaller and impossibly delicate. Purely feminine despite the tattered uniform. Now that he knew what she was, he wondered that he had been fooled.

"This is a woman?" Nicholas asked scathingly. "This is no woman, sergeant. This is an abomination of nature."

Nicholas looked her up and down, trying to fathom what he was looking at. Claire, seething inside and praying for self-control, kept her eyes level as Nicholas gazed at her as if she were a pile of putrid offal. What right did he have to look at her so. Was he not a soldier, too? Had he not killed men in the battlefield?

"What do you want me to do with her, sir?" Sergeant Grenier ventured, hoping to break the cutting look the major was using to dissect the woman next to him. Despite himself, Grenier felt sorry for the girl. Perhaps it was the way she was so silent, or perhaps it was the way the Reb who identified her was so solicitous of her. He spoke of her as if she were quality, not some bit of backwoods white trash that Grenier had initially thought her to be.

"Put her back in with the other soldiers," Nicholas said with finality and turned back to his desk.

Claire stiffened and for the first time seemed to lose some of her composure. She knew what would happen should she be returned. She had seen the looks in some of the prisoners' eyes when the young man had found her out, and she had felt a fear unlike anything she had experienced on the battlefield. Admonishing her to stay put with a firm hand on her bony shoulder, Sergeant Grenier gathered his courage and walked toward the major, who was now sitting at his desk assuming his order had been carried out. When he looked up at the sergeant, raising an eyebrow at the man's courage—or stupidity—Sergeant Grenier swallowed heavily.

"Sir, may I say something franklike?" Nicholas nodded, studying the man before him.

"Sir. If you put her back in with the men, they'll . . . abuse her, sir."

"And?"

"And I cannot, in good conscience, allow that to happen."

"No?"

"No. Sir."

Nicholas rocked back in his chair, leaning his head over just enough to see what his lady soldier was doing. He did not like what he saw. She was shaking like a leaf, her hands clenched in front of her so hard he could actually see where her fingers dug painfully into her own hands. Hell.

Keeping his eyes on the girl, he said, "More than likely, Sergeant, she was a camp whore. I'm sure the men in that room would give her nothing she hasn't gotten before." He watched as she squeezed her eyes shut and the trembling, which had become so violent he wondered that she was able to stand in one place, suddenly calmed. And he knew, if he'd been able to look into her eyes they would show nothing, not fear, not loathing, not hope. Nothing.

That theory caused Sergeant Grenier to think. It was a likely explanation, certainly more believable she was a whore than a woman passing herself off as a soldier day in and day out within a regiment of men.

"That may be true," Grenier conceded. "But some of those men are not what you'd call Southern gentlemen. I believe it would go against the rules of war to inflict that sort of punishment. Even to a whore."

"She might enjoy it," Nicholas said, only to see if he

could get some sort of reaction from the slim woman standing just yards away. She might as well have been deaf. Taking his gaze off the woman, he leaned forward in his chair and took in Grenier's look of censure.

"Of course we cannot send her back into the barracks, Sergeant Grenier," he said as if it had been the sergeant's idea all along.

Confused by the major's seeming about-face, Grenier was nevertheless pleased. No man could be as hard as the major seemed to be, despite the stories that had preceded him here. Everyone had heard of the great Major Nicholas Brooks, a Union hero, who would serve out the rest of the war in the relative safety of a prison camp thanks to two grievous injuries that would have killed a lesser man.

Seeing that the woman was swaying on her feet, Nicholas bit out, "Have her sit before she keels over." The order seemed to bring her back from whatever place she had gone to, Nicholas noted. She must be exhausted, he thought as he watched her limp beside the sergeant and sit rigidly in the chair Grenier offered her. He thought about how she had walked for miles behind that horse, not saying a word of protest. What the hell kind of female was this, anyway?

Claire Dumont was asking herself the very same question. The past two weeks seemed like a dream to her. How had she ended up here? And how could she get back. She had asked God already, very nicely, in fact, and so far He had ignored her. She looked down at her grubby feet, cut, raw, and swollen from wearing too-big boots without socks. Her hands were filthy as well, with broken nails and weeks of dirt embedded beneath them. It was 1865 dirt. She heard a rattling and realized she had begun shaking again, so hard the chair was banging against the wall. Close your eyes and disappear, she thought, her hand drifting to the locket still safely hidden in her pants. Maryellen's locket. It, like those dream memories, were the only things that helped keep her sanity.

Claire brought her head up when she heard the scrape of the major's chair against the room's plank floor. His face looked as if it were carved from granite, his eyes were certainly made of that hard, cold substance. He had not bothered to hide his disgust of her. She squeezed her eyes shut, willing herself to disappear. But when she opened them, nothing had changed. It's not working, she thought in panic. He was coming toward her, trailed by the sergeant, and she was still scared witless. Where had her strength flown, she wondered, sickened by her meekness. Time to get tough, soldier, she told herself.

She stood quickly, facing him, at attention, eyes straight ahead in an attempt to mask her anxiety. Like a good soldier.

"Sit down," Nicholas said, pushing her back into the chair, his voice tinged with impatience. "You are not a soldier, girl, and I won't have you acting as one. As soon as I can find a dress, you are to take off that damnable uniform. And bathe. You stink."

Claire opened her mouth to protest. She was a soldier and a damned good one. I bet I could outshoot this son of a bitch, she thought. But reason overcame her sudden flash of anger. She reminded herself painfully that she was in 1865. No woman fought as a soldier in those times. She had read rare accounts of women who had joined the Confederacy and remained undiscovered for a time. They were thought of as oddities. But she had never heard of one seeing combat. Most women who fought for the South did so as clever spies, using brains instead of brawn. Well, I have both, Claire figured, and kept her mouth shut and instead gave the major a look of pure hatred.

Nicholas chose to ignore the icy stare and concentrated on a more immediate problem than his prisoner's anger. He was clearly vexed. He had nowhere to put the girl except in the storeroom off his office. As the good sergeant had most helpfully pointed out, it was perfect, for the door had a lock and there was only a small single barred window. He had wanted her removed from the camp entirely, but his sergeant had also pointed out that they had little choice. It was either let her go, and he'd be damned if he did that, or bring her to the nearest women's civilian prison. But the damned woman was not a civilian, was she? She was a prisoner of war and no prison had been built to accommodate such an inmate. He could not spare a man to escort her to a civilian prison in any case. So here she would remain until he heard from his commanding officer. Let him decide, Nicholas thought wearily, giving himself a mental note to send off a letter in the morning.

Claire sat in the chair, her hands by her sides and pressing into the green stuffed leather that was nailed into the worn wooden seat, and stared at the shiny buttons on the major's uniform. She dared not lift her head, dared not look at those chilling eyes. Her anger deflated, she wondered why his scorn should bother her so much. He was nothing but a dirty outdated soldier, a Neanderthal, a foul product of his backward time.

As she sat there only half listening to their plans for her, she became overwhelmed with self-pity. For the first time since her family died, tears fell from her eyes. Why not cry, she thought, feeling an odd mixture of defiance and resignation.

Nicholas had ignored the girl as he discussed the details of her captivity with Sergeant Grenier, but looked down at his female prisoner when they were done. He could not say what made him do it, but when he saw the tracks her tears carved down her grubby face he took his forefinger and lifted up her chin so he could look into her eyes. Claire slowly brought her eyes up to meet his, past his stiff collar, the slightly cleft chin, the well-formed mouth, the patrician nose, to those hard gray eyes. She did not bother to mask the raw anguish that showed so clearly in her sky blue eyes, she did not have the energy to disappear. And so what Nicholas saw was a pain so bottomless he clenched the fist of his free hand in an involuntary reaction.

"You will not be harmed," he heard himself say gruffly, not questioning why he felt the need to reassure her. She gave him an odd smile, and her eyes made a subtle change, as if to say it would not matter if she were.

Dropping his hand, he said, "Sergeant, install the prisoner in the storeroom." Nicholas watched as Sergeant Grenier took hold of one of the girl's arms and led her down the short hall. She walked gingerly, as if walking on shards of glass.

"Sergeant, wait. Put her back in the chair." Nicholas knelt before her, grabbing a dirty foot. Embarrassed, Claire immediately pulled away.

"Let me look at your feet. You are injured," Nicholas said, his tone commanding. He let out a curse when he saw the damage the forced march had wrought. It was a wonder the girl could stand, never mind walk.

"Go fetch the doctor, Sergeant. Her feet need tending."

Sergeant Grenier grimaced. Why was it he was always giving this formidable man bad news? "Ain't here."

Nicholas let out a weary sigh. "Explain."

"The doctor. Ain't here."

Nicholas let out another curse. "Yes. I gathered that. Where the devil is the doctor?"

"We haven't had one here in, let's see now, about two months."

"And the ill prisoners?"

"Well, we haven't had an outbreak of the pox nor

other serious illness 'cept some pretty nasty diarrhea in nearly a year. Guess they didn't think we needed a doc."

Nicholas was stunned. Even a small camp of fifteen hundred men needed a doctor.

"There is a doctor in town for serious cases," Grenier volunteered. "And we got all the medicine. I could run over to the infirmary and get some bandages and salve."

Nicholas nodded. "And soap and water," he called to the departing man's back. Grenier waved a hand in acknowledgment.

When Grenier returned, Nicholas set about the task of cleaning the girl's feet himself, having had years of experience on the battlefield caring for wounded men. Grimacing at the sight of her torn feet, he tried to be gentle, but broke out in a cold sweat when she winced or let out a tiny sound of pain.

"Didn't anyone ever tell you to wear socks?" he said, dipping the cloth into the already dirty water. Holding her little feet, white and soft but for the raw wounds, Nicholas felt guilt wash over him. These wounds were because of him, because he had forced her to walk all those miles behind that horse. She had not complained once. Not once.

"They were stolen," she moaned out as he pressed the soapy cloth against her right foot.

"Gotta be damned desperate to steal a pair of socks," Grenier said, watching over Nicholas's shoulder. "Feet are a mess."

Nicholas applied the stinging salve to each wound, wincing in unison with the girl every time he touched an open wound. He knew it must hurt like hell, but she stoically took the pain, and he wondered again what type of female she was. He wrapped her feet with bandages and bid her to stand. Claire stared down at her feet, only her toes sticking out of the white cloth, and tested her weight. They already felt better. She smiled up at the major in thanks, but he had already turned away.

After the major was gone, Grenier led Claire down a short hall. Pulling out a ring of keys, he inserted one into a door, opening the room that would be her cell. Taking her left hand, he clasped one ring of a set of handcuffs to it, then told her to sit on the floor near a series of shelves. He shut the other ring through one leg of the heavily loaded shelves. A quick look around the small room told her why she had been handcuffed to the shelving. One wall of the room was lined with rifles and muskets and the shelves were loaded with boxes of ammunition. It was not the safest place to put a prisoner of war, she thought, unless they were handcuffed the way she was.

Sergeant Grenier stood awkwardly before her, rubbing one hand over his unshaven face. "You'll be all right here. Major Brooks won't allow anything to happen to you now. You're his responsibility. Good night, miss." Claire lifted her head. "Good night, Sergeant." She fell quickly into an exhausted, dreamless sleep.

In his quarters, Nicholas Brooks did not find sleep an easy escape. What to do with the girl weighed heavily on his mind. Colonel Hoffman would not be pleased to hear of these circumstances. A female prisoner of war was unheard of and certainly not something the Union Army would want to have widely known. If word that a woman was being held prisoner reached Washington, heads would roll, no matter her crimes. It was a politically volatile situation and if there was one thing Nicholas hated it was politics. He had made his way up the ranks by being a good soldier, not by greasing palms or playing patronage.

"Hell, my career's over anyway," he grumbled as he massaged his aching knee. Lying back on his hard little bed, springs creaking in protest beneath him, he stared at the ceiling, going over his options. With the war nearing its end, soon all war prisoners would be released. And that included the girl. He should release her now, he thought. Then the image of Lieutenant Phillips lying still and pale on the forest floor appeared before him and guilt filled him. He'd made the lieutenant's last days miserable with his censorious looks and unbending manner. Shouldn't the person who killed him so coldly suffer? He was torn between his duty to inform his commanding officer of the situation, and his duty toward the lieutenant. A letter to Colonel Hoffman, purposefully vague, would meet both objectives. Finally content with his plan, he allowed himself to sleep.

One of the first things Claire saw upon opening her eyes was the near toothless grin of Sergeant Grenier as he lugged a large half barrel into the storeroom.

"G'morning, miss. Brought your bath. You should have a dress to wear by the time you're done if that damned—pardon, miss—if that Corporal Barnes comes through. Got a sweetheart in town with plenty of dresses to spare, so he says."

Claire sat up, rubbing her eyes with her one free hand, eyeing that barrel the way a starving man eyes a banquet. Seeing her look at the barrel with avarice, Sergeant Grenier chuckled. "Knew there was a female underneath that Reb uniform," he said leaving the room. He reentered moments later lugging a large bucket of water, allowing a bit to slosh onto the floor. Five buckets later, the barrel had a good ten inches of tepid water.

"That'll do you," he said, pouring the last of the buckets into the barrel. Seeing that she did not leap straight up, Sergeant Grenier looked momentarily confused. Then he let out a laugh and slapped his forehead with drama.

"The cuffs. Where's my head at?" Drawing the keys out of his pocket, he unlocked both rings, freeing her.

Claire stood facing the sergeant, who seemed to be content to stand in front of her looking at her with that contagious grin of his.

"Can I have some privacy, Sergeant?" she asked, thinking he would turn his back.

Blushing, Sergeant Grenier was about to leave the room when Claire stopped him. "Er, Sergeant. I don't think Major Brooks would be pleased if you left me here alone." She jerked her head toward the considerable arsenal leaning up against one wall.

"She's right."

Sergeant Grenier turned quickly, gulping, when he saw the major in question looming in the doorway, having silently materialized. How could a man so large move so quietly, he thought with dismay.

"Remain while she bathes, Sergeant." And before either of the people in the room could utter a protest, he said, "That's an order, Sergeant," and disappeared.

Sergeant Grenier commenced to rub his jaw in consternation.

"Perhaps if you were to keep your back turned while I bathe?" Claire offered, allowing a bit of amusement to creep into her voice.

Locking his hands behind his back, Sergeant Grenier turned away from the barrel and stood rocking from heel to toe, trying not to think about the naked woman behind him. The room was murky, the only light coming from the dirty window and the door he had left open a crack so that she might see better.

She fleetingly thought of escape. It would be an easy matter to lay the Sergeant down low. But getting past the guards would be nearly impossible, and she quickly put those thoughts aside. Besides, she'd almost forgo escape for a bath. Claire peeled off the mud- and bloodstained uniform. As each item was taken from her, she felt as if a great weight were being removed. Good-bye, boots, she thought, good-bye, dying Yankee. Good-bye, shirt, good-bye, young lieutenant.

Good-bye, pants, good-bye, soldier girl. She knew it would not be easy as that to shed the past. But she wanted to pretend, if only for a little while, that she was peeling away the nightmare her life had become.

Sitting in the barrel, her knees up to her chin, Claire took the cake of harsh lye soap and breathed it in as if it smelled of roses. She began scrubbing slowly, working at her toes, her stinging feet, her ankles, up her legs, to her crotch, up her stomach, to her breasts, to her neck. By the time she got to her arms and face, the water was turning gray and cold. But she continued to scrub the dirt and filth that clung to her. Kneeling, she dunked her head in the water. Taking the soap in one hand, she rubbed it against her still-short hair, working up a weak lather. Joyously, she dunked her head in the cool, murky water and swirled her head underwater. Clean. She was clean. All the blood, gunpowder, all of the war was washed away, she told herself fiercely. Water dripping from her head, she called, "I'm done, Sergeant."

"You'll just have to sit still. The dress ain't here yet."

Now that she was finished, Claire wanted nothing more than to get out of the water that was darkened with her own pollution. She continued kneeling in the barrel, too modest to stand up even with the room so dark and the sergeant's back turned. When a knock came at the door a few minutes later, she hunkered down even lower, wrinkling her nose at the scummy water she soaked in.

"Hand 'er through the door, Corporal," Sergeant Grenier called out. Through the door came black-as-coal widow weeds in silk, and another in cotton. Two dresses! thought Claire, eyeing them greedily. She never in her life thought she would be so happy to slip on an uncomfortable dress. For as long as possible, growing up she had worn her brother's hand-me-downs, wearing a drasted dress only on Sundays and holidays. Now, she feasted on the simple black dresses as if they were a new dress uniform.

Sergeant Grenier took one at random and thrust it behind him.

"Sorry they're black," he said apologetically.

"Oh, no, Sergeant, don't be." They were clean, that is all that mattered. Using the hem of the dress to dry most of the moisture from her well-scrubbed skin and wishing she had some underclothes, Claire donned the dress quickly, reaching back to fasten as many buttons as she could. Stretching and contorting, she managed to get all but a few fastened, feeling as if she were struggling to put on a prom dress—albeit a black one.

"It's on, Sergeant," she said shyly.

Sergeant Grenier turned, his eyes wide with disbelief. Never in his wildest imaginings did he think that the girl beneath all that dirt could be the creature that stood before him now. Even with her light blond hair cropped short, she exuded femininity. Wearing the black dress, that was obviously too big for her, she looked too fragile to pick up a gun, never mind shoot and kill a soldier.

Seeing his perusal, Claire quickly looked down at herself to make sure she had not put the dress on backward, for the grizzled man was looking at her quite oddly.

"What's wrong?" she demanded, flushing in bewilderment when Sergeant Grenier began laughing. He hooted, he hollered, slapping his thigh and clutching his stomach. Claire simply stared at the spectacle, raising one eyebrow, looking at the man as if he'd lost his senses.

Catching his breath, the good sergeant said, "Girlie, when's the last time you looked in a mirror?"

"Why?" she asked, frowning.

" 'Cause I want to know what possessed you to think you could pass as a boy, that's why. I've never seen a more girlie-looking girl, never mind a boy."

Taking that as an insult, Claire stiffened. "Well, it worked, so I must look like a boy."

"Either that or those Rebs are blind fools." '

"Well then count your major in with those fools," she said heatedly.

That sobered Sergeant Grenier a bit. "Got a point there, miss. Ayup, you sure got a point there." Privately, Sergeant Grenier could not wait until the major saw his prisoner. He wanted to be around to see the look on his face when he saw this beautiful woman he had taken prisoner. Hot damn, if this wasn't going to be fun.

"Got to shackle you up again, miss," he said with regret in his eyes. Claire saw that regret and felt a need to reassure the sergeant.

"Please don't concern yourself, Sergeant. I have stayed in much more uncomfortable accommodations than these." She paused, trying to decide whether she should say more. "Sergeant, despite the fact that I am a woman, I am a prisoner or war. I deserve to be here."

Clamping the ring around her wrist, Sergeant Grenier studied her face. "No, miss. You don't deserve this. I don't know what your story is, but I'm sure you've got one. I got daughters about your age, and I was thinking last night, what would cause one of my girls to do what you done. You seem like a good girl, like my girls are. Whatever it is that led you here, it must have been something powerful or something very foolish."

Claire looked at the sergeant, grateful for his kindness and concern, even if it was misplaced. "It was something powerful, all right," Claire said with irony.

After the sergeant left her, Claire sat on the floor, worrying that her dress was getting dusty and then almost laughing aloud at the thought. The truth was, she never wanted to feel dirty again, inside or out. She could wash away the dirt and blood, but could she ever wash away the feeling of hopelessness at being trapped here? After nearly a week, Claire had accepted that something incredible had happened to her. Now she began to wonder if she would ever return to her real life. There had to be a reason she was here, she thought, fingering the locket now around her neck that she'd rescued from her uniform. But it was a complete mystery as to what that reason was. And *I have never been very good at solving mysteries,* she thought morosely.

She was still agonizing over her predicament when her noontime meal came. Sergeant Grenier came in with a hunk of bread and a bowlful of steamy stew. Claire eyed the fare suspiciously.

"Is this what the other prisoners will be eating?"

Sergeant Grenier looked affronted. "Of course not. Wouldn't want those Rebs to be eating better than our own on the field."

"Then why am I to eat this well?" she asked.

"Well . . . because you're, you know, a girl."

"I thank you, Sergeant, but I'll eat what the other prisoners are eating or not at all." She picked her chin up and crossed her arms, gestures that brooked no argument. And Sergeant Grenier could not help thinking that, she might be a camp whore, something he was beginning to doubt, but she would have made a decent officer as well with a look like that.

"Now, miss . . ."

"I mean it, Sergeant." He knew by the stubborn set of her mouth she meant every word, and he somehow felt he was obeying an order.

Backing out of the storeroom, still holding the uneaten meal that was only a slight improvement over what the prisoners ate, he nearly bumped into Major Brooks. Eyeing the untouched meal, Nicholas asked, "Our prisoner not hungry, Sergeant?"

"No, sir. I mean, she won't eat it. Says she wants what the other prisoners are eating."

"She's right again, Sergeant. How is it that our prisoner seems to want to follow the rules more than you do?"

Sergeant Grenier shuffled uneasily beneath the major's unwavering gaze.

"You are going to have to get over this, Sergeant. You are going to have to think of her as simply another Reb prisoner."

"Ain't so easy," Sergeant Grenier mumbled.

"What's that, Sergeant?" Nicholas said, scowling at the older man.

"Now that she's cleaned up and wearing a dress it sure ain't easy thinking of her as just another prisoner, sir. See for yourself."

Nicholas let out an impatient sigh. "I don't think that is necessary, Sergeant. If you continue to have trouble with your objectivity, I will be forced to assign someone else to her."

Sergeant Grenier knew that another soldier would not be as kind, nor as respectful to the girl as he was. The girl was too pretty for her own good, he thought, and might not be safe with many of the scamps here. Already the other guards were abuzz with the news of the female prisoner and he had kept his remarks to a minimum.

"Yessir," the sergeant said, but he was clearly unhappy with the situation.

It was the second time the girl had to remind the sergeant of his duties, Nicholas noted with some concern. He'd have to keep a closer eye on the situation. Clearly, the girl already had the older man wrapped around her little finger, through no fault of her own, he thought begrudgingly. He had already sent a letter to Colonel Hoffman saying that he would require the colonel's input on a question regarding a new prisoner. Purposefully vague, Major Brooks knew that the matter would get low priority, and he also knew he could point to that letter should his lady soldier create difficulties for him down the road.

"Sure is pretty, that girl," the sergeant ventured, knowing he was pushing his luck considerably, but aching to see the major's reaction to her. He followed the major to his desk, craning his neck to gauge his reaction.

Distracted, Nicholas asked, "Hmmm?"

"The girl. Sure is pretty," Sergeant Grenier said, jerking a thumb at the storeroom.

Giving the sergeant a scowl, he said, "I believe your view of what an attractive female is and my view are at opposite ends, Sergeant." The dirty little thing in the storeroom was about the most unattractive female he had ever laid eyes on. His ideal of the perfect woman was one who was soft and shy, with fluttering eyelashes and long, luxuriant hair. His ideal of the perfect woman was Diane Pendleton, his sister's best friend and the woman he intended to someday marry. That was a woman, sweet and kind and clean. The ruffian in the storeroom was none of those things. He'd meant what he'd said when he had called her an abomination. She was like no woman he had ever seen, or ever wanted to again.

The sergeant chuckled. "Yessir." But it was said in such a way that made it clear he doubted the major's words.

Ignoring the sergeant, he dismissed the man and sat down to work trying to make sense of the mess his predecessor had left behind. Nasty work, this, he thought to himself as he attempted to get organized. What the hell was he doing behind this infernal desk? he asked himself for the tenth time that day. As if in answer, his head began to throb, a dull pain to remind him of his inability to lead men into battle. This ache was nothing like the excruciating pain that assaulted him without warning. A pain so blinding it consumed him, wasting his strength, making him weak as a kitten. Although such episodes were infrequent, it was inconceivable for him to take the chance on being on the battlefield when one occurred. He could deal with the near-constant ache in his leg, it was simply mind over matter. But when his head was squeezed by that invisible vise, he was lost. Determinedly picking up a pile of orders stacked in front of him, he forced himself to get on with his work.

Nicholas was still at his desk, a dirty dinner plate beside him, when he decided to stop for the day. Tomorrow promised to be another long, grueling day, one that would begin with a tour of the prison camp and end with the paroling of five hundred prisoners. Pulling out his watch, he noted with surprise it was nearly ten o'clock. Rubbing a hand over his short-cropped sandy hair, he stopped suddenly, thinking he'd heard a strange sound. Cocking his head and concentrating, he strained to hear something in the silence. There. A cry, a whimper. A scream. Then silence.

It was the girl, he realized, grabbing his keys and lamp and walking quickly to the door. He listened at the door for just a moment, and hearing soft keening sounds, he decided to go in. The key turning the lock sounded loud in his ear, but when he entered the room it appeared the girl was lying down still asleep. He saw only a black lump and the white of her blond head as she moved restlessly on the storeroom's floor. "She should at least have a mat," he thought, a bit surprised with the sergeant for not thinking of such a simple thing himself. Even the male prisoners had a bunk and blankets.

He was about to turn to leave when the girl sat up, blue eyes wide but unseeing, screaming in a way that sent shivers up Nicholas's spine. The godawful unholy scream was bad enough, but it was the terror he saw in the girl's eyes that shook him to the core.

She began swiping at one foot in desperation, crying out over and over, "Get it off. Get it off." She strained against the arm handcuffed to the shelving so much so Nicholas thought she might snap her arm in the midst of her nightmare.

"Oh God oh God oh God oh God get it off." Nicholas acted on instinct. He put the lamp down and gripped her upper arms.

"It's off," he said sternly.

Turning her still-unseeing eyes his way, she began shaking her head in denial. He knew the exact instant she awoke, for that strangely terrifying blind sight disappeared as she focused on his face.

"It was a dream," he said, stating the obvious and dropping his hands from her arms. He expected her to begin weeping, but instead that awful shaking started.

"It was a dream," he repeated, this time more harshly, trying to get through to her. He brought the lamp closer so he could see her face, and when he did he nearly gasped. My God, he thought, the old man was right.

He stared at a near-perfect face, dominated by startlingly blue eyes. Her nose was delicate and finely shaped, but her lips . . . His gaze was riveted on those full lips that trembled still from the nightmare. Her hair, short as it was, looked like spun yellow silk that was just long enough to begin to curl around her face. It could not be, he thought in bafflement. That dirty wretch who had killed Lieutenant Phillips could not be this enchanting creature.

"It was real," she said, her voice dead. Claire looked down at her bandaged foot peeking beneath the black gown. Clean, no blood, no gore, no hands clutching her ankle, and she let out a shaky breath.

Nicholas at first crazily thought she was reading his mind, then realized she was talking about her nightmare. He followed her gaze to her handcuffed arm and swore under his breath. Her wrist was bruised and bleeding from a gouge that had been taken out of her flesh while she struggled.

Nicholas walked from the room and returned a moment later holding a jar of salve in one hand and a bandage in another. Uncuffing her, he began to expertly treat the small wound as Claire watched in silence. His movements were efficient and impersonal, but Claire was somehow comforted by his gentle touch.

"Do you have these dreams often?"

Claire tried to stop the trembling that started again, the trembling that had not stopped since that awful day on the battlefield. If the major noticed, he said not a word.

"Almost every night. I didn't dream last night and I thought . . ." Her voice trailed off. "When I was out there, I would stuff my mouth with cloth so when I screamed no one would hear me. I can do the same here."

When Nicholas finished with her arm he sat back on his haunches and studied this odd girl before him. The black gown she wore only emphasized her pale beauty, he thought, immediately wishing he had not ordered her out of her uniform. If any of his men caught a glimpse of her, there would be trouble.

"That shouldn't be necessary. I heard you this evening only because I was still at work. It's near ten o'clock."

Claire swung her gaze away from him toward the window. "Won't the guards hear me?" Claire was thankful it had been Major Brooks who had heard her. She knew that not all men would have been as solicitous.

"I will leave a standing order that should anyone hear you they are to either leave you alone or come get me."

The girl seemed to think this over. "That would be fine," she said evenly. But she knew she would use the cloth anyway.

He took her bandaged arm and slipped it into the

ring once again, clenching his jaw when he saw her wince.

"The munitions will be removed tomorrow so these won't be necessary anymore," he said, wondering why in hell he suddenly cared so much about the comfort of this prisoner. She's an abomination, right, Nicholas? he reminded himself forcefully. Right now, she just looked like a beautiful woman. He stood and Claire was forced to crane her neck to look up at him as she sat massaging her wrist. She gave him a small smile, leaving Nicholas a bit mesmerized and completely confused.

"Good night, miss."

"Good night, Major."

Chapter Five

Boredom is what got to most of them, these bedraggled men so many miles from their homes. Anything was a diversion, and the news that the camp had a new commandant and a female prisoner flew like wildfire. Walter MacDonald, whose only striking singularity heretofore was his ability to carve toothpicks that did not splinter, found himself the center of interest, having discovered the female among their ranks.

"I recognized her right away. I looked at her, and I says to myself, that there is Maryellen Hastings under that uniform. All those Hastings look alike, you know. All got that same blond hair and blue eyes. 'Course she claimed to be someone else, but I'd know Maryellen anywhere. Curious though. Can't figure why she'd lie to me."

MacDonald was interrupted by the subject of other heated discussions: Major Nicholas Brooks.

All eyes rose when Nicholas entered the room. The prisoners looked at the imposing man, their eyes guarded but missing nothing. They watched as he walked between the bunks, his boots sounding loud against the rough-planked floors in the silence of the long, narrow building. They noted his limp, slight as it was, and knew then why this man was here.

Nicholas was displeased with the conditions, although he knew many camps were worse. The barracks had been slapped together in haste to accommodate the prisoners, and the result was large gaps between the windows and frames, leaky roofs, and floors that allowed the winter wind to rush up inside. Most bunks, he noted, held no blankets, and the slop buckets nestled in one corner, tens of fat flies buzzing greedily over them, were badly in need of emptying. The smell alone, of human waste and unwashed male bodies, was enough to make him gag. The men were filthy, their clothes little more than rags. It was obvious from their gaunt, pale faces that whatever food they received was not enough to sustain them properly.

An ugly suspicion was beginning to form in Nicholas's mind. The purchase orders for supplies did not mesh with what he saw. One thousand blankets were supposed to have been delivered just one month ago, but he had yet to see evidence of that delivery.

"Is there a Walter MacDonald here?" Nicholas's deep baritone boomed.

Although Walter MacDonald suspected the reason for his being singled out, his heart still began an erratic pounding.

"Here," and he stepped forward, separating himself from the other men.

"You discovered the woman?" Nicholas asked.

"Yes. Her name is Maryellen Hastings," he said, unsure how much he should be telling the commandant.

"You know her?" Nicholas asked, groaning inwardly.

"Well . . ." And MacDonald thought of the girl's heated denial that her name was Maryellen. Could he be wrong? No. He'd known Maryellen all his life. He was certain the girl he'd seen was the girl he'd grown up with. Perhaps she was just ashamed at being discovered wearing a dirty uniform. Like Nicholas, MacDonald had a hard time believing that Maryellen had fought with a regiment. But just as unlikely was that she had taken the track of so many other women who followed regiments and prostituted themselves to survive. Both possibilities were equally shameful, MacDonald thought, knowing that Maryellen had simply done what she needed to do to survive. And as much as that thought saddened him, he believed it to be the truth.

"I grew up in the same town," he said finally. "I know her family's dead."

So, the girl was alone. "Very good, soldier."

"Uh, sir? What's going to happen to her, if you don't mind me asking."

Nicholas noted the concern on the young man's face and his own expression softened.

"For now she is being held, but I suspect I will be releasing her soon enough. She is safe, MacDonald, and will not be ill treated."

MacDonald nodded, satisfied with the commandant's answer. "She's a good girl, sir. I know she don't look it none now, but she came from a good family. She must have snapped. She pretended she didn't even recognize me. War makes a person change, makes a person do what they might normally never do."

Nicholas gave the soldier a thoughtful look. "I realize that, MacDonald. As I said, she will not be harmed."

Nicholas walked into his office, his mind reeling from what he had just seen. He had thought he had seen the worst of what war could do to a man. He had been wrong. The men he had just seen were spiritless beings. Some were homesick to the point of illness, sleeping nearly the entire day, anything to make the time here seem shorter.

Walking behind his desk, he stared blindly at the

bureaucratic garbage piled atop it, and not for the first time since the war had started, the human cost of keeping the Union together weighed down upon him. He felt stained by it. Images of the dead and wounded floated before him, mingling with the poor souls he had just seen. "Christ!" he said aloud, picking up a thin volume listing the Confederate soldiers who had died in this camp since it had opened four years before. Somehow, their deaths seemed more personal, more of a crime, than those soldiers who had died on the battlefield. Anger welled up in him and he threw the book hard into the small alcove to his left.

"Ow!"

Claire had sat quietly, watching as Nicholas strode behind his desk appearing to be lost in thought. Not wanting to disturb him, she had kept silent, hoping that he would not notice her sitting in the shadows. Sergeant Grenier had handcuffed her to the chair in which she sat while several men removed the arsenal in her cell. When he threw the book toward her, she tried to duck, but the book struck her shoulder sharply.

"What the hell are you doing there?" Nicholas spat, angry that he had lost his temper and even more so knowing he had a witness to his loss of control. He stalked over and retrieved the book, barely glancing at the girl before walking back to his desk. He tossed the small volume casually on the desk, sat, and turned in the wooden swivel chair to hear the girl's answer.

"Your men are clearing out my cell." You could have said sorry, Claire thought, giving the major a dark look. Claire crossed her arms, not giving in to the impulse to massage her shoulder where the book had struck. It hurt, and she would have a bruise, but she would not let Major Brute know.

"They are done."

"What do you expect me to do, drag the chair to

my cell and lock myself in?" she asked, jingling the handcuffs to make her point.

Nicholas narrowed his eyes at her. Apparently, she had recovered herself sufficiently to act less like the meek miss and more like a woman who had the audacity to don a uniform. He was infinitely glad, for the shy little waif she had been last night did not jibe with a woman who could have successfully infiltrated a Confederate division, no matter how desperate the Rebels were now for warm bodies. If indeed that is what she had done. It seemed so fantastical. Certainly more women had taken to prostitution in the war than had joined a regiment. If the thought of her soldiering made him angry, the thought of her whoring enraged him. Without answering her, Nicholas went in search of Sergeant Grenier.

He found him setting up the cot he had ordered for the storeroom. "As soon as you are done here, Sergeant, please put the prisoner back in her cell."

Quickly coming to attention, Sergeant Grenier gave a smart "Yessir!" Nicholas made to walk away, but the sergeant was itching to find out what the major had thought when he'd seen the girl. Grenier had seen the bandage on her arm and inquired as to how she had hurt herself and who had tended her.

"So, you seen her."

Hiding his amusement at the sergeant's transparent curiosity, Nicholas gave only a curt nod.

"She ain't so ugly," Sergeant Grenier said, an exaggerated understatement.

Nicholas actually gave out a chuckle.

"No, Sergeant. She is not ugly." Then more seriously, he added, "At least not on the outside."

"Sir, I think she's a good girl. She's just had it worse than most."

"Why do you say that?" Nicholas said, getting a bit impatient with everyone's distorted assessment of the little impostor. "Has she spoken to you?"

Sergeant Grenier shook his head, admitting that she had not. "Just something I sensed, sir. Says she ain't got nobody to write to. I thought I'd let her folks know she's okay. She said she ain't got no one. Hard to believe, but I don't take her to be one to lie."

"Her family is dead, I found out that much, Sergeant. More than likely, she's exactly what we think she is—a camp whore. I've seen it before, women following camps. Women without families to care for them, like our little prisoner. What I haven't seen, however, is women soldiering. Either way, her past is none of our concern," Nicholas said blandly, leaving the sergeant there scratching his beard and shaking his head.

Three days later, Claire opened her eyes once again to the bleakness of her cell. She could tell it was morning only by the muffled chirping of the birds and the muted sunlight that made its way through the crusty window and ill-fitting door. If she guessed right, it would be several hours before Sergeant Grenier delivered one of the two meals she received each day. After sampling the same gray gruel for days now, she almost wished she had not spoken up when the sergeant had delivered that aromatic stew the first day. Her mouth watered just thinking of the stuff.

The thought of spending another day like the previous three was immensely depressing. Lost to her own thoughts, Claire considered the impossibility that one of the prisoners seemed to have recognized her, and almost against her will her hand drifted to the locket she had placed about her neck. She hadn't been able to catch her reflection, but she was quite certain she was the same person she'd always been. It sure felt like she was in her own body. Still, it was eerie to have someone from this time seem to know her. She opened the locket, studied the girl who looked so much like she did when she was a teenager, and shivered. "Maryellen," she whispered, "are you in there somewhere? Are you hiding?"

In her more confused moments staring at the murky darkness, she could not say for certain whether she was who she thought she was. When those thoughts came, she felt a shudder of fear so violent, it took all she had not to scream. Was she truly this Maryellen Hastings who had dreamt up Claire Dumont and that life? Or was she Claire Dumont who was still in the midst of a horrid dream? Those disturbingly pleasant "memories" continued to plague her in her sleep. Scenes of Southern ladies, a woman Claire knew was her mother . . . but wasn't her mother. A father, big and robust with a thick beard and ever-present cigar. They were all strangers and yet she felt unimagined joy at seeing them.

"I know who I am," she whispered in the dark. "I am Claire Dumont who somehow ended up in another lifetime. I am Claire Dumont. I am."

When she found herself reliving the battles in hideous detail, she forced herself to think of happier days, of her family, of before this madness had begun.

How could anyone remain sane given all that had happened in the past weeks? Claire thought. She could almost picture herself lying on a therapist's couch, calmly explaining her conflicting emotions while fighting for the Confederate Army, while the therapist rubbed his hands together in glee at finding such a remarkable case of dementia. Claire brought her hands up to her head and squeezed to stop the thoughts that whirled around.

"I can't take another day here," she said aloud. "I can't I can't I can't . . ."

At a noise outside her cell, Claire stopped her chant, bringing her hands down. She stilled, straining her eyes as if she could see through the closed door. It sounded like the major settling into his office. Claire acted before she thought. Jumping up, she ran to the door and began pounding, pounding, not caring that she was hurting her hands. She shouted for the major while she continued to pound, not even stopping when the key slipped into the lock. When the door began to swing open, she backed quickly away and instantly became silent.

Nicholas could not believe that the skinny little girl who stood before him blinking her eyes from the light and massaging hands that no doubt two seconds before had been pounding on the door, had created such a racket.

"Yes?" Very polite. Very angry.

Claire swallowed and fidgeted. Why couldn't she, for once, think something through before she did it?

"I'm bored," she said, not wanting to reveal her terror of spending another day alone with her thoughts.

He cocked one eyebrow at her as if he could not quite believe what had just come out of her mouth.

"Too bad." Nicholas made to shut the door, but Claire's hand shot out to stop it.

"No. Please. I . . . I can't stand to be in here." To Claire's disgust, her voice began to quaver and Nicholas's gaze sharpened. Nicholas dropped his hand from the door and crossed his arms. The bleakness in her eyes that she tried so hard to hide touched him, but he'd be damned if he'd show it.

"I have nowhere else to put you," he said, softening his voice. "The only other place is with the men and I don't think you want that." And I wouldn't do it anyway, he added silently.

Claire, who had again fixed her gaze on his buttons, brought her head up at his words, then let her eyes drift back to his buttons so he would not see the fear there. Nicholas was relieved when she brought her gaze downward, for he found himself getting lost in those blue eyes of hers.

"No." Claire crossed one arm and rested the elbow

of another on it while biting her knuckles in thought. Then she did what Nicholas dreaded. She looked him in the eye. "If you were me, stuck in here alone, you'd go a little bonkers, wouldn't you? You wouldn't be able to stop from obsessing over every little thing that had ever happened to you, would you?" When he was silent, Claire answered for him and he became mesmerized by her lilting voice. "You would think about your family, how much you missed them, I suppose. Maybe a girl you like. Then you'd think about all the horror. Men who have died, things you have seen. You've seen some horrible things, I'm sure, Major. You would think of them, over and over, and you wouldn't be able to stop yourself."

She's suffering, he thought, trying to ignore the twinge in his gut. He understood her words, for he'd been at that place, when he was in the hospital those long, long hours with nothing to do but think about soldiers' pale faces, dead eyes staring at nothing. But he couldn't help her blot out whatever images tortured her by setting her free.

"I'm sorry. There's no other place for you."

Claire narrowed her eyes and pursed her lips. "Could I at least have a lamp at night?"

"We've not enough fuel to spare." It was an honest response, even if it was not quite believable.

Claire looked at him as if she could not believe a man could be so cold. He almost flinched from that look, but he closed the door anyway. And locked it.

Claire leaned her head against the rough wood, one hand on the smooth porcelain doorknob, the other by her side. Claire closed her eyes against the darkness of the room, willing it to disappear.

"I can't take another day here," she whispered. "I can't I can't I can't I can't . . ."

Nicholas looked at the bowl of grayish slop set before him with distaste.

"She ain't eating, sir," Sergeant Grenier said, swirling the gray matter before him to demonstrate how much of the stuff was left in the pitted bowl.

"I wouldn't eat it either," Nicholas said. Nicholas had tried without success to increase the amount and types of rations the prisoners were allowed. He'd be damned if he would starve these men to death. There was no honor in such a death. He planned to talk with Lieutenant Cunningham to have him explain why the men were being served the same gruel day in and day out when the records showed delivery of pork, flour, beef, and beans. Someone was skimming and he suspected Lieutenant Cunningham.

"She just sits there. It's awful lonely in there."

Nicholas sighed. He had tried to stop thinking about the girl and what she had said. As much as he tried to convince himself that she had brought this on herself, Nicholas could not help but think he was being too harsh. She had only wanted to escape her demons. His work allowed him not to think constantly about the men he had left behind, the men who were dying in a field somewhere, who would lie forgotten. Even the prisoners could talk to each other, whittle, or play checkers on their makeshift boards. She had no such diversion, he knew. Her eyes, those damned eyes, kept haunting him.

"I know, Sergeant. I've been thinking about moving her, but I cannot think of a place that she would be safe . . . and secure. I suppose you have a suggestion."

The older man allowed a glint of triumph to show in his murky brown eyes. "Yessir, I do. She could mend."

"Mend?"

"Yessir. Mend our uniforms." Sergeant Grenier gave him a smile, giving Nicholas an unwanted look at his holey mouth. "See, it'd keep her busy. She could sit"—Sergeant Grenier looked around the office and eyed the cubby hole off to the major's left—"there."

Nicholas swung his gaze to the small table and chair stuck haphazardly in the corner. Squares of light from a nearby window gave the little area a homey look and he could almost picture her there, her blond hair glowing in the sunlight, bent over some sewing. Something inside him tightened and he refused to acknowledge what it was. A man like him had no business wanting a woman like Claire.

"Sir?" Sergeant Grenier stood impatiently rocking from heel to ball, heel to ball.

"Four hours a day, Sergeant. No more."

"Yessir!" Sergeant Grenier turned to leave, then caught himself. "May I go inform her, sir?" Nicholas gave a curt nod, then bent over his work.

When Nicholas returned to his office later that day after a tour of the camp, she was sitting there much as he had pictured her. Except instead of sewing, she was facing the window, her eyes closed, basking in the sun.

"You're supposed to be working."

Claire literally jumped in her seat at the sound of his voice. Without a word, she took up the shirt she had started and began plunging the needle in and out of the blue cloth. When Sergeant Grenier had told her his plan, she had been overjoyed. But when she saw where she was to work, she became ecstatic. To sit in the sun, feel its warmth after nearly a week in semi-darkness almost brought tears to her eyes. Overcome, she had taken the sergeant's rough hand in hers and thanked him, unshed tears glistening in her eyes. She smiled as the thought of her mother's disbelieving expression had she known her daughter had shed joyful tears at the prospect of sewing. It was utterly ridiculous, but Claire did not care. She was free from her tormenting thoughts, and that was all that mattered.

Now, looking at her handiwork, she grimaced. "I'm not much of a sewer," she said, as if in warning. Nicholas, who had been deeply enmeshed in his work, looked over as if surprised to see her sitting there.

"What?"

"I said I can't sew." She held up the shirt to show him her uneven stitches. The only sewing she had ever done was attaching buttons, and even that was done inexpertly.

He stared at her for two beats, then bent his head and continued working. But he was thinking what sort of woman did not know how to sew? He did not like the answer that came to him. He wanted her to be of a better ilk than she apparently was, but could not think why. It was of no concern of his. Claire kept sewing, wincing when the needle stuck into her thumb.

She looked up at the major, who was so intent on his work. She watched as he massaged his knee absently as he continued writing whatever he was writing. She studied his profile, so sharply defined. Even his lips appeared to be carved from stone. The pen looked awkward in his large hand as he scratched his way across the page. Dip, scratch scratch scratch, dip, scratch scratch scratch. When the pen stopped, she brought her gaze back to his face and was surprised to see him looking at her.

"Is there something I can do for you?"

Claire flushed, embarrassed to be caught staring. "I w-was watching y-you write," she said, stammering stupidly, almost wincing at how timid she sounded.

He concluded she did not know how to write and was therefore fascinated by the process.

"You cannot sew. You cannot write. You must have other, hidden talents."

Claire, who could not only write, but do so in French and Latin as well as English, did not bother correcting this simpleton. "As a matter of fact, I do," Claire said, thinking of the way she played the piano so expertly and of how well she could fire an M-16. Piano and warfare were the furthest things from Nicholas's mind after her saucy answer. He had been right about her. For some reason he could not explain, he was disappointed. She did not look like a whore. Then again, what did a whore look like? They did not all wear bawdily colored low-cut dresses. Apparently, some wore Rebel uniforms. Wearing those modest widow's weeds, she looked beyond innocent and terribly young and the thought of her giving favors to dirty, rough men angered him.

"How old are you?"

Nicholas counted to five waiting for an answer before losing his patience. "Answer me. How old are you?"

"Twenty-two. How old are you?" she demanded, raising her head a bit.

He ignored her question, concentrating instead on her answer. The "girl" was twenty-two. His assessment of her changed; this was no girl, this was a woman. "What is your full name?"

Claire gave him a hard look. "Is this an interrogation?" She was tempted to give only her name, rank, and serial number, but decided nothing she said could possibly matter to anyone.

"Just answer the question."

"Claire Theresa Dumont."

Nicholas leaned back in his chair studying the girl— no, the woman—sitting across from him. If she sounded educated, perhaps she was exactly what Mac-Donald said she was: a good woman who had become desperate. And now was no longer a good woman.

"Your neighbor said your name was Maryellen Hastings. Why would he lie?"

The question startled Claire, but she quickly recovered. "Why would *I* lie? That man was mistaken. He doesn't know me. Believe me when I tell you that it's completely impossible for him to know me. You can bet your salary on it," Claire said, her eyes meeting his in an obvious challenge. She knew she was telling

Chapter Six

In those long, horrible hours sitting in her cell, Claire thought of only one thing—the hours spent sitting in the sunshine.

As the days passed, the major got more and more negligent about putting her back into her cell. She could not be certain, but when the time came each day to lead her back, he looked as if he did not want to do the duty. Claire knew she should not give him that pleading look she cast his way when it was time to go back. She had never been a manipulative woman, never had used her looks to get anything from a man. But she hated this dark room, this loneliness.

When she sat sewing, she could look out the window and see a few birds. She sighed contentedly, her mending forgotten on her lap. Footsteps sounded on the planked office floor, footsteps she immediately knew did not belong to Major Brooks. Her stomach tightened nervously. Other than the major and Sergeant Grenier, she had seen no one else in the camp—and no one had seen her. The hair prickled on the back of her neck as she turned to see who was approaching.

Lieutenant Cunningham had been itching to get a glimpse of the girl ever since the rumors had begun flying about camp of a female prisoner. The men claimed she was a beauty, but he wanted to see for himself. He'd waited until both Grenier and Brooks were out of the office. He'd been patient. Seeing her for himself, feeling his loins tighten painfully, knowing she was a prostitute, he wished he could have managed a private moment—a very private moment— alone with her long ago.

"Major Brooks isn't here," Claire said, her gaze level and her voice calm despite her growing discomfort. This guy was a creep, through and through.

"You don't say," Cunningham said, rubbing his mustache. "But you are, little lady. They left you all alone? Pretty lady like you?"

"Apparently."

Cunningham smiled, revealing yellow teeth, and Claire could not help but wrinkle her nose at the sight. Leaning up against Nicholas's desk, Cunningham looked her over in such a sexually repulsive way, Claire shivered.

She crossed her arms. "Do you have a problem? The major isn't here. I would think that would be obvious to you by now."

Cunningham's smile disappeared. "I don't think you're in a position to be quite so uppity, little girl." He shoved off the desk and took a step toward her before pivoting abruptly and moving out of her line of sight.

"Major. There you are. I wanted to discuss the next shipment of supplies with you."

When the two men finished their discussion, Nicholas turned toward Claire, his gaze strangely intense.

"Who was *that*?" Claire asked, her opinion of the man clear.

"Lieutenant Cunningham. Why? Did he insult you?" Nicholas had been discomforted to find Cunningham alone with Claire. He didn't like the man, though he couldn't put his finger on why. And he didn't stop to think that if his suspicions about Claire's "occupation" were correct, she would hardly have been insulted.

Claire smiled at his quaintly old-fashioned concern. "No, he didn't insult me. He just gave me the willies."

Nicholas frowned. "He gave you what?"

"You know, the heeby-jeebies. The creeps." Finally, Claire came up with a phrase Nicholas could understand. "He made me very uncomfortable."

"What did he say?" Nicholas asked, his concern growing.

Claire shrugged. "It wasn't so much what he said as the way he said it."

"He didn't . . . touch you."

Claire's face reddened. "No. Nothing like that. I was probably just imagining things. Forget it."

Nicholas swiped a hand through his hair. "You shouldn't be here," he said to himself. "You're much too pretty for your own good."

Claire threw him a smile and cocked an eyebrow. "Why, thank you, Major."

"It was not a compliment," he said, his voice hard, his eyes glittering dangerously.

"Sure sounded like one to me," Claire said, allowing herself a bit of flirtation.

Nicholas stalked over to her, his body rigid, his mouth sternly set. "It is dangerous to have you here. But damn if I know what to do with you. All I need is a bunch of lovesick soldiers waiting in line to get a glimpse of you."

"Oh, *please.* I'm not *that* good-looking."

"These men, Miss Dumont, have not been near a woman in months."

"Including you and you sure seem to be able to control yourself," Claire shot back. "Give me a break. It is completely ridiculous to think that the mere sight of a woman would drive a man to attack me."

Lord, thought Nicholas, if the chit only knew how much he wanted her right now, with her eyes spitting fire, her face flushed from their argument. Jesus, she was a beauty. He was suddenly looming above her, gazing down at her, letting her see where his thoughts had gone.

"Should I prove you wrong, Miss Dumont? Should I show you just how desirable you are?"

Claire didn't like this game anymore. So much for flirting, she thought. "No. I believe you."

"Do you?"

Claire nodded her head. "Mmmm-hmmm. I do. I can see quite clearly that you have absolutely no self-control whatsoever. I must be much more sexy than I ever imagined." She kept her voice light, emphasizing her Southern accent, hoping humor would douse the burning she saw in his eyes, eyes that traveled to her mouth and settled there.

Nicholas swallowed heavily. What the hell was he doing? He jerked back as if slapped. "I apologize if I frightened you."

Frightened? Claire had been a lot of things, but frightened certainly was not one of them. "Apology accepted, Major."

For the next few days, Claire kept her guard up, listening for unfamiliar footsteps. Maybe she had imagined the way Cunningham had looked at her, but she doubted it. Just the thought of his eyes looking her over made her faintly ill. But as the days passed without another encounter, Claire began to relax and once again enjoy the excursions from her little cubbyhole. She watched the guards walking about and sometimes spotted one or more of the prisoners. Anything out of the ordinary was savored, and Claire was a bit worried that her brain would atrophy in its idleness. The barracks within her view was vacant, so it was rare that someone passed by. Only once, just as dusk was touching the sky, did she see an officer escorting a prisoner into the barrack, something that piqued her curiosity only because it was the first time she'd seen anyone enter the building. She watched idly for a few moments, then sat straight up. It was Cunningham. Just the sight of him made her shiver. "Creepazoid," she said to her herself, and turned back to the garment on her lap. She didn't notice anyone come out of the building, for once the sun disappeared, her interest in the world outside also vanished.

Claire loved the sun. She could almost taste the sunshine when she turned her face to it. Her cell had become a hated thing, a place where she could find no peace, even in sleep. Each night she awoke sweating and shaking, her screams muffled by the cloth she stuffed into her mouth. Each morning, she sat in one corner, her eyes glued to the bit of light coming in from the small narrow window, wishing the long hours away. The worst day was Sunday, for Major Brooks was off duty and she remained in her cell.

But the hours out, mending or simply sitting in her little corner, they were heaven. Especially, she had to admit, when Major Brooks was nearby. Claire never said very much, but she was a keen watcher. She saw when Nicholas's leg was bothering him more than usual, and she watched as he massaged his head after an endless day of staring at long columns of numbers. His expression would grow fierce, then thoughtful, and he would often curse beneath his breath at something he discovered.

As Claire finished each garment, she showed it to the major, more to annoy him than to get his approval. For some reason, annoying this stern man was great fun. Today he had not even bothered to glance up at her once, not that she cared for his attention, Claire told herself. In an exaggerated Southern drawl that she used to further irritate him, Claire said, "Oh, Major. I've finished with another of these Union uniforms. I do declare, Major, these men certainly are rough with their clothing. Why, I think I've repaired this very garment three times already."

Rising to the bait, to her delight, Nicholas said, "Perhaps if you could sew better, you would not find yourself repairing the same uniform more than once." Nicholas looked up to find her suppressing a smile. He gave her a crooked smile of his own, acknowledging the little game, and turned back to his work.

Nicholas did not understand her. He did not understand why he bothered to think about her at all. But whenever he returned to his office, he found his eyes straying to that corner, to see if she was there. The few times she was not, the chair seemed utterly empty, and he would picture her in that dark room and fight the urge to go let her out. He found himself enjoying her obvious attempts to goad him, a break from the awful tedium that was his job. In a place where everything was dirty, where men spoke coarsely and stank and wore unkempt beards, she was an oasis of clean femininity. It was difficult to believe the ragged boy was this pink and washed girl.

Because she was so lovely, it was dangerous to have her around too long. He could almost trust himself with her—almost—but he knew he was looking for trouble to have such a beauty in a camp of men who had had no contact with women in months. If she had been a bucked-tooth, scraggly-haired, pock-marked hoyden, it would have been dangerous to keep her. That she was lovely, and possibly a prostitute, made keeping away from her all the more difficult for the more unscrupulous of the men. God knew his own control had been tested.

Unfortunately, protecting the girl was the least of his problems. The beaten body of a prisoner had been found in the camp's only vacant barracks. At first it had been believed the prisoner had somehow escaped when he did not appear for morning roll call. But a search of the camp revealed the gruesome remains of the man, his neck twisted at a macabre angle. It appeared that the man or men who had beaten the soldier did so with a viciousness that was disturbing. Even for a man who had seen as much death as Nicholas had, the sight of his broken body was shocking. No one, of course, knew a thing.

The prisoners were silent, their eyes filled with anger, making Nicholas suspect that they knew more than they were saying and that one of the guards had been responsible. He fleetingly thought of Lieutenant Cunningham, but immediately cast aside any suspicions. The man might be a thief, but that did not mean he was capable of murder.

When her mending was done, Claire stared out at a gray day, wishing for the sun to make an appearance. Tomorrow was a Sunday and she almost found herself crying, had she been the sort of woman who gave in easily to tears, just thinking about the long, lonely day.

"Tomorrow is Sunday."

Continuing to write, Nicholas said, "That it is."

Claire, her hands on her lap, tapped her fingertips together nervously. She stared at him, willing him to realize her dread of the next day.

"You are on leave on Sundays."

Nicholas stopped writing. "Is there a point to this conversation?"

Claire heaved a sigh. "No."

He gave her a probing look and realized suddenly why she was so concerned about it being Sunday. She would not be able to be let out without him around. He dared not assign another man to oversee her. He knew she was the topic of much discussion among both the prisoners and the guards. News that she was left unguarded would travel quickly. Few men could not be bribed, and he knew her safety would be compromised if he was not on duty.

"There is some work I need to do," he started before he could stop himself. He looked up at her and realized it was too late, she had already brightened, knowing that she would be allowed to go outside her room.

Beaming him a smile, she said thank you. That smile of hers had a strange effect on him. His chest hurt, of all things, a not unpleasant ache in the region of his heart.

The two soldiers huddled together, their backs to a sharp March wind that whipped off the river and buffeted the small fort.

"You're sure he won't be around?" the taller man asked.

"It's his day off," the second man answered.

"So, she'll be alone." His voice was laced with anticipation.

"And word is she's ready and willing, if you know what I mean. A real professional. 'Course, any woman will do, now, won't she?" the man cackled.

"No one else has had her?"

The shorter man laughed. "No one here. Major Hero been keeping her on a tight leash so far."

The other man's lean face grew taut. "He ain't had her, has he?"

The man shrugged. "Can't say for sure. But I got the definite feeling from Grenier that no one's hardly seen her but him and the major and the major don't give her the time of day. Maybe more got injured than his knee," he finished, giving another ugly cackle.

The tall man smiled, his yellowed teeth gleaming ferally. "I'll make sure she don't want no one but me when I'm through."

Claire awoke early Sunday without the same dread last Sunday had brought. It wasn't only the thought of getting out of her cell that lifted her spirits, if she was honest. It was the thought of seeing the major. She liked to watch him work, to hear his voice, to watch his expressions when she made him angry. She realized her feelings were silly and likely brought on by her strange situation, but she found herself thinking more and more about him.

For the first time in her life, Claire was allowing herself to develop a crush. Why not? she thought a bit defiantly. It's not as if she were putting her career in jeopardy here. Why not admire an incredibly handsome man without feeling overcome with panic? He was a fine-looking man, if a bit . . . remote. His eyes, when they weren't hard and cold, were beautiful to look at. His mouth, when it was not frowning or pressed into a hard line, was also beautiful. She had never looked at a man and seen such things before and she found the whole thing a bit disconcerting. Claire had never had a serious boyfriend, had rarely dated, and was a rarity in the 1990s. She was a twenty-two-year-old virgin. So focused was she in school, so consumed with her career, she hadn't had time to get serious. She refused to become like so many of her friends—besotted and starry-eyed—no matter the number of boys who had hovered about. She had more important things to do than fall into bed.

Now, sitting across from the major day after day, it seemed sex was all she could think of. She was horrified by her thoughts, or so she told herself every time she blushed red when he turned his burning gray eyes her way while she was in the midst of her rather tame fantasies. In her mind, she had never done more than kiss the major's hard mouth, but she couldn't help but wonder if reality would be as nice as her fantasy.

Claire's thoughts were interrupted by the jingling of keys at her door. Here already! she thought excitedly, jumping up to hover by the door and placing a hand on her traitorous heart. The door swung open and Claire was about to walk out when she stopped, a cold dread covering her like a chilling mist. The man silhouetted by the light was not Major Brooks nor

Sergeant Grenier, but someone thinner and somehow menacing.

"Who are you?" she asked, her voice hard and commanding despite the fear that gripped her.

"Let's just say I'm your boyfriend," Lieutenant
Cunningham said, leaning casually against the door
frame, a darkened lantern dangling from one hand.
Claire's blood ran cold when she recognized the oily
voice of Lieutenant Cunningham. "Let's get a better
look at you, girlie. Want to see if you're as tasty as I
remembered." Claire became rigid as she heard the
scrape of a match and saw the match flare revealing
Cunningham's thin face and black eyes. His mustache
drooped over his upper lip and almost disappeared
into his mouth. Hair, greasy and long, was slicked back
from a forehead shining with oil.

"You are a pretty little thing," he said, holding the
lantern up. "You know how to play, pretty little
thing?"

Claire lifted her head, her eyes glittering with fear
and anger. The man moved closer to her until the
lantern was just inches from her face, making her eyes
hurt from the light. His breath was stale and Claire's
nostrils flared in protest.

"What do you want?" Claire asked.

Cunningham chuckled. He could not believe his
good fortune. He had come here for two reasons: to
find out if she had seen him enter the barracks with
the murdered prisoner and to have a little tumble.
Seeing her, he decided to put off the first mission until
after. To have such a woman here at his disposal was
quite the dream come true. Placing the lantern on the
floor, he reached up and lay a hand by her throat,
taking his thumb and pressing just a bit against her
larynx, just enough to make the movement a threat,
not a caress.

"I'm doing what I want," he said, pressing a little
harder on her throat. "And you're going to let me."

Claire stood still, but her mind was racing, trying to plan her next move. But when he pressed even harder, she raised her hands to grip his wrist and tried to pull his hand away, letting out a thin sound of protest. Cunningham's grip tightened, and he realized with a smile that he would have to teach this little girl who was in command here. Gripping her cruelly about the throat, he pushed her hard against the wall. Claire let out a screech of pain that came out only as a hoarse moan because he squeezed her throat so tightly. Make your move now, Claire thought frantically, you've already let him do too much.

With lightning speed, Claire lifted her arms up with such force, Cunningham's grip on her neck was broken as he let out a small sound of surprise. Her head snapped back painfully as his hands became forcefully disengaged from her neck, but Claire ignored the bruising impact. In one fluid motion, Claire grabbed Cunningham's right arm and thrust one leg behind his. Before the man could let out a sound of protest, he found himself eating dirt, a knee digging painfully into the small of his back, his arm pulled onto his back with such force he thought surely it would be ripped from the socket.

"Let me go, you bitch. I'll kill you if you don't."

"I don't think you're in any position to be making threats, you oily bastard," Claire said, shoving her knee harder into his back and smiling when he gave a painful grunt. For all her bravado, Claire was not as confident as she sounded.

"The major will be here any minute," she said, praying it was true. For although her self-defense courses gave her the element of surprise, she knew she could not continue to have the upper hand should Cunningham manage to break her hold. She did not know when the major would make an appearance, but certainly he would not be here so early.

Cunningham grew very still and he tensed a bit with

fear. "Lying little bitch," he said mildly, forcing himself to relax.

Feeling the change, Claire tamped down a surge of fear. Suddenly, Cunningham bucked wildly throwing Claire off balance. It was just enough for Cunningham to twist away, with Claire rolling with him. She grabbed blindly for the arm Cunningham had jerked free and instead got an elbow to her jaw, snapping her teeth together. Then Cunningham was on top of her, straddling her, his hands painfully gripping her wrists as he looked down at her with such naked hatred she shivered.

And Claire closed her eyes and whispered a fervent prayer of thanks when she heard the major's uneven footfall on the wood planks outside. Cunningham's eyes widened in alarm. Giving Claire's wrists one last brutally tight squeeze, he released her and stood.

"Say anything and I'll kill you. Do you hear me, little girl? That's a promise." He quickly left, closing the door behind him. A few moments later Claire heard him say, "Good morning, Major, I didn't expect to see you in the office today. I was just looking for last month's purchase order. Thought I'd catch up on some of my own work."

The voices got more distant as the man walked Nicholas out of the office. Claire began to shake as her hands touched her throat, hating her lack of strength, her vulnerability. How could she possibly explain what would certainly be a bruised neck? She would have to tell the major. But then the other man would kill her, she was certain of it. Oh, God, what should I do?

When the door opened again, Claire crouched defensively in a far corner stiff with fear that the man had come back, that he had someone managed to deflect the major. She relaxed when she recognized the familiar form.

"I've decided to stay in here today," she said, surprised at how hoarse her voice sounded.

Nicholas stood in the doorway staring at her murky outline as she crouched in the corner, reminding him of a cornered animal. He tightened his jaw, knowing with a sick certainty that something had happened.

"Did he touch you?"

Claire started shaking uncontrollably as what had nearly happened overwhelmed her. Even in the gloom, Nicholas could see her shaking. Uttering an oath, he walked over to her and knelt on his good knee.

"Claire. Did he touch you?" His voice was gentle but firm. Not even a whore should be forced.

"N-no. Not the way you think. But the creep did threaten to kill me." Claire was ashamed to hear her frail whisper, and of the tears that coursed down her face.

She looked at him with those eyes so blue he could see their color even in the shadows. That bastard Cunningham. He ought to kill him.

Nicholas gripped her shoulders with strong hands. "I will not let him kill you. I will not let him anywhere near you. Tell me what happened."

Claire's shaking calmed beneath his touch. "He came in and he grabbed me by the throat. He pushed me against the wall. I threw him down and had him pinned, but he got away. I told him you were coming in and he stopped when he heard you."

"Is that all?"

"Yes. He said he'd kill me if I told anyone and I believe him. I know you are obligated to . . . do something. But there's no real harm. Just keep him away from me. That's all I want. Just keep him away." Claire meant to make her voice strong, but she could not stop the quaver in her voice.

Her eyes looked at him beseechingly, pleading with him in a way that tore at him. God, she was so frightened. Nicholas did not want to think what would have happened had he not decided to work today. He had almost rejected the idea, for it was a fine day and he did not want to feel a slave to a certain woman who had an odd claim to the soft heart he thought had been ripped from him long ago. He tightened his fists in a controlled rage thinking about the bastard Cunningham.

"I have to make sure he does not hurt you again, Claire."

Claire was not a meek woman, but neither was she a stupid one. She had seen in Cunningham a ruthlessness that only a fool could ignore. If he meant to kill her, he would. "Just let me handle it," she said.

Nicholas cupped her face in his hands, making her look at him. Her reaction was so unlike that of a woman that he was momentarily confused. Then he realized she was being brave again, ridiculously brave, and he sighed. "I will not let anyone hurt you. Do you believe that?"

Claire let out a shaky breath. "I believe that you believe that you can protect me."

Nicholas creased his brow at her response, slightly irritated that this female would doubt him. "Come into the light, let's see what the damage is."

Nicholas clenched his jaw when he saw her neck. Bruises were already appearing; he could actually pick out the thumb and index imprints on her skin. From the sound of her husky voice, Cunningham had nearly crushed her throat. Another bruise was forming at her jawline.

"Well?" she asked, then winced at the pain.

"You've bruises. He must have been squeezing like hell." His fingers touched her neck lightly, here, there, as if making to erase the deepening marks. Her skin was so soft, he thought. And her neck, so delicate he could almost encircle it with his hand. The thought of Cunningham's hands squeezing there, crushing the breath from her, brought another wave of rage and something else. A sudden and fierce need to protect her.

"I don't know what to do with you," he said, almost to himself. He was nearly convinced keeping her imprisoned was a mistake.

"I'll be fine," Claire whispered, misunderstanding what he'd meant.

Nicholas looked down at her and smiled. "You're always fine, aren't you?"

Claire shook her head. "No. I'm never fine. Not really. It's just something I say and maybe it will come true. Like saying, everything will turn out right. My mother used to say that all the time, 'Everything will turn out right, Claire, you'll see,' " she mimicked, not unkindly. "But it almost never did. That's something you say when you know nothing will turn out right."

His fingertips brushed her jaw and moved across her cheek while his eyes were somehow propelled to her mouth, exquisitely shaped and tempting him nearly beyond resistance. He could not help himself when he asked, "Did he kiss you?" The thought of Cunningham violating that exquisite softness sent fresh rage through him. Claire shook her head, and he sighed a sigh of something like relief. He thought: I will kiss you, I will make all your pain disappear. But he knew he could not, that a kiss would only give her more pain. Claire looked up at Nicholas as he touched her face, gently, and found her own eyes traveling to his lips. He was frowning.

No matter what she was, no matter what the war had driven her to do, she did not deserve to be so unhappy, he thought. She should be wearing pretty things, entertaining at parties, walking out with beaus. What man would want her now that she had sold herself, he thought idly. What life could she have now? His mind drifted to Diane, soft and pure Diane. Could she have been driven to such a life? He thought not.

Claire Dumont was an anomaly, an aberration, and, yes, an abomination. He still thought her so, he told himself. He must think her so.

Lieutenant Niles Cunningham nearly vomited from pure fear when he saw the look on Major Brooks's face as the man advanced toward him, but he was quite proud of himself for not showing a trace of discomfort. He continued to record a shipment of goods as casually as he could, noting with pride that his hand remained steady as it gripped his pen.

He even remained outwardly calm when the good major silently took his pen and clipboard from him and placed it neatly aside near the ink pot balancing on a sack of flour. But when Brooks's hand shot up and put a death grip on his throat, he began to squeal in terror knowing with certainty that Major Nicholas Brooks wanted to squeeze the life out of him.

"How does that feel?" Nicholas asked with terrible calmness. "No answer for me? Well, I'll supply your answer. This is how it feels when you are about to die, Lieutenant Cunningham." He tightened his grip, causing the man's black eyes to bulge and his thin face become mottled red. "Remember this feeling, Lieutenant. Because the next time you feel this way, it will be the very last thing you feel. Do you understand me? Lieutenant?"

Cunningham managed a frantic nod and Nicholas let him go abruptly. The man fell to his knees, gasping for air. "If you don't mind, Lieutenant, I would appreciate it if you would stop falsifying federal documents. A report will be made." Cunningham looked up at Nicholas with pure loathing. The major made to leave, but turned back. "And, Lieutenant," he said in a friendly tone, "be sure to clean yourself up before handling any more inventory."

To his utter shame, Cunningham realized he had

fouled himself. He stood awkwardly, glaring at the major's back wishing simple thoughts could kill.

Nicholas walked away, not showing the fury he'd felt inside. My God, when he'd had his hand around that bastard's throat, he'd wanted to kill him, slowly. The thought of him touching Claire, hurting her, drove him mad.

Chapter Seven

On Tuesday, Claire found herself out of her cell for most of the day, forgotten in her corner while Nicholas lost himself in reading about troop movements and battle casualties. So many times she'd wanted to reassure him that the war was nearly over, that the North would win, anything to ease the concern she read in his face.

Halfway through the day, Claire watched as the major's head jerked up and an unbelievably wide smile spread across his face. Claire watched in disbelief at how such a simple thing as a smile could completely transform a face. The hard, cold man was gone, replaced by a youthful handsome one. She felt she could stare at that face forever, then blushed when she realized where her thoughts were taking her. She could not see the man who stood in front of his desk, for her view was cut off by the wall, but she could plainly tell this was a friend and a good one.

Nicholas cast a look toward Claire and saw her raise her eyebrows in a question: "What should I do?" He gave her a subtle signal with his hand, one he hoped she would pick up, to remain where she was and remain quiet.

"It's good to see you, Harry."

"Same here, Nick."

The two had served together during the early years of the war and had become friends on equal footing, for all that Harry had maintained a superior rank. Colonel Harry Baker sat down and hoisted his crossed legs onto Nicholas's desk. Harry knew that he was probably the only man who would dare be so casual with Nicholas.

"What brings you to this paradise," Nicholas said, not bothering to hide his disgust with his assignment.

"Now, Nicky, your position here is just as important to the U.S. Army as—"

"Bullshit!" Nicholas interrupted.

Harry gave him a bitter laugh. "Yeah. Bullshit is right."

"You didn't answer my question, old friend. What brings you here. You've news?"

"Can't a man visit a friend without being interrogated?" Harry smiled.

"Harry . . ." Nicholas said, a warning tone in his voice, but a smile still touched his lips.

Harry brought his feet to the floor, signaling a change in mood. "I just came from Washington and knew you'd be here by now. It's going well. Richmond should go within weeks and you know about Sherman. I may not agree with his methods, but goddamn it, the man gets results."

"I know all that," Nicholas said with an impatient gesture. "What about my men. That's why you're here, Harry. Am I right?"

Harry smiled grimly. "I knew you'd want to know . . . Hell, Nick, it ain't pretty news." Nicholas's smile disappeared. "They got nearly wiped out, Nick. Goddamn Brimfield took 'em 'cross a bridge in Virginia without sending scouts ahead. Things have been so quiet. The Rebs, they were waiting for them. Waited until they were across, then attacked 'em from both ends. Our guys didn't have anywhere to go."

Nicholas turned deathly pale. Those men were his friends, closer to him than his family. They were his goddamn responsibility. He should have been there.

"Christ. Jesus Christ." Nicholas breathed out harshly through his nose. One fist lay clenched on the desk, the other hand continued to massage his injured knee, an unconscious gesture that claimed responsibility for his men's deaths.

"How many?" he bit out.

"Eighty percent casualties." Harry said quietly, hating to do this to his friend.

"Eighty. My God." Nicholas sat there, staring blindly ahead. Nicholas swallowed. Don't ask, he said to himself. Don't ask about Denny Clement. But he did.

"Clement?"

Harry looked at his friend and knew what he was going through. He would have done anything to shield him from this, but he knew he could not.

"Nick. It was a nightmare." Nicholas knew he had his answer, but he needed to hear it straight.

"Tell me. Clement."

"Yeah, Denny got it."

Nicholas dropped his head into his hands. "I should have been there," he said into the desk. "Goddammit! I should have been there!"

"No, Nick. Don't blame yourself. By rights, you should have gotten yours a long time ago. You weren't there. You weren't supposed to be."

Nicholas was silent for a long time, seeing the faces of his men, faces that had looked to him for guidance. Denny Clement had saved his life and now he was dead. He would never forget that skinny kid crawling toward him over the bodies, scared out of his mind but coming toward him anyway. Nicholas had been crazy with the pain and had shouted for Denny to turn back, he had pleaded with him to leave him behind. But the damned kid had kept coming with the stubbornness of a bulldog. He'd dragged him out of there, amid mortar and bullets flying, pulling him over rough ground made rougher by the battle. The last thing he remembered before falling unconscious was that kid's face smiling over him, telling him he would be all right. And now he was dead.

"It's starting to get to me, Harry. I never thought it would."

Harry sat silently watching his friend deal with the awfulness of this news. He had dreaded coming to see him, but he knew he would have to be the one who gave Nicholas the word.

"When is your next leave?"

"Sunday."

"I'll still be around. So will the whiskey. Let's say we make a date to drown our sorrows."

"Sure." He could see their faces, young, eager, ready to follow him anywhere, ready to die. Well, they'd done that, now, hadn't they. He did not realize Harry had stood up to go until his friend had begun walking away.

"Harry," he called, his voice rougher than usual. "Thanks for coming to tell me. I know it wasn't easy."

"No problem. I'll see you Sunday."

When Harry was gone, Nicholas sat in his chair, staring blindly, swallowing back the tears that threatened, clenching and unclenching his fists. A small sound drew his gaze to the corner, now in the shadows of the late afternoon.

"It wasn't your fault," the girl said, her voice sounding thick with tears.

"Spare me your sympathy," he spat. Hearing her Southern lilt irritated him beyond reason. Nicholas passed a hand over his forehead, wiping away a fine sheen of sweat. His head hurt like hell for the first time in weeks.

"What the hell are you crying about, girl? You should be celebrating. A whole division nearly wiped out. A battle for your holy Cause won. You make me

sick sitting there with tears in your eyes and Union
blood on your hands."

"You don't know what you're talking about. You
don't know anything about me. Of course I'm not glad
your men were killed. I'm sorry." Claire didn't know
what else to say to convince him. It wasn't her Cause,
but he would never understand that. He could never
know that she was not part of this war, this world.

"What are you sorry about? That they didn't all
die?" Nicholas knew he was being deliberately cruel,
but he was angry at the world and here was this pretty
little Rebel girl sitting there crying—crying of all
things—over the deaths of a few Yankees. How dare
she? He brought a trembling hand up to rub his forehead again, blinking his eyes as her stricken face went
in and out of focus.

"I don't want anyone to die," she said fiercely, fresh
tears coursing down her face, though she willed them
to stop. When had she become so blasted weak?

Nicholas stood, intending to lead her back into her
cell, to get her out of his sight. But when he stood,
the floor seemed to rotate around him. And his head,
my God, it felt as if it were being torn apart. He knew
what was happening but it was too late.

Claire watched as Nicholas put a hand blindly out
to stop himself from falling and watched as he crashed
to the floor onto his knees, clutching his hands to his
head in agony. She rushed over to him, unsure about
what to do as he writhed on the floor, letting out
groans that were just one step away from screams.

"Should I get someone?" she asked, afraid he was
going to die right there on the floor in front of her.
Surely the pain must be beyond endurance if a man
such as he was driven to the floor by it.

"No! No one!" he said, still gripping his head as
if he were holding it together. Without thinking, she
immediately looked for a phone so she could dial 911
before realizing she was on her own. She ran to her

cell and grabbed the cloth she used to muffle her nightmare screams and dipped it into some cold drinking water left on a small stand. Bringing the pitcher with her, she knelt by Nicholas and urged him to lie on his back, his head cushioned on her lap. He tried to resist, but a new wave of pain assaulted him, and he was left nearly unconscious from it. Taking the cloth, she pressed it onto the back of his neck, then she dipped the hem of her dress into the pitcher and began wiping it onto his head.

"Try to relax," she said with soft authority. "Try to breathe normally." She had no idea what she was doing, but it seemed to be having some effect. She moved her wet hem over and over across his forehead while she massaged his head with her free hand. "There," she said, "that's better. Just relax."

The instant Claire had put the cold compress on the back of his head and began massaging him, the pain began to dissipate. He listened to her soothing voice telling him over and over to relax. After a while, he was aware that the pain was long gone, but he somehow could not bring himself to stop her ministrations. It felt so good to be touched, her soft hands running through his damp hair. When was the last time he had been touched like this? When he let out a contented sigh, she stopped.

"Feeling better?" she asked.

Realizing that he was enjoying her touch, he shot up as if driven by a catapult. "I'm fine," he said, holding the edge of the desk while the room swirled around him. He blinked hard and shook his head to clear his vision.

Claire eyed him skeptically. "You don't look fine."

Nicholas felt strangely light-headed, but the intense pain was gone. Claire moved forward to touch his forehead, but he batted her hand away as if it were contaminated. "I said I am fine."

Claire backed away, suddenly angry at this ungrateful boor. She had just soothed the man who was holding her captive, who had been nothing but cranky and ill-mannered to her. "Thank you," he spat, reading her scowl correctly.

Claire gave him a snort in response to his sorry apology. "No wonder you can't fight," she said, deliberately baiting him, allowing her ill-placed worry for him to turn into anger. "Kneeling on the ground practically fainting from pain you wouldn't be worth much on the battlefield."

Already angry that he had shown weakness in front of her, Nicholas saw red. He did not bother to wonder where his famous control had flown before he roughly grabbed her shoulders, spun her around, and pushed her hard toward the hallway and her cell.

"These little jaunts of yours have just ended. I am sick and tired of treating you as if you were some sort of inconvenienced guest instead of what you are—a murdering camp whore. You are lower than the lowest Rebel soldier being held here. At least they are soldiers. At least they were fighting for something they believed in. They may be my enemy, but you are nothing. You can rot in that room for all I care."

"I am not a whore," Claire yelled, grasping the one thing in his tirade that she could take exception to.

Nicholas stalked her until her back was pressed up against one wall. "You are, and it's about time I began treating you like one."

Claire let out a little squeak when she realized what he was about to do. She tried to turn her head away but he grabbed her chin, forcing her to face him. Claire kept her lips pressed tightly, her eyes squeezed shut as Nicholas assaulted her mouth with his. Claire pressed her hands against his shoulders in a vain attempt to push him away. His mouth, crushed so hard against her, made her lips push painfully against her teeth.

Abruptly, Nicholas pulled back his head and Claire shrunk from his angry gaze.

"Please don't," Claire said, looking up into his granite eyes. She should be angry, but was unaccountably hurt that he should kiss her so roughly. Claire felt betrayed somehow that he should be such a brute, that he should be so much like that other man. Unable to stop herself, Claire began that awful shaking, and Nicholas immediately relaxed his hold. What was he doing? he thought savagely. He had never treated a woman so, not even a whore. He had never forced himself on a woman, or made a lewd comment. He had not thought this kind of behavior was in him. He had always treated women, even the loosest of them, with respect and chivalry. He was no better than Cunningham, he thought with utter disgust. He knew the fact that he had not made love with a woman for more than a year did not excuse such behavior.

"I am sorry. I do not force women," he said softly, his eyes finally softening as he looked down at her. "Stop shaking, I'm not going to hurt you." With one hand, he stroked her hair. The other soothed her jaw where he had held her roughly to him. She is so pretty, he thought, even with her short hair, even with her tainted past.

"I can't help shaking. It doesn't mean I am afraid. I'm not afraid of you. But you don't have to be such a brute," she said stubbornly. Claire looked at him, confused at his abrupt change in mood. He was touching her so gently, with so much kindness. I should be shoving him away, Claire thought dazedly, I should be kicking my knee into his groin, not hoping he'll kiss me again.

"Do you believe that I will not hurt you?" he asked, and kissed her temple. He moved his mouth to her burning cheek, kissing her softly, calming her. She felt so good beneath his lips, warm and soft and clean.

Kissing had never been like this, had never left her entire body tingling and weak.

"I don't know," she said, making him ache with her honesty.

"I promise I won't hurt you." He began kissing her lips, gently this time, making her feel even more confused. It felt good, she thought, to have a man kiss her so. Claire stood very still at first, not sure what to do, torn between her feelings and her mind that was shouting at her to stop. Then she became lost in the feel of his firm lips against hers and she found herself kissing him back in an instinctive and unknowingly provocative way. She did not want him to stop. But she asked him to anyway.

And Nicholas, who could not quite believe he was kissing her, did stop, although it was the last thing he wanted to do.

"I'm sorry." He stood before her, feeling foolish. Why in God's name had he kissed her? And why did he want to kiss her again? *Because you haven't had a woman in a very, very long time,* came the answer. *And this one is quite appealing with her soft mouth and pretty face and clear blue eyes.* More than appealing. She had asked him to stop, but he knew she had responded to him. He refused to believe those little sounds of pleasure were rehearsed.

Claire felt oddly disappointed, although she knew she should be glad. This was perhaps the strangest occurrence since she had arrived in the midst of the war. Imagine, being kissed—and enjoying it—by a Union officer who was her captor. *If I ever get back,* she thought, *this will be the most difficult part to explain.* She looked down at her hands clasped in front of her so he would not see her smile, not knowing her pose made her look impossibly innocent. It rankled Nicholas that she should look so, for she had responded to him, and she had not responded like an innocent.

When she finally looked up, he took a sharp breath and he grew instantly hard. She could not hide the want in her eyes, and he could not deny that he wanted her.

"I take it back," he said thickly, bringing his lips once more against hers. "I am not sorry I kissed you." Nicholas moved his lips against hers, coaxing her to do something she did not understand. He moved his hand to the nape of her neck, drawing her closer to him.

"You don't even like me, why are you kissing me?" Claire said, trying to keep her thoughts coherent.

Good question, Nicholas thought. Because I cannot stop, because you are here and beautiful and your lips are soft and when you stroked my head I thought I was in heaven. Aloud, he said only, "Because I want to." He kissed her neck with a whisper of lips, mouthing her, making her shiver with something that definitely was not fear. She clutched his shoulders, bringing him closer as her mind screamed for her to stop. Oh, but it was too good to stop. Too good.

"Open your mouth for me," he mumbled against her lips. Somehow, it did not seem such an odd request. Somehow, any fear Claire had been feeling had been replaced with . . . something else. She wanted to refuse to acknowledge that it felt so good for him to be holding her, for him to be moving his mouth against hers so insistently. But it did feel good, it did feel right. How was this happening, she thought druggedly, when just two minutes ago we were shouting at each other?

Claire opened her mouth beneath his questing tongue, hoping her lack of experience in kissing would not be immediately apparent. She should not be so innocent, having been born after the sexual revolution, but she was. Nearly overwhelmed by her sweetness, Nicholas thrust his tongue inside in a swirling exploration, his mouth slanting against hers. Claire jerked her head back, afraid suddenly of the response he was evoking. "What are you doing to me?" she whispered.

"Kissing you," Nicholas said, stating the obvious, bringing his mouth down on hers once again, unable to stop from tasting her, unable to stop himself from groaning aloud from the pleasure of it. Claire's claw-like grip on his shoulders loosened as she became lost in his kiss. Without realizing what she was doing, her hands crept up to his neck, where she splayed her fingers feeling his crisp sandy hair there, still damp from the cloth.

Still kissing her, for God knew nothing now could make him stop, he led her to her opened cell door, backing into the room and kicking the door closed with his booted foot. Am I mad? he thought as he brought one hand to cover her breast. At her gasp of pleasure, he pressed himself against her, allowing her to feel his hardness. He grabbed at the fabric of her skirt, pulling it up so he could touch her naked thigh.

"Don't think of anyone else, Claire, only me," he whispered harshly against one ear.

"No," she said and pressed her lips against his, not caring what was happening, only that it felt so good. I will not think about what he is doing to me, that it is stupid and probably wrong, she thought, closing her eyes as his hand skimmed her bare buttocks. Claire knew she should be shocked by the touch of his hand there, knew she should push him away. But the only sound that escaped from her throat was a moan of pleasure. I don't care, I don't care, she thought as she pulled his neck toward her even tighter. None of this matters. It might not even be really happening, she thought, convincing herself that she should continue. There was some fumbling with clothes, then he was laying her down, touching her in a place she had never been touched.

"I . . . I don't think we should," she said, quickly

reassessing the situation, but she gasped as he put his hand where she was hottest.

"Oh, I think we should, sweet Claire. So good," Nicholas said as he tested her readiness. He was nearly frantic to be inside her sweetness and the thought came to him, even as he positioned himself between her velvety thighs, that he had never wanted anything more than to be inside this woman. He was closer than he could have believed to shaming himself and he could not remember when he had felt so overpowered by his own lust. Nicholas only knew that he must have relief, he must have this woman now. He positioned himself above her, and looked down, trying to see her blue eyes in the darkness before he plunged in. And then he did, without preamble, without a second thought, closing his eyes and trying not to groan aloud at the pleasure he felt when he pushed inside her tightness and found release.

But when he heard her scream, a scream muffled by his own mouth plundering hers, his mind finally clicked on. A virgin! My God, what have I done? Nicholas thought frantically as he blindly tried to soothe the little thing beneath him.

He immediate withdrew, as if he could reverse what had happened. Claire lay there, still unsure how she had allowed it to happen, knowing only that it had hurt and that she had lost her virginity. Well, she thought with some bitterness, at least it wasn't the back seat of a Chevy. At least she would have an interesting story to tell someday: Oh, I lost my virginity to a Union soldier on the floor of my cell. But despite her attempt to make light of what had just occurred, a shame so deep, so ingrained from her mother and from her religious upbringing swept over her despite modern views on sex. She had had sex with a man who did not even love her. That had always been her rule. She might not be a virgin for the man she married, but she would not share herself with a man who did not love her.

"I didn't know," Claire heard him say the words as if spoken from a great distance. When she felt his hand on her shoulder, she stiffened, suddenly not wanting to be touched.

"My God, Claire, I am not a man who seduces virgins. I didn't know," he repeated stupidly. All his life, Nicholas Brooks had done the right thing. To be standing over this slip of a girl, her blood spilled upon him, was beyond anything in his experience. He was sickened by what he had done, by what he had thought she was.

"Please," he said, gathering her into his arms. "We can make this right."

Claire, unyielding in his arms, turned her face to him. "Listen, it's no big deal. It happens every day, I'm sure. Forget it." She tried to keep her voice light, tried to tell herself that nothing of consequence had just happened, but she could not. Nicholas was stunned by her reaction. She should be crying, or . . . something. Her blasé attitude had him thoroughly confused. "Do you understand what has happened?" he asked, thinking that no woman could be so naive.

"I understand completely," Claire said.

"That's good." Nicholas closed his eyes and swallowed. It must be done, he thought, his stomach churning at the thought. If there was a child from this reckless act, it would not be a bastard. He must do the right thing. "So you understand we must marry."

Claire pushed him away, shocked by his words. "No way. Uh, uh. I'm not marrying you. The very idea is ridiculous. Listen, just because we slept together doesn't mean we have to get married. That archaic notion was dropped a long time . . ." Claire stopped. This *was* a long time ago.

Her blunt words angered him unaccountably. What was so wrong about the idea of marrying him? he thought. "You will marry me. Whether we like it or not, a child could come of this . . . union."

Claire stared at him. "Child?" she said, as if the word were foreign to her.

"Yes, a child. Certainly you are not so innocent that you do not know where children come from."

"Of course I know where children come from. But the chances I'll get pregnant are infinitesimal. If I'm pregnant, then we'll talk about it. Marriage is tough enough without being forced to marry someone. And on top of that, I don't want to marry you."

"Too bad." Nicholas stood and massaged his head, which was beginning to ache again. Her characteristic bluntness, once so charming, was now irritating as hell. "It does not have to be permanent. If you are not with child, the marriage will be terminated."

"We could do that?" she asked, unsure of divorce laws in the 1860s.

"Of course. We could honestly say the marriage was not consummated. That we have lain together before the marriage is irrelevant. At least we will make it so. This will not happen again."

"Of course not," Claire said, so quickly Nicholas was bothered. And what she said next bothered him even more, though he told himself it should not. "We'll just pray there is no child. Pray harder than we ever have before." She did not like the idea of being forced to marry anyone.

"You do not like children?" he asked, his voice clipped.

"Of course I like children. I love kids," Claire said, surprised he had come to such an erroneous conclusion. "But a baby would make our decision more difficult. There's no law that says we have to get married even if I do get pregnant. So, we won't worry about it until we know."

Nicholas's eyes glittered dangerously. "If there is a baby, we will have long been married. I will not have a child of mine grow up a bastard. I will not have people counting the months. Are you insane? Don't you realize the stigma such a child would carry. Don't you realize what it would mean for you?"

Claire bit her cheek in thought. "I suppose it would be difficult."

"You're goddamn right it would be difficult. Surely more difficult than being married to me," he said, allowing some sarcasm to tinge his voice.

"It would be horrible. A loveless marriage is an awful thing." And I might not be here, Claire thought. I might disappear as quickly as I came. I don't want to marry you, I don't want a child I might be forced to leave behind. I don't want to fall in love with you and leave *you* behind, she thought, stunning herself.

"I agree. But we have no choice. We will marry."

Nicholas turned to leave, then cursed under his breath at his uncharacteristicly callous behavior. He felt like a cad, leaving the woman he had just deflowered, the woman he planned to be married to for at least a small time, sitting alone on a dirty floor. "Are you all right?"

Actually, Claire was scared to death and she hurt. "Yes. I'm fine," she lied. Her words came back to him then. No. I'm never fine. Not really. It's just something I say and maybe it will come true.

Before he closed the door on her, she looked up at him and he felt that now-familiar pain in his chest. "Are you going to let me out tomorrow?"

He closed his eyes for a moment, thinking that he surely must be the most vile creature on earth. "Yes." He closed the door and once again she was in darkness.

"I must not fall in love with him," she whispered aloud. "I cannot fall in love with him." But she knew, to her utter despair, that that was exactly what was happening. With everything so uncertain, with the chance she might be whisked away always a possibility, falling in love was the last thing she should do.

Nicholas returned to his office late in the evening the following day, having spent the day painstakingly going over inventory beneath the hated glare of Lieutenant Cunningham. He wanted to gather as much evidence as possible before sending off his report to Colonel Hoffman. He realized that it was likely nothing would be done, but believed it was his duty to report the crime. It was difficult to prove that Cunningham was skimming from inventory, and there were few who would harbor ill feelings toward a Union soldier whose actions caused a Confederate soldier a bit of suffering.

As he came to his desk, he automatically looked toward the dark corner, as if he expected to see her there. Claire had sneaked into his thoughts all day and more than once he had grown hard thinking of her soft body pliant against his. Although he was wracked with a consuming guilt, he knew that she had responded to him in a way no other woman had and he imagined how it would be between them now that she was not so innocent. He wanted her again and he could not stop himself from thinking of her until it became a damn irritating constant thing.

But as much as he wanted her, he did not want to marry her. The very idea was abhorrent and he was disgusted with himself that he should have been so foolish. The girl might be lovely, but he could not forget what she had been when he found her. She certainly was the last woman he thought he would marry. With God's mercy, it would be a short affair. Tomorrow he would go to town and get a license and Sunday, his day off, they would marry.

He did not intend to kiss her again, and he certainly did not intend to take her again, he told himself. But when he passed her door and heard her whimper in her sleep, he knew he must at least give her comfort. He would do so without touching her if he could, for he was not sure he could touch her and not want her.

Claire was crouched in one corner, her hands frantically swiping at her foot when Nicholas's lamp touched her with its soft light. Her eyes were open, unseeing and filled with an unimaginable terror. My God, he thought, what is she looking at that frightens her so? His heart clenched when he realized she had stuffed her mouth with a cloth to silence her screams.

Nicholas kneeled before her, and as he had done before, he took her shoulders firmly in his hands and gave her a gentle shake. "Claire. Wake up. It's all right. You're here."

Claire struggled frantically, clawing at his hands in a desperate attempt to get free. When her eyes finally cleared, Nicholas took the suffocating cloth out of her mouth and tossed it aside and pulled her to him. "Shh, shh," he said, stroking her back, calming her. "Tell me about the dream."

Claire shook her head against him. She did not want to think about the dream, she only wanted to be held, to feel safe. He pulled his head back, taking in her teary eyes, still filled with an awful dread. "Tell me, Claire."

She looked down at her hands and fiddled with her dress. "I'm so afraid."

"Of what?"

"That it will never go away."

He hugged her to him, giving her his strength, bringing one hand up to stroke her soft curls, surprised he found holding her such a simple, easy thing. "Tell me, Claire."

She pulled away, not wanting to be touched when she told this horrid tale. "It was a battle. The first real one I'd seen . . ." She told him about the soldier who clutched at her leg, who let go only when she shot him in the head. Her voice seemed dead, belying the torment behind her words. But her eyes were filled with the kind of pain only a combat veteran can recognize . . . the pain of knowing you are capable of something unthinkable.

Oh Jesus, Nicholas thought, oh Jesus have mercy, that something so horrid could happen to this girl. "Come here," he said, holding out one hand to her. She moved toward him in a sort of desperate way, and he gathered her onto his lap. He held her until the trembling ceased, until he thought she had fallen into an exhausted sleep. When he made to gently put her aside, she clung to him. "Please. Just a little while longer." She felt so safe.

Nicholas held her to him, this girl he would marry, who kept touching him softly as if to reassure herself that he was still there. That aching, that queer aching that came upon him at odd times, settled in once again as he heard her sigh softly in her sleep.

Chapter Eight

Nicholas had just sat down at his desk when Sergeant Grenier appeared before him, fidgeting and shuffling his feet. Nicholas sighed. It would be more disturbing news, that was for certain.

"Sir?"

Nicholas looked up, trying not to let his impatience with the older man show.

"Got to tell you something. Something she said to me yesterday." There was no need to explain who "she" was. "I was curious, you know, about what happened out there, about Lieutenant Phillips. She closed right up, didn't want to talk about it. I pressed her 'cause I'm real curious about how a girl like her could kill a man so coldly. Don't ring true. She said something curious, sir. She said she didn't want to fire, had yelled out to him not to shoot, but that Lieutenant Phillips fired first."

"I heard only one shot," Nicholas said, his voice getting hard. Despite everything, he was surprised the girl had lied.

"Yessir. That's just the thing. Phillips' gun jammed. He pressed the trigger first, she said, and she fired."

The only reaction Nicholas gave was a slight hardening of his jaw. "Is that all, Sergeant?"

"Yessir." Sergeant Grenier watched as the major returned his attention to his work. That's a cold fish, Grenier thought as he walked out of the office.

For several minutes Nicholas made a great show of working, but his mind was on what Sergeant Grenier had told him. Had she called out to Lieutenant Phillips not to fire? He doubted it. But if she had, then he would have to alter his view of her. Again. Unable to continue working while his mind kept drifting to the girl, and before he knew what he was doing he found himself at the camp's main arsenal where a young corporal was repairing guns. Seeing the major, he snapped to attention.

"At ease, Corporal," he said, looking about the room at the hodgepodge of rifles and parts on shelves, all neatly stacked and tagged. This small amount of order in a place with no order was pleasing to Nicholas.

"Two weeks ago, a rifle was brought in for cleaning. It belonged to Lieutenant Phillips, the man who was killed while we were traveling here. Do you still have it?"

"Yessir," the corporal turned and immediately took the rifle from its shelf.

"What condition was the gun in?"

Stroking the rifle fondly, the corporal slapped the polished butt against his palm. "It was a bit dirty sir," the corporal said, uncomfortable criticizing a dead man.

"Anything else, Corporal?"

"Well. It was pretty dirty, like I said. Which might explain why it was jammed."

Nicholas let out a short breath. "Thank you, Corporal." So, she was telling the truth, he thought as he walked across the compound to his office. He did not know why, but he found himself getting angry with the girl. Why hadn't she told him? Why be silent? He thrust the key into the storage room lock and barged in.

*　　*　　*

Claire's knees were beginning to ache. She had been kneeling in the middle of the murky little room for hours, praying. Praying that she was not pregnant, praying she could convince Major Brute they did not have to marry unless she was carrying his child. She had come to terms that should she be pregnant, she would marry him. For the child's sake. In this age where women had no rights, she must put her child's concerns above her own. She was dimly aware of the key turning in the door, but kept up her fervent petition to God.

"What the hell are you doing?" Nicholas shouted, somehow made even more angry to see her kneeling on the floor in supplication. Claire jerked her head up from her folded hands, recognizing the once-again harsh voice of the major. Stubbornly, she continued praying until her prayer was finished. Calmly she stood.

"I was praying," she said, lifting her head and staring directly at the major, who was scowling at her.

"For what? Your release?"

"I was praying for my soul."

That one threw the major. He had no response, but was bothered that she thought her soul needed saving.

"I've just come from the armory. Lieutenant Phillips' gun was jammed. Why didn't you tell me?" he demanded.

Claire tilted her head. "Why? Nothing would be different had you known. Lieutenant Phillips would still be dead and I'd still be here."

"Everything would be different, you stupid girl. Once I learned that you were female, I never would have detained you had I known. I never would have locked you in this room. Do you understand now? Do you understand that all that has happened is because of your damned self-condemnation? The one and only reason you are here was because I thought you had ambushed a man. Woman or not, I thought that deserved some sort of punishment."

"Every soldier who kills another does so in self-defense," Claire argued.

"You are not a soldier."

"I am . . . and a damn good one." Claire didn't stop to think what she was saying, so angered was she by his superior *male* attitude. "I suppose you think that just because I'm a woman I cannot be a good soldier."

Nicholas took a deep breath, a way to garner control, to recall the patience he was famous for.

"As much as you want to believe yourself a soldier," he said tightly, "the fact is, you were not. You were a woman wearing a uniform bearing a gun. That is a far cry from being a soldier. If I had known it was self-defense . . ." Nicholas rubbed his head. "Christ."

"It wasn't only self-defense. It was good soldiering," she argued. "God, it's a wonder we ever got the vote."

"It *was* self-defense. And you should have said something immediately. Then you wouldn't be here and we wouldn't be in this predicament."

"You cannot blame me for what happened. You cannot blame me. You . . . you seduced me!" she said, pointing an accusing finger at him.

Nicholas stared at her, his gray eyes stony. "You weren't so unwilling," he shot out angrily. Suddenly he wanted to prove just that, he wanted to press his lips against hers and feel her ready response.

"You'd better not . . ." Claire warned, seeing his intent. "I'll . . ." She was about to say she was going to scream, but when his insistent lips met hers, they somehow stole her thoughts. Claire meant to struggle, truly. But his mouth on hers wiped her mind clean, leaving behind a woman whose only thought was that she wanted to be kissed. She wanted to be more than kissed.

It started out as a lesson, but soon Nicholas found

himself struggling once again for control. God, she tasted sweet. He lifted his hand slowly up her body, grazing her breast, relishing her pleasure sounds. It was Nicholas who broke away, giving an almost triumphant grunt, happy to prove that he could control the raging lust he felt for this woman. Claire, drowsy-eyed, the fight kissed out of her, gave him a sloppy grin.

"What were we saying?"

Nicholas couldn't help but smile back. "That you had nothing whatsoever to do with what happened between us."

"Oh yes. That."

He wanted to draw her back into his arms, he wanted to feel her naked beneath him. But those thoughts were entirely too dangerous; it was best to get back to the business at hand, it was best not to think about how yielding her lips were, how nicely she molded to his body.

"What is done, is done," he said, forcing his voice to be cold. He did not want to think that this farce of a marriage would have been avoided had she immediately been released. It was his own folly, he thought, that had put him in this abhorrent situation. He began to pace.

"We're to be married Sunday. As soon as I can arrange it, you will go to live with my sister as a nanny or a nurse or whatever you may call it. She has three children and another on the way and needs help. My brother Matthew will bring you there. No one in my family, I repeat, no one will know of our arrangement. As soon as you know whether you are with child, you will inform me by telegram stating simply yes or no. If the answer is no, I will immediately have our marriage annulled. You may stay on with my sister if you wish. It is a good position. Or you may choose to leave. If the answer is yes, we will simply inform my family what has transpired. We will say we fell in love," he said, clenching his jaw. "You are a Southern refugee from a fine Southern family. I rescued you from the road. That is all you need to tell anyone for now."

He did not look at her while he was issuing these orders, and as if addressing a column of men he stood in front of her, his hands behind his back. Had he bothered to look as he made these life-changing pronouncements, he would have melted under her heated gaze. How dare he! Claire thought, becoming so angry her entire body was rigid.

"I will not," Claire said as calmly, as forcefully as she could manage, given the fury that was boiling just below the surface.

Nicholas looked at her as if she were not quite right in the head. "Of course you will. What choice do you have?"

What choice?! Why she could . . . she could . . . Claire felt her anger dissolve as quickly as a Bromo Seltzer in a glass of hot water. What choice do you have? She was a stranger out of time, out of place. Nicholas was the only stable force in her life right now, and she almost laughed aloud at that thought. If she were to leave, to walk out of this prison, what would she do? Where would she go? She was a soldier in her other life, an officer, a commander. Here she was a woman with no ties, no family, no husband. No useful skills.

Claire felt dead inside. This was horrid. She had not realized how awful the circumstances of what they had done were until this moment. She looked up at her tormentor, her eyes lifeless. "Go on," she said.

Nicholas stopped his pacing and stood before her, and with as much warmth as a statue, continued. "You should know that I do hope this marriage ends. You should know that I had planned to marry another, that it will be difficult for me to reconcile the fact that my plans have been thwarted. It is unfortunate for both of us, but we must do what is right. I do not blame you, I blame only myself. But I thought you should know where things stand. If you have no questions, I'll bid you good day."

"I have one question," Claire said, her voice strong, a stubborn set to her jaw. "Why must I travel to your sister's? Why can't I stay here until we know? It's absurd for me to travel to who-knows-where only to turn around a few weeks later. I'll just stay here and we'll both know at the same time and save a lot of worrying and trouble."

Her question seemed to agitate him, to break through his attempt at remaining detached from this intensely personal conversation.

"It could take several weeks before we are sure. After we are married, I cannot . . . touch you or the marriage cannot be annulled. As repelled as I am with the idea of being married to you, I find myself rather unable to . . . I find that it would be an impossible situation for you to remain in my close proximity."

Claire took that to mean he was so repulsed by her he could not stand her to be nearby. Swallowing the hurt and anger that was bubbling up, Claire asked, "Why can't we at least wait until we know before we get married? I'm not regular but I'm not *that* irregular. It will only be a week or two before I get my period. At least I think it will be about that long."

Nicholas turned red at her frank words. "No. As I said, it could be several weeks before we are certain and you cannot remain here. It could be months before I am able to join you. It is impossible. I have thought long and hard about what must be done and this the best solution. Believe me."

"This is crazy!" Claire said, her hands on her hips. "You can't force me to marry you. I still don't know why I can't stay right here. I'll stay out of your way. You won't even know I'm here."

Nicholas almost laughed out loud. He had been kept up nights thinking of her, hard and sweating until it took all the control he had not to give in to this ridiculous attraction he felt for the girl. Won't know she was there! My God, it was like saying he would not notice the sun.

"The decision has been made," he said with as much authority as he could muster considering the riotous emotions she was evoking.

"You can't make decisions for me. You can't make me do anything I don't want to do."

Nicholas wiped his hand through his short-cropped hair in an angry gesture. "What would you have me do. Just let you go? Let you walk out of here knowing you could be carrying my child?"

"No!" Claire shouted, clearly exasperated. She took a calming breath and forced herself to talk calmly. "I can simply remain here until I get my period. It's as simple as that."

It sounded so simple. Yes it did. It could only be days, he thought. But it could also be weeks. Long weeks of being tempted beyond what he knew he could endure. Never had he let his body dictate to his brain. Then again, he thought with disgust, he had never been tempted in this way, tempted by a woman he didn't even like. He was about to give in, was about to agree that he was being ridiculous, when she crossed her arms impatiently in front of her, unknowingly plumping up her small, sweet breasts. And he grew instantly hard.

His voice uncompromising, he said, "I cannot have you here. I do not want you near me. Even for a few weeks. Even for a few days. If you are not with child you will be free to go once the marriage is annulled."

"You're starting to sound like a broken record," she said with disgust, refusing to acknowledge that his words hurt her. At his blank look, she realized he didn't know what a record was. "You're starting to repeat yourself," she interrupted. Claire heaved a huge sigh. "Fine. I'll go. You win."

"Fine." But he looked so pleased, Claire wanted to slap his smug face.

It would be better, he convinced himself, to stand apart, to remain aloof. It would be better not to care what happened to her. If she carried his child, then he would care, he would force himself to.

"I will see you Sunday. I do not wish to see you until then, so you will have to endure this room for a couple of days."

Claire looked at him accusingly.

"This is no punishment, Claire," he said harshly. "I cannot look up each moment and see your damned eyes looking at me. I cannot."

"I don't understand."

"Too bad." And he stalked out of the room.

This is not happening, she told herself, closing her eyes and willing herself to wake up in her bunk in South Korea. She opened her eyes and let out a half-hearted groan, refusing to recognize the bit of relief she felt to see she was still in her cell, still here with Nicholas.

Claire Theresa Dumont and Nicholas Edward Brooks were married in a short ceremony witnessed by Capt. Harry Baker, the only person outside of the minister to know of this wedding, and the only one to know it was a sham. This, more than anything, had a sense of unreality to it. The minister, wearing his old-fashioned suit and spectacles that Claire was sure were nearly worthless, read from a battered missive as his portly wife looked on. The ceremony was so short, in fact, that Claire did not realize it was over until she heard the minister tell Nicholas that he could kiss the new Mrs. Brooks. Nicholas, who stood stiffly by her side during the entire ordeal, simply bowed to her in a slightly mocking way. Claire gave the minister a pleasant shrug, as if the slight had not wounded her heart.

After the ceremony, the minister had led them to

the wedding license, where they were to sign their names. Nicholas signed quickly, in an almost business-like manner, before handing the pen over to her. "Just put your mark there," he said, pointing to a spot near his signature. "An 'X' will do fine."

Claire almost signed her full name with her fine penmanship just to shock him, but instead put an angry X where he indicated. She would not allow him to know even that much of her. If he believed her to be ignorant trash, let him. After watching her sign the "X" with a pursed mouth, Nicholas stalked from the little chapel without looking to see if Claire followed him out into the sunlit day. After weeks of being cooped up in the commandant's office, Claire could almost forget the hurt he had unknowingly wrought, so wonderful was it to breathe the clear, clear air.

"He's distracted," Harry said, as a way of apologizing for Nicholas's crass behavior.

"He hates me, Captain," Claire said lightly, shocking the stocky man next to her.

Harry began to argue with her, but Claire stopped him with a soft hand to his arm. "Don't bother, Captain. Major Brooks hates my guts. You might ask him why, and then I'm pretty sure you might change your opinion of me as well."

"I know your entire story, Mrs. Brooks. And I can assure you that Nick does not hate you. He just feels a bit . . ."

"Trapped," Claire supplied, looking about her with a faint smile on her face. Nicholas was waiting for them by a hired carriage at the end of a narrow path. "It does feel good to be outside. I never realized how much being outdoors can affect one's outlook on life."

Harry looked aglance at the girl next to him. What a strange little thing, quite at odds with the story Nick had told. He simply could not imagine anyone believing her to be a boy, although she apparently brought it off quite well. He could not picture her grubby and unkempt wearing a Rebel uniform and shooting two soldiers. Seeing her, he could understand his friend's wanting to bed her. She was a beauty. It would not be the worst thing in the world, he thought, to be trapped in a marriage with her. Harry did not know Diane Pendleton, the woman Nicholas seemed so enamored with. But his description of her put him a bit out of sorts. Nicholas might as well have been describing a beautiful statue, an untouchable Madonna.

Claire might not be the mystical ideal, but she seemed lively and intelligent in a refreshing sort of way, the type of female who did not blush or chastise when a man swore or took out a good cigar. Enttrely female, she appeared to not have a duplicitous bone in her body and probably would have no idea how to flirt had she thought to try. Her natural buoyancy of spirit, her natural grace, made up for her lack of practiced coquetry. Why, Harry thought, if I weren't already married, I might consider her for myself. He told Nicholas that very thing when they caught up with the brooding younger man.

"And if you were not married, I would say that you could have her," Nicholas said as if he were bored.

The comment cut into Claire, but she'd be damned if she let him know how much it hurt. Even though she knew the marriage to be a sham, hearing those words, the fact they were *married*, weighed heavily on Claire's mind. Harry found himself surprised at Nicholas's behavior. He had never seen him be so rude to a woman, never mind a woman he had just married, no matter the circumstances. Perhaps, he thought, there is more that Nicholas is not telling me and he truly is pained by this marriage. Or perhaps Nicholas is trying to convince himself he does not care.

The three rode back to Fort Wilkins in silence, Claire seated next to Harry, Nicholas across from them staring morosely out the uncurtained window.

Claire looked at him with glaciers in her eyes, getting more and more angry as the moments passed. Harry shifted uncomfortably in the thick silence.

When they finally reached the commandant's office, Claire was so angry she felt like slapping Nicholas's bleak face. How dare he act like the victim here? she thought with venom. She was the one who was seduced. She was the one whose life was no longer her own. She was the one who might bear the child of a man who openly disliked her. She ignored his outstretched hand as she departed from the carriage, giving him a glare so icy, Harry was surprised Nicholas was not immediately frozen to the spot. She stalked into the building, going directly to her cell, and slammed the door behind her, welcoming the small space for the first time. That she had willingly gone into that bleak little room was enormously telling, Nicholas knew.

Harry let out a whistle. "She's mad as hell."

Nicholas gave him a bitter smile. "Yeah, well, that's better than looking at me with those damned eyes of hers. I want her mad as hell at me."

Harry gave him an assessing look. "I believe I'm beginning to understand your dilemma. You care for the girl."

His jaw stubbornly set, Nicholas said, "I do not want to be married to her."

"But you care for her."

Nicholas moved his hand in an impatient gesture. "She's been through a lot, and come out well for it all, I'll give you that. I don't care for her," he said vehemently. "At least not the way that you think. Hell. She's . . . she's not like other women."

"She's not like Diane Pendleton."

Nicholas let out a snort. "God no! Diane is the kind of woman to make a home with. She's good, and . . ."

"Pure as the driven snow and probably has the personality of a potato," Harry finished for him.

"You are very wrong, friend," Nicholas said tightly. "Diane Pendleton will be my wife if God has any mercy on me. Diane Pendleton is everything I've always wanted. Everything I've always pictured a wife should be."

Harry gave Nicholas a hard look, then slapped his friend's back, giving in for the moment. "Then I hope everything turns out well for you. Now. Don't we have an appointment with a whiskey bottle?"

Nicholas smiled, glad his friend was dropping this painful subject. He was married, for Christ's sake. Today was his wedding day. He ought to get drunk. Very drunk. He did not want to think about other things a man should do on his wedding night. He wanted to be pleasantly comatose. He wanted to forget that beautiful woman sitting in that dim room alone.

"I hate you!" Claire shouted when she was sure the two men had walked away. She had heard every word through the thin walls, suffered with every syllable he had spoken about this Diane Pendleton woman. He made her feel dirty. He had said very clearly he cared not a whit for her. Fine! She stomped around her room, kicking the door, then wincing in pain for her folly. "I pray to God this marriage ends. I pray with all my heart, Nicholas Brooks." She leaned up against one wall railing at God, at Nicholas, at herself for allowing herself to be talked into such lunacy. Now, be honest, Lieutenant Claire Dumont, she said to herself scathingly, be honest and admit that the reason you didn't fight harder against the marriage was because you actually wanted to marry him.

"I hate him! I hate, hate, hate him!" she screamed, making her voice raw, not caring should anyone pass by. Claire stood there, fists drawn up tightly by her side, willing herself not to cry, willing herself to be strong.

"I don't need him. I don't," she said aloud, but

softly. "Oh, why can't he care for me just a little?" Then she got angry with herself all over again. "Idiot!" She shoved off against the wall, walking blindly into her cot, slamming her shin painfully against the edge of it. With more strength than she thought she had, with all the anger and frustration she was feeling, Claire picked up the thing and heaved it with all her might against the wall, screaming like a banshee as she did. That felt good, she thought, marching over to the wooden cot that had suffered a crack along one side. Picking it up again, she threw it against another wall, hitting it with a loud crack, screeching all the while. Heaving from the exertion, Claire stood in the middle of the room, her eyes staring at the splintered pile of wood that had once served as her bed, a shadowed heap in a dark corner.

Hearing the major's uneven footsteps outside, Claire ran over to the cot and collected a piece of it, holding it up as a weapon. She'd run him through, she thought, if he dared say a word. She'd clock him over the head. She'd . . . the door flew open with a violence that made Claire jump back in fear.

There was Nicholas, his eyes wild, a lamp thrust forward as he quickly scanned the room. He took in the broken cot and Claire, her face red, her eyes flashing with anger, standing in the center of the room holding what appeared to be a piece of wood. She was alone. Thank God! When the guard had run to him saying he'd heard screaming and loud crashes coming from his office he'd thought only one thing—that Cunningham was a man with a death wish. The relief he felt to find her alone and well made him weak.

"What the devil happened here?" he asked, confused.

Claire, suddenly feeling foolish, dropped the piece of wood, which hit the floor, punctuating her sudden weariness. Deflated, she leaned against a wall heavily and crossed her arms, giving him a look of chagrin.

"I was angry."

"Angry."

"I suppose I was pretending that cot was your head."

"I see."

"I feel better now," Claire said, and she let out a small laugh. She covered her mouth as she felt another laugh bubble up inside her. Oh, she felt much, much better now. She looked up at Nicholas and could see the beginnings of a smile on those hard lips of his.

"Would you like to hit me now that I'm here in the flesh?" Nicholas, in all his imaginings, never thought she would take him up on his offer. She walked up to him, a smile still playing about that lovely mouth of hers, and slapped his face. Hard.

Her smile was gone as she shook her hand from the sting of the blow. She just stared at him, her eyes hard and challenging as she watched with fascination as a livid red imprint of her hand formed on his left cheek.

Nicholas clenched his jaw until it hurt. She watched him swallow, watched him search for the control he rarely lost, and bit her lip again, this time in worry.

"I'm sorry," she said. "I've never hit anyone in anger before. I've never . . . been this angry before. I don't get angry with people. But I heard you . . . You were . . ."

Nicholas sighed. "I know what I was. Perhaps the word you're looking for is 'jackass.' "

Claire appeared to think. "Yes. That one would do. But I could come up with a few more choice words."

Nicholas gave a short laugh and shook his head. "I'm sure you could." He looked at his bride, his lovely spirited bride, suddenly realizing that he had every right to hold her, every right to make love to her. The feeling washed over him unexpectedly, violently, and he knew he had been right in sending her away. He could not see her again. Not until they knew. Despite what he'd said about Diane, he almost wished

Claire was with child, just so he could have her again. He shook his head at the thought. It was insanity. What was wrong with him? He had never in all his life allowed his baser instincts to rule him. And now it seemed he was consumed by them.

Claire saw the change in him, saw the way his eyes suddenly seemed to see her. Her breathing became labored as he advanced toward her. He saw her reaction, her parted lips, the pulse quickening in her white, white throat. Just a kiss, he told himself. Just one.

He bent his head, brushing her lips with his, all the while telling himself it was all he wanted. One last kiss and then he would be healed. But he heard her give a little sound of pleasure, he felt her lips move against his, her jaw tilt so that he would have better access. Everything was by instinct, but every move she made, every sound, every breath, seemed calculated to drive him mad.

He buried his hands in her short hair, so soft against his fingers, and deepened the kiss, probing her mouth with his tongue, feeling her response beneath him. "Claire," he said, his voice breathy and taut. "Just one kiss. Just one. I swear." And his mouth came down on hers again and his body pressed against hers.

"Nicholas, does the word *annulment* mean anything to you?" Harry asked from the doorway, his voice tinged with amusement.

Claire stiffened at Harry's lazy question and Nicholas cursed under his breath. He leaned his forehead against hers, trying to gather his wits. Raising his head, he pressed an agonizingly sweet kiss against her forehead and moved away from her, leaving her dazed.

"Hello, Harry," Nicholas said with a crooked grin.

"I take it everything is all right here?" Harry simply could not suppress his smile.

"If you'll excuse me, Harry, I'll be with you in a moment."

Chapter Nine

The whiskey bottle had but a swallow left as Nicholas turned it over, emptying it into his well-used glass. He was drunk, goddammit, and it felt good. Real good. He gave Harry a bleary smile as he dangled the bottle over his glass, allowing those last few precious drops to drip, drip into the glass. The two had recounted their misadventures at West Point, carefully editing out all the fear and anxiety those days had brought, preferring to remember in their sodden state only the glory, the honor, the pranks. For a while they blubbered about men lost, the waste and carnage of war, never quite giving in to the tears they both wanted to shed, still saved for another more private time. Weren't quite drunk enough for that type of display, thank God.

"All my life, things have made sense. I obeyed my parents. I served my country. I knew where I stood. I didn't always understand why things happen the way they do, but I could put whatever happened into little categories. Right. Wrong. Good. Bad." He shook his head, the movements exaggerated by his drunkenness. "But she doesn't fit. She doesn't go anywhere. She's soft and tough and a girl and a boy. She looks at me with those damned eyes accusing me of . . . something.

Then looks at me with eyes so dead, I'd do anything to make them . . ." He stopped, still not too drunk to realize he was being a sop. "She doesn't fit," he said harshly.

"And Diane fits," Harry said knowingly.

Harry watched as a ridiculous grin came over Nicholas's face, as he relaxed his clenched fists. "Yes. Diane fits." It was as if a great realization had come over him. "Diane fits! She is good. She is soft. She is what she is supposed to be."

Harry heaved a heavy sigh, and like a father about to teach a son a serious lesson, he put a hand on Nicholas's shoulder, gripping it hard. "You, my friend, are under a delusion."

"Whassat?" he slurred.

"You believe that everything you control, is good. And everything that sits even slightly out of where you think it should, is bad. And that's simply a bunch of bullshit."

Nicholas leaned back in his seat, still grinning. "Maybe so. No. Probably so."

"I know you're drunk if you're agreeing with me."

Nicholas snorted and slapped a hand on the rough wooden table. "I have a dilemma, my friend," Nicholas said lightly.

"A dilemma?"

"I want the woman who is my wife, but I don't want her for my wife." Nicholas screwed up his face. That didn't quite make sense. "She isn't Diane," he said as if that would clarify things.

Unfortunately, it did, Harry thought.

"What happens if Claire has a baby?"

Nicholas frowned. "I will do what is right."

"Do you really think abandoning her if she is not with child is right?"

That question acted like a bucket of cold water on Nicholas, who had been enjoying his drunkenness up until then. Things were getting a bit too serious.

"I will not be abandoning her," he said tightly. "I have found her a position of respect. God knows it's better than she likely deserves. She can neither read nor write. I know nothing of her background except she likes to masquerade about as a soldier. She has no people. She's a nothing. She should be grateful."

"Then why do you feel so guilty?"

"Because nothing makes sense with her. Because she looks at me as if she knows everything going on in my head. And who the hell said I feel guilty?" Nicholas shouted.

Harry chuckled amiably. "No one, my friend. No one."

"Ah, hell, it's my owned damned fault," Nicholas said, all spit and fire suddenly gone. "I thought I was protecting her from the men and I should have had the men protecting her from me. Couldn't keep my dick where it belonged. Thought she was a whore. How was I to know?"

She had been so responsive, so willing, he thought, allowing his mind to go drunk where he would not allow it to go sober. He wanted her again, but slowly this time. He wanted to show her what pleasure he could bring her. He wanted to savor her, kiss her breasts, touch her until she was wild. He had never lost control so quickly, but she had driven him mad. Every touch, every sound. Just thinking about it made him want her.

"One can usually tell innocence," Harry said. "Unless it was the blind leading the blind?"

Nicholas laughed then. "I was blind, but not that blind," Nicholas said. "Abstinence is never a good idea, Harry. It always leads to trouble."

"Or hairy palms." The two men laughed, delighting in their off-color conversation. Then they ordered another bottle.

* * *

Rosy early-morning sunlight streamed through the dirty little window, warming Claire's face which was turned to the beam as if she were a flower kept too long in the shadows. After four days of being cooped up in her cell, that is exactly what she felt like. She had been let out only a few minutes at a time when Nicholas was not in his office, so she had caught only a glimpse of him since their wedding day. Even though he had told her he would, she could not help but be hurt that he had stayed away for so long. He must feel absolutely nothing for me, she thought, a bit bewildered.

"Remember me?" Cunningham's voice sliced through her. Claire was silent, but she knew her eyes betrayed the stark fear she felt at seeing him. "Good," he said with a smile that made Claire's stomach twist sickeningly. "Don't forget. Because I won't, little girl. You remember that."

And he was gone.

The encounter, brief as it had been, left Claire shaken. He can't hurt me, she thought. He just wants to scare me. She could only comfort herself with the knowledge that she was leaving here, that Cunningham did not know where she was going. She would be safe.

When she heard Nicholas's footsteps, so achingly familiar, Claire flushed with anger at herself for her relief that it was him, and forced her clamoring heart to quiet. She remained as she was, with her face uplifted toward the sun, pretending she did not hear him approach. With more control than she thought she had, she did not even jump when he quietly said her name.

Nicholas knew Claire would be in her corner, but he was still caught off guard by the angel lifting her face to the heavens that met his gaze. The reality of Claire was always so different from his memory, so much sweeter. Nicholas did not allow himself to think of Claire, and when he did, he tried to imagine her in the most unflattering way. To find her here, her hair burnished, her dark, gold-tipped lashes fanned out on soft cheeks, her lips, full and up-tilted and just parted, as if drinking in the warm rays, left him weak.

"Claire," he said, his voice low and rumbling. She turned toward him slowly, showing him the blue heaven of her eyes, her mouth giving him an unconsciously sensuous smile. Hell, she could have been grinning at him like a hyena and he would have thought her smile sensuous. Thank God he'd had the strength to stay away, he told himself fiercely.

"My brother Matthew is here. It's time to go."

Nervousness flooded her. Ridiculously, she found she did not want to go. Of course I want to leave, she chastised herself sternly. He awkwardly held out a cheap carpetbag and an ugly brown coat. He hadn't wanted Claire to arrive at his family home a complete pauper with nothing but the dress she wore on her back.

"Oh." It seemed that for the first time in her life, Claire could only utter a single syllable at a time. Gathering herself together, she stood to accept the bag and coat. "Thank you."

Nicholas found himself embarrassed that she should be grateful for such a paltry little gift. "I've enclosed some money for you. For clothes. And for the baby should there be one. I don't expect this war to last much longer, but it could be several months before I see you again. I've explained things to my brother."

Claire grew alarmed. "What things?"

Nicholas was quick to reassure her. "That you are a refugee. That I found you wandering alone, that your maid had died of some fever and you became lost, that you are from a good family, etcetera, etcetera."

"Oh."

"Will you please stop saying that word? Will you

stop being so damned complacent?" Nicholas nearly shouted. He'd rather have her spitting fire at him than standing there like a docile lamb. If that's what he wanted, that's what he got.

"Well what do you expect? I've had no say over what is happening. What am I supposed to do? Fight you? For what purpose? Nothing would change. You have everything figured out nicely for yourself. Your honor will be served, your conscience will be clear. You'll probably even get to marry the woman you really love. And what will I get? If I am pregnant, I get a husband who hates me, who will every day of his life wish I were someone else. If I am not, I will find myself without a home, with no friends, no family, no job, nothing. So you can just take your high principles and put them . . . put them . . . high up where the sun don't shine." Claire turned red with anger.

Now, that was much better, Nicholas thought. He had the audacity to smile.

"Don't you dare smile at me, Major. Don't you dare." Claire was so mad she could spit.

"Ah, Claire," was all he said, and he gathered her into his arms before she could push away. "That's how I want to remember you. That's the real Claire Dumont."

"How would you know?" she grumbled. She gave a couple of halfhearted punches against his rock-hard stomach, then rested her fists there, pushing against him when she wanted to pull him closer. He looked down at the top of her head, which she had stubbornly and firmly planted against his chest. He placed one roughened hand on her silky strands, allowing himself that one last caress, closing his eyes so that he might remember it.

He released her and she stepped away. "Now. If you are with child, what telegram do you send?"

She rolled her eyes. This was the third time they

had gone over this. "If I'm knocked up, just the word 'yes,'" she said, baiting him.

"What?"

"Yes if I'm with child."

He scowled, somehow knowing she was making fun. "And if you are not?"

"No."

"When I receive the annulment?"

"You send, 'It is done.'"

"And then?"

"Then I may stay or I may go. It is up to me."

"Very good," he said, as if he were talking to a simpleton. "The trip to Northford should only take one day. You'll be on the train most of the way. My brother is not the best company but you will be safe with him. He is a good man, Claire."

"I don't doubt that he is. But that is a trait I take it does not run throughout the family." She stood glaring at him, her arms folded, her hands kneading her upper arms.

Nicholas gave her a crooked grin. "Not quite. My sister is also quite good."

"And your parents?"

"Both up for sainthood."

"Well sirrah," she said in her exaggerated accent that always made him smile. "There is always hope for the black sheep. The devil can always be exorcised. But I do declare, that in you, the good Lord does have his work cut out for Him."

Clasping a hand to his heart, playing along one last time, he said. "I am cut to the quick that you should think my heart so black."

"Oh bull. As if you gave a rat's tail what I think."

"You wound me!"

Claire abruptly stopped the game at the sound of a carriage outside.

"I suppose I should go."

"Yes." Claire walked down the short hall to the

door that stood open on this unusually warm March day. "Good-bye, Major," she said, holding out her hand.

Nicholas stared at her, working his jaw, his eyes suddenly intense.

"Aw hell," he said, and with one motion pulled her toward him and kicked the door closed. He gripped her head in two hands, savagely but so gently, and brought his head down for a quick hard kiss. "If you carry my child, our child, I will try, Claire. I promise I will try. But that is all I can promise."

Claire looked at his eyes, no longer cold granite, but a softer, morning mist gray, then dropped her gaze down to his throat, where his stiff collar bit slightly into his neck. "I know." She turned quickly, opening the door, and rushed to the carriage.

Claire could not say she had not been warned about Nicholas' brooding brother. But the reality of the man was so much more disconcerting than the brief description that he was "not the best company" the major had felt forced to give, that Claire found herself still taken aback.

Claire thought she had reconciled the fact that she was somehow alive and living in the year 1865, but she was still a bit bewildered to find herself stepping aboard a horse-drawn carriage. She nodded to the driver, not knowing whether she should or not, and stepped carefully into the carriage that shifted beneath even her slight weight. It seemed a novelty to be stepping into a rich carriage with gleaming burgundy leather seats and gold velvet curtains covering the windows. Although it was a sharp, sunny day, the inside of the carriage was dark and murky from cigar smoke. Claire automatically searched the ceiling for a light before realizing with a blush there would be none.

Claire decided to take the seat opposite the shadowy figure leaning against one corner of the seat, stepping over a leg placed carelessly in her way. Trying to carry her small carpetbag in one hand and brace herself for balance with the other, Claire tripped heavily over the limb blocking the narrow aisle. She landed in a heap on a cushioned seat no worse for the wear, but was immediately concerned she may have injured the gentleman's leg, so hard did she hit it with her booted foot.

"I'm sorry," Claire said, wincing at what she perceived as the man's pain. She rested a hand on his leg and was immediately puzzled. The leg felt so . . . odd.

"I'm afraid it is quite impossible to injure that leg, miss, unless you knocked into it so hard it splintered," came the sardonic reply from the shadow man.

Ridiculously, Claire continued touching the odd leg until it dawned on her impossibly thick skull. It was an artificial limb. Jerking her hand away and blushing red, Claire quickly explained. "I'm so sorry, Mr. Brooks. I did not realize it was, uh, a prosthesis." Then, allowing a bit of censor into her voice: "Your brother did not explain."

Claire sat back, still feeling the awful heat of her blunder, and clamped her mouth shut. If she could simply keep her mouth shut, this long trip would not be so difficult, she told herself. The two rode in silence for several long minutes. The silence was so uncomfortable for Claire she began humming a tuneless song under her breath. But that seemed to make things worse. The creaking of the leather and the springs beneath the seats, in Claire's mind, only amplified the fact that she was sitting across from Nicholas Brooks's brother, being utterly rude by ignoring him. She gave no thought to the fact that he had leaned his head back into the corner and appeared to be sleeping and was being just as rude by ignoring her.

"Did you injure your leg in the war, Mr. Brooks?" The question seemed so loud in that creaking carriage, it seemed as if Claire had shouted the words.

By now Claire's vision had adjusted to the gloom and she was able to watch as his eyes drifted slowly open. He lifted the still-smoldering cigar to his lips and inhaled until the tip glowed red.

"No."

"Oh."

Wracked with curiosity, Claire sat silently for a few seconds formulating her next question.

"Then how did you injure it?" she asked, deciding her characteristic bluntness would work quite well in this situation.

"How can that possibly be any of your business, Miss Dumont?" The question was asked so politely, so calmly, that the menace behind it was all the more apparent.

Answering his question on face value, Claire said, "I suppose it's not any of my business. I'm simply curious."

He stared at her, tapped his good foot twice, and shook his head. "I lost it in a boating accident," he said, amazing himself.

"A boating accident? Your brother never mentioned it."

Matthew raised an eyebrow, not surprised his unusually reticent brother had not shared any information about his family.

"It was a long time ago," he said in an attempt to end the conversation. But Claire, though she recognized this attempt, was still consumed with curiosity.

"Was it in a storm?" In her limited knowledge of boating and of accidents, it seemed to her they always occurred during some sort of storm.

"Yes." Perhaps, he thought, if he kept his answers short this woman would shut up.

"It must have been awful." Not waiting for a reply, for she believed she had pushed Matthew Brooks as far as she could, she continued to hold her own conversation. "I hope my being Southern doesn't bother you too much. Your being Northern doesn't bother me. I have a unique perspective on such things," and Claire could not help but smile. "War is the enemy, I've decided. Funny I should say something like a pacifist, with my upbringing what it was. But now I know war makes us our own enemy." Claire was rambling, she knew.

Something in her tone tugged at Matthew and made him take a better look at the slight woman sitting across from him. She looked out the window, her eyes moving lively, as if trying to capture every item out there to store it in her memory. She was a pretty thing, though he did not care much for her hair, and he noted with some interest that she wore no hat or gloves.

"You were lucky," Claire said, nodding at his leg.

"I'm afraid you don't know what you're talking about, Miss Dumont." His voice was hard, reminding her of Nicholas.

She turned toward him, her eyes holding something fathomless, something he recognized for he'd seen it in his own mirror. Old eyes.

"I'm sorry. I didn't mean to trivialize what happened to you." She gave a small laugh. "Everyone thinks their own hell is the worst. I forgot, Mr. Brooks. I can't believe that I did. Hell is hell is hell."

Despite himself, Matthew was intrigued. What a serious female she was.

"Explain."

"I was thinking, wrongly I admit, that because you did not lose your leg in the war, it was somehow not as horrid. But I don't know the circumstances. In my limited view, the worst that could happen to a man— or a woman—is war. But that's not right, is it? That's what I meant. Your hell is just as hellish as mine, or the major's. Because it's yours."

"You must have driven Nicholas crazy," Matthew

said, dismissing her. But he simply wanted her to shut up. He did not need to discuss what he already knew.

At the mention of Nicholas's name, Claire's expression closed. "He was much better at ignoring me than you are."

Matthew leaned his head back and closed his eyes. "Then I will simply have to practice."

Claire found herself unaccountably hurt. What was it about the Brooks men? Maybe it's not them, she thought. Maybe it's me. And she flushed when she realized what she had said. Could she not learn to keep her mouth shut? Why must every thought that flew into her head come out of her mouth? She sat silently as the carriage bounced roughly over the rutted road, bracing one hand on the seat and the other on the small windowsill.

Matthew appeared to be sleeping, but she suspected he was pretending, to avoid conversation. He was tall, like his brother, but he was more lean and more forbidding. Why, Nicholas was jolly compared to this man, Claire thought, then she immediately chastised herself. She knew nothing of this man. He was on the unwelcome chore of fetching little more than a servant to a new position.

A *servant*.

Without knowing she was doing so, Claire had put a death grip on the soft leather seat, her fingers turning white at their tips, her nails digging in. Her other hand clutched the locket painfully hard. This is awful, she thought. What am I doing here? I shouldn't be here. I should be trying to figure a way out of this, not sitting here like some sort of zombie. She turned quickly to look out the window, as if that would give her some answer, as if somewhere written on the still-brown hills, it would be carved vividly for her to see. What will I do, what will I do?

"Is something wrong, Miss Dumont?"

Claire jumped at the sound of his voice, wrenching

her head toward the shadowed corner where she could only see the shiny glint of Matthew's eyes. Somehow she could tell he was looking at her hand clutching the leather seat, and she immediately let go and thrust her hands onto her lap.

"No. I . . . no." What could she tell him? That she suddenly realized what was happening? That until that very moment, it had not dawned on her what she was?

"I've never been a servant before," she said, surprising herself and the man across from her.

"I could hardly call being a nanny being a servant."

Claire swallowed. "Yes. But. It's just occurred to me, that's all."

Matthew was silent for a long moment. This girl is not what she appears to be, not even what Nicholas thinks she is, he decided. "Nicholas doesn't know, does he?"

Claire's blue eyes widened. "Doesn't know what?"

"He doesn't know you are educated. That you come from a wealthy background, that you are what some would call quality."

Claire flushed. "We were not so rich. But yes, I am educated. I come from an old Southern military family."

"And lived in a grand house, I suppose," he guessed.

"Well, yes. I suppose some would call it grand. It was not so big, but very beautiful." Claire allowed herself a wistful smile of the home she had not had the heart to sell. A beautifully restored row house, it had been built in 1892, and so would not even exist yet.

He leaned forward, giving Claire the first good look at the hard planes of his handsome face, at the glittering green-blue eyes, the color of the sea on a stormy day. "What are you to my brother, Miss Dumont?"

Startled, Claire involuntarily moved back from his penetrating stare. "N-n-nothing," she said before she could compose herself. And then, calmly, and truthfully, she said, "I am nothing to your brother."

But Matthew had his answer. Her words were strong and honest, but her eyes could not hide the truth. She may not be anything to Nicholas, but he was something to her. He let it rest for the moment, satisfied that he was still capable of reading people so well even though it had been years since he had tried.

Chapter Ten

March 15, 1865

Abigail Carr was exhausted. Five months' pregnant with three children underfoot, she found herself almost looking forward to the arrival of the woman Nicholas had described in his letter, even though she'd had grave doubts about the entire idea. He was right, of course, she could use the help. But Abigail had always been a bit of an oddity for a woman of her class, hiring a minimum number of servants and caring for her children herself. The thought of having another woman with her children, one she did not know, and one from the South of all things, was a bit disconcerting. It was more than disconcerting, it was alarming.

Abigail looked out the window, yet again having imagined the sound of a carriage outside. The drive was empty.

"You're going to pull that curtain down, Abigail," her husband said dryly, eyeing the material she was worrying in her hand.

"Oh, George, why is it nothing bothers you. The entire house could be aflame and you would say, 'Abigail, my dear, I think it would be prudent to leave the house, do please fetch the children and we'll be off.' "

George laughed, not at all bothered by his wife's accurate mimicry.

"What do you think she's like?" Abigail said, not for the first time since she had received the rather cryptic letter from Nicholas. She could have refused to take the woman, of course. She should have refused. But she could never, ever say no to Nick, especially when she had not seen him since his injury. She would do anything for her big brother, she would hire the entire displaced South had he wanted her to, so grateful was she that he'd survived his wounds. She had gone to church every day to pray and plead with God to save her Nick when they'd received word of his injuries, and had run until she was breathless to thank Him when she finally received a letter in her brother's own handwriting.

It was completely unlike her brother to pick up a foundling and help her, and she wondered if her brother's wound had softened him a bit. She could not understand what he was thinking of, sending the poor woman to Northford. He had offered little information in his letter, only that she was a refugee from the war, stranded alone and lost in Yankee territory when he discovered her. He said she seemed "respectable and clean" and hoped his sister would see fit to give her a position as nanny. Abigail pictured an older, matronly woman, given her brother's only description in the letter was "respectable and clean."

George eyed his fidgeting wife with humor. She was in a positive state over this event and had plagued him with endless questions that he could not answer any more than she could.

"I'm sure she has two heads and is foaming rabid at the mouth," he said into his newspaper.

Abigail put her hands to her hips, a pose that she meant to look threatening but only made her look adorable, George thought, his brown eyes traveling warmly down to her gently swelling stomach.

"I'm just trying to think how I would feel if things were reversed. Imagine me, George, getting lost in say, Virginia, and being sent to Mississippi to work in a Southern home. I can't think of anything more horrid. Why would a woman do such a thing?"

"Perhaps she is a woman with few choices. Nick wrote she had no family, so perhaps this is the best she could hope for," George said, his tone matter of fact.

"Or," Abigail said, her eyes growing narrow, "perhaps she's a Rebel spy."

George let a laugh explode from him. "Oh yes, she will be quite dangerous in Northford, the center of the Union intelligence activity. Really, Abby, don't you dare think any such thing. The poor woman has been through quite enough without you casting such suspicions her way." He shook his paper, showing Abigail his irritation with such a fanciful notion. "And do not mention that thought to Diane. The next thing we'll know a lynch mob will be forming outside our doors demanding that we give up the Rebel spy."

"I was simply speculating," Abigail said, pouting a bit. "And I didn't actually think such a thing. I was simply having a bit of fun." Abigail gave her husband a dark look. The war was one subject that her usually jovial husband never joked about. It more than bothered him that he was rejected from the Army because he was deaf in one ear, a leftover remnant of childhood ear infections.

"And Diane is not the addlebrain you take her for," Abigail added, staunchly defending her friend. Diane would be stopping by in the afternoon, as she usually did, but this afternoon's visit was specifically so she might meet the new nanny and grill her about Nicholas. The two were best friends, having grown up together like sisters. Their parents were quite close, so it was only natural that Diane and Abigail, who were just a few months apart in age, also be close. Even Abigail's early marriage did nothing to mar their friendship. If Diane was jealous of Abigail's husband and children, she did not show it. She was the sweetest person Abigail knew, and she was counting on Nicholas to make them truly sisters. Everyone in the family knew the match was inevitable, for every time Nicholas had managed to make it home, Diane was always by his side. Diane had prayed right alongside Abigail for Nicholas's safe return, and had cried tears of joy when Abigail read his letter aloud to her. Nicholas had written, "Give Diane my warmest regards," and Diane made Abigail read that section twice.

"Warmest regards," Diane had said dreamily. "Oh, I wish this war would end, Abby. Then Nicholas would be home and we could—" Diane stopped herself, pretending to be shocked by what she was about to blurt out. But Abigail knew her friend and knew she had been pining for her big brother for years. She was Diane's partner in crime, managing to have her friend present for each family event Nicholas managed to attend in the past ten years.

Before the war began, Nicholas had been twenty-two and Diane fifteen, too young for the young soldier to openly court. But when Diane turned eighteen, it seemed as if she had also, overnight, turned into a woman, and the two began acting the way both had been longing to. Nicholas had not wanted to make promises, not when he could die in battle. He did not want Diane pining for him when so much could change before the war ended. Though nothing was said aloud, both knew Diane was waiting for Nicholas, and while he could not express his gratitude in so many words, his kind mentions in letters, his warm looks when he was on leave, told her he was glad she did. It had been enough to satisfy them both.

Had Claire known what she was stepping into when she stepped down from the carriage, she would have jumped back in and barred the door. She and Matthew had said little more of consequence through their long trip. They had come to a sort of mutual understanding of sorts. Matthew had figured her out, but would not give up the game. And Claire had gotten under the skin of a man who had made an art of not letting anyone in.

"Are you coming in?" Claire asked, peeking through the carriage window at the simple but large house before her, its features barely distinguishable in the oncoming dusk.

"No."

Matthew watched as she gathered herself together, taking a fortifying breath and throwing a falsely brave smile his way.

"Thank you for accompanying me, Mr. Brooks," Claire said, more to stall the inevitable than to express her gratitude. She had already thanked him on the train.

"I suppose I should go in now."

"I suppose you should."

Claire threw him an irritated look. "You could be a bit more helpful, you know."

"I could be," Matthew said, a crooked little smile forming before he could stop himself.

Claire smiled, giving him this victory, and thrust out her hand. "Good-bye, Mr. Brooks. And thank you again."

She opened the door and stepped from the carriage a bit awkwardly, unused to maneuvering in long skirts, and closed the door without glancing back at the brooding man who studied her so closely. Her eyes were peeled on the house that would be her home at least for the next few weeks and possibly longer, if she was pregnant. If I can go through with this craziness, Claire corrected silently. It was a massive house squatting at the end of a long drive. Three stories high, the house appeared rather ordinary from the front, like many New England homes built in the early part of the eighteenth century. But additions over the years produced a somehow charming hodgepodge of architecture resulting in a home of huge, if not sloppy, proportions. Painted white with black shutters, it could have looked forbidding, but instead it was a welcoming warm place and Claire found herself smiling.

"My God, George, look. She's just a baby," Abigail held the curtain opened just enough for one blue eye to look outside. The young hatless woman stood looking up at the house, a whimsical smile playing about her mouth. She wore a black dress and a cheap, thin cloak that probably did nothing to shield her from the brisk wind coming off Miller's Cove. As if suddenly aware of the chill in the air, the young woman shivered and gathered the brown cloak about her, and seemed unsure of what to do next. Abigail frowned as Matthew's carriage disappeared down the drive. He should have stayed with the girl, she thought, but was not surprised that her brother had retreated to his sanctuary on Willow's Point.

"She's not wearing a hat or gloves," Abigail informed her husband. "And, unless I'm greatly mistaken, it does not appear she is wearing any petticoats." Abigail was unable to hide her shock at the state of undress this young woman had arrived in.

"Perhaps petticoats are not worn in the South," George offered.

Abigail rolled her eyes. "Don't be ridiculous. Petticoats are very much worn in the South. Mounds of them. Quite over down there, if you ask me. Oh what has Nicholas sent us?" Abigail asked worriedly.

"Abigail," George said with a bit of the censor in his tone. "You certainly aren't judging the poor girl based on her wardrobe, or lack of it, are you?"

"Of course not. It's simply a curiosity. I'm sure I can scrounge up something for her. Are you coming with me, George?" He answered her by getting up from his spot near the fire and joining his wife as she walked toward the front door.

"Well. We suspect she has no petticoats. Does she have two heads, my dear?" he asked, pretending rapt curiosity.

Abigail's answer was to purse her lips and give him a playful punch on the arm. "Three heads."

George opened the door, letting in a gust of cold air, startling the young woman, who had just begun to reach for the door knocker.

"Oh." Claire's eyes were huge as the door swung open revealing a jovial-looking bearded man standing next to a pretty brunette. The woman was smiling at her. Claire hadn't been sure if she should use the front door and was glad to see a smiling face.

"Hello. You must be Claire Dumont. I am Abigail Carr, Nicholas's sister. And this is my husband, George. Please come in, you must be cold."

Claire walked in, feeling the immediate warmth of a household that makes good use of its fireplaces. After the coldness of Fort Wilkins and the carriage, it felt almost luxurious, making Claire realize how long it had been since she'd been truly toasty warm. Despite the smiles and the warmth of this house, she clutched her carpetbag in her hands and wished she were back in her dark little room.

"Hello, Mr. Carr, Mrs. Carr." Abigail took her cloak, and Claire was mildly surprised that no servants had appeared to do the task. She'd somehow gotten the impression that everyone with money had large numbers of servants in the good old days. Abigail was a tiny woman with a huge unruly mop of brown hair that was currently piled artlessly atop her head. She bore little resemblance to her brothers, other than her sharp, intelligent eyes. It was almost inconceivable that the same parents who produced two giants for sons could have also had this petite woman.

"You're so tiny," Claire blurted, immediately grimacing.

Abigail laughed. "That's what most people think

when they meet my two bear brothers." Abigail paused, studying the slender woman before her. Her face was pale and drawn and dark smudges under her startling blue eyes told of her weariness. Her black dress hung on her as if she had recently lost a great deal of weight, or else borrowed it from a heavier woman. The dress was clean, but slightly faded, as if it had seen a few too many vigorous washings. And of course, there were no petticoats.

"Welcome to Northford. You must be exhausted, so I'll show you around the house when you're rested. The children are with their grandparents for the afternoon. I didn't want to overwhelm you with them."

Claire *was* exhausted. After spending long weeks in the prison camp, the full day of relentless travel was unexpectedly tiring. "I am tired," Claire said, suddenly feeling that she would not be able to take another step without sleeping.

"I wasn't sure which room to give you," Abigail said as she started up the stairs, the steps giving up homey creaks. "You should be near the children, but we have no real nursery here except on the third floor and I didn't want to put you there and I don't keep the children up there. It's so cold in the winter and almost unbearably hot in the summer. And I thought you might like to face south." Abigail blushed. "You know, for the sun."

"My room at home had a southern exposure," Claire offered. "Please don't feel awkward about my being Southern, Mrs. Carr. I realize this is a bit strange for both of us. And it's not as if we can ignore it, can we. Every time I open my mouth, it's a reminder. I just hope I don't make you feel uncomfortable, knowing I am Southern and having a brother in the Union Army."

"Apparently it did not make my brother uncomfortable. I trust his judgment. I do have one question, though. How old are you, if you don't mind my asking?"

"Twenty-two."

Abigail's eyes widened. "When I first saw you, I thought you were much younger," she said, realizing that Claire's short hair and the overlarge black dress combined to give her a waiflike appearance. But the girl's demeanor, her grace in a situation that must be nerve-wracking, impressed Abigail. Even though she was two years her senior, married, and with children, Abigail felt like the younger woman. She could hear her mother's voice in her ear: "Hardship has a way of forcing people to grow up." Perhaps this is what she was sensing in this woman, she thought.

Claire self-consciously brought a hand up to touch her still-short locks when she saw Abigail's eyes drift to her hair. "I singed it in a camp fire," Claire improvised quickly, "and had to cut it off. It's growing back."

"Oh, that must have been awful. It's lucky you were not injured."

"Yes, quite lucky," Claire said weakly. She hated to lie, hated that she must play false with these good people who were taking her into their home.

The two walked down a long dim hall, Abigail pointing out a small study, the children's rooms, and the Carrs'. The hallway seemed to stop at a narrow set of stairs that led up to the small servants' quarters and down to the kitchen, but a door almost hidden behind the steps led to another wing and Claire's room.

"Here we are," Abigail said, opening a door to a room with slanted ceilings and deeply encased windows. "It gets a bit chilly in here in the winter without a fire because of all the windows, but I adore this room. Most of the house is three stories, but this part is two, so you get these odd ceilings."

Claire walked in behind Abigail and immediately

smiled. The bed was tucked in one corner opposite a bank of tall windows covered with lacy curtains. A small fire danced in the fireplace situated near the door, its bricks whitewashed. Abigail walked to a small windowed cubbyhole where a writing desk with an inkwell built in was located and peered out. "If you look through those trees, you can see Miller's Cove."

Claire followed her direction until she could see the sparkle of the small cove. "It's lovely," she said, her voice husky and low. "Thank you. I love old homes."

"I'm glad you like it, but the house is really quite new compared to many houses you passed along Main Street." Claire gave herself a mental slap, a reminder that she was living in the 1860s.

"This room is one of my favorites in this monster, but it's so out of the way, we really don't have a use for it. It's wonderful in the summer, though, with all these windows, and I imagine you don't mind the heat too much. I'll let you get settled and send someone up for you in a few hours. Have a nice rest."

Claire hung her spare dress in a tall wardrobe and tucked her carpetbag in the bottom before sitting on the bed and bouncing a bit. The mattress gave a crinkling sound beneath her, but seemed comfortable enough. Then, trying not to wrinkle her dress, she lay back and stared sleepily at the fire.

"I'll imagine I am here for a visit," she whispered. "I'll imagine they are Northern relatives I have never seen who live in a quaint bed and breakfast and I won't think about why I am really here." But she did think about it and her stomach gave a queasy turn. "Disappear, disappear," she mumbled, and fell asleep.

Claire awoke feeling disoriented and chilled. The fire had long gone out and the room was dark, telling her the sun had disappeared beneath the horizon. When she heard a small knock on the door, she realized it must have been a knock that had awakened her.

"Come in," Claire called, her voice hoarse from sleep.

A portly, gray-haired woman entered the room, carrying a lamp and what appeared to be a mountain of frothy material with her. "Hello, Miss Dumont. I'm Mrs. Tillinghast, the housekeeper. Mrs. Carr wanted me to come fetch you to the parlor."

"Oh, yes. Thank you," Claire said, standing quickly and smoothing out her dress. She brought a hand up to her hair, fluffing it a bit, but knowing it was likely a mess.

"There's a mirror in that corner if you'd like to see," Mrs. Tillinghast offered brusquely. "There aren't many servants here. Just me, the cook, and two others. This isn't a grand household." Claire knew then that Mrs. Tillinghast resented her presence.

"I'm not used to grandness, Mrs. Tillinghast," she said.

"Well, it's just as well you aren't, I suppose. It's not that the Carrs can't afford to take on more servants, don't get me wrong. We just make do, seeing how the country is at war. It's a time for sacrifice. A time for doing without."

Claire flushed at the mention of the war. She was not sure the older woman felt that way because she was from the South or because she believed having a nanny was excessive in these hard times. She got her answer almost immediately.

"My son Carl is fighting. Fighting for the Union," she said, as if Claire could have made a mistake and thought her son was fighting for the Confederacy.

"Then I hope he is safe, Mrs. Tillinghast," Claire said softly. She had no desire to make enemies here.

Mrs. Tillinghast gave a little "hmpfh" and handed the lamp to Claire so that she might see herself better in the small mirror. Claire blinked at the image re-

flected back at her and brought a hand up to her face,
almost to reassure herself that the woman she saw was
actually her. While she felt a bit of relief to actually
see her own face peering back at her, she realized she
looked simply awful. Her hair was uneven and in need
of a good brushing, her cheekbones, always promi-
nent, were absurdly so because she was so thin. Her
eyes looked ridiculously large in her head. Claire tried
ineffectually to tame her hair, as she grew hot beneath
the stern, assessing gaze of Mrs. Tillinghast. Claire
gave a nervous little laugh.

"I haven't seen myself in weeks," she said. "It's
almost like seeing a stranger."

Grimacing, she turned to find Mrs. Tillinghast's eyes
hard on her.

"Mrs. Carr was kind enough to find some petticoats
for you to wear," the older woman said, thrusting the
material toward her.

Claire took the undergarments cautiously. "Petticoats?"

"Two should be sufficient, although I understand in
some parts of the country, women wastefully wear
more," Mrs. Tillinghast said, her tone mean and hard.

Claire shook out two of the petticoats and folded
the other neatly on her bed. Petticoats, for goodness
sakes. What was next? A corset? As if reading her
mind, Mrs. Tillinghast said crisply, "I'll also inform
Mrs. Carr you are in need of a corset. This is a respectable household, Miss Dumont."

Claire inwardly grimaced, but realized that she
would probably have to wear one of the torture de-
vices in order to appear "respectable." Maybe this is
hell, she thought grimly as she pulled on the rustling
petticoats.

"Would you please show me to Mrs. Carr?" she
asked, smoothing her skirts.

"That's what I'm here for." The woman turned and
led her down the long hall to the sweeping front stair-

case, Claire smiling at the unfamiliar sound of her rustling petticoats. They walked down a carpeted hall that eventually opened up into a high-ceilinged parlor, warm and cozy from a fireplace that was almost large enough to stand up in. Most of the room was cast in shadows, the only lamp lit was by Mrs. Carr, who was busy working on a sampler.

Sitting in an overstuffed, comfortable-looking chair not far from the fire, Abigail beckoned Claire to sit across from her. The room glowed warmly from the fire and a table lamp with its flame turned low.

"I hope you had a nice rest," Abigail began. "My brother said very little in his letter. You have no family?"

"No. They died in a plane . . . They died." Claire said, tensing at her mistake, and immediately changed the subject. "How old are your children?"

Abigail smiled, warming immediately to the new subject. "Mabel is just eighteen months, Nathan is five, and Emily is three." Abigail folded her hands and became pensive. "I've always cared for my children, Miss Dumont, so I'm not entirely at ease with this arrangement. Please do not take this to heart. My brother and my husband agree I do need help even when my mother is here, and I admit they are right. But I'd like to ease into this, if possible. I know this is not what you were expecting, but I'd still like to care for my children as much as possible. I'm afraid I would miss them terribly if I were to simply put them into your hands. At least until this one is born," Abigail said, placing a hand on her slightly swollen belly. "I will be with the children several hours each day, so that means you will have more free time than I imagine you expected."

Claire relaxed, hearing the uncertainty in Abigail's voice. She was as unused to having a nanny as Claire was to being a nanny. "I've never been a nanny, Mrs.

Carr, and I appreciate this position. I'm sure we'll work things through."

Not for the first time did Abigail wonder what her brother had been thinking. This woman sitting across from her staring at her with those disconcertingly expressive eyes was nothing what she expected. It was so unlike her brother to act so impulsively, promising a position to a woman he did not know, who had no experience caring for children, and who came from the South.

"Nathan is a bit rambunctious, so if you're not used to boys, it may be difficult for you. Mabel is precious. She's just starting to talk, to say things you can recognize as words. But she's constantly getting into things because of her incessant curiosity. And Emily is her older brother's shadow. She's discovered throwing tantrums can be quite effective in getting my attention. It can be difficult. They are so active." Claire noticed Abigail twisting a handkerchief in her hands, and realized that relinquishing her children to a complete stranger was distressing her. Claire made an immediate decision—it was better for her to put the woman at ease than to pretend she was some ignorant hick, as Nicholas thought her. She had no idea what Nicholas had written, but she decided to put the record straight.

"Mrs. Carr, I grew up in a wealthy family in Virginia. I had two older brothers whom I was able to keep up with quite well. My family is gone now, but when I was young, my brothers were my best friends and I could not be separated from them. I am probably overeducated by today's standards for women. In addition to literature, calculus, physics, and biochemistry, I am fluent in French and Latin and speak and read both."

Abigail smiled. "And church? My brother said very little," she said to explain her trepidation.

"Your brother knows very little," Claire said, attempting at lightness. "I go to church." Sometimes.

At the sound of a commotion toward the front of the house, Abigail threw Claire an apologetic look. "Claire, my dearest friend Diane has arrived. I hope you don't mind, but she's a bit taken with Nicholas and . . ." Abigail flushed. "I'm afraid Diane will try to get you to describe in intricate detail how he is. Diane is very sweet, but she's just a complete idiot over Nicholas."

"I . . . I don't know what I could say. I . . . didn't see much of him," Claire stuttered. To her horror, she felt herself blushing and prayed Abigail would not read anything into that blush. To see Diane so quickly, to describe Nicholas to her—how could God be so cruel, she thought. She was married to the man, could be carrying his child, and Diane, the woman he loved, who loved him, would be standing before her bright-eyed and flushed. . . . Oh, damn, damn, damn, Claire thought, her heart beating painfully in her chest.

The rustle of skirts announced the legendary Diane, who stepped quickly into the room, bringing the crisp, fresh smell of outdoors with her. Claire tried not to stare, but could not help herself. Here she was, the woman Nicholas wanted for his wife. And here Claire sat, this skinny bedraggled thing in borrowed clothes with uneven, sleep-mussed hair, his wife in fact.

Diane was, indeed, perfection. A jaunty hat sat atop dark brown hair elegantly styled, her figure was trim, but shapely, her brown eyes sparkled with a joy and innocence Claire had long forgotten was possible. She was fresh and pretty, wore lovely, intricately made clothes, and had a sweet girlish voice when she noticed Claire sitting uncomfortably in the chair. How she managed to look so elegant wearing all that godawful material was beyond Claire.

"You must be Miss Dumont, the one Nicholas sent to us," Diane said, offering Claire a gloved hand. Claire didn't like the possessive way she talked about Nicholas, nor the way she talked about her as if Claire were some sort of object that Nicholas had sent by United Parcel.

Abigail smiled at her friend and gave her a little hug. "I've already warned Claire that the only reason you've come over today was to grill her about Nicholas, so you don't have to beat around the bush, darling."

Diane blushed prettily and threw Claire an apologetic look before taking off her cloak and hat and seating herself daintily in a nearby chair and demanding a full report.

"How is he?" Diane asked, leaning forward in her chair, her hands folded in front of her, her eyes intent on Claire.

Absurdly, Claire felt like blurting, "My husband is fine." This sudden and inexplicable possessiveness was completely unexpected and almost brought a bit of hysterical laughter bubbling up. Instead, she fought for control, and weighed her words carefully so as not to reveal too much.

"I didn't see him for long," Claire began cautiously, waiting for God to send a bolt of lightning crashing through the house for her blatant lies. "He appeared well."

Diane sat back, disappointed. "But his injuries. Are they apparent? He was wounded on his head, you know."

Yes, I know, I held him as he writhed on the ground in pain. I watched as he massaged his knee as he heard that his men had died. Claire realized her resentment toward this woman was caused by one thing—jealousy—but she could not help it.

"He seems to suffer from headaches. But, no, the scar is not apparent. He was injured on the side of his head and his hair covers most of the scar."

Diane put a delicate hand to her throat. "A scar?"

Claire could not help herself. She could not. "Yes. Grievous wounds typically do leave scars." She smiled serenely, leaving Diane wondering whether Miss Dumont was making fun of her or simply being kind by explaining. "And he has a slight limp in his left leg that appears to worsen if he sits for long periods of time." Claire cursed to herself: too much, you've said too much.

"How observant of you," Diane said, a smile touching her own lips. Somehow, both women knew some sort of battle line had been drawn. Diane might just suspect, might simply be the sort of woman who was jealous out of hand, but Claire felt sure she had seen through her. Poor Abigail sat looking at the two women, sensing something was wrong, but not quite understanding what was happening.

"Does he seem to be in much pain?" Abigail asked, her voice tinged with worry.

"I know his head injury is worse than his leg injury. He limps, so I imagine his leg pains him. We never discussed his wounds in any detail."

"And what did you discuss?" Diane asked, sounding chirpy and false.

I'm not your enemy, Claire thought miserably. Nicholas loves you, he loves you. "We talked about the war," Claire said honestly.

Diane seemed to brighten. Certainly there was no threat discussing such a dreary subject as war. And Claire, not knowing why she did so, threw Diane a bone. "He mentioned you, Miss Pendleton."

"Oh?" And her smile could have lit a darkened room.

Now that she admitted it, Claire did not know what to say, but forged ahead anyway. "I forget what the topic was. He was actually speaking with a Colonel West at the time and I happened to be nearby." In my cell, right after my wedding. "He described you as, let me think, good and pure, I believe."

"Why that's rather boring, darling, isn't it," Diane

said to Abigail, a frown forming on her lovely face. "Did he say anything else to this colonel?"

He had said more. He had said that Diane Pendleton was the kind of woman to make a home with. That she was everything he'd always wanted. Everything he pictured a wife should be.

But Claire could not tell her that. It would be too cruel if she turned out to be carrying his child. "No. At least not that I can remember," and she made a mental note to ask God to forgive her the lies she told. "But he seemed to hold you in high regard," she said, pleased she had thought of something ambiguous to say.

Diane sat back, well pleased that Nicholas had spoken of her. From all accounts, the war was nearing its end and no doubt Nicholas would soon be home. That smile cut into Claire, adding to her intense discomfort. Nicholas must have known that Diane spent a great deal of her time with Abigail, that Claire would be forced to keep company with the very woman he wanted for his wife. For Claire, it was gentle torture to meet in the flesh the woman Nicholas had placed so high on a pedestal and to find that she seemed to actually belong there. Any pettiness she noticed on Diane's part, Claire decided, was her own jealousy poking through like a sharp new blade of grass. Claire looked at Diane, bright and clean, and above all, innocent.

It dawned on her with sickening awareness, that perhaps a reason Nicholas had kissed her, had held her, perhaps the *only* reason, was that she was a woman and he had not been near a woman in a very long time. He had told her as much. She had asked him why he kissed her, and he had simply told her it was because he wanted to. He had not said she was beautiful, as Diane certainly was. He had believed her to be a prostitute. Any woman would have done, even one as unappealing as herself. What a little fool I am, to think a man such as Nicholas Brooks would look twice at me in normal circumstances, she thought. And what a bigger fool I am to care.

"Miss Dumont? Did you hear me?" Abigail's voice forced its way through Claire's morose thoughts. Bringing her head up, she turned to the woman who was smiling gently at her. "I asked if you were ready to meet the children?"

Claire returned her smile. "Oh, yes. I would love to meet them."

Claire turned in her chair to watch the three children approach their mother, Nathan leading the way, trailed by Emily holding little Mabel's hand as she moved awkwardly on her chubby little legs. Claire groaned inwardly, knowing a horrible truth. If it turned out she was free to go, leaving these three little babies would be the most difficult thing she would ever do. Damn Nicholas and damn her unprotected heart.

Chapter Eleven

The days whirled past for Claire, who numbingly accepted her role in what she quickly learned was a lively household. Claire often found herself with free time, as George would suddenly arrive home from work and swoop the children away for some adventure or other. Not knowing what else to do, Claire would more often than not retire to her room until they returned. The total lack of events, the utter safety of this world, put Claire into a wonderful complacency about events around her. The war, the time she had spent in prison, her other life, seemed like years ago, or else a vividly real dream that was fading more and more every day. The only thing that was real from her days in prison was Nicholas, and no matter how much she tried, she could not banish him from her thoughts. It's because I don't want to forget him, she chastised herself silently many times. She would relive, over and over, every laugh they'd shared, every kiss, every touch, until she was quite sure she was engaging in a sort of self-torture. Once I know, it will be easier, she thought. This living in limbo, she decided, was why she was so willing to simply drift along like so much flotsam on a slowly rolling sea. She knew she had not truly accepted that she was living in the past. But with every day that slipped away, her old life faded more and more, almost as if it had never existed at all.

Eight days after her arrival, Claire knew she was not pregnant. She looked at her bloodstained underclothes, suddenly aware of the crampiness, a slight headache, and felt her throat constrict as an inexplicable sadness washed over her. "Oh, God," she whispered aloud. She had not known what she would feel, but had she guessed, she would not have, not in a hundred years, believed she would feel this overwhelming sense of loss. Well, you knew you weren't, she told herself, trying to buck up. She would have to send a telegram, of course. She cruelly pictured Nicholas's happy face at the good news. He would be free to marry Diane. And she could go.

At supper that night, alone in her room, Claire thought about what she should do. "I know what I should do," Claire thought as her stomach clenched. "I should leave." But even as she said the words aloud, as if to give herself resolve, Claire knew she could not.

The telegram lay unopened on the desk before him. Nicholas stared at it, drumming his fingers on either side of the small envelope. It will be no, he thought, it has to be no. It has arrived too quickly for it to be yes. The chances she is with child are too remote, so remote, he thought, I should not have bothered to marry her. I could have lasted a week with her here, he told himself, even though he knew he likely could not have. Not with her so near, not when he wanted her so much still.

He opened the letter and read the single word, letting out a breath he did not know he had been holding. He stared at the message, trying to feel the relief he knew he should feel, trying to garner even a bit of happiness. But for some reason he could not. He crumpled up the telegram, holding the thin bit of

Chapter Twelve

April 1865

On the day the newspaper arrived with the news that Richmond had fallen, Claire stayed as far away from everyone as possible. The mood in the Carr household was joyous, and Claire felt nothing but overwhelming sadness for the lives lost, for the hate and turmoil that was yet to come. She felt strangely detached from the events around her, and yet it had become an integral part of her life. It is all just history, people you'll never know, people who are long dead, she told herself. But telling herself this did not make it so. These events were happening now. And they were happening to her whether she acknowledged it or not.

She ignored the smug looks from Mrs. Tillinghast and the overloud comments from that petty woman, but she could not ignore the tolling bells, the guns shot in air in celebration. How alone she felt when all around her were completely happy. Abigail and George were understanding, and few in the household but for Mrs. Tillinghast were outright rude, but Claire felt like an outcast nonetheless. Strangely, the one person she believed could understand how she felt was Nicholas. If he were here, she thought, he would comfort me. Ah, but perhaps that was not true. Perhaps if Nicholas were here, he would be with his Diane, she thought, forcing herself to be realistic.

Less than a week later, General Lee surrendered. The Carr family huddled in the parlor, Abigail shushing the children who did not understand the significance of the news, while George solemnly read news accounts and printed letters from Lee and Grant. Claire prayed that day, for General Lee, for his soldiers, for all those men who had died only to lose in the end. She thanked God the war was near its end. But war had not finished punishing the country, she knew. So much would happen over the next decades, so much pain and change.

She could not recall the exact date Lincoln was assassinated, but knew it was coming. How awful to know an event so horrid was about to happen and know she could do nothing to stop it. On Saturday, April 16, the newsboy shouted the awful report while handing out the black-bordered newspaper. Lincoln had been assassinated. Even the Carrs could not help but give Claire censorious looks. For she was Southern and surely the entire South was guilty of this evil deed.

George, the newspaper rustling in his shaking hands, his voice thick with unshed tears, read the horrific account to his dazed family. "A hasty examination found that the President had been shot through the head above the temporal bone and that some of the"—he stopped, sickened by what he read—"some of the brain was oozing out," he finished.

Claire listened, hidden in the doorway. Claire might have known Lincoln would die, but living it, seeing people mourn, made his assassination as fresh and new as if it were happening for the first time.

"What are you *spying* on?" Mrs. Tillinghast asked, her voice cutting into Claire. She jerked and her face colored with a guilty flush for having been caught eavesdropping. "I was simply listening to Mr. Carr reading the awful news."

"You Rebs did it. You murdered him as much as if you had been holding the trigger yourself. I don't know what you're doing here, Miss Dumont, but I know you ain't telling the Carrs the whole truth. You're hiding something. I knew it the minute I laid eyes on you." All the hate for the South and for the war Mrs. Tillinghast directed on Claire as she spewed out her venom. And despite Claire knowing the older woman was a mean, petty person, her acid words hurt just the same. "You don't belong here. Why don't you go back South where you belong."

"Mrs. Tillinghast! That is quite enough!" Abigail's face was red with anger. "Claire is as much a part of this household as you are. She is welcome here as much as you are. And if you don't like that, *you* can leave."

At first affronted, Mrs. Tillinghast's pasty face flushed as her flat blue eyes took on a hunted look. Gathering herself together and lifting her loose chin, she said, "I'm sure you are correct, Mrs. Carr. I've got lunch to attend to if you will allow me to."

Abigail let out a small sigh. "Of course." To Claire she gave a pained look of apology. "It's her son. She hasn't heard from him in days now and the papers are still filled with news about fighting even though Lee surrendered."

Claire clutched her skirt, horrified to be the center of attention on this day. "I understand her attack was not personal, Mrs. Carr. If you don't mind, I'd like to take the children out for a short walk until lunch." The children loved Claire unconditionally and were too young to associate the tragic news of Lincoln's death with their nanny who had a distinctive Southern drawl. She wondered if she should take Mrs. Tillinghast's advice and leave. Certainly she should. She had no ties here other than the children and it would be better to leave now, before she became impossibly attached to them, than wait any longer. But when she thought of actually leaving this haven, she felt nearly paralyzed with uncertainty and fear. She had nowhere to go. She could go South, to Alexandria. At least the accents and some of the buildings would be familiar. In her heart, she believed it would be better to stay put, to put her hometown away in her heart and remember only the good times when her family was whole. If she went back now, when people were suffering and bitter from the long years of war, all her good memories of her childhood of her family would disappear forever.

And if she chose to look deep into her heart, which she chose not to do, there was another reason to stay. Nicholas would come home someday and she wanted to be here.

Chapter Thirteen

June 11, 1865

Claire felt like throwing up. She clutched a hand to her roiling stomach and looked again at her reflection in her small hand mirror propped on her wardrobe. Swallowing heavily in an attempt to calm her queasiness, Claire inexpertly twisted her hair and clipped it at her nape trying to avoid looking at her face. One look and anyone could see she was ridiculously nervous.

He was coming home today.

Claire let out another shaky breath and closed her eyes to search for some calmness. She had always known this day would come. But everything seemed to have happened so quickly. Wasn't it only weeks ago when she was climbing aboard the Blackhawk in South Korea? Wasn't it only days since she had sent her telegram to Nicholas. She had heard from him only once, the horrid telegram with the words, "It is done." Even though this is what they had decided, Claire found she was hurt he had not sent a more personal message.

Even if their marriage had been a sham, for a little while they had been husband and wife. They had lain together and held each other. They were not complete strangers. Those cold three words were like a slap in the face. To her utter disgust, she realized she still loved him. No, she thought, I love the man I thought he was—a kind man with honor. How many times would she have to tell herself he did not care for her before she began to believe her own arguments? How many times would she have to listen to Diane go on and on about how wonderful Nicholas Brooks was before she got it through her thick skull that it was Diane Nicholas loved.

Claire told herself she did not know whether she was more frightened he would ignore her, or appear glad to see her. But she did know. In her weakest moments, as she lay in her dark room she would imagine him coming to her first for a welcoming hug. She would imagine Diane's shocked face, her utter horror, that the man she loved instead loved Claire. How delicious were those fantasies. And how cruel. Claire knew how silly she was being, but she could not help herself. She missed him. And now he was coming home.

Claire smoothed her new dress. It was dark gray with a little white collar and white cuffs. She wore two petticoats and a new whalebone corset. Diane had joked that she looked a bit like a Quaker, and Claire supposed she did. It was appropriate attire for a nanny, Claire knew, for she had seen other nannies leading their charges around Northford. In the three months Claire had been in Northford, she had gotten used to wearing a corset, though she refused to cinch them to the point of her breathing being impaired. The first time Abigail had assisted her, she had nearly fainted as the woman violently pulled on the ribbons. If Abigail thought it strange that Claire had never worn a corset before, she never let on. And she only raised an eyebrow when Claire asked which undergarments went under which. Wearing so many layers was patently absurd to Claire, but Abigail patiently explained the petticoats, corset, chemise, stockings, and pantaloons.

Claire longed for jeans and a T-shirt, for her Hanes panties and bra. But instead she forced herself to conform, grumbling to herself nearly every morning as she began the dressing ritual. She tried to do without the corset, without the petticoats, but the dresses she had purchased hung oddly, and without the corset she could barely button them.

She was slowly becoming used to living in this century. She still found herself waving her arm along the wall of a darkened room searching for a light switch even as she carried a candle in her other hand. She still groaned when she walked out to the outhouse or squatted over the chamberpot. She got used to washing her hair in lukewarm water and rinsing it with cold, but oh, how she longed for an endless hot shower, the water beating down so hard and so hot it hurt.

Claire's thoughts were interrupted by Abigail, who stuck her head through her door. "Oh, there you are Claire. Could you please watch the children while we're at the train station. I think it might be too much for everyone with the children running about."

Claire smiled at Abigail, who looked even more disheveled than usual. "Of course. Where are they?"

"Where are they? Oh. In our bedroom. It's really too much right now. I'm a mess. Nicholas won't recognize me." She put her hands to her mop of hair, trying to tuck stray strands back into a large bun at the top of her head. "I hate to go out about like this, but I refuse, absolutely refuse, to have Nicholas step from that train and not see me there," she said, putting both hands on her swollen belly. At eight months' pregnant, she looked almost as round as she was tall. "I even convinced Matthew to be there, even though he saw him just those months ago."

Claire followed Abigail down the hall to the Carrs' bedroom, where she could already hear the excited chatter of the children. No doubt Nathan was beside himself not being able to join the adults in welcoming his uncle home. One look at his tearstained face and Claire knew she had been right.

"Come, children, let's go down to the beach and look for some shells to give to Uncle Nicholas."

Emily jumped up and down in excitement and Mabel followed suit, but Nathan refused to be baited with such a paltry offer when what he truly wanted to do was meet Uncle Nicholas coming off the train. He never got to do anything fun.

Claire knelt down to talk to the scowling little boy. "If we meet him here, Nat, then it will be like two welcome homes for Uncle Nicholas. Won't that be better than one? He'll be expecting people to greet him at the train, but just think how surprised he'll be when you come running out of the house to welcome him."

Nathan seemed to think about it and Claire held her breath. "No! I want to go!"

George decided to step in. "That's quite enough, young man. You will go with Nanny. I want not another word from you, do you hear me?"

His father so rarely used such a stern tone, Nathan was immediately chastised. "Yessir."

George lay a hand on top of his son's head. "That's better." He watched as Claire led his little family away, and turning to his wife, said, "Is everyone ready?"

"Your parents are waiting for us down in the foyer. Matthew said he'd meet us there. Oh, I wish Mom and Dad were here, too. They knew the war ended weeks ago." The Brooks had been gone for months on a European tour.

"They'll be here soon enough," George said in a way that made Abigail scowl. She knew her parents could be difficult, and living all together was wearisome, but she loved them dearly just the same.

The Carrs pressed into the carriage together, all

chattering excitedly about the homecoming. As the carriage pulled out of their drive, the Pendletons followed in behind them. A whole entourage of people would be there to greet Nicholas home, one of Northford's true heroes. Since the war had ended, it seemed like a great smothering fog had lifted, as if it were suddenly acceptable to laugh, to plan parties, to dance and not feel a twinge of guilt.

As the train pulled into Northford Junction, Nicholas felt his own stomach give a queasy turn. He had cried silently when he heard the war was officially over. He had watched with gladness in his heart as the Confederate prisoners walked out that gate and began their long trek homeward. But the end of the war, as joyous as that was, meant for Nicholas the end of a career. He'd always imagined himself either dying on a battlefield or retiring. He'd not imagined this sort of limbo. For the first time in his life, he did not know what or who he was. Harry Baker had joked that all he needed to do was put his name on a ballot and he would be elected in any race he cared to run in. The thought of running for office, the thought of any political career, was repugnant to Nicholas—especially after what had happened to Lieutenant Cunningham.

Nicholas had gathered an enormous amount of evidence against the man, going back years at Fort Wilkins. That he was guilty of stealing from the government was without doubt. But when he tried to pursue the matter, he'd found out just what politics were for. It turned out Cunningham had friends in high places. The matter was dropped and it was all Nicholas could do not to take justice into his own capable hands. Cunningham, smug and feeling untouchable, still was not stupid enough to throw his victory in his commanding officer's face. Nicholas had waited for him to say something—anything—so that he could justify throttling the man. But the war ended before Cunningham could be baited into laying himself open.

As the train ground to a halt, Nicholas bent to look out the murky, coal dust–covered window, and just made out the hazy figure of Diane. Even through the coal, she looked lovely, and Nicholas smiled. Claire's face, once so vivid, was finally, blessedly fading. Because Abigail was a notoriously bad correspondent, he did not know where she was and he told himself he did not care. She was a mistake, a short, not entirely unpleasant episode in what he hoped was a long and happy life. No one need ever know how close he had come to being with her for the rest of his life.

As Nicholas stepped from the train, he found himself surrounded by family and friends. Abigail, tears running down her face, awkwardly hugged her brother, who was forced to bend nearly in half to accommodate her neck-wrenching embrace. George slapped his back heartily and smiled as he wiped his own tears. Matthew's son Samuel appeared before him and accepted a bear hug and then disappeared into the crowd. He waved to Edgar and Mary Pendleton over the heads of George and Abigail and his eyes strayed to the woman standing next to them. Diane. More beautiful than he remembered. She did not throw herself into his arms, but held out both hands for him to grip, looking up at him with watery eyes.

"Welcome home, Nicholas," she said, her voice sounding sweet to his ears.

"It's good to be home. Strange, but good." Nicholas glanced around, seeing so many familiar faces, all smiling and waving, some with tiny American flags. Home. He had not been home, not truly, since he left for West Point all those years ago. Now he was here to stay, and it was finally beginning to sink in. These people would be part of his life. The woman standing in front of him would be his wife. It was overwhelming.

He felt a firm hand on his shoulder begin to pull

him through the crowd. "Let's get the hell out of here," he heard his brother growl. If there was one thing Matthew hated, it was crowds. Nicholas good-naturedly allowed himself to be dragged away from the throng, shrugging an apology as if he had no choice in the matter. The truth was, he was ecstatic his brother had pulled him away.

Matthew led him to a buggy and with a sharp snap of the reins, the two left the crowd behind looking confused and choking on their dust. "Abigail is going to be madder than hell with you, Matt."

"She sure is," Matt agreed good-naturedly. "I saw that look on your face. You were dying to get out of there. Admit it."

"You're right. I didn't expect such a welcome. I just wanted to quietly come home."

Matthew snorted. "Abigail doesn't do a thing quietly."

As they made the short ride home, Nicholas relaxed and gazed at the town he'd grown up in. Tall elm trees lined the dusty street, protecting colonial homes that dated as far back as the 1700s. The houses gave the town a sense of permanence, Nicholas thought contentedly. Once in a while, a driver would recognize the brothers and stop to chat, but Matthew simply waved and continued onward until Nicholas thought he would cry from the laughs he was trying to suppress. "I see you haven't changed a bit," Nicholas said dryly.

When Matthew turned up the drive, Nicholas felt overcome with sentiment. The old rambling house he grew up in stood at the end of the narrow dirt drive like an old friend. As he got closer, he saw that his nieces and nephews were hurtling themselves down the dirt stretch to greet him. In the confusion at the train, he had not realized they were not there to meet him. He smiled as Emily tried valiantly to keep up with her brother, and chuckled at little Mabel's unsteady gait. His laughter died in his throat when he caught a fleeting glimpse of a woman standing in the doorway watching the children's progress before disappearing inside.

Claire. She was still here. His heart began hammering in his chest, a reaction so unexpected Nicholas was momentarily astounded. He forced himself to smile as the children reached the buggy. Matthew, a smile of his own on his unusually stern face, pulled back on the reins, stopping the horse.

"Uncle Nick, Uncle Nick. Wait there!" Nathan yelled. The little boy, clutching a large piece of paper rolled up in one hand, took charge of his little sisters and lined them up. Looking as if they were about to engage in the most difficult task, the three stood on the side of the drive. This was an important moment. Slowly they unfurled the cloth. Painted neatly on it, were the words WELCOME HOME UNCLE NICHOLAS. Little handprints dotted the paper; each child's signature. Emily's smiling eyes peaked over the cloth, but the only part of Mabel he could see were two chubby hands clutching the end of the sign.

"Thank you. That was a much better welcome than at the train station."

"You can say that again," Matthew said under his breath. Nicholas stifled a laugh.

"You all did a nice job on the sign, too. I especially like your hand signatures," Nicholas praised.

The children beamed at him. "Nanny helped," Emily said, her voice high and loud.

"Did she," he said thoughtfully. Considering Claire could not write, he suspected she did not help all that much. His eyes strayed to the door where Claire had stood moments before. What the hell was she still doing here?

The remainder of the day was spent catching up on old times. The war, the six years that had separated him from his family was barely mentioned. It was as if by some pact everyone had agreed to not talk about it, except in vague ways when asking about his injuries. Nicholas thought it was just as well. He did not wish to discuss the war any more than his family and friends wanted to. They would not understand, and he did not have the energy to make them understand. Instead they talked about shared memories, stories they had all told and heard a hundred times before, laughing, as they always did, as if it were the first time the tale had been told.

Nicholas was acutely aware of Diane, of every word, every gesture. For the first time since he'd made the decision to marry her, he could stake a claim officially. He would have felt completely content, completely happy, if not for Claire.

After a dinner of fresh flounder and early vegetables from the kitchen garden, Nicholas asked Diane to take a stroll with him. It would be the first time they had been completely alone in their adult life and for some reason, Nicholas was as nervous as a fourteen-year-old with his first crush. He walked beside Diane, feeling awkward and oafish. Women almost always made him feel this way, he thought with disgust, through no fault of their own. After living exclusively with men for so many years, they were like foreign creatures to him—soft, delicate. And Diane was the epitome of womanhood, so elegant and cool, so self-assured, so much a lady. Her auburn hair was pulled high atop her head, leaving her graceful neck exposed, white and creamy and untouchable.

His hands clamped tightly behind his back, he wondered when he would feel comfortable with the woman he had promised himself would be his wife. Why did Diane make him behave like a gaping, buck-toothed boy, swallowing heavily in fear of saying the wrong thing? She was just a woman, goddammit. The master strategist had no strategy for courting.

"Thank you for asking me for a walk," Diane said, casting a sidelong look at Nicholas. She pressed her hands together to stop their trembling. After all this time, after all this waiting, Nicholas Brooks had asked her to walk out with him. Her mind raced ahead to the weeks and months to come, to parties and dances and, of course, to the inevitable wedding. She would be the wife of one of the most admired men in the county. Everyone said he had great potential, could name the political office he wanted. Some even said he was presidential material, although Diane dared not hope for so much. Being a senator or governor's wife would be wonderful enough. And she would fit that role perfectly, she thought. It was everything she had been trained to be—a good hostess, a thoughtful companion, a loving wife. Her life would be perfect.

She placed one hand softly in the crook of Nicholas's arm. "It's a beautiful evening," she said.

Nicholas swallowed. How long had he waited for this moment, had he dreamt about this meeting? Diane was everything he remembered and more. She was a lady, pure, clean, modest, beautiful. He realized that he was mentally comparing her to Claire, marking off a checklist in his mind of everything Diane was that Claire was not. Claire was . . . Claire. He forced her impish face from his mind, he quashed the image of her upturned face, her tempting mouth, her blue eyes burning with desire.

Clearing his throat, Nicholas turned to look at Diane, unknowingly standing at ease before her. "I have asked your father's permission to court you, Diane Pendleton, and now I ask yours."

He's actually nervous, Diane thought with glee. "You have my permission, Nicholas," she said softly, lowering her eyes shyly. For some reason, that lowering of the eyes irritated Nicholas, but he did not know why.

They continued walking along the brick path, strolling slowly and silently. Once Nicholas spit out what he came here to say, he found himself at a loss for words. He had rehearsed that little speech a hundred times in his head, but had put little thought into what came next. What could he possibly talk to this creature about? Knitting? Fashion? She baffled him, she was so much the opposite of what he was, it was fascinating.

He stopped again and she stopped with him, tilting her lovely head up and laying a small smile upon her beautiful lips. "May I kiss you?" he asked, surprising himself. For when had he ever asked permission for a kiss? He was again reminded of Claire. Why was that infernal girl entering his thoughts at a time like this?

"You may." Diane closed her eyes, her stomach clenching excitedly in anticipation and nervousness, for she had never before been kissed.

Nicholas brought his mouth down, telling himself to go slowly, not to frighten this woman. He found himself smiling against her firmly closed mouth.

"Relax," he whispered, and felt a slight tension leave her taut lips. He moved his mouth against hers, putting his hands on her shoulders. "Relax," he said again, after feeling her arms tense beneath his touch.

He continued kissing her, feeling a bit frustrated by her lack of experience, her lack of involvement. "Open your mouth," he said gently, brushing his tongue against her lips. He remembered saying those same words to Claire. He remembered that she had, letting out a small moan as she did. Again he chastised himself for thinking of Claire when all he wanted was standing right in front of him.

"What?" Diane asked, pulling her head back quickly. She was clearly disgusted by the suggestion she open her mouth and she brought her hand up to wipe away where his tongue had passed. Seeing Nicholas's confused look, Diane said, "I'm sorry, Nicholas. I'm not very experienced at this."

"I know," he said softly. "That's why I'm teaching you."

He bent down to kiss her again, feeling pursed lips beneath his. "Diane. Don't be afraid. Open your mouth."

Her eyes tightly closed, Diane did as he commanded, her stomach twisting in fear, her entire body becoming rigid. When she felt his tongue enter her mouth and begin to swirl around, her first feeling was repugnance. She knew enough from talking to Abigail that repugnance was the last thing she should feel, so she continued on with the kiss in the best way she could.

After a few long moments of what seemed to her to be pointless and rather offensive activities with their tongues, she pushed him gently away. "We mustn't," Diane said, thinking this is what she should say.

Nicholas smiled down at her. "You will become accustomed to kissing. And even enjoy it."

"I enjoy it now," Diane lied. But Nicholas knew better. She had given him no response. Indeed, he had given her none. He might as well have been kissing a tree, but that would change. He did not stop to think that a man who had not lain with a woman in months should feel a bit more . . . something. They did not know each other enough, he told himself, they were not yet comfortable in each other's company. Indeed, he probably should not have taken such liberties with her. Without being conscious of it, his eyes stole back toward the house and sought the room where Claire slept. A light was on. She's still awake, he thought, then jerked his head away when he realized what he had been thinking. Kissing Diane had only made him think of Claire, of her ready response to him.

"Let's go back inside," he said abruptly, steering her down the path toward the well-lit house.

Claire was dreaming again, of running in that bloodied battlefield, of hearing the moans and screams of dying men. But before the bad part, before the soldier, she started awake. Sitting up, her heart pounding, Claire heard again the sound that had brought her out of the dream—a soft knock on the door. Pulling on a thin cotton robe and lighting a lamp by her bed, Claire walked to the door and opened it, expecting to see one of the children.

"Claire."

"Major, what do you want?" Claire whispered, hiding her surprise at seeing Nicholas Brooks at her door. "What time is it?"

Nicholas walked in the door, closing it behind him, forcing Claire to step back into the room. "It's early. Only eleven or so. You really shouldn't call me major anymore."

Walking to her bedstand, Claire placed the lamp down, leaving much of the small room in shadows. She fiddled with the flame, stalling, praying that her beating heart could not be heard clear across the room where Nicholas stood. He looked magnificent, she thought, better than her memories. He was cleanly shaven, revealing a strong jaw, and his hair, still short, had lightened in the summer sun, making his face appear even more tanned, his eyes more striking. By the time she turned around, she had composed herself.

"What do you want?"

Nicholas had no answer, no reason for coming to her door in the middle of the night. He told himself he wanted to be sure she was happy here, to reassure himself that he had made the right decision when offering her a home and a position in his sister's house. He was not prepared for the impact of seeing her wearing that demure cotton nightgown. It was as if someone had sucker-punched him in the gut, looking at her again. Tall and lithe, her eyes were steady and calm, challenging and direct. So unlike most women who cast him shy and modest looks. So unlike Diane with her dark, delicate beauty.

"You were having another dream," he said. Claire bit her lip, wondering whether she had been screaming in her sleep. Those dreams of hers were the only weakness she showed, and it was only when she was unaware of doing so. She had not awoken screaming in weeks and had thought she was finally rid of her nightmares.

Seeing her worrying her lip, Nicholas made to reassure her. "I was walking by your room." He stopped, a small smile on his lips, realizing she would see through the lie as her room was so isolated from the rest of the house. "Actually, I was coming to see you but was waiting outside. I . . . I heard you whimpering. It was not loud. No one else would have heard."

Claire plopped down on her bed, completely unaware how inappropriate it was for a single woman to have a man in her bedroom late at night. It did not seem so strange or alarming that he was here with her alone, it did not make her nervous, or shy to be with Nicholas after so many weeks without seeing him.

"I was having the bad one," she said, a look of impatience on her face. "When will it stop?"

"It will."

"Have yours stopped?"

It struck him that there was probably not another female in this world who could have asked him that question with the empathy that Claire did.

"Almost."

"Your head?"

"Only twice since you left." And it was hell without you there, he added silently.

They stared at each other in silence. Nicholas stood in the middle of the room, his hands behind his back, his feet planted on an old rag rug that lay on the wood floor. Claire sat on her bed, her legs swinging, revealing that she was just a touch nervous. Claire thought he looked good out of uniform. She had only seen him at a distance since he had come home, and now, close up, she realized just how handsome he was. Claire found herself wanting to touch his smooth, beardless cheek. His shirt was unbuttoned, giving him an uncharacteristically ruffled look.

"You said you wanted to see me. Certainly you could have waited until the morning. Or sought me out earlier this evening."

"I was busy tonight," Nicholas said, wondering why he was being evasive with the only woman he'd ever spoken frankly with. "I was entertaining Abigail's friend, Diane." He said it almost as a challenge, to see what her reaction would be, but for the life of him, he could not say why.

"Diane is very pretty," Claire said noncommittally, as if describing a vase. Inside, a rage that she instantly recognized as jealousy erupted. Stupid girl, she thought, of course he would like a girl like Diane. But not two months ago, he had been married to *her,* even if their marriage had been a farce.

"Yes. And smart, too. I have asked permission to court her. She has agreed. I saw no reason to postpone our future. Hers and mine." Now why was he telling her this? He had not even told his sister the news.

Claire swallowed and looked away for the first time. She could not bear to see the pride and happiness in Nicholas's eyes as he spoke about another woman, yet she could not let him know how she felt about him, she thought with mortification. Oh, wouldn't that be grand. The little Southern girl soldier in love with her captor. How awfully predictable. How wonderfully charming.

"I wouldn't think you would have asked permission," she said, and immediately wished she had not. It was a transparent reminder of the virginity he had taken without asking. Kisses she had freely given.

Nicholas narrowed his eyes, recognizing the jibe for what it was. "With some women, a man knows he must act a certain way," he said cruelly.

Claire brought her gaze back to his then, unable to shield the hurt and anger in her eyes before masking it with indifference. "That was not fair. Nor very nice," she said blandly, picking at her bedspread in an effort to appear nonplussed.

Nicholas heaved a sigh. He did not know why he continued to be cruel to Claire. He gave her a curt nod. "Forgive me," he said with about as much warmth as an iceberg.

Claire let out a laugh and rolled her eyes comically. "Oh, Major, with your sweet words and gallant ways, I am quite sure your precious Diane will be swooning at your feet in no time a'tall."

He laughed. He could not help himself, watching her dramatics and listening to her magnified Southern belle imitation. It was during these moments that Claire allowed her real self through, where he caught a glimpse of the happy, carefree woman she once was. Taken with the moment, he immediately got down on bended knee and swooped up one of her hands, pressing it to his lips. Keeping with the playacted scene, Claire pressed the back of one hand against her forehead and tilted her head back, personifying the tortured belle.

"Please forgive me, my sweet, sweet Claire."

"Never!" Claire said, withdrawing her hand from his grasp with much flourish. A part of Nicholas knew that had any of his fellow officers or troops witnessed this ridiculous spectacle, he would have been the butt of jokes for years to come. He would only have solace in knowing that so out of character was this playful scene, that few would have believed even reliable witnesses.

Claire gave up the act and laughed. "You know, I was only half kidding, Major. You can't say mean things to me and expect me to accept it."

Nicholas sobered. "I know. And, really, Claire,

please call me Nicholas. Or at least Mr. Brooks. I was your husband, after all."

Claire snorted. "You were never really my husband. Not truly. And I can't think of you as anything but Major."

"And do you think of me?" He'd meant it to come out lightly, but somehow the question did not, and the air around them seemed to change, instantly becoming warmer, thicker, and charged. He was still at her feet, his hands resting on her knees. Only two thin layers of cotton separated his warm hands from her thighs. Although he had placed his hands there casually, suddenly they became aware of just how intimate their positions were.

Claire looked at Nicholas, a little crease forming between her troubled eyes. Think of him? My God, it seemed it was all she did in her moments of solitude. "Of course I think of you," she said quietly.

Warning bells were pealing inside Nicholas's head. He recognized the signs now. He knew what could happen unless he got up this instant, and walked away. But for some reason he did not. Instead, he did the one thing he told himself he would never do again, the one thing he knew would only cause Claire more pain. But God, how he wanted her! He never thought himself a weak man. Why, then, when it came to this girl, did he suddenly throw away all his resolve, all his good sense?

Instead of listening to his common sense, Nicholas raised one hand to the side of Claire's burning cheek. "Your hair is longer," he said, as if that gave him an excuse to bring his hand to the side of her head and comb his fingers through her silky strands. "Soft," he whispered, staring at his hand as it brushed her hair.

Claire closed her eyes and concentrated on breathing. Oh, why did this have to feel so good? Why couldn't she simply push him away as she knew she should? "Nicholas." She opened her eyes and looked into his gray ones, so intense they burned into her. A smile touched his hard lips, changing them completely, and her eyes strayed there before returning to his eyes. His hand went to the back of her head and he drew her suddenly toward him, but stopped just as his mouth was about to envelop hers.

"May I kiss you, Claire?"

Claire's breath came out in shaky spurts, her tongue darted out to moisten her lips. Still he waited for her answer. She closed her eyes and took a deep breath.

"No, Nicholas. You may not."

He let out a harsh laugh and rested his forehead against hers. "Just answer me this," he let out roughly. "Do you want to kiss me?"

She did not think. She simply said the first words that came to her. "Yes. More than anything."

Nicholas grew so hard at her answer, he was in pain. Honest Claire. She should have lied, he thought. It would have made everything so much easier.

Nicholas stood up abruptly and turned away so she would not know his condition. He gripped her bureau so hard, his knuckles turned white and the muscles in his back bunched with exertion. Claire followed him to the bureau, unsure why Nicholas suddenly stood, but he appeared to be hurting.

"Nicholas, what's wrong? I'm sorry I did not kiss you. But you have to understand that you can't come to me and kiss me and leave and then think that I can continue to live as I have. You can't kiss Diane and then come to me for more."

Nicholas squeezed his eyes shut. So, she had seen them. He had already hurt her. Ashamed he had put Claire in such a position, in pain from his need to have her, he remained silent. But when he felt a shy and tentative hand on his back, it was too much.

"Don't touch me," he said harshly, willing himself not to turn and thrust her into his arms. He knew she would not resist, and that made it all the more difficult.

"I don't understand," Claire said, sounding hurt and a little angry.

"Then I'll tell you," Nicholas said, whipping around and grabbing both her arms in a firm grip. "I cannot be near you without . . . I thought I could, but I cannot. It is why I sent you away."

Claire looked up at him worriedly. "I still don't understand."

Frustrated, angry at himself, he took her hand and pressed it against his hardness. "Do you feel that Claire? This is what you do to me. God, you are so innocent. How can you still be so innocent? I want to be inside you again. I want to fuck you." He chose the basest language he could in order to shock her, in order to drive her away. He thrust away the hand he had held against himself with disgust, as if she had put it there against his will.

Claire backed away from him, frightened of him for the first time.

"Yes. You should be afraid of me, Claire. Because that is all I want from you. That is all. Do you understand me? Do you?"

Claire swallowed heavily. She knew exactly what he meant. He would use her because his body wanted her. But he would never love her. Those things were delegated to his Diane.

He saw the change, he watched as she gathered her strength from whatever place she hid it, and his heart gave an odd twist. Holding her head up, she forced her trembling hands to still.

"I understand completely, Nicholas. Please remember, though, that you came here to see me. I did not invite you. Never come to my room again. Never seek me out alone again." Her voice was strong, steady, belying the horrible fact that she was dying inside.

Filled with remorse and regret over his actions, Nicholas turned to go.

She turned away then, no longer able to keep the wall in place that shielded what her heart truly felt. Go, go, go, she silently said over and over. It was only when she heard the soft click of the door closing that she allowed herself to feel. She swayed against the grief, breathing in and out as if she could not get enough oxygen in her lungs. But she did not cry.

Seeing her older brother approaching her, Abigail leaned forward expectantly, a conspirator's look on her lovely face.

"You must tell me what happened, Nicky! I couldn't get Diane alone last night before her parents whisked her way. What happened? She positively glowed all evening."

Nicholas smiled at his spirited sister and sat down at the table situated in the sun a few yards from the house. Formal silver graced the top of the sturdy wicker table, and he poured himself a cup of coffee, frowning at the delicate teacup he held in his hand. He would rather have had a sturdy—and large—tin mug for his coffee than this tiny thing, he thought. The sound of children's laughter took his attention away from his sister. There, in the distance, his nieces and nephew romped together, apparently trying in vain to capture a butterfly. Laughing and romping just as enthusiastically was the children's nanny. Entranced, Nicholas stared at the slim-figured woman who played so unself-consciously with her charges.

"Well? Are you, Nicholas? Are you going to ask her to marry you?"

Startled, Nicholas for just a moment thought his sister was talking about Claire. "Marry her?" he asked.

"Of course! You don't have to tell me but . . . Oh, please, please tell me. Do you plan on asking Diane to marry you?"

Nicholas smiled indulgently at his sister. "Why on earth would I tell you before I tell Diane?"

Abigail clasped her hands together happily. "So you are going to ask her."

"I didn't say that," Nicholas said with a warning in his voice. "I've simply asked permission to court her."

Abigail waved an impatient hand at her brother. "That's the same thing," she said.

In mock horror, Nicholas said, "Good God, I hope not! I still have a few good remaining months of bachelorhood left in me."

"I hope you do marry her, Nicholas. She's my greatest friend. And don't you dare say a word to her, but I know she's been in love with you for some time. She's perfect for you."

Nicholas nodded his agreement. "She does seem to be nice."

Abigail let out a light little laugh. "Don't you ever call her nice to her face. Certainly you can come out with better descriptives than that, big brother. She's beautiful, intelligent—but not bookish, she plays the piano, she loves children, she sews and cooks and does everything any man would want."

"You don't have to list her attributes to me, Abigail. I am well aware that any man would be a fool to pass her up. Why do you think I'm courting her?"

Nicholas took a sip from his steaming coffee, allowing himself to glance once again at Claire, who was now sitting in a circle with the children, the littlest, Mabel, on her lap.

Seeing where Nicholas's eyes strayed, Abigail said, "Have you said hello to Miss Dumont yet?"

"No," he lied.

"I think you should at least say hello. After all, it was you who recommended her. She's turned out to be such a godsend and the children adore her. I could never have done it this time, not with three and me big as a cow," Abigail said, patting her enlarged belly. She was becoming more and more sluggish every day.

"I'm glad it's working out," Nicholas said, dragging his eyes away from Claire.

"It's more than working out. She's teaching the children French and even a bit of Latin, flowers' names and such, and Lord knows we're not paying her a proper wage for what she's worth. She should be a governess or a schoolteacher. Really, Nicholas, she is absolutely wonderful."

Nicholas gave his sister an incredulous look. "French? Latin?"

"Didn't you know? She is one of the most educated females I have ever met. Apparently her parents were very modern."

Nicholas gazed intently at the lithe young woman dancing among the toddlers. "Apparently."

"Go say hello," Abigail persisted.

Nicholas clenched his jaw. The last thing he wanted to do was stand next to Claire with his curious sister watching. But if he continued to resist, it would only raise her curiosity to a high level, he knew. Reluctantly he stood and walked toward the happy little group.

As soon as Nathan spied his favorite war-hero uncle walking toward them, he left the little circle and ran full speed to greet him, unknowingly throwing himself hard against the man's injured knee. Nicholas grunted softly, but only the keenest observer would have noticed his pain.

Nicholas effortlessly heaved the boy atop his shoulders and walked toward Claire, who stood up when she realized who was approaching. Without meaning to, her eyes shifted to his knee, then back to his face. She said not a word, but Nicholas knew she was aware of his discomfort. Damn her and her knowing eyes, he thought harshly.

"You don't follow orders very well for an officer,"

Claire said, shooting blue daggers at him with her eyes.

"My sister suggested I 'at least say hello.' That is what I am doing."

Claire felt a tug at her hemline and looked down at Emily, immediately lifting the little girl into her arms. Claire's face changed so dramatically Nicholas almost forgot to breathe. She looked down at the little girl with a softness, a tenderness he had never seen there before. She was lovely, standing there, holding Emily on her hip. It looked so natural for her to have a baby in her arms. She lay a gentle hand on top of the little girl's head, a gesture that somehow showed more than if she had kissed one chubby cheek.

"I'm sorry if I hurt you," he ground out.

"You're flattering yourself. In order to hurt someone, they have to care. I do not."

Nicholas clenched his jaw. He felt himself becoming angry.

"You lie."

"Why should it matter to you if it is a lie? Which it is not."

"Why, indeed."

Just then, the two adults, so busy sparring they forgot they were not alone, were interrupted by a shy little voice coming from above Nicholas. "Are you and nanny fighting, Uncle Nick?"

"Of course not," they said in unison, both flushing from embarrassment.

"It sounded like you was."

"It sounded like you were," Claire corrected automatically.

"It sounded like you were," the little boy parroted.

"We were disagreeing. There is a difference," Claire explained.

Nicholas took Nathan from his shoulders and placed him on the ground. "Go check on Mabel," he said, nodding toward the little girl so enraptured by a dandelion gone to seed she was quite ignoring the excitement of two adults arguing.

Bored, Emily held out one hand to her uncle, wanting him now to hold her. Nicholas took her from Claire, his hand accidentally brushing against the gentle swell of her breast. Stepping away quickly, Nicholas covered his immediate and searing reaction to that slight touch by shifting Emily to one shoulder. He winced as the little girl clutched his hair to keep her balance.

"Careful, she's not used to that," Claire said.

Nicholas shifted Emily to his chest, more to relieve the hair-pulling than to follow orders from Claire. "I wouldn't allow her to be hurt," he said defensively.

"I know that. But sometimes you can hurt without meaning to."

Nicholas gazed intently at Claire, who turned to check on the children, but not before he saw her face flush. So, he thought, she does care. For some reason, one he refused to acknowledge, he smiled.

"Parlez vous français, mademoiselle?" Nicholas asked, his pronunciation slightly less than perfect.

"Qu'est-ce que?" Claire was so distracted by the children, she did not realize he had asked the question in French and she had said "What?" in that language as well, until it was too late.

She turned giving him a grin that was part triumph, part guilt.

"And you read and write. And I imagine you know how to sign your name," he said, recalling the angry "X" she had written on their wedding license.

"Quite well."

Why was she never what she seemed? Why could she not be what he had already decided she was? It was damned disorienting. Nothing he thought about her was true. She was not a boy, but a beautiful, desirable woman. She was not a whore, but a virgin. She was not ignorant. Quite the opposite. She appeared to be more educated than he, at least in the finer arts. The more he thought about it, the angrier he got.

"Is there anything about you that is not a lie?" he said more harshly than he'd intended.

Claire was taken aback by the viciousness of that statement, by the look of dislike in his eyes. She had thought, had fantasized that he would be pleased. But he disliked her even more.

"I never told you anything. You assumed. You never asked. You always thought the worst of me, Major. And now when you find out you were wrong, you are angry with me? What a crock! I should be mad at you. Where you got this idea that women are either whores or virgins, with nothing in between is beyond me."

"It is mostly true."

Claire rolled her eyes in disgust. "Ah, 'mostly.' So I see you're willing to leave some room for doubt."

"You were the one wearing that goddamn filthy uniform. You were the one who shot . . ." He stopped when he saw her wince at his last word. "What was I supposed to think, Claire?" he added softly, his voice tinged with regret.

She looked at him with those eyes so bleak they pierced his heart beyond the armor he thought he had placed there. She just shook her head and, with false cheerfulness gathered up the children for a game of tag.

He watched her go, resisting the terrible urge to go after her. It would do no good. And anyway, it wouldn't be right.

Chapter Fourteen

Five days later, Claire escorted the children, scrubbed and wearing their finest, into the parlor where the Carrs' guests had gathered to listen to Diane Pendleton play the piano. She had admonished them most sternly that they were to be on their best behavior. The privilege of being in the parlor with the adults was a high honor, she explained, and one that could be revoked should the children not live up to the high standard that she believed they could. Claire stifled a smile at the solemn little nods both Nathan and Emily gave her. Mabel, still too little to understand the importance of the event or her stern message, instead played with Claire's shoelaces. Settling the children next to their parents, Claire removed herself to the back of the room where she could be summoned at a moment's notice if one of the children got too restless.

Claire had worn her best dress as well, a dark navy silk with creamy lace at her wrists and neckline. She told herself that she wore it for the special event and certainly not for any particular man's perusal. Claire scanned the small crowd, a group of about twelve dinner guests. Somehow, Diane always seemed to be at the center of a laughing group. She stood in the midst of a small group, all of whom listened enraptured at whatever she was saying. How could anything she had to say be so interesting, Claire thought meanly. Petite and shapely, Diane Pendleton looked composed, graceful, and beautiful. Claire had always felt tall and gawky, and she felt that way even more so when standing next to a paragon of female beauty such as Diane. No wonder he loves her, she thought.

Diane sat at the piano, smiling sweetly at the guests, her hands folded calmly on her lap, looking lovely in the soft lamplight. If it were me, Claire thought, I'd be wiping my sweaty palms on my dress and wishing everyone would disappear. Claire played the piano with more skill than most, but she had never played for anyone other than herself, her teacher, and her family. Despite her confidence in her skill, the thought of playing the piano in front of a crowd made Claire sick to her stomach.

And there sat Diane. Serene, lovely, saving a special look, a special smile for Nicholas. Claire clenched her fists, then quickly reminded herself that she was angry at Nicholas, and Diane was welcome to the heartless cad. Despite herself, she could not help staring at the back of his head, willing him to turn around and acknowledge her. Claire's iron will dissolved like sugar in a cup of hot tea when it came to that man, she thought with dismay.

When Diane began playing, the room became silent. Claire watched as the small audience became entranced by what she thought was a rather stiff performance. While technically good, Diane's play was emotionless, as if she had no inkling of what Chopin was trying to say when he wrote those mournful melodies. From the applause the small crowd gave her, it was as if they had never heard a better performance, Claire thought with some annoyance. She watched as Nicholas clapped the loudest and the longest, a soppy, ridiculous display, she thought. It was torture standing in the back, watching Nicholas watch Diane. Claire rolled her eyes in disgust more than once as Diane gave Nicholas a special shy little smile. She wished, just this once, that she had the courage to perform. Claire realized she was being spiteful, but she did not care. Why was Nicholas so blind to this woman who was so obviously manipulating him by batting her eyelashes and gazing up at him as if he were some sort of god? She had seen her type in high school, the ones who always had boyfriends, while Claire accumulated an odd bunch of "buddies."

As the performance ended, Diane stood and executed a perfect curtsy, accepting accolades and words of praise. She held out two hands to Nicholas, who pulled her close and whispered "Well done" in her ear, beaming down at her as if she were his creation. Claire chewed on her bottom lip, taking in the tender scene. It hurt so much, she thought, I've got to stop letting the fact that Nicholas feels nothing for me rip me apart. She forced herself to look away, but before she knew it, her eyes had once again sought him out. Her stomach twisted painfully as she watched Nicholas pass a hand across his forehead as he listened to Diane, her upturned face animated. Was that hand trembling? Claire thought, suddenly casting aside her jealousy and watching Nicholas with a new intensity. She could see a fine sheen of sweat on his forehead, and watched as he again touched it. He is trembling, she thought with deepening concern. His head is hurting him.

Recognizing the signs of an oncoming attack, Claire immediately looked for his sister. Spying her introducing the children to some of the guests, Claire made her way over to the woman, keeping one eye on Nicholas. There! He stumbled a bit and blinked his eyes as if he were having trouble focusing. She hastened her pace.

"Mrs. Carr, may I have a moment . . ."

Distracted, Abigail acknowledged Claire, but continued her conversation.

"Mrs. Carr, this is quite urgent."

Smiling her apologies, Abigail gave Claire her attention. "What is it, Miss Dumont?" she asked, allowing just a bit of impatience to enter her voice.

"It's Mr. Brooks. He's about to have one of his headaches," Claire explained quickly.

Abigail shook her head in confusion.

"Has he told you this?" she asked.

Claire flushed slightly. "No. But I can tell."

Relaxing, Abigail dismissed Claire's concern. "I'm sure if Nicholas were about to have a headache, or if, indeed, he had a headache, he would know and would take the proper precautions."

Claire breathed out of her nose in frustration. "That's just it, Mrs. Carr. He always has a slight headache. It's a constant thing. But he's about to have a very severe one and I'm sure he's not even aware of it."

Giving Claire an indulgent smile, she said, "Thank you for your concern, I'll mention it to him . . ." She was cut off by a woman's scream.

Hopelessly, Claire looked over to where Nicholas knelt on the floor clutching his head and rocking to and fro in the throes of unimaginable pain. Abigail gave Claire a disbelieving and apologetic look before rushing over to her brother. She had never seen her big brother so helpless, and was unsure what to do. Diane hovered above him, wringing her hands, repeating over and over, "What's wrong with him? What's wrong with him?"

Abigail kneeled by her brother, gripping him firmly on his shoulders. "What can I do to help, Nicky. Tell me."

Through the red hot pain that enveloped him, he heard his sister's question. Breathing in and out harshly through clenched teeth, he managed to say the only thing that came to his mind. "Get Claire."

Claire was already on her way, having run to the dining room and grabbed two napkins, which she dipped into the iced water used to cool the wine. Pushing her way through the crowd, Claire moved behind Nicholas as she had done before and brought him back gently until the back of his head rested on her lap. Placing an ice-cold cloth on the back of his neck, she ran the other over his head, massaging him gently. The effect was almost immediate. Nicholas unclenched his fists and flexed them painfully and then opened his eyes to find ten pairs of eyes looking down at him with such worry and concern he almost laughed. His head still hurt too much to give in to that impulse, so instead he smiled. Closing his eyes, he sighed as Claire seemed to draw the pain out of him with her hands. He wondered how she knew exactly what to do, exactly where to touch him to ease the agonizing pressure. The headaches he had suffered without her were excruciating and seemingly unending.

"You must show me what your secret is," Diane said, her voice uncharacteristically clipped.

"Miss Dumont knew Nicholas was going to have an attack even before he did," Abigail said, her voice tinged with confusion and a bit of awe. "How could you possibly know, Miss Dumont?"

Nicholas felt Claire stiffen. She clearly did not want this crowd of people to know they had spent so much time together, for that would certainly lead to probing questions they both preferred to go unanswered.

"I mentioned in passing that I was not feeling well," Nicholas lied smoothly.

"You didn't mention anything to me," Diane said, sounding petulant.

"I didn't want to worry you," Nicholas said, smiling up into her worried eyes and holding up a hand for her to grasp. Seeing that utterly sickening exchange, Claire abruptly got up, allowing Nicholas's head to bounce onto the carpeted floor.

"Oh. Sorry." He sat up, giving Claire a knowing grin, then proceeded to accept Diane's assistance with relish, making Claire want to slap that smug smile off his face. Despite herself, she gave him an intense, searching look to make sure he was better and not simply acting tough for his girl. Satisfied he was better, Claire turned to collect the children, but Abigail pulled her aside.

"How *did* you know, Miss Dumont?"

"I could see it. He was trembling . . . he kept touching his forehead as if something were bothering him. He lost his balance. I could tell." Claire shrugged.

Abigail did not ask why Claire was studying her brother so intently she was able to see something the people standing directly in front of him could not. But she was still curious.

"How did you know how to help?"

Claire blushed. "I don't know. It happened before . . . in Maryland. I just knew what to do. It's as if I can feel his pain, as if I know where it hurts the most."

"Well, since I noticed Nicholas did not thank you, I will."

The next day, the guests who had decided to stay gathered up a picnic lunch and headed to a small pond well known for attracting large numbers of swans. Abigail decided to take the children and care for them herself, giving Claire an unexpected day off.

Claire walked about the huge house feeling awkward and foreign. Aimlessly walking from room to room, Claire stopped in the parlor and stared at the piano. For three months, that piano had sat there and Claire had no urge to play it. But now, just one day after Diane Pendleton's performance, her fingers itched to rest on those cool ivory keys. It was the perfect time, she told herself, with no one in the house but servants. And should one of them mention to the Carrs that Claire could play the piano, she would tell them she was simply playing to pass the time, that she was actually quite dreadful and was mortified that anyone had even heard her.

Closing the door behind her, she walked up to the beautiful mahogany instrument and caressed the wood, savoring the moment before sitting down on the padded bench. Cracking her knuckles with flourish, she closed her eyes and began to play, letting her soul fill up with the sound. She grimaced, realizing she was a bit rusty, but as the minutes passed, it was as if she had never stepped away from the instrument. She was lost in the music, her heart was filled with it. I missed it so much and did not even know it, she thought, smiling as her fingers flew over the keys.

Nicholas heard the music while he was still outside tying up his horse. The day had grown chilly and when Diane had commented on the thinness of her clothing, he immediately offered to return to fetch her a cloak.

This courting ritual was becoming more and more of a nuisance, Nicholas thought as he tied his horse up to the carved granite hitching post. He found himself acting in a way that went completely against his grain. His first reaction when Diane pouted about the cool weather was to berate her for being foolish enough to leave the house without her cloak in the first place, but he remained silent. It was quite apparent within moments of leaving the house that the wind whipping off Miller's Cove was cooler than normal. Instead, he smiled sweetly and gallantly offered to fetch her cloak, all the time wondering when he had become such a mealymouthed sop. Being with Diane was such an effort. Used to being around soldiers, he found himself constantly being aware of not cursing, of considering her female sensibilities. It was getting to be downright exhausting.

Still, he found her completely captivating, entirely

satisfying to be with. He watched her keenly as she walked among his sister's friends. She was so much a part of this world, she belonged so thoroughly, it was impossible to imagine her anywhere else. After years of war, of filth and pain, Nicholas wanted to live in a gentler place, where ladies wore beautiful gowns and did not have to worry about spoiled meat or whether they had enough thread to mend a tattered dress. He wanted simply to live a normal life and if bending a bit to a woman's whims was what it took he would do it. If he was not a true fit to the life he imagined himself living, the life Diane lived now, then he would simply cram his big, awkward body into the proper shape.

Hearing the music, he was momentarily confused. Diane was still with the party and he knew no one else who could play the piano, never mind with such expertise. Curious, he followed the sound to the parlor and silently opened the door. He stood there, stunned, for several moments staring at what could not be. Claire, her wispy hair a curling cloud about her shoulders, was playing the piano with such passion, with such feeling Nicholas was quite literally made speechless. He had thought he knew all her surprises. He was quite wrong. Her hands flew over the keys, fingers a pale blur, eyes closed, one foot stepping on the pedals beneath her. Her entire body was playing the piano. Unlike Diane, who sat rigidly upon the bench in perfect posture, Claire was humped over the keys, her head tilted to one side as if she were consuming the notes that she played. When she stopped, the silence that followed was almost a tangible thing. Her fingers lay on the keys, lightly touching them as she took a deep breath and smiled ethereally.

Suddenly Claire stiffened, aware that she was no longer alone in the room. Nicholas watched as she slowly turned her head and smiled, too distracted by the music to put up a guard.

"I didn't know you were still here," she said.

That smile arrested him and he decided he would not chastise her again for hiding a part of herself from him. "I came back for something. You . . . My God, Claire, you play beautifully. You should have played last night."

Shifting uncomfortably, Claire said quietly, "I only play for myself. I can't play for anyone."

He walked over to her looking at her as if he had never seen her before and he noticed the tears tracking down her face for the first time. "You're crying," he said, bringing his hand to her face and brushing his thumb across one tear.

"Am I?" Mortified, Claire lifted her hands to her cheeks to feel for proof, her hand pushing his away. Her cheeks burned with embarrassment. "Sometimes when I play, I cry. I'm not even aware I'm doing it. That's one reason I can't play in public. If I get lost like that, I'm completely unaware of anything or anyone. My mother always said the house could burn down around me and I would't know it. My brothers always teased me about what I look like. They called me a piano-playing hunchback." She let out a little laugh.

"No, no." Nicholas shook his head and searched for words to describe what he had just witnessed. "You're beautiful when you play, like the music." I want to kiss her, he thought, and his mind was assaulted by the memory of her soft lips against his. Incredible how vivid that memory is, he thought as his eyes drifted to her lips. But with her there, a mere inches away, her clean, undefinable scent filling him, it was impossible not to remember, impossible not to want to remember.

Claire felt his gaze drift to her mouth and drew back. "Diane is also beautiful when she plays," she said pointedly. How dare he look at her like that. How dare he make her want him.

"It's probably just as well you didn't play last night, you would have made Diane look like such a novice," he said, as if his mind were still on their innocent conversation.

"She's technically quite good," Claire said, but even that charitable comment almost stuck in her throat.

Nicholas laughed. "She was mediocre at best, let's be honest."

Claire's eyes widened in surprise. "But you told her she was wonderful. You clapped so loud and . . ." Claire clamped her mouth shut, afraid she had already said too much.

"Of course I did. I'm courting her for godsakes. What the hell was I supposed to say, 'Fair job, my love'?"

"So she's your love now?" Claire said, snorting, not caring how petty she sounded.

"Diane is . . . My God, Diane! I almost forgot why I'm here." He ran from the room not bothering to say good-bye. Curious, Claire peered out the window waiting for Nicholas to reappear. When he did, Claire let out a sound of pure disgust. In his hands he carried Diane's red woolen coat.

"Miss Dumont! Miss Dumont!" Claire smiled at the sound of Nathan's husky little voice as he shouted for her down the hall. She peeked her head out of the nursery door, trying in vain to put a stern look on her face.

"You shouldn't yell so loud," Claire said.

"But Mama told me to fetch you. We're getting our 'graph taken. And you must come so that we behave."

"A picture? How wonderful! And you're all to be in it? This is very, very special."

Nathan, his hair slicked back for the occasion, nodded solemnly. Claire took the little boy's hand as they marched importantly down the stairs and to the parlor, where all the Carrs and their remaining guests had gathered.

"It was supposed to be outside, but it's raining," Nathan said, explaining the crowded room.

Emily came running over, and Claire bent down to give the little girl a kiss. "My don't you look pretty." Her hair was in ringlets held by two red bows and she was wearing her finest dress. "Your mommy should have called me to help."

"I should have," Abigail said tiredly. "I forgot how much work it is getting these three little squirmy things dressed." Abigail sighed and massaged her back, making her already large stomach appear larger. Looking down at herself, Abigail groaned.

"George is insisting that all the Carrs be in the picture," she said, rolling her eyes toward her jovial husband. "It is quite embarrassing having a photograph taken of oneself looking like a cow."

Claire smiled at Abigail's misery. "You look beautiful, Mrs. Carr." Abigail threw her a disbelieving look.

"Be that as it may, I've insisted to be standing and well hidden. If that's possible." She laughed. Abigail massaged her back again. "If you could just make sure the children don't get too messy before the photographer is ready. It seems he's been setting up for hours over there."

"I will give it the ol' college try," Claire said.

"College?"

Claire sighed. "I'll try my best."

Claire gathered all three children about her and tried to capture their attention by looking at the huge draped camera that the photographer was still fiddling with.

"Attention, everyone! We are ready. If you would all gather around," the photographer yelled. Then came the shuffling and debates about who should stand where, who should sit next to whom, and even whether they should smile or not. In the picture were

the Carrs, their children, George's parents, Grand-
mother Carr, Diane Pendleton and her parents, and
Nicholas, Matthew, and Samuel, the latter two looking
as miserable as the weather outside. The elder Brooks
were still in Europe and there had been much debate
about whether to go ahead with the photograph without them here. They had been due to arrive a week
ago, but had decided to stay another month in Paris
instead.

Last to join the assembled group were the children.
Mabel went on George's lap, and Emily and Nathan
on either side of their proud father.

"What are the children holding?" asked the harried
photographer, coming out from behind the black
shrouded camera. Claire rushed forward and confis-
cated a small glass of milk from Nathan and Emily.
She stood back with the other guests who were not to
be in the photo, clutching the two glasses to her, feeling strangely left out. She knew she had no place in
the photograph, but this obvious separation drove
home that she would likely never be included in such
a family portrait. Claire was lost in her thoughts of
her family, longing for them in a fresh way, when the
photographer's bulb exploded near her ear. She did
not think, she acted. At the burst, Claire flung the
glasses from her and crouched to the floor. She dis-
tantly heard women's startled oh's but it took several
agonizingly long seconds to realize what she had done.
She had been diving for cover.

Mortified, Claire slowly rose to her feet, looking
about her at the startled expressions. She was dimly
aware that people were asking if she was all right,
and she could hear one woman—Diane Pendleton?—
exclaiming that her dress was wet with milk. She saw
Nicholas's look of concern, saw that he was coming
toward her as the others seemed to gather their wits
and also began approaching her.

"I'm sorry," she whispered, her Southernness accentuated absurdly in this Northern parlor silence. "I . . . I thought . . ." She swallowed, her face hot and red from shame. Without another word, she walked quickly from the room, leaving behind a crowd of confused onlookers.

The moment Nicholas heard the explosion and saw Claire dive for the floor, he had known what had happened. He, too, had flinched from the sound even though he had been expecting it. Weeks of being conditioned to hitting the ground at the sound of mortar and gunfire could not be driven out in a few short weeks. Claire had been fresh from the battlefield when he had found her, and not enough time had passed for that conditioned response to abate.

He found her in the small second-floor library, her back to the door, staring blindly at the cold hearth.

"Claire."

She did not turn, she only breathed in deeply at the sound of his voice. He walked up behind her and lay a hand on her shoulder, turning her into his chest. He held her to him with one warm hand on her neck as she rested her forehead against his chest. One hand clutched his lapel, the other hung loosely by her side. Her eyes were dry, but they were closed. *He makes me feel safe,* she thought with terrible longing. *Who will make me feel safe when he is gone, when he is with her forever? If I go back.*

"When I first got out of the hospital this last time, the same thing happened to me," Nicholas said, his lips brushing against her hair. "I had just stepped off the train and someone was unloading some crates. One was dropped and hit the porch with a loud crack. I was eating dirt before I knew what happened." He chuckled, and Claire could feel the deep rumble in his chest more than she could hear it. "I felt very foolish at the time. But as I stood up, I saw another man brushing off his knees. I remember looking at him, a complete stranger, it was like looking into a mirror. I saw that same look in your eyes."

"But it's been so long," Claire said, her voice muffled against his lapel.

Nicholas chuckled again. "Not so long." He breathed deeply and Claire found herself listening to that breath, so strong and solid and alive. "Claire, what happened in the parlor is nothing to be ashamed of. Do you really care what those old biddies think of you?"

Claire looked up at him and gave him a sad smile. "I'm afraid I do. They could never understand. Never . . . forgive."

Nicholas took his thumb and stroked her cheek. "I understand." His gaze moved over her face, impossibly beautiful, so at odds with what she had done. He bent his head and touched his lips to hers, soft and undemanding. "And I forgive." And saying the words, he found that he did. That what she had done, that what she was, no longer mattered.

Claire gave him the sweetest smile, moving him beyond what he thought she could. She placed her forehead back on his chest and breathed deeply, as if breathing him into her soul. I love him, she thought, wishing it made her happy instead of filling her with dread. I truly love him. It came to her as subtle and silent as a freight train barreling through her mind, that given a choice now to stay or go back to her old life, she would stay. Such a thought should have frightened her. Instead, she was oddly comforted. Perhaps, she thought, this was meant to happen.

"There you are. It seems every time you two are together, I find you in each other's arms." Diane Pendleton tried to keep her tone light, but seeing her future husband holding another woman in his arms— and a nanny at that!—was almost more than her well-practiced coolness could take.

Nicholas felt Claire tense and make to move away,

but for some reason he would not have been able to explain had he been pressed, he held her to him as if sheltering her.

"Is Miss Dumont ill?" Diane asked, her voice beginning to get tight and clipped.

"Claire had a fright, that is all."

Claire made to pull away and this time she was successful. "Really. I'm fine. Thank you for your concern, Miss Pendleton."

"The South cannot be as backward as all that. Certainly you have cameras."

Claire flushed beneath the woman's gaze. Clearly Miss Pendleton did not like Claire any more than Claire liked her. To her dismay, she heard Nicholas chuckle, as if sharing the nasty little joke with Diane.

Seeing that she had gained Nicholas's favor, Diane continued. "Perhaps that is why we Yankees won the war so handily. We should have given our soldiers cameras instead of guns and maybe it would have ended sooner."

"Perhaps," Nicholas said lightly, but his eyes wandered to Claire, whose face was flushed, whose back was stiff and straight.

"Ah, well, war is such a dreary topic. Shall we go down and join the others?" She walked over to Nicholas and grabbed his arm possessively, leaning in to him so that he might feel her breast against his arm. As they disappeared through the door, Claire could hear Nicholas chuckle again and wondered with awful insecurity if she was the topic of their little joke.

Chapter Fifteen

Diane tugged nervously at her gloves, glancing down at her burgundy-colored silk dress to make sure it was not getting too wrinkled in the buggy. She could have walked to the Carrs', for it was less than a mile from her own home, but preferred to arrive in a buggy, which allowed her to remain fresh. More than anything else today, she wanted to look pretty for Nicholas. Her stomach churned uneasily each time she thought about Claire in his arms, his hand holding her head protectively against his chest. She had congratulated herself on her cool reaction to coming upon the two in what was an impossibly intimate moment. The appearance of innocence, for she had convinced herself that it was completely innocent, somehow overshadowed by . . . something almost charged. But that simply couldn't be. She must be imagining things, allowing a petty jealousy to confuse what had obviously been an employer comforting an employee. Still, Miss Dumont was the *nanny*, for goodness sakes. That was the crux of it and that was why she could not put the incident out of her mind. Nothing must come between her and her vision of the future, a vision fed over the years by girlish fantasies and the reality of Nicholas's true affection.

These past few days had been heavenly, Diane thought, except for that nanny. If not for her, she could thoroughly enjoy Nicholas without concern. She knew she should not think of the skinny girl as a rival for Nicholas's love, the idea was absurd! But she wanted to make sure, to put her mind at ease, as ridiculous as she was certain her doubts were. She had tossed and turned the entire night, doubts assailing her, making her almost ill with fright. Over and over, she saw Nicholas's hand, almost completely enveloping Miss Dumont's head, her face pressed against him. Why, Diane had never been that close to Nicholas!

Despite the bluish smudges under her eyes from her sleepless night torturing herself, she realized she must talk to Nicholas immediately about her fears and explain her silly doubts. She must hear from his lips that Miss Dumont meant nothing to him and she prayed he would not think her forward or witless. She had been invited to the Carrs' for luncheon, but planned to arrive an hour early so that she might talk to Nicholas in private.

Stepping down from the carriage, Diane smoothed her dress and tugged again at her gloves. In a practiced gesture, she adjusted her hat, a jaunty little thing with a burgundy feather and a wide navy ribbon, and stepped to the door. She almost gave a little shriek of surprise when it was Claire who opened the door before she had a chance to let the knocker fall.

Correctly interpreting Diane's surprised look, Claire explained, "I was just about to go out, Miss Pendleton. Should I let Mrs. Carr know you've arrived?"

"No. I've come to see Nicholas, actually. Do you know where he is?" Claire did not, Diane was pleased to discover, but said she would inquire.

"I'll be in the sitting room, Miss Dumont, if you would be good enough to fetch him for me," Diane called as she walked down the hall to the private little room tucked in one of the house's many haphazard additions. Claire threw her dirty look at her receding back. The way the woman had dismissed her like a servant irked her. What riled Claire most was that she indeed was a servant of sorts, but only Diane Pendleton seemed to make her feel that way. Upon finding Nicholas alone and buried by the paper in the parlor, she said, "Your girlfriend sent me to 'fetch you,' Major. She's in the sitting room."

Nicholas ignored her jibe, so engrossed was he in whatever he was reading in the newspaper. When he did finally look up, his eyes were filled with anger and Claire was momentarily startled.

"What's wrong?"

He shook his head as if he did not want to share with her what he had been reading. So Claire marched over and searched the page over his shoulder. He knew she had discovered the correct article when he heard the sharp intake of her breath.

"I'll be damned. That scumbag is running for city council?" Claire quickly scanned the rest of the article announcing the candidacy of one Nelson Cunningham for Boston City Council.

"Apparently. It doesn't surprise me, but I wonder what his constituency would say if they knew what I know about him," Nicholas said dryly.

"Do you mean what he tried to do to me?"

"That and other things. The bastard. He's got no right holding office representing decent people. I know he's a molester of women and a thief and I've a good suspicion a murderer as well. He'll get away with it, with all of it." Nicholas wanted to spit to rid his mouth of the bad taste that developed at the thought of Nelson Cunningham.

"Murder?" Claire asked, her eyes growing wide.

Nicholas backed down a bit, feeling guilty about the accusation even though he loathed the man. "Well, I've no proof really. I suppose I shouldn't say such things publicly. But there's something evil about that man. Something putrid eating him inside."

"Yuck," Claire uttered at his graphic imagery. "But what made you say that? About him being a murderer. Something happened at Fort Wilkins. Tell me."

Nicholas tore his gaze away from Claire to stare at the offending newspaper article. "It happened while you were there. We found a prisoner badly beaten in a vacant barracks. It was brutal. It was as if he had been beaten long after he was dead. I suspected Cunningham for no other reason than I didn't like him. And that's not enough to accuse a man. Not nearly enough."

Claire felt her stomach clench, her heart beat quicken. "Nicholas? I think I saw something." She swallowed, not quite believing that she may have been a witness to a murder. He turned to her and gripped her arms. "Tell me."

"It wasn't much. The body. Was it found in the barracks on the south side of your office? Would I be able to have seen it from my window?"

He paused, brows creased in thought as he mentally mapped out the camp. "By God, yes, Claire. What did you see?"

"I saw Cunningham go into the barracks with a prisoner one day right before sundown. I remember because the prisoner had bright red hair like my brother."

A gleam entered Nicholas's eye, and a smile that wasn't quite a smile formed on his lips. "That's it, Claire. You saw Cunningham with a murdered prisoner. He did it. *He goddamn did it,* that son of a bitch." He slapped his fist loudly into his hand.

"But that still doesn't prove anything," Claire said. "We don't even know if what I saw happened at the time of the murder."

"Of course. But now we have something to go on. Now we have a suspect. And I'd bet that someone in that camp knew it was Cunningham or had a damned good suspicion. The guards and the prisoners were afraid of him. They didn't talk then, but maybe they'd talk now."

Claire smiled suddenly. "The murder, did it happen before or after Cunningham attacked me?"

Nicholas thought. "Before. A day or two before." Nicholas whipped his head up and gave her a look of triumph. "Of course, Claire. He saw you in the window. He got scared."

"He wasn't there to rape me," she said, her voice soft, almost a whisper. "He was there to kill me." Her mouth gaped open at the horror of it. "He wanted to kill me! That rat!" Claire was stunned, affronted, angry. "We have to tell someone. We have to let them know what we know."

"I'm not sure who would handle such a case," Nicholas said, thinking aloud. "But we can start with the War Department and go from there. There is a chance, Claire, that nothing will be done. It was war and the man was a prisoner. I'll do my best to see justice done, but Cunningham already slipped through my hands once. He may do it again."

"But murder is murder. Couldn't he be accused of some sort of war crime?"

"That's what I'm going to find out. You'll have to sign an affidavit, I'm sure. Do you want to do that, Claire?"

"You're goddamn right I do, Major." Nicholas raised one eyebrow at Claire's tone and a smile quirked on his lips. Brave Claire.

Claire smiled back, sharing the small victory, their common cause. But the smile dropped abruptly from her face when she recalled her reason for seeking Nicholas out.

"Diane is waiting to see you in the parlor," she said, trying to keep her voice bland. "Like I said before, she sent me to fetch you."

Claire could never hide what she was feeling, he thought, noticing how her blue eyes, normally bright like a summer sky, were dark as dusk. He correctly read the situation. "You might bring us a bit of tea," he said, purposefully goading her.

"I'll have one of the maids do so, if you don't mind," Claire retorted belligerently. "I may just get confused between the sugar and the salt. You just know how ignorant we Southerners are, Major Brooks." It was all Nicholas could do to stop from laughing at Claire's dart about last night's incident and Diane's comments. He gave her a condescending pat on the head as he passed her and eagerly left the room to seek out Diane.

Claire glared at his back. He just knew how he infuriated her and he actually enjoyed it! I should get over this silly notion that I care for that wretch, she thought savagely. But even that condescending little smile and that pat on her head made her heart quicken a beat. I must force myself to hate him, I must not allow myself to think a kind thought about him, she thought, her hands gripping her skirt so tightly the material became wrinkled.

A wicked thought entered her head and she shoved it immediately away. But it came back with a force Claire could not stamp out. How she wanted to spy on the two of them! Nicholas always made a sap of himself in her presence, to Claire's disgust. Maybe that was just what she needed. Maybe it would dampen these ridiculous feelings she had for Nicholas if she heard him profess his love for Diane. Biting both lips between her teeth, she tried to talk herself out of such a horrid notion. It would be dangerous to eavesdrop. And it would have to be done, she thought.

Once they were seated in a sunny little parlor, Diane in a chair and Nicholas across from her on a small couch, Diane almost lost her nerve.

"Nicholas, I feel rather awkward right now," she admitted, still looking into her lap and letting out a nervous little laugh.

"You look anything but awkward," he said, an automatic response to put her at ease. She actually did look quite lovely and shy, but then, she always did.

Diane took a deep and fortifying breath. "What do you think of Miss Dumont?" There it is out.

For just a moment, something flashed in his eyes, but Diane was too nervous to take note. "I'm certain I don't think of Miss Dumont at all," he lied blithely.

The fact was, he found himself thinking too damn much about the girl, but he was confused and angry with himself for such thoughts. *Why is it when I finally have the woman of my dreams all I can think about is that irritating slip of a girl?* Claire visited him in his dreams, leaving him hurting and sweating in his need. Perhaps if he denied he had any feelings for Claire aloud, it would become true, and so he lied to the woman he would marry.

Diane was relieved at his answer, but not convinced. "I'm sure you do not think of her," she said, finally lifting her gaze and giving him a tremulous smile. "Please don't think me silly, Nicholas. It's just when I saw her last night, with you, in your arms, I'm afraid I got a bit jealous."

"Oh, my dear Diane," Nicholas said, crossing over to her to grasp one cold hand. "You needn't be. Of Miss Dumont? You are all that is lovely and good. She is, why, she is coarse, she doesn't hold a candle to you, my dear. I comforted her as I might." He stopped, searching for the right words. "Why as I might an injured animal. That is all."

Diane smiled truly this time and Nicholas basked in her loveliness. "Oh, Nicholas! You don't know how happy that makes me. I was so worried. I know it was silly. Especially to think you would be attracted to someone like Miss Dumont. I realize she is pathetic in a way, and that can be a rather endearing quality to a strong man. That's what I was thinking."

"It was silly, Diane. Miss Dumont is rather pathetic, but that is not a quality I find very attractive." Nicholas heard himself lie, and was rather amazed that he was so good at it, for he had never lied so blatantly before. He nearly winced as he said the last, but he'd be damned if he would lose this woman because of his stupid infatuation with Claire Dumont, because he was too weak to deny his physical needs. Certainly it would pass. It was an attraction, one he must put out of his mind. Despite his resolve, he felt hellish for what he had uttered to the point he nearly reneged. But Diane was in front of him, looking so very happy, and his heart melted to see her heart so clearly in her eyes. He kissed her, a quick warm kiss on her soft lips, but he frowned when he saw the color leap into her cheeks as she looked down demurely at her lap. He wished, just once, he would kiss her and she would uplift her face for more instead of looking down into her lap as if she'd just committed an unpardonable sin.

Claire clutched a hand over her mouth to stop the sob that threatened to burst from her throat. She had not thought to hear such ruthless comments, she had not thought she would be the topic of any conversation between the two of them. She felt betrayed and hurt beyond anything she had ever endured. To hear him say such things. For him to have called her pathetic. Pathetic! It was too much for her already-fragile heart. How could he have held her so tenderly the night before, stroking her head, sharing a part of the pain he had felt, and then say such dreadful things. "I comforted her as I might comfort an injured animal." What a cruel thing to overhear, certainly the small sin of eavesdropping was not worthy of this terrible hurt. And it did hurt, more than Claire would have imagined. It's what you wanted, she thought brutally, to hear the truth, to hear something so horrid you would get over him.

Claire flew down the hall, keeping an eye out for servants or the Carrs, and ran up the stairs, taking them two at a time, lifting her skirts much higher than decency allowed, all the time holding back the tears that threatened to erupt at any moment. Unable to keep them at bay a moment longer, she ran into the small second-floor library, knowing she would be alone. No one used the room but Mr. Carr, and he was out this morning with the children. Claire closed the door as quietly as her raging emotions would allow and flung herself down onto the floor, laying her head on the nearest chair, and released in a violent flood the tears that had threatened. She tried as much as possible not to be noisy, aware of how humiliating discovery would be. She couldn't bear the concern, she couldn't bear lying about her tears. Claire let out tears that had been lying dormant for months, her chest heaving painfully as she tried to cry silently, her throat aching almost as much as her heart. She cried about Nicholas, about the soldiers, about her lost life, her lost family. "Oh God. Oh God," she sobbed into her arms, allowing herself to completely lose herself in her grief, suddenly not caring who might pass by. When she felt a warm hand on her shoulder, she shrieked "Oh God!" and spun around in fear, gazing up into the frowning face of Matthew Brooks.

"What is wrong?" he said, both concern and firmness in his voice.

"N-Nothing," Claire choked out between gulping hiccups. Matthew gave her a withering look of disbelief.

Claire gathered herself up enough to sit heavily into the chair she had made wet with her tears and found a handkerchief thrust in front of her. "Thank you," she said, the words coming out thick from her stuffed nose.

"I'm fine now, Mr. Brooks. Really." She looked up at him and tried to make her expression bland. He almost smiled at her effort. Clearly the girl's heart was breaking.

"You're in love with him, aren't you?" he asked, his voice surprisingly soft. It was a guess, but he knew his answer from her reaction. Claire feigned a look of confusion, but not before he read the truth in her eyes.

"In love with who?"

"Nicholas."

Claire tried to lie, really she did, but it rang so false, even to her own ears, that she faltered and fresh tears began to fall. She felt like a complete and utter fool to be blubbering in front of Matthew this way, to admit she loved a man who felt nothing for her but a bit of concern.

"It's awful, I know," she said looking up at him, fearing he would laugh. Surprisingly, he was completely serious.

"Tell me what happened," Matthew demanded.

Claire shook her head. "Oh, no. It's all too awful. I'm such an idiot," she finished, mostly to herself.

Matthew turned and sat down in the shadows, where he had been before Claire burst in and dropped to the floor in despair.

"Miss Dumont, I do not take you for a frivolous girl, one to fall in love so easily. How does Nicholas feel about you?"

Claire flushed crimson. "He feels nothing."

"I think you are very wrong," Matthew said, causing Claire to lift her head up in surprise. "I think Nicholas feels a great deal for you, but he's so wrapped up in what he thinks he wants, he does not realize it."

"Diane," Claire said dully. "He loves her. He told her he found me pathetic. I overheard them talking. I know I shouldn't have listened, but I did. And I'm glad I did because now I know."

"And that is what the tears were for?"

Claire did not answer him. She felt oddly drained and listless.

Matthew leaned forward, giving Claire an uncomfortably penetrating look. "I'd like to share something with you, Miss Dumont. And in exchange, I want to know all about you. Everything. I want to help you and I want to help my brother and I think I can do both." Matthew sparked her curiosity.

"Are we agreed?" And Claire thought, what did it matter if Matthew knew about her. What, indeed, did anything matter?

"Agreed."

Matthew leaned back, apparently satisfied. "My brother, Miss Dumont, is making a complete ass of himself over Diane. I like the girl, don't get me wrong, but she is entirely too complacent for him. He loves the idea of Diane. He's turning into a buffoon over that girl. It's sickening. You know that dog of hers? That little white thing that looks like an overgrown rat? I know for a fact that Nicholas loathes the thing, he's made jokes about making slippers of it." And Matthew laughed, obviously sharing his opinion of the creature. "But in front of Diane he dotes on the animal. Carries it for her, pets the damn thing. It's enough to make one ill. Do you see what I mean, Miss Dumont? He is not himself when he is with her. He's a complete and utter idiot."

"People in love are often idiotic. Just look at me," Claire noted, her tone depressed.

"I believe he loves you, Miss Dumont. We just have to make him realize it."

While Claire's heart soared at those words, her intellect rebelled. "Why would you think such a thing?"

"You didn't see his face when you were frightened by that bulb exploding. He looked . . . scared to death. And he follows you with his eyes. He cannot help himself. He watches you then gets irritated when he realizes what he's doing. He's fighting it, true, but I'll wager it's a losing battle."

Claire shook her head. "You must be mistaken. You didn't hear him talking with Diane. I did." She was beginning to get angry with Matthew for giving her even a bit of hope.

"He's just trying to convince himself," Matthew spat.

"Well, then, he's done a good job of it. And of convincing me."

Matthew glared at her. She was a stubborn little thing, wasn't she, and he half wondered why he even bothered trying to assist the two of them. Still, he persisted.

"Nicholas needs a woman who will fight him. Who he can fight with, who can outshout him. He will marry Diane, then wake up one morning, look into those vacant eyes, and realize he has made a grievous mistake. A man needs a woman who loves him because she understands him, not understands him because she loves him."

"Nicholas believes he has found what he wants in Diane. Who are you, or I, to say he is wrong?" Claire countered.

"I am his brother," Matthew bit out. "And you . . ."

"And me?"

"I don't know what you are."

Despite herself, Claire chuckled. "Perhaps that's the problem. Nicholas doesn't know what I am either."

"Tell me what you are."

Claire immediately sobered. "Can I renege on our deal?"

Claire could see a flash of white as Matthew smiled from his seat in the shadows. "Not a chance, lady."

And so she told him. Everything. She left out only that she had come from 1995. And that she and Nicholas had made love and were married. That was Nicholas's to tell, she decided, and much too personal to share with this man. Throughout her monologue, Matthew was silent, the only sound a sharp intake of breath when she described the battle in clipped silences. Matthew could not believe what he was hearing, that this woman who had cried over his thick-skulled brother had been to hell and back and remained sane. And beautiful. And kind.

After she finished, the room was thick with silence and Claire feared he was as disgusted by her as Nicholas.

"My brother is a bigger fool than I thought," he said absently. "Nicholas needs to see you in another light, Miss Dumont. I wonder what Nicholas's reaction would be if his little brother staked a claim?"

"What do you mean?" Claire asked, wrinkling her brow.

"I wonder what he would do if he thought someone else showed some interest in you? If you are correct, he will not care. If I am correct, it will drive him mad."

"Too dangerous," Claire said, a wicked gleam in her eye seeing finally what Matthew was thinking. "You would fall madly in love with me and then what a pickle we'd be in!"

"I believe I can resist your infinite charms, m'lady."

Claire bit her lip. It was the oldest ploy in the book, and one that she could not recall having worked except in books and bad movies. "Do you really think he'd care?"

"There is only one way to find out. What do you say?"

Claire's smile broadened, making Matthew wonder once again at his brother's stupidity. The idea of playing this game with Claire was infinitely uplifting to Matthew. It would be the most fun he'd had in years.

Chapter Sixteen

Abigail stared at her younger brother, a look of complete astonishment upon her face. For the third time in as many days, Matthew Brooks, who had not graced his parents' home three times in the past year, had decided to eat dinner with his family. And Abigail was beginning to suspect that, as unbelievable as it was, the true reason Matthew was visiting was not his family, but his family's nanny. As much as Abigail liked the girl, she was a bit bothered that her brother, who had not so much as spoken to a woman since his wife died six years before, appeared to be so enthralled with Miss Dumont.

Abigail sat on the small side porch, waving a fan in front of her face as much to discourage the pesky gnats as to encourage some sort of cooling breeze, her troubled gaze taking in the scene before her. Matthew stood by Miss Dumont, their backs to the house, and watched as her children and Samuel played a game of keep away. Miss Dumont would join in periodically, her skirts flying about exposing a flash of ankle and calf in her enthusiasm, then return to Matthew who appeared completely enthralled by the game—and by Miss Dumont herself. Thank God her parents were returning tomorrow. Certainly Papa would take Matthew aside and lecture him about the dangers of dallying with the staff, even with someone as apparently refined and respectable as Miss Dumont. The hollow sound of footsteps on the porch brought her head around.

"Matthew's here. Again," she informed Nicholas, although his gray eyes were already taking in the quaint scene.

Silence.

"He seems to be taking an uncommon amount of interest in our Miss Dumont," Abigail ventured, praying Nicholas would agree and volunteer to talk to his younger brother.

"Does that concern you?" Nicholas asked, his eyes narrowing as he watched Matthew pick a bit of something from Claire's hair.

"Well . . . a bit. This is the third day in a row he's kept Miss Dumont's company."

"Third day?" Nicholas asked, trying to keep the alarm from his voice. What the devil was his brother thinking of, he thought. And then he got his answer. His brother was thinking that here was a beautiful, unattached, intelligent, lively woman. Why wouldn't he be attracted to someone like Miss Dumont? Why, for that matter, wouldn't any man? It was something he had not contemplated and he found that seeing Claire appear so enraptured with another man—and his brother for God's sake—bothered him when it should not. Not when he felt nothing for the girl, as he had told himself over and over.

"Yes. Third day. In a row." They continued to watch the pair in silence for several minutes before Abigail spoke.

"Nicky," she said, her voice sweet and beseeching, telling Nicholas his little sister was about to ask a favor.

"No."

Abigail frowned. "You don't know what I was going to ask."

"It doesn't matter. When you call me Nicky and look at me like that, I know I don't want to do whatever it is you're planning. The last time you looked at me like that I ended up kidnapping a pig."

"Saving a pig from murder. And it was very gallant of you."

"And got me whipped."

Abigail pouted. "This will not be such a dangerous thing, Nicky. All I want you to do is find out Matthew's intentions. If he has none, then I can immediately reassure Mother and Father and avoid a messy situation."

"No. If you are so curious, ask him yourself."

Abigail stood up, hands on hips, and craned her neck to look Nicholas straight in the eye with her sternest look. "You know he will not tell me the truth! He will pat me on the head and tell me not to worry my little head about it. And I will end up breaking my new fan over his big head." She shook the fan at him as if she might smash it over his own head.

Nicholas stifled a grin at his feisty little sister's scowling face. "You could not reach his head with that fan, squirt."

Abigail let out a disgusted breath, her anger deflating.

"And I think you are exaggerating Mother and Father's reaction to Matthew talking with the nanny. He's not courting her, after all, and he's not asked her to marry him."

"Perhaps. But that does not mean he will not."

Nicholas ignored the sick lurch his stomach gave at the thought of Claire being courted by Matthew, or any man for that matter. Of her holding his hand, or touching his face, or kissing his lips. Or inviting another man into her bed.

"I'll talk to him," he said, suddenly desperate to know what his brother was up to.

Brother and sister turned then at the uncommon sound of their brother laughing, scowls on both their faces.

"I'll talk to him," Nicholas repeated, mostly to himself.

Matthew, his back to his brother, a slight smile on his lips, studied the brandy in his glass. He had wondered what had taken so long for someone in his meddlesome family to broach the subject of his interest in one Miss Dumont. He noted that Nicholas had taken pains to be casual in his questioning, and if Matthew did not know Nicholas so well he would not have known that his brother was so furious he could barely keep up the facade of polite conversation. He turned to face Nicholas, almost letting the smile that threatened show itself upon seeing the look on his brother's face. When had Nicholas lost his great ability to hide his emotions? Matthew wondered.

"She is a sweet little number, I have to admit," Matthew said, purposely coarse. "She seems receptive to my . . . advances so far. And you do know what they say about Southern girls. They teach them the finer arts of love early. It's the heat, you know. Those long, hot summers. I'm sure she's not as innocent as she seems to be. She's no virgin, that one. I'm not all *that* stupid, Nick."

Nicholas was almost shaking in rage. "She seems rather innocent to me," he choked out, not quite believing his brother could be so crude.

"Even so. She's ripe for the picking," Matthew said, turning around quickly before he lost control and laughed aloud at his brother's expression. He poured himself another fingerful of brandy, breathing deeply to regain control. Christ, this was fun.

Nicholas stared at his brother's back, his hands

curled into fists by his side. By God, he wanted to pummel the living daylights out of the man. He would, too, if he said one word, one more word castigating Claire.

"I don't think you mean to say such things, Matthew. I don't think the girl is what you think."

"Who cares?" Matthew said, waving one hand in a dismissive way. "It's been a long time since a female has interested me as much as this one, and I mean to take advantage of it. Whores have never been to my taste. Claire has a sweet quality, but I suspect not far beneath that sugar coating is something hot."

Nicholas nearly choked on his drink. "*Miss Dumont* is your nephew and nieces' nanny. She is not some . . . tart for you to taste."

Matthew smiled a hard smile, his eyes narrowing in anger. "You are not presuming to tell me what female I can and cannot keep company with, are you, brother? You implied not long ago that the girl had no background, was little more than poor white trash. I'm afraid I'm confused, Nicholas. I'm afraid I haven't the slightest idea why you should concern yourself with our sister's *nanny* and whether I might show some interest in the girl. It is really none of your business."

Nicholas swallowed and threw his brother a frustrated look. Of course it was none of his business. Not anymore. He had severed all ties with Claire. What did it matter if his brother showed interest in her?

"Perhaps you should simply be careful," Nicholas said, a tone of weary defeat in his voice. "Abigail likes the girl and if anything should happen, if she should choose to leave her position, Abigail would be upset. The babe's due anytime, now. Abby needs Miss Dumont. Just keep that in mind."

"Claire is not a child, Nicholas. You can be assured I will try to be discreet." Matthew walked from the room, his steps as jaunty as his wooden leg would allow.

Nicholas's gray eyes smoldered. Discreet! He would try to be discreet! By God, if he touched the girl, he'd . . . He'd what? Beat his brother? His one-legged brother? How could he condemn his brother for the same feelings he had for Claire himself? At least Matthew was honest and up front about the whole thing. Unlike he, who secretly thought of Claire, who dreamed of kissing her, of loving her, while pretending to feel nothing. It was the height of hypocrisy for him to feel anything but happiness for Matthew, for finally finding a woman he was attracted to, even if his intentions were far less than honorable. How honorable were his intentions that night he had first made love to her, that night of unfettered passion on the storage room floor?

It truly was none of his business whether Claire succumbed to his brother's charms. He must tell himself that, he must remind himself that he cared not whether Claire fell in love with Matthew, or whether she allowed him to make love to her. Nicholas wiped a hand through his hair in an angry gesture. Claire, Claire, Claire, he thought wildly, desperately.

Please say no.

Nicholas walked slowly to the front of the house and gazed morosely out the window only to see Claire clasp Matthew's hands in pure happiness before they turned and walked side by side toward the cove. Nicholas's nostrils flared and his entire body ignited in rage as he watched Matthew's hand rest on the small of Claire's back as they strolled.

"I see your little talk with Matthew did wonders," Abigail said derisively, her eyes glued to the couple.

Nicholas grunted in reply.

"Why her? Why her of all the beautiful girls who have mooned over Matthew? He's become the town's tragic, romantic figure, you know, Nick."

"Perhaps because she is so beautiful herself. And sweet. She is very sweet."

Abigail gave her brother a hard look. "You think her beautiful?"

Nicholas snapped out of his reverie. "I can see how some men might think her beautiful."

"She doesn't hold a candle to Diane," Abigail said pointedly.

Nicholas smiled and looked down at his sister's worried face. "No need to worry that both brothers are becoming enamored with your little nanny."

"Of course not!" Abigail said, as if that were the farthest thing from her mind. And indeed it was. Miss Dumont was so unlike Diane that it was inconceivable that a man could be attracted to both women.

"Diane should be here any minute. I've had the croquet set up. I'll watch from the porch with the children. George insists he'll beat you this time. You wouldn't let him win, just once, would you, Nick?"

"Sorry, sis. My generosity is never extended towards games of skill."

Nicholas was about to win—again—when he happened to glance up and catch Matthew and Claire in the distance beneath a huge box elder tree. Matthew was facing him, his hands on Claire's shoulders, her face uplifted. Telling himself to ignore the romantic little scene that played out not one hundred yards from his spot, he set up his shot, an easy smack of the ball through the final set of wickets. It was at the moment of impact of his mallet against the grooved wooden ball, that, out of the corner of his eye, he saw Matthew bend toward Claire. My God, was he kissing her? The ball went sailing wide, hit far harder than was necessary, and missed its mark by a considerable amount.

"Is he looking?" Claire asked, her mouth just an inch away from Matthew's.

"Oh yes. He's looking. He missed his shot."

"He did? Do you think it was because he was distracted?"

Matthew pulled his head up, ending the overlong mock kiss, and surreptitiously watched his brother as he angrily stalked to his ball, his eyes glued to the couple beneath the tree. "I would definitely say he was distracted by our little scene."

Claire giggled, then became serious. "Are you sure? You are not simply saying so to spare my feelings?"

Matthew switched positions with Claire. "See for yourself." Claire spied Nicholas standing off the course awaiting his turn. He appeared to be facing her, his eyes boring into hers, his hands clutching the mallet as if it were a weapon.

"Put your hands on my shoulders. What's he doing now?"

Claire peeked over Matthew's shoulder. "He's just standing there."

"Kiss my cheek. Put your hand to my face first. What a tender scene this is, my dear." Claire giggled again. She lifted her face to Matthew's, her eyes on Nicholas. Her lips touched Matthew's rough-shaven cheek, her eyes growing large as Nicholas took a step, then another, toward them before recovering sufficiently and stopping. Claire put her forehead against Matthew's chest and stifled a laugh of happiness.

"It does appear to bother him, doesn't it," she said, trying not to let her heart soar too high at the sight of Nicholas's discomfort. She clasped her hands in front of her, as if she could capture her excitement before it flew out of control.

Matthew looked down at Claire's face, so full of happiness and hope, and his heart expanded just a bit. She will be so good for Nicholas, he thought. She will give him life and fire and joy. For the first time in a long time, Matthew wished he had someone in his life who would do the same.

"I think we'll end Nicholas's suffering for this evening," Matthew said, a smile in his voice. He shifted to lean heavily on his good leg, turning slightly ashen as a sharp pain sliced through him.

"And your own suffering," Claire said, pointedly looking at Matthew's leg. Claire smiled gently at the slight tinge of redness that appeared on his cheeks.

"I've noticed that if you stand in one spot for too long your leg hurts you." She watched as he clenched his jaw, his good humor gone with the reminder of his weakness. "I only mention it because I need you in top form to drive Nicholas insane with jealousy."

He relented then, smiling at her. Of course Claire would notice he was troubled by his leg. "I'll walk you to your buggy," she said, taking his arm.

In the waning light, Nicholas, standing beside Diane, watched the two figures walk across the lawn toward the drive. No one looking at him would have guessed at the turmoil in his heart. Not Abigail. Not George. And certainly not Diane, who at that very moment glanced up and followed Nicholas's eyes to the departing pair.

"I'm glad for Matthew, despite what Abigail thinks," said Diane, who as a woman in love wished everyone else to be in love as well.

The next day dawned gray and heavy. The old-timers who gathered at the town dock each morning pretending to fish as they smoked stinking cigars, spat their tobacco and nipped at their flasks, sniffed the air like old hound dogs, and predicted a storm. The air was still, but the water on the bay was choppy, a telltale sign that a storm was brewing off the coast. Although the townspeople went about their business, eyes frequently looked to the sky and all the talk was about the coming storm. Not whether it would hit, for those living by the sea recognized the signs—the way the seagulls hovered in the still air, the way the swans stayed in their protective inlets without venturing onto the open water—but when. Perhaps the most telling news came from a man who had just arrived from Rabbitt Island's rocky coast, where waves were crashing ashore and so many striped bass danced in the watery curls you could catch them with a net.

In the Brooks household, talk was not of the storm, but of the arrival of the elder Brooks, and the arrival of the youngest. For Martha and Joseph had barely stepped through the door, complaining loudly about their rough trip home, when Abigail went into labor with a surprised screech. It was as if their newest grandchild had waited patiently until their return, then wanted to meet them immediately.

Claire gathered up the children and brought them outside into the thick humid air where they would not be able to hear the childbirthing screams of their mother. Claire, noting the leaden sky, prayed the weather would hold until after the babe was born so that the youngsters were spared not only hearing their mother's pain, but seeing their father's frantic worry. Not a week ago, a woman of their acquaintance had died in childbirth, and George was beside himself with fear that the same fate awaited his Abigail.

She took the children to their favorite place, a marsh that always drew graceful white egrets, their beady yellow eyes somehow spotting tiny fish beneath the surface. The children loved to play near the shallow water, collecting tiny shells and smooth rocks. As the afternoon wore on, a balmy breeze blew little ripples in the glassy water and the leaves in the trees above began clattering together. Claire closed her eyes, at first enjoying the wind as it buffeted around her, then becoming concerned that the wind was a precursor of rain to follow.

She tried to calculate how long the little group had been gone from the house and guessed it had been several hours. They had eaten lunch, and the children had even napped on the grassy hill above the marsh.

"Children, I think we should return home before it begins to rain," Claire called. The children, excited about the possibility that a little brother or sister could be awaiting them upon their return, immediately came running. As they walked through the woods, following a narrow little path that led to the house, the trees above them began a crazy dance in a sudden strong gust that caused a few dead twigs to fall around them. Claire, for the first time growing alarmed at the intensifying storm, hurried the children along, giving a sigh of relief when they cleared the woods and the house came into view. Pretending to start a foot race, Claire, carrying Mabel in her arms, made a quick dash across the lawn just as the first drops of rain began to fall. The sporadic drops left tiny dusty puddles in the drive and the air was filled with the scent of rain. Claire was herding the children through the door when Emily turned to her, a stricken look on her face.

"Annabelle!" she cried, and tried to push past Claire.

Claire grabbed the little girl gently. "Honey, she'll be all right. A little wind and rain won't hurt such a sturdy dolly as Annabelle."

Claire's assurances did little to soothe Emily, who appeared to grow even more agitated when Claire mentioned the wind and rain. "I want Annabelle!" she screamed, her little face becoming red and mottled.

"Shh. Shhh. Emily! Do you remember where you left her?"

Sensing her nanny was about to help, Emily stopped her screams. She appeared to think, then her face screwed up in horror when she realized she could not remember where she had left her precious doll. "Nooo," she cried in complete anguish. Emily began crying real tears of heartbreak, her imagination picturing her doll washed away in some violent torrent. Claire bit her lip.

"I'll go look for her. Nathan, you take your sisters to Cook so she can watch you. I'll be right back."

With that, Claire opened the door, which nearly blew out of her hands from the force of the gale. Groaning under her breath and cursing her soft heart, she bent her head against the windswept rain that stung her face and headed back to the marsh.

Nicholas had just finished toasting his brother-in-law's new son when he spied Emily gazing out the window with an intensity that was comical.

"Hey, princess. You're not worried about the storm are you?"

"No." But her gaze never wavered from the window.

Nicholas bent down beside her so he could see from her level what was so fascinating out in the storm. The window rattled, but Nicholas did not believe there was any danger yet that it would shatter. From the looks of the storm, however, it would not be long before he ushered the entire family into a safer area, away from large-paned windows facing the brunt of the storm. Outside was gray—the rain coming down so heavy in the steamy air, Nicholas could not see clearly further than the drive. The distant woods were nothing more than a dark gray blur on the horizon.

"What are you looking at?" Nicholas asked, smiling at his niece's serious face.

"I'm waiting for Nanny to come back with Annabelle."

Nicholas's body went cold, his heart seemed to stop. "Where did Nanny go, and who is Annabelle?" he asked as calmly as he could, not wanting to frighten the girl.

Emily finally turned her China blue eyes to her

uncle. "Annabelle is my dolly. And Nanny went to find her."

"Nanny went to find her."

"In the woods near the marsh," Emily cheerfully volunteered.

Nicholas swallowed, trying to stem the panic that threatened to rise up in him. He stalked to the mud room and grabbed two slickers, purposely trying to be methodical, to be calm, to stop the urge to simply dash out into the storm and search blindly for her. Brave Claire, stupid Claire, he thought as he pushed out the door, the wind blowing in his face, stealing his breath away. Risking her neck for a little girl's doll. What a perfectly idiotic thing to do. He'd throttle her when he found her. He'd . . . My God, he prayed, leaning hard against the blasting gale, please let her be safe.

He entered the woods, his eyes above him, watching for falling branches and trees. The roar of the wind through the trees, the rain beating on the leaves and the hood of his slicker made shouting useless. His stomach clenched tightly as he saw a large branch crash ahead of him as his mind's eye pictured Claire being crushed beneath the limb. Where the hell was she? Following the path he guessed Claire and the children had taken to the marsh, his eyes strained the gloom for her familiar form. A movement! And he saw her, struggling with her wet and wind-torn skirts that flapped around her legs wildly. She held one hand up to her forehead, a desperate and futile attempt to keep the rain from falling into her eyes. The other hand held the doll. Nicholas ran toward her, heedless of the falling branches, of the trees twisting dangerously above him, groaning and snapping.

Claire knew within two steps of entering the woods that she had made a mistake. But having come so far, she was determined to find the doll. How could she return to Emily empty-handed? How could she fail yet again? By the time she found the doll sitting safely against a fallen log, Claire was as frightened as she had ever been on the battlefield. Although she had seen intense thunderstorms back home, she had never witnessed such a violent tempest. Every step was a monumental effort, with her skirts seeming to take a life of their own as they wrapped around her legs and tripped her time and time again. A small branch slashed against her cheek, leaving behind a stinging, bleeding cut, and all around her larger branches thundered to the sodden ground. Blinded by the rain, Claire tried to follow the narrow path as best she could, but was finding it more and more difficult to navigate. Briers pulled at her skirts, tearing the light material and cutting into her flesh. She tripped on a rock, falling hard to the ground, where she lay breathless and near to tears, her hands clutching a handful of soggy, rotted leaves.

Strong hands suddenly gripped her shoulders, and Claire knew without looking that it was Nicholas. She flung her arms around him, sobbing uncontrollably as he held her to him so tightly she could barely gather enough breath to fuel her cries. Thank you, God, Nicholas said over and over in his head as he pressed her against his. It seemed they stayed that way for hours, both kneeling on the wet ground, heedless of the storm battering them. Finally, Nicholas dragged her up with him and struggled to throw the extra slicker over her, fighting the wind that threatened to snap it out of his hands. Claire shivered as she numbly complied to his shouted commands to lift her arms so that he could pull the coat over her. Throwing an arm around her waist, he began pulling her down the path toward the house. Suddenly, Claire refused to follow and fought to go back. He turned her roughly to him, his face contorted with anger.

"Where the hell do you think you're going?" he shouted, trying to be heard above the storm's clamor. Claire simply shook her head and tried to pull away.

"No, Claire." He shook her and began dragging her down the path.

"The doll!" she screamed. "I have to get the doll!"

Nicholas looked behind them, his eyes finding the sodden rag doll lying in a puddle a few feet away. "God-*dammit*!" He pushed around her and retrieved the doll, thrusting it angrily into Claire's hands. She had the effrontery to smile up into his face before bending her head once again into the wind.

By the time they got back to the house, both so weary they could barely take a step, Nicholas's fury had grown to almost uncontrollable proportions. Finally through the door, the silence of the house almost tomblike compared to the outside, Nicholas stared at her with utter disbelief. Even when a weeping Emily came to claim her Annabelle, his expression did not soften. Claire simply crossed her arms and stared up at him, daring him to shout at her. He took a deep breath, letting it out harshly through his nose, closing his eyes and searching for a reason not to take her over his knee. Before he could say a word, she spoke.

"I had to get the doll. I did not realize the storm had grown so dangerous. Thank you for saving me." Her voice was clipped and businesslike, as if she were thanking a servant for bringing her wrap. Her eyes challenged him, her jaw was stubbornly set and one foot tapped impatiently.

His eyes narrowed dangerously, his mouth opened, then shut. "You're welcome," he spat.

And Claire, her face still beaded with rain and spattered with mud, smiled. Even with her hair plastered against her head, even wearing the shapeless rain slicker, she looked uncommonly beautiful. Nicholas, despite himself, let out a puff of laughter and shook his head.

"Claire, you could have been killed," he said heavily. "For a doll."

"And you could have been killed trying to help me." She took one of his hands, surprisingly warm despite the cold rain, and leaned forward laying her lips softly on one wind-kissed cheek. He clenched his jaw and swallowed. "Thank you, Nicholas," she said before turning away.

"You say it's not serious?" Nicholas's father, a large man grown larger still on his trip to Europe, stood looking out the window taking in the uncommon sight of his younger son talking to a woman.

"No. Not serious the way you mean," Nicholas said, conveying his concern with his tone.

"Yes. Indeed. I don't believe Matthew is contemplating marriage, either. We mustn't have any Brooks bastards running about the place. We'll have to discharge her, of course. I'll talk to Abigail about it. I'm sure she'll listen to reason."

"I don't believe that will be necessary, sir," Nicholas said quickly.

His father looked up at his son quickly and began stroking his salt-and-pepper beard. "Of course it's necessary. What else do you suggest?"

Noting his father's intense gaze, Nicholas lowered his eyes, chastising himself for allowing his confusing emotions for Claire to cloud his judgment. His father was not a stupid man. His father must not suspect that he had any relationship with the girl, other than as a concerned employer. And, of course, he did not, he told himself.

"I don't believe Matthew is that taken with the girl. And Abigail has come to rely heavily on her. That reliance will only increase with the baby. I suggest Matthew be told to curb his interest in her. After all, no good can come from it. The girl will end up hurt. Or pregnant," Nicholas stopped, nearly choking on the word, on the thought of Claire carrying anyone's babe. Except perhaps his. He closed his eyes to banish that reckless, impossible thought.

Joseph Brooks, his eyes still peeled on Matthew, did not see the flash of agony that crossed his older son's face. Had he, he would have known without a doubt which son he should be wasting his worry on. Instead, rubbing his beard as if that action somehow stimulated his brain into decision, he said into the glass, "You are right. There are plenty of young women Matthew can attend to. Abigail does seem to like the girl and she does appear to do her job well. The children obviously care for her." The older man paused and turned to Nicholas. "Why do you think Matthew is so enamored with this one? You've been gone a long time, Nick, you have not seen how your brother is. He does not speak to women, he does not seek them out. I'd begun to think he was not quite . . . normal. A man. Well, my boy, you know a man must . . . It's not natural to go so long without a woman. He's not a priest or a monk, after all."

Nicholas stepped next to his father. "I didn't know. It must be Anne. He must still be missing her."

Joseph grunted. "After all these years? No. He's punishing himself. It's why he stays in that godforsaken lighthouse. He doesn't count himself worthy of human company. She is a pretty thing, I must admit. She does have a certain . . . charm to her. It's that accent, I suppose. But she's no more special than anyone already here."

Nicholas watched as Claire bent to wipe a smudge from Nathan's face as the boy grimaced from her attention. She apparently told him something funny, for the little boy laughed. So did Matthew, throwing his head back with abandon.

"He's laughing," Joseph said with awe in his voice. "Perhaps I have not given the girl enough credit. Anyone who can make Matthew laugh certainly demands higher consideration. Perhaps I've been a bit hasty in my judgment of the girl."

Nicholas felt his stomach knot nervously. My God, all he needed was for his father to sanction their relationship. If Claire found an ally in his father, Matthew was as good as married. And the thought of Claire being married to anyone made him literally ill. Though it should not. Certainly not. He should be happy. For both of them. Yes. Happy.

"She may make him laugh, but she certainly is not suitable as a wife," Nicholas bit out before common sense could tell him to keep his mouth shut.

"Good heavens no. Of course not," his father said, and relief washed over Nicholas. What his father said next, though, was more than unsettling. "It certainly will not hurt to allow Matthew a bit of . . . diversion, however. He has become much too morose. It is not good for him nor his son. Samuel is such a brooding little boy. 'Tisn't natural. But he will not listen to me. Or your mother. He gets angry and stalks away whenever we so much as hint that he should get on with his life. That damn leg won't let him forget, I suppose. And if that is what this girl has done, make him forget, then good for her. Let him have his fun."

Nicholas clenched his jaw until it hurt. "You don't mean to say you are sanctioning this . . . relationship."

"That's exactly what I mean," Joseph Brooks said, pulling out a Cuban and deftly clipping off one end. He paused to light the cigar, puffing lightly. "Don't tell your mother about this," he said, indicating the cigar.

He watched as his father took several thoughtful puffs.

"We'll just have to tell him to be careful. About a child, I mean," Joseph said.

Rage. It coursed through his blood, it made his ears ring, it nearly blinded him. Matthew would not have her. By God, he would not. She is my . . . What? She is my nothing, he realized. He had no rights over her. He had no right to stop her from falling in love, no right to be angry. Diane. I must think of Diane. The woman I love. He forced himself to look at the couple with detachment. She is nothing to me, he fairly shouted in his head, trying to stem the panic that was rising in his chest.

He turned to find his father looking at him strangely, as if he could read his riotous thoughts. Nicholas, to his utter shame, blushed beneath his father's scrutiny.

"Abigail tells me you found the girl. That she had become lost." His tone was thoughtful, calm.

"Yes. She, um, needed a position and I thought of Abigail. That she was about to have a child and would need the help."

"Hmmm."

Nicholas crossed his arms and leaned up against the wall, in control now, his casual stance appearing unforced.

"You must have made a rather quick assessment of her character then," he father said, clearly fishing for information. Nicholas's suspicions were correct. His father had read his face as he had stared with such heat at Claire standing beside his brother.

"She appeared to be clean and respectable," he said, trying to repeat the noncommittal description he had given of Claire in his cryptic letter to his sister.

"And young and beautiful," his father said.

Nicholas felt the tension working its way up from his shoulders to his neck. Hell. He'd better just confront whatever his father was trying to get at.

"Yessir. She is both those things. But she is a pale version of Diane," he said, willing himself to believe the words that sounded hollow even to his own ears. "It is Diane whom I plan to marry," he added more forcefully.

But it is Claire who you love, his father couldn't help but think. A man did not look at a woman the way his son just had unless he loved her. If it was true, at least his son had the sense to ignore such soft feelings and marry the woman who was more suited to him, he thought. His father grunted, apparently satisfied, and puffed on his cigar.

He knew his sons would do the right thing.

Chapter Seventeen

If Nelson Cunningham was surprised to find a Union officer at his door, he did not show it. And if he felt just a twinge of trepidation when the officer informed him he was from Colonel Hoffman's office, head of prisons during the war, he managed to hide that as well. Never had Cunningham felt safer. He was home, he was a hero, he was about to be elected to the city council in a special election. Nelson Cunningham believed himself to be a powerful man with powerful friends. Hadn't he proved that already?

And so when the officer, not more than twenty-five years old, stepped uncomfortably into his parlor, Cunningham exuded confidence.

"Sorry to inconvenience you, sir, but I'm here investigating an incident that occurred at Fort Wilkins back in March. I'm Lieutenant Young. Carl Young." The young officer's tone was apologetic, but his eyes were cutting and shrewd and Cunningham felt his uneasiness grow.

"If this is about commissary records, Lieutenant, I'm afraid you've made a wasted trip. That matter has been cleared. I have a letter to that effect." Cunningham stood and moved to his desk as if to search for the document.

"No, sir. I just have some routine questions to ask about the death of one of the prisoners."

"Many prisoners died, Lieutenant. It was unfortunate but inevitable." I am smooth, I am confident, he thought.

"One of the prisoners was murdered, sir, and we've recently received additional information on the matter. Perhaps you recall the incident."

Cunningham felt a bit of panic building, but he calmly shook his head. "No. I don't believe I recall a *murder*."

"The prisoner was found beaten in a vacant barracks, sir," Lieutenant Young offered, his eyes seeming to read Cunningham's mind.

Don't lie, he thought with an inward smile. You can beat him at this game. "Oh yes. I remember now. I thought it must have been one of the other prisoners."

Lieutenant Young smiled politely. "We have reason to believe, sir, that one of the guards or officers could have been involved."

Cunningham widened his eyes in shock. "Really? One of ours?" And he couldn't help himself, for he had to know just how much "information" this *boy* had. "What have you learned?"

The young officer smiled again and might as well have pointed an accusing finger at Cunningham for the effect that smile had on Cunningham's roiling stomach. Keep calm. He knows nothing. Nothing!

Ignoring the question, Young asked, "Do you recall where you were the night of the murder?"

Was that a trick question? Had anyone ever determined whether the beating had taken place at night?

"I was on duty until six or so. Then I suppose I went to my quarters. I really don't recall."

"Did you perhaps enter barracks number 14, that's the vacant one, the night of the murder at any time, sir? Perhaps with a prisoner?"

The girl. The *bitch*. She opened her little mouth.

She had them believing he was a murderer. God-dammit I should have killed her when I had the chance. I . . .

"Sir?"

Cunningham jerked his head up. He smiled at Young. Yes, I'm fine. They have no proof other than that bitch's word that she saw me go into that barracks. Surely not enough to convict. Surely not enough even to charge.

"I'm sorry, I was thinking." He shook his head, an apologetic expression on his face. "I just don't recall, although I doubt it. I can see no reason why I would have gone into an empty barracks. Certainly not with a prisoner." I'm being too polite, he thought suddenly. I should be affronted by such a question.

"You certainly don't think I had anything to do with the murder, sir. Why, such an idea is preposterous. I am running for city council. I am a decorated veteran!"

Young smiled again. That same knowing, calm smile as if Cunningham had just admitted to beating the prisoner. "No, sir. I was thinking perhaps if you had been in that barracks you might have seen something that could help with our investigation. As I said, these questions are just routine. If you think of something, please contact me in Washington." Young brought out a card and handed it to Cunningham. He walked to the front door, Cunningham following behind him. "Again, thank you for your time, sir."

"Yes. Happy to assist, Lieutenant," he said, opening the door for the officer. When he closed the door, Cunningham brought a fist to his mouth and chewed nervously, his eyes darting about as if looking for some answer as to what he should do. His breath came in spurts and he felt sweat trickle through his thinning hair and down the side of his face. My God, he thought with horror, did Young see me sweat?

Cunningham walked back to his desk and sat down

heavily. "What am I going to do," he said aloud, his voice unusually high-pitched. "What am I going to do?"

She must not be allowed to testify. Without her, there would be no other witnesses. He was sure of it. And there was only one way to stop her, he thought as his breathing returning to normal. "It must be done, Nelson, ol' boy," he said aloud, his voice, now calm and smooth, comforting him. "Tsk. Tsk. Too bad. Such a beautiful young woman. Such a waste." And he grew hard thinking about her delicate neck beneath his hands and how she would be after. Pale and cold and lifeless.

Chapter Eighteen

July 4, 1865

It was only nine o'clock in the morning and already the air was filled with the periodic blasts of fireworks and the acrid smell of gunpowder and singed paper, a scent that seemed to excite the children as much as the blasts themselves. Claire's stomach clenched nervously hearing yet another loud boom and she wondered how Nicholas, who had seen many more battles than she, could stand it. She could see him in the distance on the tiny cove beach working with George to build a huge pile of driftwood for the bonfire that would be lit later that night. Each time a fireworks was lit, she jolted as if it had been lit just feet away. She could not be sure, but she thought she saw Nicholas jerk as well and felt an overwhelming urge to go to him, if only to show that she understood. She thought: It is not your place to comfort him. Though that chastising thought did nothing to stop the longing she felt each time she looked at him, each time she sensed that he was near. Another blast and Claire clenched her entire body against the urge to run into a closet and hide for the day. She watched Nicholas pick up a large branch and throw it angrily into the pile, and she knew he was angry at himself for allowing something as innocuous as fireworks to rattle him.

The children, however, oblivious that such noise could have a sinister meaning, rushed to the windows to see if they could pinpoint from which direction the blast came, excitedly searching for the telltale smoke that would drift up from the explosion. As much as she hated the blasts now, she remembered when she and her brothers were children. How they loved the Fourth of July with its picnics and games and most of all, its fireworks. The Dumonts would head to Washington, D.C., and gather with thousands of others to picnic, listen to bands, and watch fireworks near the reflecting pool on the mall with the Lincoln Memorial looming behind them.

A particularly loud blast sounded, followed by Nathan's excited whoop, jarring Claire back to the present. Tonight would be worse, she knew. From what Matthew had told her, the entire town gathered at Northford Cove Beach each year, and this Fourth of July celebration would likely be all the more well attended. She dreaded it. She did not want to be among a crowd of Northerners as they celebrated the South's defeat. She did not want to be close by when the fireworks display was lit. But her duties would likely require her to be on hand, and she was unwilling to ask Abigail to give her the evening off so that she might stay safely in her room. Baby Alex was already ensconced safely at George's parents' home in Kingstown, so Claire had no excuse to remain in the house. She knew such a request would only bring loud protests from everyone—especially the children.

Matthew would not be at the picnic. The thought of being in such a crowd of people was abhorrent to him, Claire knew. And so she must endure not only the good people of Northford alone, but the prospect of seeing Nicholas and Diane snuggling together watching the fireworks display. At least when Matthew was about, she could pretend that part of Nicholas's attention was drawn to the two of them. She was thoroughly convinced that Nicholas became even more doting, more utterly sickening with Diane when she was about—a situation that was magnified tenfold when Matthew was standing dutifully by her. It was this alone that made her dare believe Matthew was correct when he'd told her they were getting under Nicholas's skin.

"Boom!" Mabel screamed after another firecracker was set off. "Boom, boom, boom."

The solemn conversation immediately forgotten, Nathan and Emily joined their little sister in creating their own fireworks noises. "Boom, boom, boom."

Boom! The sound reverberated between the houses like a clap of thunder exploding overhead. Claire simply closed her eyes, having conditioned herself throughout the endless day to the constant blasts. The Carrs, the Pendletons, and the Brooks, with the exception of Nicholas's parents, had decided to walk the mile to the town beach. The streets were filled with families lugging picnic baskets and harried parents trying to control their wayward children. Carriages and buggies were logjammed on the narrow dirt street, carrying frustrated passengers who watched as the walkers passed them with ease. The sweet smell of honeysuckle mingled with the smell of outdoor cooking, and Claire again was transported back—or was it forward—to her summers of childhood.

Claire held hands with Nathan and Emily, clutching them tightly so as not to lose them in the crowd. In front her, Mabel smiled at her over her father's shoulder as she happily bounced along. Nicholas and Diane walked behind Claire with Samuel. She could hear them talking, Nicholas sounding falsely jovial and Diane sounding impossibly perky and sweet. Samuel, as usual, was silent. The sun was still high in the western sky, but the light was just beginning to soften into what would become twilight. Mosquitoes and tiny black flies made walking with both hands occupied rather frustrating. Claire blew into the air, hoping to drive the pesky insects away from her face, wishing for a can of insect repellent. A trickle of sweat tickled her neck and Claire longed to wipe it away, but with Nathan and Emily straining against her hands in their excitement, she didn't dare let a hand go. Instead, she contorted her neck in an unsuccessful attempt to scratch the spot with her shoulder. But when a mosquito decided the back of her neck looked like a tasty place for a meal, she let go of Nathan's hand to swat at it. Free, Nathan started to dart away and would have made good his excited escape had Claire not been quick to grab him.

"You've got to stay by me, Nathan, 'else you'll be lost in this crowd. Imagine how upset your mother would be to be looking for you rather than watching the fireworks." Claire tried to be stern, but when Nathan lifted up his head and smiled, charming her completely, she found herself smiling back. In a mockingly stern tone, she said, "I mean it, young man."

The next time a mosquito landed, Claire gritted her teeth and wished she had a tail so she could swish it away.

"Here, I'll take them." Nicholas took each child, his warm hands brushing her own. It was the first sentence Nicholas had said directly to her in days, Claire realized, relinquishing her wards to him. Her heart beat crazily as she looked up into his gray eyes and smiled. He gave her a heart-stopping grin in return before hoisting Nathan onto his shoulders.

Although Nicholas had been chatting with Diane, his eyes had been glued to the woman walking in front of him struggling with his excited niece and nephew. He watched that bead of sweat as it made its way from her hair, made dark with dampness, drop down her neck, to disappear below her collar. He saw when her shoulders, held so straight, jerked a bit when a firecracker was lit nearby, and saw her lift her head, knowing she was trying to be strong. He'd wondered how she was handling the noise, for his own nerves had been rubbed raw from the day no matter how many times he told himself the blasts were simply fireworks. Now he knew that she, too, had suffered through this day. He wanted to hold her, just to comfort her, he told himself. And maybe give her one kiss. Yes. Just one so that he might taste her salty summer skin.

When she let that pesky mosquito complete its evening meal without batting it away for fear of losing the antsy Nathan, he simply could not stop himself from coming to her aid. And when she smiled up at him, stealing away his breath, making his heart stop—yes it did stop—he could not help but smile back. And Diane Pendleton and her jealousies be damned. It was only a smile, after all.

For a few steps, Claire found herself walking beside Nicholas, feeling awkward but wonderfully happy. But Diane edged her way up, and taking Emily's free hand, subtly forced Claire to step back and walk with Samuel. It was not an unfriendly movement, simply an acknowledgment that somehow the balance was wrong, and Diane was simply stepping up to correct it. Diane might as well have shouted in Claire's ear: "Hands off! He's mine!" But the gesture was so polite, so *correct,* that Claire could do nothing but step back into her proper place and pray no one could read what her burning cheeks proclaimed.

When Nicholas turned to see Diane once again beside him, it hit him like a blow. His heart went cold. Even when she beamed him her best smile, he could not for the life of him feel anything but annoyance that she had managed to step up and replace Claire.

What the hell.

He gave Diane her smile, but turned his head back quickly to the front, so stunned was he, so afraid his thoughts were readable. For those few steps as he walked beside Claire, separated only by one little girl, it had felt . . . natural. He threw Diane another quick look and turned back again, his brows creased with worry. I love *Diane,* he told himself fervently. Then why can I feel Claire behind me, feel her as if she were draped upon my back. Without realizing he was doing so, Nicholas stopped dead in his tracks, lifting his free hand to massage his temple. Samuel and Claire, engaged in a quiet conversation, nearly ran into the little group in front of them.

"Are you all right, darling?" Diane asked, her concern real. "Is it your head?"

Nicholas shook his head, as if surprised to find himself stopped on the walkway with Diane looking up at him with worry etched on her lovely face.

"No," he said in a distracted way that caused Diane's face to crease in even more worry. "No. I was just lost in my thoughts," Nicholas said with forced joviality, and he gave Diane a smile that caused Claire's stomach to clench. Nicholas remained mostly silent for the remainder of the short walk, allowing the children's chatter to cover his obvious preoccupation.

The group made its way to a portion of the grassy lawn that had not already been taken by the hundreds of families already at the beach. Many men wore their uniforms and Claire wondered why Nicholas, one of the most highly decorated officers from Northford, chose to dress as a civilian. Children ran, sparklers hissing in their hands, as mothers and fathers lounged on blankets or unpacked their picnics. The village band played in the bandstand, mostly ignored by the crowd busy with their own entertainments. Claire helped as the Carrs and the Pendletons and the Brooks laid down their blankets and began unpacking their bundles. Samuel, Nathan, Mabel, and Emily were momentarily astounded to be in such a large area with so many people, and were, for once, subdued and obedient—a state that Claire knew would not last long.

"Hey, kids, why don't you help make the blanket straight," Claire fairly shouted over the din of the crowd. A few heads turned, hearing the Southern drawl, and Claire's face went bright red. More quietly, she gave the children instructions, but she felt that every eye was on her, that every giggle and laugh and conversation had somehow turned her way. She thought she heard someone say something about "a dirty Rebel" and was convinced they were talking about her. She felt as if she were wearing the Confederate flag instead of the light cotton summer dress she wore. Already agitated when a young boy let off a firecracker not ten feet away, Claire clenched her eyes shut and brought her hands up to cover her ears. She quickly recovered, opening her eyes to see Nicholas staring at her, his expression unreadable. Claire immediately busied herself tucking in Nathan's shirt, a fruitless effort, she knew, but one that allowed her to drag her eyes away from Nicholas's. Her hands shook as she smoothed the little boy's already-wrinkled shirt.

"Are you all right, Miss Dumont?" Abigail asked kindly.

Claire gave her a tremulous smile. "Actually, this is not the easiest thing for me, Mrs. Carr. I fear I stick out like a sore thumb here. I feel very out of place."

Abigail paused to think. "Stay for a while, just until the children are settled down a bit. They are insane with excitement. If you still want to go, then go. I understand, Miss Dumont, truly."

Claire smiled and felt absurdly relieved. "Thank you."

Claire resolved to stay the entire evening after Abigail's thoughtfulness, but as the day bled into night Claire's agitation grew worse. She found herself in a constant state of tension waiting for the next firecracker, the next censorious look, the next overheard mean little comment about the South. Her head was splitting when she finally decided she must leave or become ill. Chastising herself for her weakness, she told Abigail she would have to go home. Having finally resolved to leave, Claire felt immensely better as she pictured herself safe in her room, her windows shutting out the celebration.

"Oh, but it's too dark for you to be walking all that way alone. Let me get George to walk you back," Abigail said sternly.

"I'll be fine, Mrs. Carr. I hate to take him away from the children. He's having so much fun," Claire said, watching as George rolled about on the grass with his three children. Even Samuel was joining in on the fun.

"I'll walk her."

Claire's entire body tensed at the sound of Nicholas's deep voice.

"No. That's quite all right," Claire said quickly. Too quickly.

He firmly grasped her upper arm and began pulling her away from the blanket, giving his sister a wink that told her he had the situation well in control.

"I find I am not enjoying this evening myself," he told Claire as he continued to lead her away.

"What about Diane?" Claire forced herself to ask.

"What about her?"

"Won't she wonder where you are?"

Nicholas stopped then and looked down at her uplifted face, her cheeks a peachy red in the last light of the day. "I find I don't really care. Does that shock you? I see that it does."

Claire was indeed shocked that Nicholas would say anything that could even remotely be construed as being against Diane. They continued walking, side by side, but no longer touching.

"How have you been today," he asked, his voice oddly clipped.

"Fine."

He turned to give her a knowing grin. "Liar."

Claire shrugged, acknowledging her fib. "Actually, today was not an easy day. It is why I am going back to the house. I feel so incredibly Southern today."

Nicholas gave a laugh. "Yes, I imagine you would."

"And you. How have you been?" She pictured him on the beach, angrily throwing a branch into the pile.

"Today was not an easy day," he said, echoing her words.

They walked in silence as a group of boys rushed past them, fists filled with firecrackers, their faces flushed with excitement.

"I remember that feeling," Claire said, nodding toward the shouting boys. "I remember thinking the only thing better than the Fourth of July was Christmas."

"Fifteen years ago, that would have been Matthew and me running like that. Where is Matthew, anyway?" He had to ask.

"I believe he is at the lighthouse. You know he does not like crowds."

That Claire knew even that much about his brother rankled. He knew his brother did not have good intentions toward Claire, and that was one thing. But should Claire feel something for Matthew, if she should love him. Well, that was something else entirely. He would ask her, he decided, while a voice in his head shouted that it was none of his concern. Ah, but it was, said another voice. For how would it feel if the woman he loved, loved another? He did love Claire. It had hit him as he had walked beside Diane, it had hit him hard, like a bullet to the gut. He stared at Claire with such intensity she was startled.

"What? What's wrong, Major?"

He shook his head and let out a humorless laugh.

"I've found myself in love, Claire. It is not the blissful thing I thought it would be."

"Oh." Claire felt as if her chest were being crushed, as if her heart had forgotten to beat. Her eyes burned, her throat ached, and she turned her head away so that he might not see, suddenly enthralled by the houses they passed. It was no surprise, she told herself. She had known for quite some time that Nicholas loved Diane. But to hear him say it, say the words out loud to her this way, after she had begun to hope that perhaps he was bothered by Matthew's attention. Little fool, she thought angrily. Stupid, stupid little fool!

"I'm happy for you," Claire wrenched out, cringing when she heard her own voice sounding constricted. Nicholas gave her an odd little smile and allowed her to misunderstand.

They were alone now, having made the turn down the road leading to the house, and Claire wished she could simply run away as fast as she could up to the house and throw herself on her bed and cry her bitter tears. As they reached the long drive, Claire made to turn toward the house, but Nicholas stopped her.

"I thought the two of us could get the bonfire going. It takes a good hour for it to be good and hot. By the time the others return it'll be ready for them."

"No. I just want to go up to my room."

"Come, Claire. Just for a little while," he said, grabbing her hand in his and pulling her away from the drive. "We'll make some fun of this night and the fire will drown out the noise of the fireworks."

Claire sighed. The last thing she wanted was to be alone with Nicholas right now. And it was the thing she wished for the most.

"Okay."

"You might think I was asking you to join me in gutting a load of fish," Nicholas said, laughing. "Surely my company isn't that abhorrent."

"Almost," Claire said, grumbling, but she found herself smiling up at Nicholas. He could be so very charming when he wanted to be, she thought begrudgingly.

When they reached the huge pile of wood, Nicholas stood at attention. "Your first duty is to collect eel grass, Rebel."

Claire bit her lips to stifle her grin. "But sirrah. Mah hands are much too delicate for such duty. Perhaps you could think of something a bit more sedate for me to do." Claire appeared to think, then smiled coyly at him in her best Southern Belle, eye-batting manner. "Why, you're so big and strong and I'm just a girl, after all, I think mah duties should be limited to watching you."

"Your hands, eh? Let me see them," Nicholas said with mock sternness. She held them out limply, palms up, and Nicholas grasped them in his two larger hands, his thumbs running over her palms, testing for calluses. What had been a game, suddenly was not. Claire found her whole being was focused on those two thumbs, moving back and forth in her palms. How could such a simple and innocent caress cause such a riot of feelings within her. My God, she thought with disgust, I am depraved. She pulled her hands away. "I'll go get the grass."

Nicholas took a deep, steadying breath and watched her go as she practically ran across the coarse sand toward the tall eelgrass. He was hard and hurting. From holding her goddamn hands! He knew then that he should not have allowed himself to be alone with her. Hell, he'd known he should not be alone with her from the beginning. But he had contrived a way to be with her anyway. He simply could not stay away any longer.

Claire stared with frustration at the smoldering bit of wood that simply refused to light. "I wonder how forests catch fire with all that green wood when we can't even start a fire with dried stuff." She sat on her haunches and bent her head down low to blow softly on the glowing ember. The sun had disappeared behind the horizon an hour ago, leaving only a faint glow in the west. "Oooo!" Claire squealed as she saw a flame begin giving tentative, lazy licks at a branch. "Catch, you stubborn thing, catch."

That was about the time she heard the telltale sound of a crackling fire. Walking around the pile to investigate, she let out an angry sound seeing Nicholas's face visible in the glow of a lively fire. He stood there, pant legs rolled up, exposing powerful calves, his bulky arms crossed over his chest, a triumphant smirk on his handsome face.

"How are you coming along?" Nicholas said, correctly reading Claire's scowl.

"It's coming," she said stubbornly. She felt as if she were ten years old again, competing with her infuriatingly superior brothers.

"Let's see," Nicholas said, beginning to walk around toward Claire's weak little flame.

Claire attempted to stop him. "No, no, you just worry about your fire and I'll worry about my fire."

"What fire?" Nicholas asked, having successfully maneuvered around her. All that was left of Claire's success was a dimly glowing ember and a small thread of smoke. Claire crossed her arms and stared at the traitorous fire with daggers. Nicholas walked over to where the fire was crackling and spitting up sparks to gather a gnarled torch so that he might set the entire pile afire. It wasn't long before a healthy blaze was going. The two watched the flames, entranced, until a loud pop sent a cascade of sparks toward them. Nicholas grabbed Claire's waist and pulled her toward him and away from the fire, stopping only when he thought they were a safe distance from the spitting pyre. He did not drop his hands and Claire felt as if his hands were two hot embers on each side. She did not move away even though her common sense screamed at her to do so. But it felt so good to have his hands there, so safe and right. And why shouldn't she for once feel safe and right. So she stood there, Nicholas standing behind her so close she could feel his soft breath on her neck, with his hands at her waist.

Nicholas wanted to pull her close, but feared she would pull away. In fact, he was surprised she had not already. She stared at the fire, but Nicholas stared at the place where her neck curved toward her shoulder. It was soft there, smooth and glowing red in the fire's reflection. Her hair, still too short to successfully put up atop her head, was gathered at her nape and a few curling tendrils, which had escaped the small nest of hair, caressed her neck in the gentle breeze. He watched, fascinated, as one curl brushed on the very spot he longed to put his lips. Maybe he would, he thought. Just a brush of his lips on that spot where her neck curved toward her shoulder.

Claire closed her eyes when she felt just the hint of his lips on her neck. Tell him to stop, she screamed to herself as she felt her body sway slightly. Without meaning to, without consciously thinking it, Claire tilted her head, just so, so that he would have better access. And she felt those lips, warm and moist, brushing her neck, again amazed that such a light caress could produce such a riot of sensation throughout her. She tilted her head more, shaking her head at the same time she allowed him to kiss her, and let out a little sound. Nicholas could not tell whether that little sound was one of pleasure or protest. All he knew was that she tasted as sweet as she looked, like the summer air. His kisses became more aggressive and he pulled her toward him, still keeping his hands on each side of her waist. Her hands covered his and he thought, just for a moment, that she was going to throw them off. Instead, she grasped them and pulled them around her, hugging them to her. So wicked, she thought, I'm so wicked. And she smiled as she felt his tongue lick at her.

Nicholas suddenly, almost violently, turned her around in his arms. He brought his hands up to her jaw, grasping her head, his fingers buried in her hair. His eyes, looking black in the firelight, searched her face, touching her eyes, her winged brows, flushed cheeks, and finally her exquisite mouth. His breathing was shallow, his jaw clenched tight, and Claire would have been frightened by his look if she had not been so enraptured by his touch.

"Are you in love with my brother?" he demanded. And so fierce was his look that Claire wondered if she would have lied even if she were. Her eyes wide, she shook her head. "No. And he doesn't love me."

Nicholas closed his eyes fleetingly, relief flooding him. "May I kiss you, Miss Dumont," he said, his voice husky. And Claire knew he would whether she acquiesced or not.

"Yes. Nicholas, oh please."

He brought his mouth down on hers then with a groan of triumph and pleasure, his tongue, his lips moving against hers with almost desperation. He stepped backward, bringing her with him, until he was leaning up against the low stone wall that bordered the beach, until they were out of the light cast by the bonfire. He brought her up against him, hard and straining in his breeches, one hand on her buttocks, pressing her against him until it was almost painful.

"Claire. Claire," he said against her lips. "I have wanted to kiss you for so long. You are so sweet."

Claire's only answer was a whimpered protest that he had stopped for a moment to talk instead of kiss her, and she pressed her lips against his, licking his lips, his tongue, tasting him finally. She could feel his want, she knew what it meant, and she pressed against him feeling herself turn to liquid as she pushed against the hardness. Nicholas brought his breath in with a hiss and moved against her in a tortuous rhythm that drove them both mad with wanting. He brought a hand to one breast, caressing it, feeling her erect nipple through the material. He brushed his thumb back and forth, causing Claire to squirm and driving him almost insane.

With trembling fingers, he fumbled with her buttons until he revealed a pretty white cotton shift with tiny rose-colored bows. He stopped and looked up at Claire's half-closed eyes, her swollen moist lips. Although the air was filled with the roar of the bonfire and the distant booms of the night's fireworks, the only sound they heard was each other's labored breathing. One by one he pulled at the ribbons, slowly, as if giving her a chance to pull away.

I want him to touch my breasts, she thought wickedly. I want him there, I want him everywhere, I don't care, I don't care if he loves Diane. Please God, I don't care. He was making her feel wonderful and strange and filled with a want so strong she could do nothing but want more. She had enjoyed his kisses before. But now she knew that making love entailed so much more pleasure than she imagined. Raw, base pleasure that she was sure no one must feel 'else they would constantly be kissing and touching this way. The last ribbon was undone and Nicholas tore his gaze from her eyes to the small, but perfectly shaped breasts he uncovered.

He swallowed, finding that simple function difficult. "You are so beautiful." And he brought his mouth down to kiss one breast. Claire did not know such pleasure could exist as she felt his mouth on her hard nipple. She let out a sound, unable to stop her moans, and pulled his head closer. Hearing that sound drove Nicholas to the brink. He stopped his caresses, his breathing labored. Claire stood there, leaning heavily against him in a daze of want and need. She did not want him to stop. She did not. And so she brought her hand between his legs and pressed it against his hardness.

Nicholas clenched his jaw so tightly he thought certainly he would shatter his teeth. "Don't," he ground out, his body tensing, centered on that one spot, that one place where she held her hand. Despite himself, he pressed against her hand, then let out a frustrated groan. Claire smiled, knowing she had pleased him, relishing the feeling of power she had over him. "We cannot. Not here, love. Oh God, Claire. Oh God."

He gently took her hand away, wondering if he were the biggest fool on earth. Still trying to catch his breath, he eased Claire away from him. Claire felt suddenly awkward in front of him. What had she been thinking, putting her hand there on Nicholas's crotch? She was quite sure Diane would not have done such a thing. Mortified, Claire began buttoning up her dress, not bothering with the little ribbons on her shift. Nicholas grasped her hands, stopping her, and pulled her to him again, laying her head on his shoulder and kissing the top of her head, her hair soft and warm against his lips.

"You turn me into a cad," Nicholas said, a smile in his voice. "You turn me into a man I don't recognize." The sound of voices in the distance caused them both to jerk their heads up, their cheeks equally red from a guilty flush. Without a sound, Claire pushed away from Nicholas and climbed the short wall to the grassy lawn and ran all the way to the house, as if she could run away from the burning flame Nicholas had ignited in her heart.

By the time Matthew and his son made their way to the beach, Nicholas had gathered himself together. Barely. Still, he was relieved to find his brother making his way down the shallow steps to the beach and not his sister. Or, God forbid, Diane and her parents.

"Who was that running across the lawn?" Matthew asked as he limped heavily toward his brother, his peg sinking annoyingly deep into the sand.

"Claire," he said, trying to sound casual.

"Well, I'll just go fetch her. Nothing more romantic than a roaring fire, eh, Nick?" Matthew turned as if to go, but was stopped by a steel grip on his arm.

"You will damn well stay here, Matt," Nicholas said. He'd be damned if he would be tormented by watching his brother try to seduce Claire. Matthew raised his eyebrows in feigned surprise at his brother's harsh tone.

"I've never let you tell me what to do, big brother, and I'm not about to start now," Matthew said, his voice softly menacing.

Nicholas took a breath. "She said she wasn't feeling well," he said lamely.

Matthew almost laughed aloud. "She appeared to be doing well when she was in your arms," he said as casually as he would discussing the weather. Nicholas's head snapped up in alarm, but it took only seconds before he recognized the easy grin on Matthew's face.

Nicholas's gaze went to Samuel, who was entranced by the bonfire, to make sure the boy was out of earshot.

"You don't mind?" Nicholas asked.

"Hardly," Matthew said. "I was only interested in a dalliance. And Claire is not the type of girl a man should simply dally with. Don't you agree, Nick?" Matthew gave his brother a hard look.

"I agree." Nicholas looked at the fire a long moment, trying to decide how much he should tell his brother.

"I'm in love with her, Matt." He shook his head as if he could not believe the news himself. Matthew smiled broadly. He felt like whooping with happiness for his brother and for Claire and would have if Nicholas had not looked so distraught.

"What about Diane?" Matthew prompted, accurately reading Nicholas's bleak expression.

"Yes, indeed. What about Diane. I don't want to hurt her, but I will. And Abigail and, God, Mother and Father will absolutely go insane. What a mess."

"Here comes the mess," Matthew said, jerking his head toward the advancing crowd.

Diane, looking a bit miffed, and her parents led the little party as they approached the bonfire. "When are you going to tell her?" Matthew whispered in Nicholas's ear.

"Not tonight, that's for sure."

"Good thinking."

Surrounded by his and Diane's parents, his sister and her husband was the absolute worst time to tell the woman who had waited for him to come home from the war that he had fallen in love with another.

"I thought you were coming back," Diane said, sounding hurt.

She is lovely, Nicholas thought, looking down at the woman he'd thought for years would be his wife. Her image had helped him through some of the war's worst moments, he realized. But it was an image he had clung to, not a real woman. He cared for Diane. He never meant to hurt her, but he knew with a certainty that he would. As long as there was Claire, he could never look at Diane with anything more than admiration. It was Claire he wanted, Claire who plagued his dreams, who made him laugh, who made him whole. Whom he loved.

"I'm sorry. I thought I would get the bonfire going for the children. But I see they're going to miss it." All three Carr children were fast asleep on a blanket Abigail had spread out for them on the lawn.

"You missed the fireworks. They were splendid this year. Everyone seemed so happy. I wish you could have been there. So many people asked after you. You're very popular, you know, Nicholas."

"Am I?"

"Of course," Diane said, taking his arm. "You are an official war hero, Nicholas Brooks. You should take advantage of it while you still can. Councilman Hoyt thought you should run for town council, but I said you had grander aspirations than all that. I said you would make a wonderful governor, or perhaps a senator. Then we . . . I mean you . . . could go to Washington. Wouldn't that be grand?"

"Hmmmm."

"Nicholas."

"Hmmm?"

Diane looked up at him, tilting her head in mock anger. "You haven't heard a single word I've said."

"Yes I have. You were talking to Councilman Hoyt, who wants to run for senator. Am I right?"

Diane good-naturedly rolled her eyes. "Not even close. I thought *you* would make a good senator."

Nicholas was truly startled. "Good God, why?"

Diane blushed and stammered, "Because you are so well liked. Because you are well suited to such a position."

"Do you really think so, Diane?"

Believing he was looking for approval, Diane beamed, "Oh, yes, Nicholas. You would be wonderful." She gave his arm a little squeeze and commenced to imagine herself as a senator's wife. How wonderful it would be hearing their names announced at parties. Senator and Mrs. Brooks. Diane became happily lost in her own fantasy, not even realizing that Nicholas stood next to her, still as a statue staring into the fire, praying it would go out so he would have an excuse to leave. He must see Claire again, he thought, shifting uncomfortably as the mere thought of her caused his loins to stir. He must see her again tonight.

The night had long grown still, the type of sultry summer night when the air remained heavy and even the far-off sounds of the channel bells were muffled. After tossing sleepless for what seemed like hours, sheets twisted uselessly at her feet, Claire finally slipped into an uneasy sleep. She remained restless, even in her slumber, as visions of Nicholas's face, his body, his voice, plagued her. So when she felt a soft touch on her cheek, she at first thought it was part of a dream. She slowly opened her eyes, and there was Nicholas, smiling at her, his thumb caressing her jawline. She smiled back.

Nicholas! She started, pulling away, and sat up in bed as her hands blindly and frantically searched for the sheets still bunched up at the foot of the bed. She wore only her thinnest cotton nightgown, which left her arms bare and Claire, now used to wearing unrevealing clothes, felt practically naked.

"What are you doing here?" she whispered harshly.

Nicholas kneeled on the floor and negligently leaned onto the bed, his eyes sparkling in the darkness.

"I forgot to tell you something earlier," he said softly, and Claire flushed at the memory of the kisses by the bonfire.

"So tell me. Then get out. Are you crazy? You shouldn't be here."

Nicholas ignored her and smiled stupidly at her. Lord, she was beautiful. Even when she scowled at him. He climbed onto her bed causing Claire's eyes to widen before she scooted over, pressing against the wall, her head slightly bent to accommodate the slanted ceiling. Nicholas's shirt was open at the neck and was untucked. She had never seen him look so disheveled, so absolutely unconcerned about his appearance. His hair was ruffled, his cheeks burned from the sun and the fire, giving him an innocent boyish look. Claire blinked, knowing the image and reality were poles apart.

"Get off my bed," she said harshly.

"Not until I've said what I've come to say," Nicholas said, and Claire could see the stubborn set to his jaw even in the darkness.

"Fine. Speak."

"First I want a kiss," Nicholas said, knowing he was pushing her goodwill.

Claire bit her lip. She knew what happened when they kissed. She knew there was nothing to stop them from doing more, and she was not sure she would be the one to stop. She hadn't been able to stop earlier that evening. She had wantonly pressed herself against him. She had touched him on his crotch, for crying out loud.

"One kiss."

To her surprise, Nicholas pressed a chaste kiss on her pursed lips and pulled back. She frowned, unable to hide her disappointment, and Nicholas almost laughed aloud.

He put a hand on the side of her face, his thumb caressing her tender bottom lip, still swollen from the night's earlier kisses. "I love you, Claire."

Claire's eyes widened. She swallowed thickly. "W-What?"

Nicholas chuckled. "That is not the response I anticipated. I love you. I want to make love to you. Do you understand what that means?"

Claire dared not smile as she thought how the last time they had made love they had gotten married. Nicholas had insisted. She looked at him, her brows creased, her blue eyes troubled.

"You love me."

She could see him grin, his white teeth flashing.

"It's not so hard to believe, is it?" he asked, bending for another kiss, this one lingering and so sweet Claire's heart felt it would burst.

"Yes it is. It *is* that hard to believe." Claire shook her head and her eyes filled with tears. "I mean to say, I've loved you so long I thought I was insane, loving someone who could barely stand to be in the same room as me. You made me leave Maryland. You've barely even spoken with me since you came home. And every time you do look at me, you look as if you hate me. It is that hard to believe," she repeated.

"Claire. I made you leave because I couldn't trust myself with you. I wanted you so then, I could not be near you and not have you. You drive me insane with want. I think I loved you even then, even on our wedding day." He kissed the tears on her cheeks. "If I could take away all your pain, I would. Please don't cry, Claire, it breaks my heart so. I know I've been a brute and I hate myself for it. You confused me, Claire. I've never met a woman like you. Every day you were someone different. The thing is, I found myself loving every one of those people." Nicholas placed both hands gently on her shoulders. "Please let me love you."

Claire hesitated. Would it be forever? Did she have a forever or would she one day be whisked away by some unknown power, leaving Nicholas behind? It seemed she had been denying herself happiness her entire life. Here it was, placed in her lap, and even if it was for a short time, dare she throw this chance at love away? No way!

She threw herself into his arms, peppering his face with kisses. "I do love you. Oh, I do, Nicholas."

"I'm very pleased, love. You *are* my love, my heart. You do know that. You do believe me." His hands moved up and down her bare arms, sending shivers through her. He bent his head for a long and languid kiss, pressing her against him almost fiercely. He had never thought to feel this much, to love this much. He lifted the thin nightgown over her head, watching as her hair bounced back into place. She was not self-conscious to find herself kneeling on her bed naked in front of him. She looked straight into his smoldering gray eyes and smiled a welcome that no man could have resisted. Where is this woman coming from, she thought, this woman who wants to love this man thoroughly and without compunction.

Lifting her chin gently, he looked into her eyes, thrilling at her confidence. "You are beautiful, Claire. You are more than I imagined." He chuckled. "And I did imagine, believe me." Claire's mouth lifted to a smile. "Kiss me," she said, placing her hands on his shoulders and drawing him to her.

With a throaty moan, he complied. So sweet, so hot, was all he could think. As the kiss deepened, Claire made those little noises that drove Nicholas insane with need. His tongue swirled with her, plunging deeply, tasting her as she tasted him. Her hands were at the nape of his neck, clutching him there almost painfully, pulling so close he felt he could devour her.

He pulled away, gasping for breath as he tore at the buttons of his shirt, wanting suddenly to have her pressed against him, to feel flesh on flesh. She was there, in his arms, feeling delicious and warm and molding her body to his. Claire felt his hands travel up and down her back, resting on her buttocks, pulling her closer as they knelt together on her bed. He was so warm and solid. She could feel his arousal at her belly and she pressed closer, amazed at her own wantonness and the rush of pleasure his hardness gave her. She wanted to touch him there, she wanted to know him, but flushed just thinking about such a caress. Modern as she was, she was still an inexperienced woman.

He grazed her breasts with the back of his hand, then turned it, cupping one soft mound in his hand. Keep control, he admonished himself, go slow. Oh, God, but it was difficult with her here naked and warm and squirming with pleasure beneath his hands. He wanted to throw her down and enter her, swiftly and hard. But he also wanted to savor every caress, every

kiss. His thumbs moved over her nipples, and Claire
gasped, arching against his hands. Shards of pleasure
coursed through her, centering on the place between
her legs. She pulled him closer still, her hands clutching his head, her fingers lost in his thick hair.

He lay her down, trying to kiss her as he took off
his breeches. When he, too, was naked, he lay down
beside her, running a hand to her breasts, down her
stomach, down to between her legs, where it was hot
and moist. He wanted to please her, he wanted to
show her that what had happened in her cell held no
resemblance to what a man and woman in love did.
The thought of what he had done to her, taking her
so roughly when she was so utterly innocent about
what happened between a man and a woman filled
him with shame. I will make this good, he vowed, his
hands shaking as he tried to maintain control.

Claire closed her eyes, becoming lost in the sensa-
tions as his hands seemed to burn over all of her at
once. She sighed with pleasure, knowing this was right,
that they would marry and spend a lifetime touching
each other like this, if only God would let her. Oh, it
was wonderful, simply wonderful to have him touch
her this way, to touch him as well. He listened to her
soft pleasure sighs as he touched her, as he licked her
hard nipples, as he moved against her, unable to put
off his own pleasure completely.

Nicholas had touched her before in that spot between her legs that tingled and ached whenever they
kissed, Claire knew, but nothing she remembered
about that quick coupling in her cell prepared her for
the onslaught of feeling he produced with his seeking
fingers. He touched her, moving his hand until Claire
was wild with . . . something.

He stroked her and kissed her until she thought she
would scream unless something happened, for surely
the pleasure, building, building, must have some end,
some release.

She'd read all about orgasms in magazines, and heard them discussed in detail on some of the more lurid talk shows, but nothing could have prepared her for the burning bliss she was feeling. When she finally arched her back, letting out a small screech of surprised pleasure that he muffled with his mouth, she found out. Wave after wave of shivering warmth spread out until her lips and the tips of her toes and fingers tingled with life. Just as the storm was subsiding, Nicholas moved between her legs and entered her slowly, savoring each moment, torturing himself with her warm tightness. "My God, Claire, you are too good to be true," he said roughly, before becoming lost in sensation, driving into her over and over until she was clutching at him frantically, until she arched her back once again, until he pulsed into her with near violence. He unwrapped them slowly, their bodies slick with sweat. They lay side by side, staring at the ceiling each with their own odd little smile on their lips, holding hands like children.

"So. *That's* what making love is all about. Very cool."

Nicholas chuckled. "I'd say it was more like hot."

"That's what I meant. I think I like it."

"Me, too."

Claire lifted herself up on one elbow, feeling free and beautiful. "Let's do it again."

Nicholas laughed again. "I'm still recovering."

"Are you?" And Claire, feeling very bold and very much in love, lay her hand between his legs and touched him, exploring as her curiosity overrode her lust momentarily. Nicholas jerked beneath her hand as he grew hard for her again.

"I believe you have recovered," Claire said, laying atop him and kissing him expertly.

"So I have." And he pulled her down onto him.

Much later, as the eastern sky was just beginning to hint at a new day, Nicholas eased out of Claire's bed.

She stirred, holding out a hand for him to hold before he went about the task of dressing, as she watched with sleepy eyes. Somehow it seemed natural to watch him dress, to notice how he put both pant legs on at the same time, hopping into his breeches, to hear the soft snap of his cotton shirt as he brought it over his broad shoulders. Finished, he again knelt beside the bed, resting his head on his arms as he gazed at his drowsy love, a smile touching his lips. "I'll see you later," he whispered and watched as she closed her eyes in a happy sigh. He leaned over for one last kiss. "I love you, Claire."

Closing her eyes again as sleep beckoned, she mumbled "Love you," and managed another drugged smile before she drifted off again. He stood, looking down at her, wanting nothing more than to climb back into bed with her. Had he ever been this happy, this content? Had he ever imagined feeling this way? He walked stealthily to her door, pausing to look at her once more, her curling blond hair sleep-mussed, her cheeks flushed from slumber. Jesus, she's beautiful, he thought, an unexpected stab of possessiveness nearly overwhelming him.

And almost as unexpectedly, he was awash with guilt about Diane. He would have to deal with her today, he thought as he made his way to his own room, tiptoeing carefully past his sister's room. He would have to try to find a way to tell her gently, but knew he could not avoid hurting her. He dreaded it more than anything he'd dreaded before. His stomach knotted in a sickening twist as he pictured the scene.

Nicholas, having made his way to his own bed in a hopeless attempt to get more sleep, lay staring at the ceiling, his eyes wide open. What a goddamn mess.

Chapter Nineteen

The little group stood on the bluff looking down at Northford Cove, where Nicholas and George, each captaining his own catboat, tacked around a channel marker and headed for a buoy on a windward reach. Nicholas, everyone noted with some surprise, was doing poorly.

"Perhaps he's out of practice," Abigail ventured, profoundly proud of her George, but unwilling to be smug in front of Diane.

"He seems a bit distracted," Diane said, then let out a happy giggle. Nicholas had begun losing, she recalled, when he'd noted the little group standing on the bluff—Abigail, Diane, Claire, and the children. They sat upon a blanket atop the grassy bluff enjoying the breeze off the bay and the beauty of two white sails cutting across the deep blue water. Diane continued to giggle, she could not help herself, she was so happy. Claire, for once not irritated with Diane, so blissful was she herself, gave the other woman a curious look.

"Oh, don't mind her, Miss Dumont, Diane is positively glowing today. Brimming with goodwill and happier than a pig wallowing in the muck."

"Abigail," Diane chastised, then was once again

overcome with mirth. "Oh, I simply cannot help it. I am so very, very happy."

And Claire thought rather meanly, You won't be so happy when you discover Nicholas and I are to be married. She immediately felt contrite even thinking so meanly. For as much as Diane irritated her, Claire knew the girl would be crushed. Oh well, Claire thought happily, such is life.

The three sat in relative silence looking dreamily out to the sailors, each lost in her own thoughts. The only noise was the contented gurgling of Alex and the soft whispers of the children as they strung together dandelions in order to make their mother a surprise present. From their vantage point, they could see Matthew and Samuel standing on the lighthouse's lookout, watching the race. Abigail stood and waved at her older brother, hoping he would leave his spot to join them, but Matthew simply acknowledged his sister with a small salute and remained where he was. Sighing over Matthew's less-than-enthusiastic response, Abigail turned her eyes back to the race, which her husband, never a skilled sailor, was winning handily.

"See what love can do?" Abigail teased her friend.

"I don't think it's love as much as the impending wedding. I've never seen Nicky so nervous as he was this morning," Diane answered.

Claire, who had been watching the children, suddenly stiffened at Diane's casual remark. Her body became so hot, her skin prickled almost painfully, and her head felt thick. She turned her head slowly to look at Diane, whose face was glowing and serene. She had seen an expression like that before—on her own face this very morning as she looked at her reflection in her handheld mirror.

"Wedding?" she managed to choke out.

Diane's smile became brilliant and she hugged herself, barely able to contain her joy. "Yes. Nicholas finally asked me to marry him this morning."

Claire would never know how she managed the next few minutes. For as strong as she was, for as many hardships as she had faced, she had never experienced a pain quite so piercing as what she felt in her heart that moment. She smiled at Diane. She actually smiled, saying "Congratulations," in a husky voice. I sound sincere, she thought, I sound as if I mean it.

I must get away from here, Claire thought wildly. I must . . . I must. She looked out onto the bay and took a breath. And another, until a strange calm stole over her, as if her mind were wiped clean and allowed only a single thought. Go. *Go now.*

She waited what seemed like an hour before cheerfully claiming she was cold and would return to the house for a wrap. She saw the women's faces, saw that they were surprised that anyone could feel cold on what was a hot and humid July day. But they let her go without a second thought, dismissing her as they prattled on about the wedding. The wedding!

Claire stood behind them for a few moments, her eyes on Nicholas's boat, on the stark white sail and the blue-painted hull. He was hidden by the sail. All she could see was one arm, strong and brown, holding the tiller.

Good-bye, she said, staring at that arm. Good-bye.

Abigail Carr was furious. In her hand she held the hastily written note from her former nanny announcing her abrupt departure. There was no explanation, just a pretty apology and a plea that the children be told that she loved them with all her heart. What utter rot! she thought, pacing angrily around the parlor, the note crackling in her hand as she waved it yet again in front of her husband's sun- and wind-burned face.

"To think we let her into our home sight unseen, welcomed her here, and for her to have abandoned us this way. I simply cannot believe it, George. I simply would not have thought her capable of such, such . . ."

"Capriciousness."

Abigail stopped in midstride. "Yes. Exactly. She seemed such a solid person. She knew how much I relied on her. Oh how could she do this?"

George was as baffled as Abigail. Indeed, leaving suddenly, with absolutely no warning was so unlike what he thought Claire to be, he would have been alarmed if not for the note. Although it appeared to have been quickly composed, it was coherent and well thought-out. He detected no panic.

"We never do know what goes on inside another's head, dear. I'm sure she had her reasons for leaving. And to her they were probably quite good ones. I do know she was upset at last night's picnic. The fireworks, the celebration. Perhaps she decided she did not fit in. Perhaps she simply decided now that the war is over, to go home."

Abigail paused to think on that theory, tapping one foot soundlessly on the carpet. "No. Miss Dumont would have talked to me. She would have given notice. No."

George gave a heavy sigh, already weary of this stressful topic. "We'll probably never know her reasons. What we must concentrate on now is getting another nanny to take her place."

Abigail's face screwed up in anger once again. "Impossible. The children love her. I trusted her. I'll never trust anyone again," she announced with drama. "The children will be heartbroken. How can I take the chance that this will happen again?"

Nicholas chose that moment to step into the parlor to inquire as to the whereabouts of one Claire Theresa Dumont, the woman he intended to be his wife. Unfortunately, in his attempt to set things right, he had gained an unwanted fiancée and likely hurt the woman he loved. His stomach twisted sickeningly when he thought about the horrible turn the day had taken.

That morning, Diane Pendleton, wearing her very prettiest dress, had sat perched at the end of a small couch, her stomach a nervous bundle of buzzing bees. This was *it*, she had thought happily. Nicholas had been so distracted lately, and she just knew it was because he was trying to garner the courage to ask for her hand. And now he had asked her to wait for him in the parlor. He wanted to speak to her about a matter of utmost importance. Diane could barely contain herself. Nicholas Brooks, the man of her dreams, was about to answer her most fervent prayers. He was going to ask her to be his wife.

Diane took a deep and calming breath. It would not do for her to look as if she were anticipating the question. But oh! She could not, she thought desperately. She could not be calm when her life was about to begin this very day. When she heard footsteps outside the door, muffled by the thick carpet, she smoothed out nonexistent wrinkles from her skirt and took another fortifying breath.

There he was, so handsome in his buff-colored pants and white shirt, his hair neatly combed, his jaw freshly shaved. Was there a more handsome man? she thought. Was there a luckier girl than she? Instead of sitting across from her, as Nicholas usually did in strict conformation to society's courting rules, he took the seat next to her on the little couch. It is why she had sat there, it is why she had left enough room for him to fit his overlarge frame. Diane clenched her stomach in anticipation, telling herself to remain calm.

"Diane," Nicholas managed to choke out as he looked somewhere off behind the beauty sitting next to him.

"Yes, Nicholas?"

"We must talk, you and I. You know that I hold you in the highest esteem," Nicholas said, wincing at his stilted words. Just get on with it, man, this delaying will not help matters, he thought wretchedly.

Diane bent her head, more to hide the excitement in her eyes, than to play at being shy. She waited one beat, two, before lifting her eyes up again to meet with his troubled gray ones. He's nervous, she thought happily. He is so sweet.

"This is not easy for me, Diane. I am not a man who is good with words, and these are perhaps the most difficult words I've had to speak." There, thought Nicholas, that was much better.

Diane held her breath, waiting, waiting for him to say the words. Nicholas looked bleakly at her face, so filled with anticipation. How could he say what he had to say? How could he break this girl's heart? Then he thought of Claire, the way she had looked as he escaped from her room, and suddenly his task became more easily done. He would ask her not to hate him. He would beg her not to, for he would always want Diane to be his friend. He would miss her, the gentleness, her way of carrying herself, her presence. And he *did* care for her, enough to not want to hurt her. Nicholas managed to smile, a sad smile of good-bye.

"Diane, I beg of you . . ."

"Yes! Nicholas, yes!" Diane shouted, throwing herself on him so forcefully she did not see his astonished face, his look of utter surprise. "Oh, Nicky, you have made me so happy," and she covered his face with little kisses. "I've got to go tell Abigail, and Mother! Oh, Nick! You have made me so happy. More happy than I ever thought I could be." She jumped up and ran out of the room, waving happily when she heard him call her name. Had she not been so excited, she would have heard the almost frantic tone of his voice as he tried to call her back. His face, filled with panic and compunction, would have registered. But it did not.

Nicholas, left sitting on that uncomfortable little

couch, slapped his forehead painfully. "Idiot. You goddamn idiot!" He had managed to make things vastly worse. He had meant to say, "I beg you not to hate me for what I am about to say." Why had he begun his sentence that way? Of course Diane would misunderstand. He had bungled things, true, but it was nothing, thank God, that could not be put to right.

But he had failed again. Diane had fled to her home with the good news before he could catch her, and Nicholas, for once in his life, had taken the coward's way out. He put off what would likely be a horrid confrontation with her parents, and instead made good on his sailing wager with George. Now all he wanted was to see Claire and explain what had happened.

Having just spent the last twenty minutes searching the grounds and house for her, the man who entered the parlor was not only exasperated, but beginning to feel a twinge of worry.

"Where is Miss Dumont?"

"That, brother mine, is exactly what I would like to know," Abigail said, marching over to Nicholas and thrusting Claire's note in his hand. Abigail's look of anger changed to one of worry as she watched her brother's face go deathly pale.

"Oh Jesus." Nicholas sat down heavily in the nearest chair, the note dangling from one hand. He dropped the paper to the ground and lay his head in his hands as he made a monumental effort to calm himself.

"Nicholas? What's wrong? She's just a nanny. A good one, but only a nanny. We'll get another." Abigail, feeling a bit odd to be comforting her brother over the loss of the nanny, looked over Nicholas's head to her husband and shrugged.

Nicholas let out a bitter laugh. "What a mess. What a goddamn mess. Jesus!" He shouted the last word, making Abigail flinch.

George was looking at Nicholas with sudden intensity. "Perhaps you should tell us why this news is so upsetting to you, Nicholas." George said in a soothing tone that caused his wife to look at George a bit strangely.

Nicholas suddenly sprung up from the chair as if catapulted. "How long ago did she leave?"

"I've no idea," Abigail said. "We've been home about an hour. Miss Dumont left us on the bluff, what, two hours, ago? I'm not sure."

"Two hours. Maybe three. She couldn't get far. Unless she got on a train." Nicholas was thinking out loud, walking back and forth between Abigail and George. "She hasn't got much money. Abigail. How much money would you say . . . *Dammit.* She had plenty of money from the baby." Abigail let out a startled squeak.

"What baby?"

Nicholas looked up at his sister as if surprised to find her still in front of him. "There was no baby," he bit out, and Abigail crossed her arms in frustration. "And knowing Claire, she probably didn't take the damn money. Did you check her room?"

Abigail scowled at her brother. She did not like his tone one bit. "Yes."

"Well, I'm going to check it again. How much did you pay her each month?"

"Nicholas. Why are you asking me all these questions. What does it matter . . ."

"Just answer me," Nicholas said in a tone he would have used for the greenest private.

Abigail narrowed her eyes, but answered anyway. "Twenty-five dollars a month."

Nicholas slapped his fist into his palm. "Good. Good. She must be going home. She cannot live in a hotel for long. She'll know that. She must be going home." Nicholas seemed to calm down, then his face contorted with anger once again. "Goddamn it! I don't know where she's from. Abigail, did she ever say where she was from?"

Still angry, Abigail found herself getting caught up in Nicholas's excitement just the same. "Virginia. She's from Virginia," she said triumphantly.

"Yes, yes. What town?"

Abigail deflated. "I don't know. She was very private. Oh, Nicholas. What is all this about?"

As Nicholas ran out of the room and headed up the stairs, he shouted back, "I plan to marry your nanny, Abigail. I'm in love with her."

Had George not been so quick, Abigail would have slid to the floor in a dead faint.

Chapter Twenty

Nicholas stared at Claire's neatly made bed, not quite believing that just that morning he had lain there beside her, holding her close to him, breathing in her scent. It looked so awfully empty now.

He opened the wardrobe, vacant except for the two black mourning dresses, so ragged they were almost unwearable, and a small package. Nicholas knew without even looking that that package contained much of the money he had given her. He reached out and touched one sleeve of the dress she had most often worn, his mind seeing her, face uptilted toward the sun as she sat in the little office alcove. Shaking his head to clear his thoughts, he jammed the packet into his pants pocket.

Claire had lost everything she had ever had, and now she believed she had lost him. He was such a damned fool. How could a man, a master strategist, who maintained a cool head in the heat of smoke-choked battle, have managed to make such a complete muddle of things? He did not want to think about what she must be feeling, what she must believe of him. She would think him the vilest of creatures. Imagine making love to one woman and not a few hours later proposing to another. It would have been laughable if the outcome were not so tragic. He cringed with regret when he realized he had not asked her outright to marry him. He had simply let it be understood. And now she would wonder whether marriage was what he'd intended. She would believe he had used her. Again.

He only knew that once he found her, if he found her, he would make her understand. I'll find her, he thought, fighting back the panic that was beginning to grow. Surely, I will find her.

He turned to find Abigail approaching, her face mottled red, her always unruly hair coming undone from a somewhat sloppy bun. He would have smiled at his adorable little sister had he not been so distracted with worry.

"I don't believe I understood you correctly, Nick. Please tell me I did not understand you. Please tell me you do not intend to break it off with Diane and marry my nanny." Abigail had begun rather calmly, Nicholas noted with admiration, but by the time she ended she was fairly screaming.

"I don't have time to argue this right now, Abigail. But no, you did not misunderstand me. I love Claire. She loves me. And she has been terribly hurt by what was a misunderstanding by Diane."

"Misunderstanding! You proposed to the girl not six hours ago." Her expression was one of complete bafflement.

Nicholas was beginning to get angry. "I brought Diane into the parlor to break it off. She jumped to the wrong conclusion and before I could stop her, she had spread the news like a town crier."

Abigail's face went rigid. "Don't you dare blame Diane for this. She, of anyone, is innocent."

Nicholas heaved a heavy sigh. "You are right. I am the only one to blame. I am, little sister, an idiot."

"You are an idiot to give up Diane for Miss Dumont. For goodness sakes, Nicky, what are you thinking of? How could you?" Abigail was beginning to cry, making Nicholas feel like an even bigger heel. He clenched his jaw, hating that this was happening, hating that he had somehow lost control of his life. He brushed past Abigail, then turned and lay a gentle hand on her shoulder, which was shaking from her tears.

"I'm going to look for Claire. We'll talk later."

"Diane is coming over this evening. I'm not going to say a word about this to her, Nick. Not one word. And I'm going to pray Miss Dumont is long gone. Forever gone. I'm going to pray harder than I've ever prayed before."

Her words, spoken so vehemently, sliced into Nicholas's heart. He stood there watching and listening as his sister cried, her back still to him, then he turned away to begin his search.

"I'm leaving for Boston within the hour," Nicholas announced, his voice curt. The others at the dinner table, his family, except for Matthew and Samuel, and the Pendletons all turned to Nicholas, surprise etched on all their faces. Except Abigail. Her eyes held alarm and a combination of warning and pleading that her big brother not say too much. They had not spoken since their argument earlier that day, and already Abigail regretted her harsh words, if not her position supporting her best friend.

Nicholas ignored Abigail's warning look. Nothing would stop him from searching for Claire. He had thanked God a hundred times when the railroad clerk had not only remembered Claire, but had recalled her ultimate destination was Maine—and that meant a lengthy layover in Boston. Claire's train would not depart for Maine until the following morning, giving Nicholas more than enough time to travel to Boston and intercept her.

"What's this about Boston?" Joseph Brooks said in an overloud voice, more to compensate for his own bad hearing than to be heard over the din that Nicholas's abrupt announcement had created.

Nicholas finished chewing a mouthful of thick steak, purposely taking his time before answering. "I need to see an old friend," he said vaguely. He turned back to his meal, sawing away another portion of the tender meat before he was once again interrupted.

"How long will you be gone, dear? It seems you've just gotten home," Nicholas's mother said.

"I should return within a few days. But I'm not entirely certain," and he ignored the disappointed gasp from Diane. He found he could not even look at her without the overwhelming urge to run from the room. Never had he felt more uncomfortable in the presence of the Pendletons, who had been almost like an aunt and uncle to him. He had dreaded sitting down at a meal with them and pretending that all was well in the world. He accepted their hearty congratulations as he would have accepted an order to slog through a stinking, muck-filled pond—stoically, but with little emotion. If they wondered at his reticence, at his seeming lack of enthusiasm at the topic of his marriage, they said nothing.

After dinner, Abigail grabbed her brother's arm and led him to the second-floor library where she knew they could speak privately.

"She is gone. She wanted to leave. So let her go." As Abigail stamped her foot, a large bit of hair drifted out of her heavy bun.

Nicholas let out a sigh. He did not want to argue with Abigail, but it was apparent she had not changed her mind.

"No. I've hurt Claire, Abigail. I must find her. You seem to forget that I love Claire. I do not love Diane."

"Suddenly you love my nanny. Three days ago, you loved Diane. And they say women are fickle. My goodness, Nicholas, do you not see how ridiculous this all is? Why, she was with Matthew not one week ago. We were all worried that she would become . . ." Abigail stopped, blushing furiously.

The way Abigail had portrayed the sequence of events, indeed, from her perspective, Nicholas's behavior did seem a bit irrational, he knew.

"I've loved Claire since Maryland, Abigail. I just didn't realize it."

Abigail rolled her eyes in disgust. "I thought you had a level head."

Nicholas let out a short laugh. "I thought I did, too. That's what she does to me, Abby, I love her."

Abigail bit her lip in frustration. "And what about Diane? You suddenly have fallen out of love with Diane?"

"I was never in love with Diane. I loved what Diane was. What she represented. During the war, when I was lying in mud and breathing in smoke and death, I would think of home. I would think of Diane. But I loved that image, not the person."

"What poppycock," Abigail snorted. "Diane waited for you. She prayed with me when you were injured. She cried when we learned you would live. She lived for any little line you added to your letters mentioning her. She'd read them over and over. You are all she has had for the past six years. Six years, Nicholas! You cannot abandon her for some woman, some *stranger,* that suddenly comes on the scene. She is nothing. Nothing!" Abigail began to cry, heart-wrenching sobs that tore at Nicholas. But he was not swayed from his resolve to set things straight.

"I intend to tell Diane the truth tonight. Now."

"No!" Abigail lunged toward her brother and clutched his shirt, her teary face looking up at him, pleading, imploring, frantic. "Please, Nicky. Not yet. She's so happy. You've no idea how happy."

Nicholas clenched his jaw. "It is a lie. Her happiness is a lie."

"If you don't find Claire . . ."

"I still will not marry Diane."

Chapter Twenty-one

Twelve hours had not seemed like such a long time that afternoon when the ticket master had told her that was the wait she would face when she arrived in Boston. But after six hours of sitting on a hard wooden bench in a hot, dusty, and nearly deserted train station, Claire was regretting not spending some of the little money she had for a hotel. At least then she could have been completely alone, for even the threat that someone might come upon her stopped her tears.

During the two-hour train trip to Boston, Claire had stared out the gritty window, letting the scenery pass by without interest. The farms, the little children who waved, the smoky towns, the quaint villages all blurred together, evoking no response save relief that every clack of the wheels brought her further away from Nicholas.

She allowed her eyes to burn out a few tears, but that was all. She was as angry with herself as she was with the man she loved still, despite her repeated silent proclamations that she hated Nicholas Brooks with every cell, every molecule in her body. She had proven to be as stupid as any woman, as gullible, as susceptible to a gorgeous face and a rock-hard body.

Years of putting up walls to avoid this sort of hurt had done nothing to protect her heart.

And so she sat, as alone as a human being could possibly be, heading to the only person on this earth who had been genuinely kind to her, who had never judged her, and who had offered her a sanctuary on the chance she would need it. When Stanley Grenier had told her he would always have a place for her on his rocky little potato farm in Maine, she never thought she would go. Yet here she sat, rather pathetic, her heart wrenched from her, heading to Maine.

"I'd be there right now if I had my Bronco," Claire thought with disgust, again adjusting herself in a vain attempt to get comfortable. "And I'd be a hell of a lot more comfortable if I had on my jeans." She longed to loosen her corset and throw the damned thing into the trash. Maybe I will, she thought defiantly. It was better to think about too-tight corsets than where she was heading and why. Stanley Grenier would welcome her, of that she was sure. She had sent him a telegram when she arrived in Boston and had prayed it would arrive before she did. And when she was there, she would try to find a way back to her own time. She no longer had a reason to want to stay. There must be a way, something she had overlooked, something she had not seen because her heart had been in the way.

Even now, even with her heart aching inside, the thought of leaving Nicholas behind left her numb.

Claire's stomach rumbled loudly, for she had not eaten since her picnic with the children more than eight hours earlier. The children. Just the thought of them sent a fresh burning to her eyes as they filled with tears. They would not understand why she left, they would miss her as she desperately missed them. She regretted already that she had not said her good-byes in person, rather than leave behind a note that she knew sounded trite and insincere, though it was not. But she had been nearly overwhelmed by the feeling that she had to leave before Nicholas confronted her, before he convinced her with all his charm and faithless endearments that he loved her, that they would somehow be together despite Diane.

For she knew that had he found her, had he held her in his arms, she would have been lost. She would have stayed and somehow endured the shame of being "the other woman" as long as she was convinced of his love. Some modern woman, she thought with an audible snort. Hadn't she stayed while he courted Diane, hadn't she made a fool of herself over a man who did not deserve the pure love she had offered? And that is why she left, she told herself with brutal honesty. Because you are weak and pathetic and you are stupid enough to still love him.

Her thoughts had traveled as fast as the train. One minute she was cursing him, the next she missed him and felt weepy. By the time the train pulled into the Boston station, she almost had herself convinced she had fallen in love with the romance of it all—not that she had ever considered herself a romantic. But what woman, thrust back into the 1860s, wouldn't have fallen for the handsome and heroic, and very maddeningly charming, Nicholas Brooks? She had thought his complete lack of vanity was rather endearing. Now she had herself half convinced that was merely his dirty ploy.

I should have stayed around and kicked his ass, Claire thought, crossing her arms and creasing her brow. I could have done it, too. I could have laid him low and made him suffer. And then laughed at him. Ha!

During the long hours sitting on the bench, she willed her mind blank. Finally, exhausted, she fell asleep, her head drooping wearily to her chest.

He found her sleeping in the deserted train station, sitting up on a hard wooden bench, her head resting on her chest, her fingers still grasping what he guessed to be a ticket to Maine. He could not believe his good fortune. It was as if God had a hand in helping him to find Claire.

Stepping from the last train to pull into Boston for the evening, Nicholas had been prepared to sit alone in the train station waiting for Claire to arrive for the morning train to Maine. The relief that came over him upon seeing her sleeping form was so profound he nearly wept with joy. She looked so alone, so young sitting on that bench, her feet turned into each other like a child's.

"Claire."

She murmured in her sleep but did not awaken. She must be exhausted, Nicholas thought, gazing at her with tenderness. It was nearing midnight. She had likely tried valiantly to stay awake, but had obviously failed.

"Claire," he said again, this time laying a hand on her shoulder and giving it a gentle shake.

Claire's eyes snapped open and she became instantly and completely awake. Horrified to have been found so quickly, Claire leapt up, clutching her carpetbag in her arms, and began backing away from Nicholas. Without a word, she spun around and began running toward the nearest door.

"Claire, goddammit, wait!" Nicholas caught her before she was able to throw open the door, his hands gripping her upper arms. At his touch, Claire became still, as if she had been turned to stone.

"I have nothing to say to you. Leave me alone," she gritted out, convinced she was long past shedding tears over this man.

"But I have something to say to you, Claire." He squeezed her arms almost painfully in his desperation. "I love you and—"

His heartfelt plea was interrupted by her overloud snort as she struggled once again to be released.

"What crap! I've heard enough of your talk of love to last me a lifetime. I gag every time I think that I believed you. Now let me go."

Nicholas spun her around until her back was to the door. She refused to look at him, preferring instead to keep her eyes trained on the dirty planked floor. He dropped his hands, knowing she was trapped between him and the closed door.

"Claire, please listen to me. It was a mistake." He lifted one hand to caress the side of her face, but she jerked away. Claire clenched her jaw, willing the tears that threatened to stay where they were. Oh why did he have to come for her? Why put her through this torture? He was talking to her but she did not want to listen, she did not want to grow weak and fall into his arms the way she longed to. Keep strong, she pleaded with herself, don't let him get to you.

"Diane misunderstood my intentions. It was a mistake."

Claire jerked her head toward Nicholas, looking into his eyes for the first time. She breathed in sharply when she saw his beautiful gray eyes were brimming with unshed tears.

"Wh-what did you say?"

Nicholas swallowed, feeling renewed hope. Until that moment he believed Claire was slipping away from him even as she stood before him.

"I meant to break off with Diane but she misunderstood. It was a nightmare. She just ran off thinking she'd just been engaged and I sat their stunned that I had been such an idiot. I couldn't find you, Claire, to tell you. I was a damned coward. I thought I could wait to set things right, let things settle down. If I had known you would hear it from her then . . . go away. Claire, please, believe me. It was a mistake." Nicholas stopped, his throat constricting, making speech nearly impossible. She must believe him. She must.

He lay a trembling hand on her face, closing his

eyes at the surge of joy that ran through his body at her velvety softness.

"You see, Claire, I find I'm only half a person when you're gone. It's the strangest thing. So you must marry me. You must forgive me, for I will hound you for the rest of your days until you do." He smiled and was uplifted when he saw Claire's lips curve ever so slightly upward. "I know I was wrong not to set things right immediately. But I'll make up for that mistake every day for the rest of my life."

Claire pursed her lips in thought. "You meant to break off with Diane?"

"Yes."

"And have you?"

"I suppose it will become clear when I introduce you as my wife." She smiled again. Begrudgingly.

"Don't you think that is a bit cruel? After all, she does love you."

"Perhaps."

"Maybe it would be better coming from me. Maybe I should introduce myself." She bit her lip to stop the smile.

"Maybe."

Claire pursed her lips and gave him a thoughtful look. "Okay," she said, as if accepting a portion of mashed potatoes.

"Okay?"

"Okay I forgive you. Okay I'll marry you. Okay I'll make you pay for your grievous mistake every day of your life. Okay!" Claire flung herself into Nicholas's arms, letting out a happy squeal.

He crushed her to him, whispering harshly, "Thank God. Oh thank you, God."

Claire nuzzled her face against his shirt, slightly moist from sweat, for the night was unusually humid. She breathed in, loving his musky, horse-and-man outdoorsy scent. She tilted her head up to look in his eyes. "Nicholas, I never want to feel that way again.

I never want to be so alone. I realize I don't like it. I thought I did, but now that I have you, being without you will . . ." She stopped, for it hurt even to talk about the pain she'd felt. "Just don't ever leave me, Nicholas. I couldn't bear it." *I'm not the person I was,* she added silently, *I've become someone who needs to be loved.*

Nicholas kissed her then, a warm and lingering kiss. "How could I leave you, Claire? It would be like leaving my heart behind. I would die." His words were gruff with emotion.

"Well, you might not *die,* but I hope you would be completely miserable."

"You say! I would die as certain as the flowers die without the sun," he said dramatically.

Claire laughed. "You should be in the movies."

"The what?"

"The stage, then," Claire amended with a laugh. Then she gasped, her eyes becoming wide. "Oh my God. It's him."

Nicholas turned to see what had startled Claire so much. And when he spied the poster, it was his turn to be stunned. Nelson Cunningham's face stared back at them from a political poster, his smile just as oily in black and white as it was in person.

"It makes my skin crawl just looking at him," Claire said, wrinkling her nose in distaste. "Have you heard anything since I signed that affidavit?"

Nicholas gave Claire's shoulders a reassuring squeeze. "Only that an investigation has begun."

Claire couldn't take her eyes off Cunningham's face. In her mind, he was leering at her. "How could anyone vote for that scum?"

He let out a bitter laugh. "They don't know he *is* scum."

Claire shivered and turned away from the poster. "I would never take back the affidavit and I don't regret for a minute that I might be the person who sends him to prison. But seeing him again . . . He is so evil, Nicholas.''

Nicholas gripped both sides of Claire's face as if he could absorb her fear with his hands. "I won't let him hurt you. Is that what you were thinking?"

"I suppose." She let out a sigh and forced a smile, hugging Nicholas to her. "There is one thing, though. He doesn't know my name and he doesn't know where I am. I'm safe, I know I am."

But Claire was wrong. For at that very moment, Nelson Cunningham was planning a trip to Northford, hoping to put an end to the devious little bitch who dared to call him a murderer.

Two days later, Claire Theresa Dumont and Nicholas Edward Brooks were married in Northford in a small church on the north side of town that no Brooks or Pendleton had ever entered. This time, the only witness to the nuptials was the minister's apple-cheeked wife. They decided to get married privately, believing it was better to get the deed done and face the music later. That way, there could be no arguing and objections would be fruitless. They both knew the scenes that awaited them would be nasty and tear-filled. Nicholas might receive the brunt of the verbal abuse, but it would be Claire who would be seen as the culprit in this affair. Not five miles from home, they rented a small room in an inn along Boston Neck Road that was barely respectable but very private, and celebrated their wedding night.

Hours after their wedding, a very naked Claire lay upon Nicholas's chest and swirled her fingertips non-chalantly around one brown and puckered nipple. He lay with his hands behind his head, relishing her touch, the slight weight of her body lying on his, the way her soft breasts felt against his hard stomach. He gave a little gasp of pleasure when she flicked her tongue against that sensitive spot and let out a happy chuckle.

"I didn't know men liked that, too," she said, her eyes half closed and drowsy.

"I like everything you do to me," he said.

"Such as when I do this?" And she shifted so that her hand could wrap around his very hard member. His entire body stiffened and he gritted out, "Particularly when you do that."

"How about when I do this?" And he thought he was the luckiest man on earth when she flicked her tongue along his shaft.

"Two can play at that game, you wanton girl," he said as he rolled over her to begin his own erotic game. His tongue laved her nipple as his hand found her burning center and began stroking her until she was squirming beneath him. And then, as she had done to him, he flicked his tongue where she was hot and wet until she was almost frantic. Heeding her pleas, he moved up between her legs and entered her, thrusting almost violently into her tight heat. They began a frenzied rhythm as they both sought that blistering pleasure they knew would burst through them. Never had they been so impatient to find their release, never had they touched and kissed and pounded into one another with such abandon.

Sweaty and exhausted, they lay back dazed.

"This can't be normal," Claire said, breathless.

Nicholas chuckled. "It isn't. We, wife-of-mine, have something very rare and very wonderful."

Claire couldn't help thinking at that moment how very rare their relationship truly was. How many 1990s women made love to a Civil War hero. She giggled, turning her head against his chest. "We are a miracle," Claire said softly. "We are what happens when there is love."

Chapter Twenty-two

Telling his family was not as bad as Nicholas thought it would be. Abigail, of course, was livid, but his parents were remarkably understanding and Nicholas had a good idea that Matthew was behind their surprisingly calm reaction to the news of their marriage. Though a bit stiff and transparently insincere, both his mother and father welcomed Claire to the family—his mother with a light embrace, his father with a small kiss to her cheek. Matthew scooped Claire up and gave her a resounding kiss right on her mouth and was so enthusiastic Nicholas found himself clenching his fists at the fond display. Even after Matthew and Claire had explained their little ploy to make him jealous, he found he could not easily watch Matthew kiss his new wife.

Telling Diane, however, was a different story. Nicholas decided to do the chore by himself, his stomach churning at the thought. Claire gave him a kiss for courage and a firm shove in the direction of the Pendleton house. "Cruel to be kind," she called after him, as if that gave him comfort.

The Pendletons were delighted to see Nicholas, their future son-in-law, the man who had made their little girl so utterly happy. He decided to tell them first, so they would be prepared to comfort their daughter.

Nicholas watched with dread as their smiles turned into shock, then to anger. "I couldn't be more sorry to hurt you, to hurt Diane. It was unplanned, completely uncalculated. I know I am a cad, I know I deserve every evil thought you think of me. But please believe me when I say I never intended to hurt Diane. I do love her, after a fashion. Like a sister or a friend. And I will mourn the loss of her friendship. I love Claire, I have for a long time. I am sorry."

"This will kill her," Mrs. Pendleton announced succinctly. "You are vile, Nicholas, to do this to her. To cast her off for some Southern trash tramp is beyond me."

Nicholas clenched his jaw. "Please remember, Mrs. Pendleton, that as much as I respect you, I will not allow anyone to castigate my wife either to my face or behind my back. Claire is a kind and good woman. I have never heard her say one thing against Diane."

Mr. Pendleton recovered first. "Nicholas is correct, my dear. We should refrain from such pettiness. However, Nicholas, once you have explained things to Diane, you will no longer be welcome in this house. You have been like a . . . son to me, boy. To do this . . ." Mr. Pendleton stopped and Nicholas's heart beat painfully in his chest. To hurt these people, who had been so good to him, was like hurting his own parents.

"I understand, Mr. Pendleton. I'm so sorry. Sorry what this has done to us, but I am not sorry I married Claire. I hope someday you can forgive me."

"Never!" Mrs. Pendleton said, and proceeded to weep against her husband's shoulder.

"Diane is behind the house, reading in the garden," Mr. Pendleton said, his voice clipped. "Try to be kind, Nicholas."

Nicholas was truly miserable. "I will."

He left the distraught couple in their parlor, clinging

to one another, and despite himself Nicholas let out a guilty sigh of relief. It was nearly over. Thank God.

He found Diane looking serene and beautiful, sitting on a wicker chair, her book forgotten in her lap as she looked out to the bay.

"Hello, Diane."

At the sound of his voice, Diane's head whirled around and an expression of pure happiness lit up her face, making Nicholas's heart wrench. "You're back!"

"Yes." Diane took in Nicholas's serious expression and her smile faltered. She had wanted to rush into his arms, but somehow knew such a gesture would be unwelcome and an awful feeling of dread enveloped her.

Nicholas stood in front of her, his arms behind his back, facing the bay, and she looked at his stern profile, a small crease in her lovely brow. "I have made a terrible error, Diane, and I accept full and complete responsibility for that error." He turned to her finally, refusing to again be a coward. Getting down on his haunches before her, he held her hands and looked into her worried eyes.

"That day in the parlor, I never meant to propose marriage, Diane. I never meant for you to misunderstand that way. It was my fault, I know. Oh, Diane, I don't want to hurt you. You must know that. But that day you thought I proposed, I meant to break off."

Diane pulled her hands from him, her expression cold. "I don't understand. Are you saying we are not to be married? Ever?"

Nicholas swallowed heavily. God, this was difficult. "I already am married, Diane. To Claire, two days ago. I'm sorry."

Diane let out a harsh breath and cocked her head as if she could not have heard him quite right. "You are married. To Claire. The nanny." And then Diane did something Nicholas never expected. She laughed.

"You married the nanny. Instead of me? Why, Nicholas, that is the most ridiculous thing I've ever heard. I would think you were joking if you didn't look so serious. You married the nanny. Instead of me." She let out one more laugh, then her eyes filled with tears. "Oh, how could you, Nicky. How could you?" she asked quietly, shaking her head.

"I love her, Diane. I never wanted to hurt you."

She lifted one eyebrow. "Well, you have." She clenched her jaw and pressed her hands together. "Would you mind leaving now, Nicholas?"

Nicholas felt so ashamed, but so relieved she would not make a scene. He should have known she would not. Perfect Diane. "Of course. Good-bye, Diane."

She waited until he was no longer in sight before bending her head to her hands to weep.

One month after their arrival at Northford, Claire and Nicholas sat at dinner as they had nearly every night since their return, eating silently in an atmosphere so tense it was impossible to enjoy even the tastiest meal. Belligerently, Claire stabbed her fork into the pot roast and shoved the meat into her mouth. She was angry at her in-laws, she was angry at Nicholas for not confronting what was becoming an impossible situation. They had argued just that night about his parents' and sister's treatment of her. Even the children were a bit standoffish, knowing something was wrong and that Claire was the cause of it all. "Give it time," he had said, and then drew her to him, knowing she could not argue while she was in his arms. The manipulative jerk.

Claire wanted to move out, wanted them to have a home of their own, but Nicholas, to her complete bafflement, was against the idea. In her experience, the chicks left the nest as soon as they knew how to fly. This living together stuff was silly, to Claire's thinking, though she knew many couples stayed at home in these backward days. Nicholas had begun toying with the idea of joining his father at the bank.

And that was fine. But working with his father did not mean he had to live with him.

"I'll never be welcome here, Nicholas. They'll always look at me and wish I were Diane. Don't you see that? Don't you see how they look at me, how they talk to me?"

"We knew it wouldn't be easy," he'd said in a condescending tone that drove Claire out of the house. About the only thing they had agreed on since their marriage was lovemaking. They agreed on that, on where and when and how and . . . yes, that they more than agreed on.

But now, sitting at this table, silverware clinking musically against the china, Claire felt she was about to scream. She felt it building, this rebelliousness, she felt her mouth open before she knew what was going to come out.

"Nicholas and I are getting our own place. We feel it would be best for all if we did . . ."

"Claire."

Claire shot a glance at Nicholas, took in his look of warning, and ignored it.

"After all," she continued, as if Nicholas had not rudely interrupted her. "We are adults. We'll soon be starting a family and this house is only so big. So . . ."

"Claire!"

"So as upset as I'm sure this will make all of you," she said, allowing as much sarcasm into her tone as was physically possible, "that is our decision."

Silence. Claire met everyone's startled gaze with her own, including Nicholas, who appeared angrier than she had ever seen him. His eyes, a dark, murky gray, were narrowed, his lips compressed to a white line, the muscles of his jaw bulging.

"For crying out loud, Nicholas. You wouldn't listen. And now you are." Claire, despite the fear that she had made Nicholas so angry, was glad it was finally out in the open.

Nicholas threw his napkin on the table. "Claire, we are going for a walk. We must talk."

Claire stood, her face blushing red, with as much grace as she could and followed Nicholas out the door.

"You made me do that. You wouldn't listen to me. They hate me. And I hate them," Claire said, knowing she sounded like a child but not caring one bit.

Nicholas continued walking and Claire struggled to keep up, battling skirts and stays and uncomfortable shoes. "Say something."

"I'm too angry to talk right now. I might say something I'd regret," Nicholas hissed.

"Like what? Like Diane would never act this way?" Claire knew she was being ridiculous, that she was baiting him, but he had been so *silent* lately about everything. She wanted him to shout. She wanted him to get angry, to show some sort of emotion.

Nicholas stopped abruptly and glared at her, his nostrils flaring. Then without a word he turned and began walking once again. Claire let him take a few steps by himself then hurried to keep up.

"I know I should have talked about it with you first before I made that announcement. It's not as if we haven't discussed this. But you've been so, so, unresponsive lately. Except in bed." She smiled, hoping he would also, but it was if his face were made of stone.

They walked until they were in town. The streets were nearly deserted as the sun had set an hour before. "I don't want to have a fight in the middle of town," Claire announced as they passed by the post office.

Nicholas glared at her, then grabbed her arm and pulled her around the building until they were in a small alley, two brick walls looming above them. "You would rather fight in front of my family? By God, Claire, you have no sense of timing. I have been thinking about what you've said in the past week. And believe it or not, I agree with most of what you've said. But do not defy me in front of my family. Do. Not. Ever. Again."

"You aren't the boss of me," Claire said, recalling one of her favorite childhood comebacks.

"By God, Claire, I am your husband. I . . ." He stopped, his head pounding painfully. "Damn . . . Claire . . . my head . . ." He dropped to the ground with a suddenness that frightened Claire. Never had she seen one of his headaches attack so quickly and with so much force. Overwhelmed by guilt, Claire dropped to the ground beside Nicholas, who appeared to have blacked out.

"Nicholas. Oh my God, Nicholas, wake up." She felt for a pulse and sighed with relief when she found it strong and steady. She was unsure what to do, whether to stay by his side or try to find someone to run to fetch a doctor. At the sound of footsteps behind her, Claire turned, grateful that a passerby was on hand who could help her.

Before she could ask for help, a steely arm encircled her neck. "I imagine you know why you're about to die, you little bitch, and I imagine you know by whom. Say good-bye to your husband." Claire's eyes bulged in shock as she recognized the voice grating in her ear, and she let out a soft squeal when she felt something sharp on her neck. She didn't have time to fight back.

She didn't even have time to say good-bye.

Chapter Twenty-three

Claire awoke to the sound of beeping. I must be in the hospital, she thought wearily, recognizing the sound of a heart monitor. She opened her eyes slowly and lay still as her surroundings slowly came into focus. Above her was acoustic tile, and turning her head, she made out the heart monitor and a bag of fluids that was no doubt dripping into her arm. I'm all right, she thought, trying to keep her eyes open. Nothing hurt, and all she felt was an overwhelming desire to close her eyes and go back to sleep. She looked to her right and stared at an empty orange vinyl-covered chair. I wonder where Nicholas is? she thought lazily, closing her eyes. Her hand moved to her chest, searching for the comfort that the locket always seemed to give her and then moved up to her neck to feel for the chain, an automatic almost careless gesture. The locket was gone.

Suddenly she sat up, her head spinning crazily, her heart pounding painfully in her chest. Heart monitor? IV? Hospital? "Nicholas! Nicholas!" she shouted at the top of her lungs, but her voice was scratchy and her throat so dry she was barely croaking out his name. Breathing in short gasps, Claire ripped the IV from her arm and put her legs over the side of the bed. "No, no, no, no," she said over and over. When her bare feet touched the cold floor, her legs, weakened by long weeks in the coma, collapsed beneath her.

"No! Oh, God, no. Nicholas! Nicholas!" She could hear footsteps rushing down the hall, squeaky sneakers on polished tile.

Donna Pritchard, her big face lined with worry, rushed over to find one of her favorite coma patients on the floor, crying her eyes out.

"Here, honey, up you go. I know you're confused. Everything's all right, now. You're in the hospital, honey. What a miracle. I can't believe it, I never really believed I'd see this day."

Claire looked into the nurse's beady, but kind eyes, unable to hide the horror she felt at finding herself in a modern hospital. "What year is it?" she asked miserably.

The nurse smiled. "You've only been in a coma a few weeks, honey. It's still 1995."

Claire's face crumpled at the news. She had known it was true, but hearing it said aloud rammed it home. "What's wrong, honey?"

"Nicholas needs my help. And I can't get to him. He needs me. He had one of his headaches. We were fighting and now . . . now I have to go back. I can't be here. Oh, God, this can't be happening. I have to go back!" Claire looked up at the nurse, choking on her tears. "But I can't, can I?"

"Go back where?"

Claire lay down, her eyes glued to the tile above her. "Nowhere. It doesn't exist. It was just a dream. He was just a dream." She shook her head, her tears staining the pillow on each side of her face. "But it was so real. Oh, Nicholas."

Across the hall, Coleman Brennan stirred. He felt he needed to wake up, had to wake up, but his eyes refused to open, his arms refused to move. He could hear someone calling his name. A woman, calling from a great distance, sounding desperate and sad.

"Maryellen," he whispered. "Maryellen."

"Holy shit!" Janice Downes exchanged looks with Donna as she paused outside the man's room. "He's coming out of it, too. Go call Dr. Hanley. And Dr. Tauerbaum. This is unbelievable. This is so weird."

As Donna rushed down the hall, Janice turned back to the man who was struggling to bring himself out of his coma. His eyes opened so suddenly, Janice drew back in surprise.

"Maryellen," he said, his voice husky.

Janice bent down close to his head and lay a calming hand on his shoulder. "Who is Maryellen, Captain?"

Coleman blinked rapidly several times before turning to the nurse. "Where am I?" His throat was scratchy and raw.

"You are in the Veterans' Memorial Hospital in Baltimore. You've been in a coma. The doctor will be here soon to explain things to you."

Coleman closed his eyes, too tired to think about what the nurse had just told him. A coma? For how long? He tried to shut his brain down, to fall back into oblivion, but he could not. Dormant for so long, his brain had kicked into high gear, despite his exhaustion. The crash. There had been a crash. Was he the only survivor? He did a mental check list of his body, his eyes still closed, moving his right leg easily, but finding his left leg immovable. Opening his eyes, he groaned when he saw his bandaged leg suspended slightly above the bed. Everything else seem to be in fine working order.

He was still gazing at his leg with disgust when a woman with fuzzy red hair and startling blue eyes approached the bed. "I'm Dr. Hanley, Captain. Welcome to the land of the living. I just want to test some basic responses. Do you know your name?"

"Captain Coleman Brennan."

"Your birthday?"

"October twenty-eight. Doctor, my brain appears in fine working order," he said, letting some impatience creep into his voice.

Dr. Hanley smiled. "It seems to be, yes. But it is not uncommon for coma patients to have memory loss, Captain."

She leaned over, flashing a penlight into each eye. She touched his right leg. "Feel that?" Getting a positive response, she grabbed a toe on his left leg. "And that? Good." After a series of pokes and prods, Hanley appeared satisfied. "We'll do more extensive tests later and get you into physical therapy as soon as possible. Your muscles atrophied just a bit while you were in coma. We'll take things slowly, but you should be back to normal physically in about a month or less." Hanley smiled.

"The crew. What happened to them? Do you know anything about what happened?" Coleman croaked out.

Hanley's smile turned into pursed lips. "Lieutenant Colonel Bertsch has been notified of your condition. He's flying in from D.C. tomorrow A.M. He'll brief you then. I'm not putting you off, Captain, I simply do not have any answers for you. One other member of the crew is in this facility, a Lieutenant Dumont."

Coleman creased his brow. "Dumont? The woman?"

"Yes. Apparently she made a similar recovery. She woke just a few minutes before you did." Hanley hesitated, as if debating whether she should say something.

"Do you know Dumont well, Captain?"

"I met her just before climbing aboard the helicopter," Coleman said. In a flash, he remembered the nightmarish images and odd joy that leapt into him when he touched Dumont's hand. And he remembered taking her hand in his as the helicopter spiraled to the ground, but he said nothing to the doctor.

His answer seemed to intrigue Hanley, but she remained silent. "One more thing, Captain. Just before you awoke, the nurse heard you call out for a Maryellen. Is that someone whom we should contact?"

"Maryellen?" Coleman mentally went through a list of girlfriends he'd had over the past two years, but came up dry. Shaking his head, "I don't know any Maryellens."

"Oh well. If you would like to call family or friends, feel free to," Hanley said, nodding to the bedside phone. "Your parents kept up a pretty intensive vigil in the first two weeks. They were out of their minds with worry. And I've never seen such a contingent of friends—male and female." Hanley was trying not to laugh at Coleman's obvious discomfort.

He grimaced. "Yes, well, I'm a popular guy." He had no doubt who some of the women had been who visited him as he lay unconscious, and the thought of some of them hovering over his helpless body was downright disquieting.

Hanley left as Coleman was picking up the phone and headed across the hall to Claire Dumont.

"Lieutenant, I'm Dr. Hanley."

Claire turned her head to look at the doctor, then brought it back to stare once again at the hated acoustic tile. "Hello, Doctor."

Hanley went through the same routine she had with Coleman as Claire listlessly responded. The doctor noted Claire's red, puffy eyes, but said nothing. But she couldn't help thinking how odd it was that the two patients were reacting to waking up so differently—especially since their conditions had been almost identical during the coma.

"Do you have any questions, Lieutenant?"

Claire almost laughed that someone was calling her by her rank. Oh yeah, real funny. "No."

"Is there anyone you need to call?"

"No. No one." And Claire remembered Sergeant Grenier asking her if she had someone she needed to write to, someone who would care whether she had disappeared. Her answer now was the same, she thought, allowing for a bit of self-pity.

Claire turned her head away from the doctor and stared at the empty bed next to hers. She felt a bit of resentment build when she heard the soft footsteps of the doctor moving around the bed. When Hanley sat down on the vacant bed, Claire moved her eyes to the doctor's and scowled.

"The nurse told me you were rather agitated when you first awoke. Can you tell me what you were experiencing?"

Heartbreak. "I was having a dream. That's all. No big deal." No big deal. My God, Nicholas, you were my everything. You were my life. And now you're nothing but a dream, a chemical reaction in my damaged brain.

"All right." But it was obvious Hanley had not accepted that explanation. "Lieutenant Colonel Bertsch will be here tomorrow to brief you and Captain Brennan."

Finally, Claire's interest was piqued. "Captain Brennan? He's here? Who else is here?"

"Only you and the captain. I don't know about the other crew members, I'm sorry. Lieutenant Colonel Bertsch will brief you."

Brennan. Coleman Brennan. Claire remembered him. In fact, her memory of him was amazingly vivid given that they had exchanged only a few words. But she would never forget his hand, warm and strong and so . . . comforting as it held hers. And his eyes. Gray eyes telling her to be brave, intense and penetrating, looking at her in a way that only Nicholas . . . Claire took a quick breath.

"I'd like to be alone now," Claire choked out, trying

to stop the panic that was building from showing in her voice.

Claire closed her eyes and tried to recall exactly what Coleman Brennan looked like. He was tall and athletic. Like Nicholas. She did not know the color of his hair, for it had been covered by his helmet. But his eyebrows were . . . sandy, his eyes, gray. Like Nicholas's. Claire shook her head in disgust. She had transformed Coleman Brennan into Nicholas Brooks in her dream. It was so obvious, it was almost embarrassing. Mystery solved, old girl, she thought bitterly.

She had an overwhelming need to find out for sure. Claire slowly worked her way to the side of the bed and gingerly placed her feet onto the tile. Keeping one hand on the mattress, she slowly walked toward the foot of the bed, amazed that she was so weak. Looking up, she could see across the hall into Brennan's room, and she shuffled toward her door. Feeling like she was doing something wrong, she peeked into the hallway, looking both ways, then lurched toward the opposite side.

"Hello!"

"Oh God. Oh my God. Nicholas," Claire whispered. She couldn't believe what she was seeing. It was Nicholas, his charming smile, his short-cropped sandy hair, his beautiful gray eyes, his sculpted mouth.

Seeing Claire's distress, Coleman called out, "Is something wrong, Lieutenant? Should I call for someone?"

Lieutenant. Nicholas would never call her lieutenant. Because this man, this mirror image of her husband, was not Nicholas. "No. No, I'm all right. I'm just a little winded," Claire said wearily. Mystery completely solved, she thought. I somehow manufactured a whole other life in my subconscious. She instinctively rebelled against that notion, for the details of that life were so vivid still in her mind, but no other explanation made sense.

"Hello, Captain. How're you feeling?" Claire made her way slowly over to his bed and leaned on it.

"Better than you, I think. Sit down." Claire did, heaving herself up near the foot of the bed. She eyed his suspended leg. "Broke your leg?"

"Ripped the cartilage in my knee." The two were silent for a while. "Lieutenant, you're staring at me."

Claire looked startled. "I'm sorry. You just look and sound like someone I once knew. I feel rather strange, to be honest with you. I don't feel like I'm myself. I feel like I lost myself, as if my real self is still in a coma." Claire stopped, blushing. "I know I'm not making any sense."

"No. You are. Except that's the way I always feel." Coleman laughed, but his expression briefly held a tinge of bitterness. "The nurses say we both made miraculous recoveries. That no one thought we'd come out of this intact," Coleman said.

"I'm not so sure I have," Claire admitted, letting out a nervous laugh.

Coleman sat up a bit, giving Claire his full attention. "What do you mean?"

Claire shrugged. "It's just that I had this incredibly realistic dream when I was out. It was so real. It's left me a bit disoriented." Claire shrugged again and looked at Coleman, seeing only Nicholas. Nicholas was still so real to her and she missed him. But she felt like a complete fool missing a figment of her imagination. It would be so easy just to close her eyes and listen to Coleman talk and imagine it was Nicholas. *There is no Nicholas,* her mind rebelled, even as her heart wrenched painfully.

"Must have been some dream," Coleman said. "You look really shaken. Do you want to tell me about it?"

Surprisingly, Claire realized that she did. "Promise not to laugh," she said, smiling. "It sounds absurd, but I dreamt I was a soldier in the Confederate Army."

So began an hour-long story that both stunned and moved Coleman. He was astounded at the detail of her dream, her recollection of specific conversations, her description of Northford, of the house and the people who were part of her dreamworld. He held her hand when she cried as she talked about the Carr children—she missed them so much—and when she talked about the dream's end, her fight with her dream husband, and the dream's abrupt end.

"It's funny, that last is a bit foggy. I remember our fighting and Nicholas collapsing. Someone came up behind me and . . ." Claire screwed up her face in thought. "It won't come to me. But it was someone dangerous, evil."

When she was finished, all Coleman could say was, "Jesus. That was one hell of a dream. No wonder you're a bit disoriented."

Somehow, Claire's and Coleman's hands had become entwined during her long speech. Looking down, Claire's heart twisted. Nicholas's hands were holding hers.

"I left out one thing," Claire said hesitantly.

Coleman looked a bit shocked. "There's more?"

She let out a little puff of air. "Nicholas, my husband. Well, he looked exactly like you. Exactly."

Coleman grinned, his male ego given a tremendous boost, and Claire threw him a withering look. "I knew I shouldn't have told you that," she grumbled.

Coleman instantly sobered. "No. No. It makes sense. I was the last person you saw before the crash."

"Yes, but . . ." It was the details, the way the irises in his gray eyes were circled by a darker gray, the small gold flecks near the pupils, his beard that came in reddish gold (how could she know that when Coleman was clean-shaven when they'd met?), the crinkles that appeared around his eyes when he smiled. "I didn't look that closely at you."

"Maybe you didn't, but your brain remembered,"

Coleman suggested. Claire sighed an agreement, but she was still skeptical.

"Did you dream at all?" Claire asked hopefully.

Coleman shook his head. "Not that I know of, thank God. The past month is a complete void. Strange, isn't it? To lose an entire month." He snapped his fingers. "It's gone forever."

Claire felt she had lost more than a month. She had lost a life. No, she told herself sternly, you lost nothing.

"You're thinking of that dream. It's really gotten to you, hasn't it?"

Claire smiled that she had been so transparent. "I feel like an idiot. I'm so confused. I'm sure I'll feel better tomorrow. Once it fades, I'll be better." She tried to say it forcefully in an attempt to convince herself, but it was no use. Her intellect rebelled against the idea she had dreamt up Nicholas, just as much as it had rebelled when she first found herself in the middle of the Civil War. "I'm going nuts," she groaned, lifting her hands up to either side of her head.

"Hey," Coleman said, gently taking one of her hands again. "You've just woken up from a coma, for God's sake, give yourself a break!"

"I guess you're right." Claire let out another audible sigh and decided to change the subject. "Did the doctor say when she would discharge you?"

"No, but she said it'd be about a month before I was back to normal. I wouldn't imagine we'll be in here much longer." Coleman yawned. "God, I hate to fall asleep. I've been sleeping for thirty days. I feel like Rip Van Winkle."

"I'm tired, too. I guess I'll leave you alone now. Good night, Coleman."

"Good night, Claire."

And Claire shivered. He sounded exactly like Nicholas the first night she'd spent in her cell. Exactly.

Chapter Twenty-four

"No! Jesus God, no!"

Claire sat up in bed, her heart pounding. Nicholas. Nicholas was shouting. . . .

She heard the voice again, and slowly she became aware of where she was and what she was hearing. It was Coleman, of course, not Nicholas, and he was apparently having some sort of nightmare. She lay stiffly under the sheets for several minutes, straining to hear the sounds from the next room, unsure whether she should see if he was okay. Coleman was moaning, as if he were in some awful pain, and Claire immediately made the decision to see if something was wrong. She carefully made her way to his room, which was only dimly lit. By the time she made it to his bedside, Coleman was awake, his head in his hands. He lifted up his head when he heard Claire, and she almost gasped at the naked pain she saw in his face.

"A bad dream?"

Coleman let out a bitter laugh. "You could say that." He was still breathing hard from whatever plagued his sleeping mind. Claire suddenly felt awkward standing by his bed in her hospital gown. "Should I get someone?"

"No. There's nothing they could do." Coleman

clenched his jaw and swallowed heavily. "God-dammit!" he gritted out suddenly, causing Claire to jump. Coleman looked up at her, having seen her re-action. "I'm sorry. It's just that I hoped the coma would erase something. I hoped . . . I've been having these nightmares for as long as I can remember. Horri-ble things. I wake up every night in a cold sweat."

Claire put one hand on his bed, wanting to take his hand, but was unsure whether it would be welcome. "Every night?"

"Yeah. I can't even drink myself out of it. I've tried, believe me. But I wake up with the nightmare *and* a hangover."

"Have you been to a doctor, some sort of sleep specialist?" Claire asked.

"I've done all that."

Claire gathered up her courage and took his hand. It was oddly comforting to see her hand swallowed up by his. "What are the nightmares about? Are they always the same?"

Coleman immediately bristled. He never talked about his dreams to anyone. He was about to tell her so, when he stopped. This woman had spilled her guts to him just that day, how could he push her aside now?

"They're always the same," he said, his voice low. Claire sat on the bed, her hand still gripping his. "Here, I'll make room," Coleman said and scooted over. Without even thinking a moment, Claire stretched out next to him and they lay there not touch-ing except for their hands as Coleman described his dream.

"There's always blood and screaming, but I can't tell if it's a man or a woman. But that's not the worst part. It's as if someone I love is about to be hurt or is already hurt and I try and try to stop it from hap-pening, but I can't. Something . . . evil is out there and I'm completely helpless, like I'm paralyzed. I look down and my hands are covered with blood. I know you're not supposed to be able to smell in dreams, but I can smell the blood. At least in the dream I can. It's always the same. I look down and see my bloody hands and I know, somehow I know, that the evil thing is me." He stopped letting out a shuddering breath.

"Oh, Coleman. It's every night? How awful."

"It messes me up every time. For a while I thought I was going crazy, but I've come to expect it, I guess. Still. Tonight it seemed more real. Maybe because I had fooled myself into thinking it wouldn't happen."

They lay in silence for a long moment, Claire giving Coleman's hand a squeeze. "No one knows, Claire. No one. I . . . I've never spent the night with a woman because of it."

Claire gave him a shocked look before she could stop herself, and Coleman immediately laughed aloud, knowing what she was thinking.

"I don't mean I'm a virgin. Hardly. I mean I've never spent the whole night with a woman. The last thing I need is to scare the shit out of someone I've just made incredibly happy."

"Oh really," Claire said dryly.

Coleman laughed. "Really." He sobered then. "I keep hoping it will stop. But it never does."

Claire's mind drifted to her own nightmares experienced after her battle. . . . Stop! she silently told herself. Those nightmares, the battles, *everything* was a dream and was nothing like what Coleman was experiencing.

"Cole? Have you ever heard of someone dreaming within a dream? I had nightmares during my dream. I can remember them, but only vaguely, the way you remember a dream. And the funny thing is, they acted like dreams. My nightmares didn't always make sense, but my dream did."

"Mmmmm."

"Cole. Are you falling asleep?"

"Mmmmm."

"I'd better go then." Claire began easing herself away, but Coleman's hand gripped hers more tightly. "I can't stay here," she whispered. "Coleman! Let go!"

"Just a little while," he mumbled. "Just until I fall 'sleep."

"Okay," she whispered begrudgingly. It was only a few minutes before his grip on her hand relaxed and his breathing became deep and even. Still, she lay there, ashamed that she enjoyed his presence. He's not Nicholas, she told herself when she felt herself weakening. He is Coleman Brennan. A stranger, who looked and sounded and smelled—she turned her face and breathed in deeply—yes, even smelled like Nicholas. There were differences. Coleman appeared to be more open, less serious than Nicholas. He talked like a modern man, he smiled more, revealing teeth that were straighter than Nicholas's.

Later, as Claire pulled her own blanket up to her chin, her mind was on the man across the hall. As she sleepily thought about their conversation, she turned slowly to her left side, extending one arm. At that same moment, Coleman turned to his right, his hand outstretched.

Claire woke with a start, sitting up so quickly she felt light-headed. The hospital was quiet, finally, except for the soft snoring from Claire's roommate, an overweight army recruit who had suffered a concussion after a nasty fall on an obstacle course. Claire had been moved to another room, away from the other coma patients. When Claire was moved from the room she had occupied for nearly a month, she stared at the patients in the coma ward, Nurse Pritchard a calming presence beside her, and she felt oddly in commune with them and terribly sad that they were still trapped in their silence.

Her new room looked much the same as the old one, but it was a place where the living recuperated, where the murmur of voices could be heard coming from open doors, where even a groan of pain was a welcome sound. Even a woman's soft snores at one o'clock in the morning.

Claire grimaced, thinking how even in sleep this woman was noisy. She knew everything about Paula Inez, from her favorite foods to her favorite sex position, in a matter of minutes. No matter how many times Claire had said, "You really don't have to tell me this," hoping the gabby woman would get the not-so-veiled hint, she prattled on until Claire thought she'd strangle her.

Claire had a long and tiring day of tests and physical therapy, and her exhausting meeting with Lieutenant Colonel Bertsch. Only she and Coleman had been badly injured in the crash, which was officially being called an accident—and certainly that is what it was. Friendly fire from a panicky second lieutenant brought down the copter far from the demilitarized zone, far from any North Korean.

Both she and Coleman had been given extended leaves to recuperate and regroup and to decide whether a return to military service was what each wanted. For the first time in Claire's life, she was uncertain whether she wanted to be a soldier. She knew what she wanted, she thought morosely.

I want to go back.

Claire, still weak, carefully made her way out of her bed after staring at the ceiling hoping sleep would come. She felt exhausted, but each time she closed her eyes, they had snapped open. I need . . . I need . . .

"Hello." Coleman, smiling a bit sheepishly, hovered outside her door, leaning heavily on a single crutch.

Yes, Claire thought, this is what I need, then frowned at the thought.

"You okay?" Coleman asked after seeing her frown.

Claire smiled. "What are you doing here?"

Coleman could only shrug. He had no idea. In fact, he hadn't known where her room was until that moment or that he had been looking for it. But having come upon her, he knew instantly why he was roaming the halls. He had awakened suddenly with an odd urge to do . . . something. And so he had carefully made his way down the hall, hoping none of the night staff would catch him wandering about, and he had ended up outside Claire's door.

"Where were *you* going?" he asked Claire.

Claire creased her brow. "I think to find you." She sounded a bit amazed at her conclusion . . . not only that it was true, but that she had actually said it aloud.

Coleman didn't seem pleased or perplexed, just accepting.

"We've been through something," he said hesitantly as he backed from the door to allow Claire to follow. "I don't know much about the brain and how it works, but something happened to us."

Claire gave a little shiver, unwilling to give in to the eeriness of his statement. "We both knocked our heads and went into a coma. That's something, all right."

"And woke up within seconds of each other?"

"Yes. A coincidence," Claire said firmly.

"And wake up in the middle of the night, both with some sort of weird urge to see each other? Virtual strangers?"

"But you're not a stranger," Claire blurted before she could stop herself.

"No. I'm not," Coleman said, surprising her. "And

I'm not talking about your dream. I'm talking about this . . . thing that's happening."

Claire shook her head. "Nothing is happening. I'm just confused because you look like Nicholas."

Coleman shook his head in an angry gesture, and Claire had to close her eyes, for in that moment of frustration he had looked so much like . . . No!

"Maybe that dream is just confusing things for you. But I know something is happening. Did that nurse Donna tell you about when we were still under?" Claire shook her head. "They couldn't separate us. We both went spastic or something when they put us apart. They almost had to keep us in the same room together."

"But the regulations . . ." Claire said, trying to maintain some control.

"Of course they couldn't. That's why they had us across the hall from one another. No matter how they positioned us, we turned toward one another. They were afraid we'd develop bed sores on our sides. Turn me on my back, and I turned toward you. It was the same for you. Explain that. I can't. Can you?" Coleman was fierce, and a little bit afraid. He had never been so drawn to another human in his life. It was more than that she was beautiful. It was almost as if she were a part of him, a part that had been missing, but one that God had finally given back. Didn't she feel it? Was he imagining it?

Claire crossed her arms in a protective gesture. "No. I can't explain it. But that doesn't mean there isn't a medical explanation."

Coleman stopped in the hall and placed a hand on each of her shoulders, gazing into her blue eyes with an intensity Claire found discomforting. "You don't really believe that. Do you?"

Claire flared her nostrils and the crease between her eyes deepened. "I don't know what to believe," she whispered. I only know that I want you to hold me right now, she thought. The urge was overwhelming, and Claire, feeling weak and disoriented by their conversation, gave in to it. She stepped into his arms and lay her head against his chest, not caring that this man was nearly a stranger, not caring about anything but that she needed to be held. And somehow, she knew, she needed to be held by this man. She felt his arms come slowly around her, as if the gesture was almost reluctant, and she heard the deep rumble of a troubled sigh.

"My God, Claire," Coleman whispered harshly. "This . . . You feel. . . ."

"I know. I know." She said the words into his chest. She did know. This was right, it was somehow, impossibly right. What was happening to them?

Coleman gently pulled away, then put both hands on either side of her face, and bent for a kiss. It was soft and undemanding and the most beautiful thing either had ever felt. When Coleman pulled away, there were tears in his eyes.

"I'm scared witless," he said with a short laugh.

"Me, too."

Coleman had never felt so out of control in his life. He *did not* act this way. Not over a woman. Not over anything.

"Will you, please, Claire, I know we don't know each other very well, but will you sleep with me tonight. Just for a little while. I just want to hold you." The intense look was replaced by a grin. "At least I'll try just to hold you. I promise."

Claire gave him a speculative look and then a small smile. "Okay."

They walked hand-in-hand back to his room. Folding around each other like spoons, they fell asleep almost immediately. And when Coleman awoke, sweating and shaking from his nightmare, Claire was there for him, to hold him, to comfort him and whis-

Chapter Twenty-five

It wasn't fading like dreams should. One week later, Claire felt the same ache, the same heart pain she had felt the first day she awoke and realized she was back home. Except this time, this place no longer felt like home. She kept it to herself, knowing that had she shared her dream, she'd have been put in the psychological ward and would be on her way to a Section 8. No one knew. No one except Coleman, and even he did not know the extent of it.

How I miss them, Claire thought, visualizing Nathan, Mabel, and Emily. Even if they had been real, they were long dead now, hardly remembered even by relatives, nothing but old-fashioned people wearing old-fashioned clothing in faded sepia-toned photographs. Were they real? Had they lived? How could I have dreamt in such detail, Claire thought. I can still remember their laugh. When I close my eyes, I can still smell Nicholas's scent wrapped around me. Oh, God, please let me go back—even if it means back to a dream, even if it means I am insane.

Claire sat in an orange vinyl-covered chair near the hospital's entrance, her knees pulled up tight against her body, ignoring the chitchat going on around her. Certainly Coleman's parents found her rather strange, this solemn woman whose eyes always appeared to be on the verge of tears. She knew they darted quick looks at her and wondered what their boisterous son could possibly see in her. She wanted to scream: "This isn't me. I'm a happy person. But everything I've ever loved is gone."

Coleman needed more physical therapy on his knee, but had insisted on being discharged and becoming an outpatient. Claire, discharged the day before, spent a sleepless night in a Marriott, fighting the almost overwhelming urge to return to the hospital so that she might be with Coleman. She had actually gotten dressed, pulling on stiff new jeans and a T-shirt, and touched the room's door before pulling back. "He is not Nicholas," she had said out loud. But she knew in her heart she was going to Coleman, not Nicholas. That it was Coleman she wanted to hold—and to have hold her. It was guilt that kept her in that room, she finally admitted to herself. Loyalty to a figment of her overactive imagination.

Claire lifted her head when she heard Coleman's voice. She watched, a small smile on her lips as he gave both his mother and father an enthusiastic hug.

"Who are you all again?" he asked, feigning confusion. But at his mother's worried look, he laughed and hugged her again.

"Don't you dare do that again," his mother said, giving him a cuff on his shoulder.

Claire swallowed thickly when his smiling gray eyes searched her out. God, he's beautiful, she thought. She wondered if she would have thought so if she hadn't had her dream and decided, yes, she would think him beautiful. She would think him breathtaking.

"Claire." He held out one hand to her and Claire unfolded herself from the chair and approached the happy group. Feeling safe once his arm drew her close to him, she said to his parents, "I'm sorry I wasn't much company to you when we were waiting. I still feel a bit out of place."

"Of course you do, Claire," Mrs. Brennan said kindly.

Mr. Brennan cleared his throat. "Thought we'd take you both out to dinner. To celebrate."

Coleman felt Claire stiffen almost imperceptibly next to him and he felt a sharp pang of protectiveness toward her. "No, Dad. I think Claire and I need to be alone right now. We're going to her house in Virginia for a few days. To regroup."

At a disappointed sound from his mother, Coleman said, "I know you've been looking forward to my getting out of this place, but I think right now I just need to be with Claire."

"All right, Coleman. It's just that you were taken from us. And now you're back." Mrs. Brennan covered her face, embarrassed by the sudden tears that appeared. "I'm sorry," she said, laughing a bit. "You two go on. Stop by in a couple of weeks. When you're ready. You're welcome, too, Claire."

Claire bit her lip, thinking of her own mother, who would have reacted in much the same way—except perhaps her mother would have gushed a few more tears. "Thank you."

Claire grew up in a beautiful row house in the Old Town section of Alexandria. Her parents had renovated the Queen Street house long before it had been in vogue to do so, meticulously scraping away years of paint and grime from the neglected home. She had warned Coleman the house had been unoccupied since her family's death. Until now, Claire had been unable to return, afraid seeing the familiar old place would be too overwhelming. But somehow now instead of tears, she felt a smile on her lips. It was good to be home, good to see her parents' favorite things, good to feel close to them again.

"You okay?" Coleman asked, searching for signs this homecoming would be too much.

Claire let out a long shuddering breath. "Yes. Better than I thought I'd be. God it's so dusty. My mother would have a fit if she saw it." Claire drew a finger along one end table, grimacing at the thick layer of dust that had settled there.

"It's a beautiful place."

"Yes. I'm glad I came here," Claire said forcefully. "It puts things in perspective. *This* was my home." Claire felt anchored. That horrible feeling of floating between two worlds diminished the moment she stepped into the foyer. Memories flooded her head. Real memories, of people who had existed and events that had actually happened.

"You look . . . relieved."

"Oh, I am. C'mon. I'll give you the grand tour."

Coleman's mood also lightened. He had never seen Claire look so carefree. It made her even more beautiful. Since that day in the hospital hallway, Coleman had not kissed Claire, although they had managed to sleep together nearly every night, at least part of the way through. More than once he had awoken during the night immediately and painfully aware of the soft feminine form sleeping next to him. If she ever noticed what he thought must be his obvious and rather embarrassing desire for her, she gave no indication.

They made their way up a curving staircase to the second floor, Coleman trailing a bit and struggling with his new metal cane, where yet another staircase led up to a third floor. Long and narrow, the rooms were also both elegant and inviting despite the grime that had accumulated.

"This was my room," Claire said, an odd expression on her face.

Coleman took in the white eyelet curtains, the delicate white wicker rocking chair, the canopied bed. "It's so . . ."

"Feminine," Claire finished. "I know. I'm a psychiatrist's dream. You should see how my fatigues looked draped on that vanity. I've always had a girlie room. I don't know why."

"Maybe because you are a girl." Coleman said, his voice suddenly gruff. Claire looked at him then and saw the raw desire he didn't bother trying to hide. She felt it, too, God knew she did. But . . .

Coleman advanced toward her, not caring that her eyes suddenly looked wary. He stopped inches from her, his face looming over hers, causing Claire to tilt her head up. His eyes searched hers for some sort of answer, any sign that he was welcome. He waited, his mouth just inches from hers, his lips hard, his eyes burning. He must have read something in her blue depths, for he suddenly turned away, roughly taking a hand and rubbing the back of his neck.

"I want to know why," he bit out, turning his head in an almost angry gesture so he could better hear her answer.

"I hardly know you. I . . ."

"No. Not good enough," Coleman said, spinning around to confront her. "We know each other better than most people ever do. Not good enough, Claire. I want to know why."

"I told you. It's. . . ." And she stopped, her eyes glued unseeingly to a distant corner, she shook her head slightly. "I'm not ready."

"Because of him? Because of Nicholas?" Coleman didn't want to say it, for the thought that the woman he loved could be in love with someone from a dream was unthinkable.

"Yes." It was no more than a whisper. Claire closed her eyes. So much for putting the dream behind her. Coleman began to walk out of the room. He could not fight a dream, and he did not want to. It was insanity.

"Please, Coleman. Don't go. I'm sorry."

Coleman turned to her, his face hard. "It's been

more than a week, Claire. I'm trying to understand what you're going through, but it's not easy. It was a dream. Nicholas doesn't exist."

Claire tugged nervously at the front of her T-shirt. "I know. I know it's crazy. Maybe I'm crazy. But, Cole, it was all so real. As real as this is. I'm afraid I'll wake up and you'll be gone. I don't want to . . ." I don't want to love you, Claire thought. I don't want to lose someone else.

"You don't want to what?"

"I don't want to fall in love with you," she whispered, her eyes filled with pain. Her admission seemed to calm Coleman and was as soothing to him as a declaration of love.

"But you will. Because it's already happened to me, Claire. I love you."

Claire shook her head back and forth, letting out little puffs of air. This can't be happening, she thought desperately. She felt Coleman's hands gripping her shoulders.

"Claire. Why is that so horrible? I have never in my life told a woman that. You don't know what . . . You've no idea." Coleman stopped again, unable to lay himself exposed before her, not when she was looking at him as if the last thing she wanted was for him to love her. He had thought that something connected them, something more than physical attraction or a shared tragedy. Maybe he was making too much of it all. Maybe he just wanted so much for her to love him, he was willing to convince himself of any fairy tale.

Defeated, Coleman stepped away once again. But this time, there was no anger in his stance, no challenge in his smoldering gray eyes. "All right, Claire. I'll try to be patient. Maybe I'm the one who's crazy."

"No, Cole, not you. And not me either. I've just . . . been through something. I need time. But I need you here, Cole. Please don't leave." God how she needed him, so much so she didn't care if she sounded weak or pathetic. She only knew that he must stay. It was a physical need to have him with her.

Coleman drew her into his arms, wrapping himself around her, and she sighed against his chest. "I love you, Cole," she said, her words muffled against his shirt. "And that scares the hell out of me."

Coleman pulled back enough so that he could look down and read her face. "Did I just hear you correctly?" He wanted to whoop aloud in joy, but knew that admission had somehow frightened her even more.

"You heard me," she said, a bit grumbly now. "But I just want to make sure . . ."

"That it's me you really love?"

Claire looked up at him, amazed at the understanding she saw in his eyes. "Oh, God," she said miserably. "I know it's crazy. I know."

"Yeah. And I'm probably just as crazy to wait for a woman until she figures out it's flesh and blood she loves and not some dream man," he said, more harshly than he meant. "I'm sorry, Claire. It's just that I look at you and I want to make love with you. I want us to be everything."

Claire gave him an impish look. "Maybe we could start off slowly. How about a kiss?" Claire lifted her face up to his, heard him let out a small groan, then felt his wonderful lips upon hers. She had meant to give a warm, affectionate, slightly more-than-a-peck kiss. But as soon as her lips touched his, the heat between them grew at an almost frightening rate, taking them both by surprise.

This was a mistake, she thought wildly. For it was as if they had been kissing each other for a lifetime, as if they each knew what the other craved. Never in her life had Claire experienced such immediate and fiery desire. Pressing into each other, their mouths were melded together, tongues probing, exploring, twisting together. Coleman cupped her buttocks and pressed her against him, unable to stop wanting what he knew he could not have. At least not yet. But when he brought a hand up to her breast, when he passed his thumb over one erect nipple and heard her whimper in pleasure, he was nearly lost.

It was Coleman who pulled away, his eyes burning, his breath labored and hot against Claire's cheek. "Claire. God, Claire, if we don't stop now . . . I want you so damn much."

Claire was almost too stunned by her reaction to his kisses to respond coherently. "Wow. I didn't expect . . . I don't want to stop either, Cole. But . . ."

Coleman tensed, trying to stop the flood of anger that surged through his body at that "but." "We don't have to," he said, but pressed against her, contradicting his own words.

Claire felt if they shared just one more kiss she would surely melt into him. She wanted him, every cell in her body cried out for her to continue. And yet, she was afraid of what she was feeling, of what she was thinking, afraid that she was somehow betraying Nicholas's memory. She did not want to give herself to someone completely, and then be left alone. If she gave herself to Coleman, it would be the last time she gave herself to anyone. Her heart, still so fragile, could not stand to lose another love.

"Cole, Cole," she said, kissing his neck, tasting him, her hands kneading his shoulders in an almost desperate way. "I want to make love to you." This time, she left the "but" unsaid, but it was there just the same and Coleman couldn't help but let out a strangled moan. Claire stepped back, her hands lightly resting on his chest.

"I'm pretty sure I'm a virgin," she said, shamelessly falling back on her untouched state to cool his ardor—and hers.

"Pretty sure?" Coleman asked, and couldn't help but smile just a little.

Claire bit her lip. She was quite certain she did not lose her virginity while in a coma with a man who did not exist. "I'm a virgin," she said with more force.

Coleman was unprepared for the surge of possessiveness that swept through him. She is mine! he thought, allowing some primitive male emotion to rule his senses.

"I'm glad," Coleman said, his voice deep.

"I know you love me," Claire began hesitantly. "And it's not as if there is some religious meaning to my present state, at least not entirely. I never even put much thought to it. I've never cared about anyone enough to even think about making love. Not even close. With you, it's more. Suddenly it's become important. Do you understand?"

"I think I do." Coleman placed his hands on either side of her neck, his thumbs caressing her jawline. "I want to marry you, Claire, not just make love to you. I want to hold you every night until I die. I never thought I'd want that with anyone. I thought there was something wrong with me." He let out a bitter laugh. "But, my God, Claire, this thing between us is almost scary."

"I know," Claire said in a small voice. Marriage! That frightened her more than anything. For what if something went wrong? What if this was just another dream?

"What do you say we get married, Claire?" Coleman's attempt at making his tone light would have worked if Claire hadn't looked into his intense gaze.

Coleman swallowed his disappointment and anger as he watched her shake her head.

"Let me work through some things, Cole," Claire said when she saw his face harden. "You don't want a wife who's still screwed up in the head, do you?"

Coleman let out a short laugh, but his eyes were

still bleak. "Okay, Claire. We'll wait. To make love,
to get married. But I can't promise the marriage will
come first. Fair enough?"

Claire hugged him to her, squeezing her eyes shut.
"More than fair."

Claire lay in bed, staring blankly at the ceiling, and
listened to the partyers from the King Street pubs
make their way noisily to their cars. Coleman slept
through it all, oblivious to the drunken laughter and
the tense woman sleeping next to him. She bit her lip:
Don't think about it. Don't think about it. But she
could not stop her thoughts from traveling to that little
town where she had "lived" all those months. She
could almost smell the honeysuckles mingling with the
salty-fresh air, so unlike the musty smell of the Poto-
mac that flowed not one mile away.

Claire eased out of bed, careful not to disturb Coleman and tiptoed to the door. But once out of the
room, she ran down the carpeted stairs to the small
study that still carried the lingering scent of her father's pipe. Turning on the light, Claire went immediately to the large bookcase that contained, among
other things, an atlas of the United States.

"It probably doesn't exist," she said aloud. Wiping
sweaty palms against her cotton robe, she took in a
mighty breath to calm her loudly beating heart. Flipping through the pages, she stopped at Rhode Island
and began scanning the list of towns with a
trembling finger.

"Oh my God," she whispered when she saw Northford listed. Her eyes darted to the map of the tiny
state, following the coast, praying that it was there.
And praying that it was not. Claire had never been to
New England, had never even heard of Northford before slipping into the coma.

When she spotted the town, no more than a little
dot and a word on a map, she pressed her palm against

her mouth to stifle the sob that erupted. Breathing in and out harshly, Claire stared at that little spot until her eyes burned. "Okay. It's there. It exists. Oh my God. Northford exists!"

Could that mean that Nicholas existed? That the rambling old colonial, the dusty, tree-lined street, the little beach . . . could they all exist? She had to find out. She had to put this to rest. Grabbing the map, she ran up the stairs, puffing from the exertion, and rudely flipped on the overhead light in her room.

Coleman immediately woke up. "What's going on?" he said, sounding as grumpy as he was, squinting against the bright light.

"It exists! It's here," Claire said, slapping the atlas. "I'm not crazy. At least not completely crazy."

"That's debatable," Coleman said, still shielding his eyes from the light. "What's this all about?"

Claire plopped down on the bed and placed the atlas in front of him, her finger near the word "Northford."

"See?"

Coleman slowly focused on that word until the meaning of what she was showing him slammed into his still-sleepy head. And something else happened as they stared at that word, at the town that hugged a body of water called Narragansett Bay. Fear. It tingled along his scalp, it twisted in his gut. The feeling was gone so quickly, Coleman was able to dismiss it as excitement for Claire rather than fear.

"It's just where I thought it would be, Cole. Exactly where. I've got to go. Tomorrow. I've got to find out," Claire said forcefully.

"I'll go with you. It is amazing. You've never been to Rhode Island?"

"Never."

"You might not find anything, Claire," he said.

"I almost hope I don't. I don't know what I'll do if

it's just as I remember. What if it's all there? The
town, the house. Where if I was really there?"

Coleman shook his head. "But that's impossible."

Claire wrapped her arms around herself to stop a
shiver. "I know it's impossible. But I just have this
feeling that it's all there. And if it is . . . I'm afraid,
Cole. I'm afraid I'm going to find out that everything
really happened. And then I'm really going to go off
the deep end."

Coleman chuckled and kissed her forehead creased
with worry. "I'll be there to catch you," he said.

Chapter Twenty-six

Coleman swallowed the sickening bile that kept rising to his throat, physical evidence of the near-paralyzing fear that had gripped him ever since they reached the little village of Northford. He was nearly oblivious to Claire's excited chatter as she pointed out landmarks she recognized.

"That used to be a bank. I'm sure of it," Claire said, pointing to a three-story brick building that now housed the town's small newspaper. "And that's the telegraph office. At least it used to be. Cole, pull over and park. This is incredible. Unbelievable."

Claire was beside herself, her brain overloaded by everything she saw, and everything it meant. Some buildings were gone, the street was now paved, and intermingled among the old buildings were some twentieth-century structures looking oddly out of place. But it was Northford, the Northford of her dreams, where she had lived and loved a man named Nicholas Brooks. Claire was so excited to find she had not imagined such a place that she refused to think of what all this meant. She didn't notice the fine sheen of sweat on Coleman's face, the sick pallor, his silence, so consumed was she by what she was seeing.

Coleman eased the car to the side of the street, his

hands gripping the wheel so tightly his knuckles shone white. His breathing was rapid and shallow as he tried to fight the fear, the incredible fear, that brought him close to screaming. Clenching his teeth and shutting his eyes, he willed his hands to open and forced his body out of the rental car. My God, he thought, what the hell is wrong with me? With sickening dread, he closed the car door, its bang sounding impossibly loud in his pounding head. For the first time, Claire noticed something was wrong and felt ashamed.

"Are you okay, Cole? You look horrible."

Leaning one hand on the roof of the car, Cole said harshly, "I feel pretty horrible, too. Like some sort of goddamn anxiety attack or something. Jesus." He closed his eyes, not wanting to take in the surroundings, not wanting to look at the quaint buildings crammed along the tree-lined main street. They were all terribly familiar. And they shouldn't be. He had not dreamt of this town. He had never been to Rhode Island. But he knew without looking that at the end of this street was a wharf and a street that would be lined with graceful homes overlooking Northford Cove.

Claire came around the side of the car and led him carefully to the sidewalk. "Cole, what's wrong?" He could only shake his head. It was insane. As insane as Claire falling in love with a dream man—and as impossible.

"If I'd known this would bother you so much, I never would have brought you."

He shook his head again. "It's not that," he moaned, his head feeling as if an ever-tightening steel band were wrapped around it. Claire led him to a park bench stationed outside the local barber shop and helped him sit down. He looked at Claire finally, and she almost gasped. His eyes were filled with the same utter emptiness that filled them after one of his nightmares. Truly worried now, Claire put one hand behind his neck in a comforting gesture. "My God, Cole, *what's wrong?*"

"It's this place," he said, his voice hollow. "Claire, I . . ." He rested his head on one hand, his elbow on his knee, and gazed at the concrete sidewalk. "I've been here before. I know this place. As well as I know my hometown. As well as you apparently know it."

Claire felt a tingling in her scalp. "What do you mean?"

"I don't know. All I know is this is all familiar." He began pointing out various shops, mostly tourist places with knickknacks, T-shirts, and antiques. "Post office. Bank. Bait shop. Tailor. Bakery. Stationer."

Claire blinked, following his finger as he pointed out the various stores that no longer housed the businesses he rattled off. Though once they had. "Am I right?"

Her voice sounding small and frightened, Claire asked, "How?"

Coleman swallowed the bile once more as his eyes strayed to the alley between what was now the newspaper and a small boutique. "I don't know."

The crease between Claire's troubled blue eyes deepened. "Could you have had a similar dream in your coma and not remembered it until now?" she asked.

Coleman shook his head. "Not a dream. A memory."

"But that's how I feel about my dream. It seems more like a memory to me. It seemed real," she said stubbornly.

His eyes strayed to the alley again and he began to shake.

"C'mon. Let's walk." Claire pulled him up and they walked down a serene-looking street lined with colonial houses. Little historical markers were tacked onto most of the homes, with the dates and names of the original owners. Claire felt almost detached from her body, and when she looked over to see how Coleman was doing, she was so overwhelmed by the image of Nicholas, she swayed and her knees grew weak.

"Down that street," she said.

"The house," Coleman said woodenly. Claire gave Coleman a startled look, but remained silent. The street ended at a small cove, just as each knew it would, and to their left, set back from the road, was the Brooks home, looking much as it did as they remembered it. Even the drive was still unpaved. In unison, they began walking toward the old house, noting a small addition and other changes. The house appeared to have been carved up into small apartments.

Coleman stared at the house, almost in a trance. His gaze went to a small portion of the house, a section that was two stories, not three, with windows banking the southern side. He smiled.

"Maryellen," he whispered, his smile widening.

Claire's head turned to Coleman sharply. His eyes appeared glazed, and she found that smile oddly disconcerting. "Cole?" She touched his sleeve lightly, not wanting to disturb him. He turned toward her, his eyes crinkling in pleasure. "Maryellen." Claire shivered.

"Cole!" she said sharply, hoping to bring him back from wherever he had just traveled. Coleman blinked rapidly. "What," he said, irritation in his voice.

"You were in a trance or something."

"Don't be ridiculous," he said. Staring at that house just for a moment, he had felt peace wrap itself around him like a mother's welcoming arms.

"This is weird," Claire said, her voice tinged with fear. "I don't know what's happening, but I don't like it. I want some answers. This is not normal. We should *not* know this place. And yet we do. Both of us do." Claire folded her arms angrily. She felt out of control, as if she were being manipulated by some sadistic puppet master.

"What do you suggest?" Coleman asked, his gaze still riveted on the house.

"That we find out who the hell Nicholas and Maryellen were."

Claire wrinkled her nose at the musty smell of the records room in the town hall. The clerk had happily showed them the bound volumes with vital statistics for the 1800s; he was used to having genealogists perusing the old records. Except for a lawyer who sat scribbling at a table, the long, narrow room was empty.

Spying the 1865 volume, Claire pointed it out. Her stomach roiled nervously as Coleman heaved the thin bound book from the shelf. They sat across from the lawyer and stared at the volume as if it were about to turn into a writhing snake.

"Oh, this is silly," Claire said and opened the book. They were immediately assaulted by the smell of old paper and dust. The volume was broken into three sections: marriages, births, and deaths, all duly recorded in a beautiful script.

"Marriages first," Claire said, trying to keep her voice calm. "We ... *They* would have been married in July. July seventh." She turned the fragile pages slowly, both from fear of tearing them and fear of what she might find. The clerk had written only one entry that day: "Brooks, Nicholas to Hastings, Maryellen."

Claire had told herself she would not see her name there, but seeing Nicholas's name tied to another nearly knocked the wind out of her. "It wasn't me," she said in a small voice.

Coleman stared at that name Maryellen for a long moment. "Of course it wasn't," he said kindly. "It couldn't have been."

"I know." But tears swam in her eyes just the same. She looked at the entry again. Maryellen. My God.

"You've said that name, Cole. Maryellen. You said it after one of your nightmares and you said it again today when you were looking at the house."

"What?"

"Maryellen. That's the name you've been saying. And in my dream, I was mistaken for a Maryellen in the prison camp," Claire said excitedly, as if she had made a great discovery. The thing was she didn't know what she had discovered yet. "Does that name mean anything to you?"

Coleman was about to give an automatic no, but he stopped. Maryellen, he thought, and he smiled a smile so close to the one he had smiled outside the house, Claire shivered. "It's so strange," Coleman finally said. "I feel happy and incredibly sad. It that possible?"

"I'm starting to believe anything is possible, Cole," Claire said as she began flipping to the deaths. "This might be more difficult to find," Claire said, moving her finger through July, scanning the page for the name Brooks. She stopped suddenly on August eleventh. "There she is." Suddenly Claire remembered the alley. I must have died that day, she thought. Oh, poor Nicholas.

Coleman was unprepared for the assault on his senses, seeing the entry on Maryellen Hastings Brooks. He wanted to weep, cry out a denial, but stopped himself, realizing how foolish it was to mourn a death that had occurred more than one hundred years before. The death of a stranger. "I wonder how she died," he said, his voice tight with emotion.

"I think she was killed," Claire said. "In the alley near that newspaper. It used to be the post office."

Fear nearly smothered Cole. "Why do you say that? How could you possibly know that?" He knew he sounded nearly hysterical, but he didn't care. He ignored the irritated look the lawyer threw his way.

"Because that's where *I* was when my dream ended," Claire said. "Let's see if we can find Nicholas, though he could be anywhere." Claire tried to remain detached, tried to remind herself that she was looking for the death of a person she did not know. But when she found his name, recorded just two months after Maryellen's, she gave a little cry and folded her head into her hands. Oh, Nicholas, she thought, I miss you. As ridiculous as that thought was, it was true. She felt Coleman's hand drift to her shoulder and give it a squeeze. "I understand," he whispered into her ear and kissed her cheek.

The whir of the microfilm was grating on both their fried nerves as they scrolled to the August twelfth edition of the *Northford Times* in the town library. Claire sat in a yellow plastic chair that reminded her of grammar school, and Coleman hovered behind her, one hand resting gently on her shoulder as they both peered at the tiny type.

"Here is it," Claire said with a touch of triumph as her eyes scanned the page. It seemed to be filled with nothing but advertisements for Dr. Whitney's Elixir and Houston's Fine Whale Bone Corsets and the like, as well as nonsensical stories that had nothing to do with the news of the day. Moving to the next page, Claire adjusted the focus on the old machine when Coleman jabbed out a finger. "There!"

The headline, which seemed almost as long as the story, read: *Shocking News! Local Hero Falls! Admits to Murdering Southern Belle Wife!*

Claire, her eyes riveted to the flowery story, began shaking her head. "No. That's not right. That's not how it happened." Her lips moved soundlessly as she read the reporter's account. "Found with a dripping shard of glass in his hand, his wife's bloodied, nearly decapitated body by his side, local war hero Nicholas Brooks could do nothing more but admit his heinous crime to Chief Preston. With confession in hand, Chief

Preston regrettably told the citizens of Northford that execution was certain."

Claire closed her eyes trying to remember that horrible day. They had been fighting, true. But then Nicholas had been overcome by one of his headaches. And someone . . . Yes! Someone had come up from behind. Someone . . . Who? Someone evil. She remembered a voice in her ear, a horrible voice that had paralyzed her with fear. Cunningham. My God, it was Niles Cunningham. And Nicholas died believing he had murdered her!

Claire turned to share her revelation with Coleman, but he was nowhere in sight. Then she heard a strangled whimper coming from her right. Huddled in a corner, staring at his hands in utter horror, Coleman let out another almost inhuman sound of anguish.

"I've murdered Maryellen. I've murdered my love," he said, staring at Claire blindly.

"No. No. You didn't, Nicholas. You didn't kill me. Cunningham did. You were innocent."

Coleman looked at Claire, still not seeing her, seeing another woman. "Maryellen?" he said, his voice strangled and incredulous.

Claire swallowed. "Yes, Nick. It's me. You didn't kill me. You must believe that. You must."

"No. I would never. How could I kill my love? Would be like killing myself, wouldn't it. Ah, God, Mar, I was so afraid. So afraid." Coleman clutched Claire to him blindly, burying his face against her neck, letting out sobs of joy.

"I know. I know." Claire clung to him until he calmed, her mind racing. This cannot be, she told herself. It was not possible that Coleman could be Nicholas. And yet, she knew in her heart she held Nicholas in her arms. And he held Maryellen.

Coleman finally calmed and brought his head back to look at Claire, who gave him a tentative smile.

"Cole?"

"Yeah." She could tell by his tone, that he was aware of what had just happened. "Man, I'm drained," he said, letting out a humorless laugh.

"Well," Claire said, a bit of mischief in her voice, "you just traveled one hundred, thirty years back and returned."

Coleman shook his head. "It's impossible."

"Apparently not. It explains an awful lot if we were them." Just saying it aloud seemed so ridiculous. And yet . . . "There's no other explanation. Except I still don't know what happened to me. I still don't know if it was just a detailed dream or I actually was living that life. Or reliving Maryellen's life." She added more forcefully, "I was here, I fell in love with a man named Nicholas Brooks. I know I did."

Coleman put an arm around her. "Hell. No wonder I fell for you hook, line, and sinker. No wonder you were so damned confused. Jesus. No one's going to believe this. I'm not even sure I believe it."

Claire moved to sit beside him on the floor, one hand resting on his thigh. "It needed to be resolved. Nicholas needed to know he didn't kill me . . . I mean Maryellen. That's why I went back. When there is that kind of love between two people, I guess it doesn't die." Claire shivered.

"The nightmares." Coleman said. "All those years. How tortured he must have been. My God, to die believing he had killed the woman he loved. How he must have suffered."

Claire leaned her head against his shoulder. "And how you suffered."

They sat in silence for a long time, each lost in their own thoughts, their own memories. "Do you think we have to get married again, or do you think the old wedding is valid?" Coleman asked, laughter in his voice.

Claire, pretending to consider the question, rested

her chin on her hand. "Oh, I think we'll have to do it all over again."

Coleman smiled. "Is that a yes?"

"Yup."

"Good," he said, giving her a chaste kiss.

"I was thinking. . . ." Claire said, looking at him from the corner of her eye.

"About?"

Claire blushed, she actually blushed, and Coleman was charmed. "Kids."

"What about them."

"Well. I was thinking. If we were to have, say, a boy and a girl, what do you think of the names Nicholas and Maryellen?"

Coleman gave her another kiss, this one long and lingering. "I think, future wife, those are two of my favorite names."

WE NEED YOUR HELP
To continue to bring you quality romance
that meets your personal expectations,
we at TOPAZ books want to hear from you.
Help us by filling out this questionnaire, and in exchange
we will give you a **free gift** as a token of our gratitude.

- Is this the first TOPAZ book you've purchased? (circle one)

  YES   NO

  The title and author of this book is: _____

- If this was not the first TOPAZ book you've purchased, how many have
  you bought in the past year?

  a: 0 - 5   b 6 - 10   c: more than 10   d: more than 20

- How many romances in total did you buy in the past year?

  a: 0 - 5   b: 6 - 10   c: more than 10   d: more than 20 ____

- How would you rate your overall satisfaction with this book?

  a: Excellent   b: Good   c: Fair   d: Poor

- What was the main reason you bought this book?

  a: It is a TOPAZ novel, and I know that TOPAZ stands
     for quality romance fiction
  b: I liked the cover
  c: The story-line intrigued me
  d: I love this author
  e: I really liked the setting
  f: I love the cover models
  g: Other: _____

- Where did you buy this TOPAZ novel?

  a: Bookstore   b: Airport   c: Warehouse Club
  d: Department Store   e: Supermarket   f: Drugstore
  g: Other: _____

- Did you pay the full cover price for this TOPAZ novel? (circle one)

  YES   NO

  If you did not, what price did you pay? _____

- Who are your favorite TOPAZ authors? (Please list)

- How did you first hear about TOPAZ books?

  a: I saw the books in a bookstore
  b: I saw the TOPAZ Man on TV or at a signing
  c: A friend told me about TOPAZ
  d: I saw an advertisement in_____magazine
  e: Other: _____

- What type of romance do you generally prefer?

  a: Historical   b: Contemporary
  c: Romantic Suspense   d: Paranormal (time travel,
     futuristic, vampires, ghosts, warlocks, etc.)
  d: Regency   e: Other: _____

- What historical settings do you prefer?

  a: England   b: Regency England   c: Scotland
  e: Ireland   f: America   g: Western Americana
  h: American Indian   i: Other: _____

- What type of story do you prefer?
    - a: Very sexy
    - b: Sweet, less explicit
    - c: Light and humorous
    - d: More emotionally intense
    - e: Dealing with darker issues
    - f: Other

- What kind of covers do you prefer?
    - a: Illustrating both hero and heroine
    - b: Hero alone
    - c: No people (art only)
    - d: Other_____

- What other genres do you like to read (circle all that apply)

    Mystery   Medical Thrillers   Science Fiction
    Suspense   Fantasy   Self-help
    Classics   General Fiction   Legal Thrillers
    Historical Fiction

- Who is your favorite author, and why?_____
  _____

- What magazines do you like to read? (circle all that apply)
    - a: *People*
    - b: *Time/Newsweek*
    - c: *Entertainment Weekly*
    - d: *Romantic Times*
    - e: *Star*
    - f: *National Enquirer*
    - g: *Cosmopolitan*
    - h: *Woman's Day*
    - i: *Ladies' Home Journal*
    - j: *Redbook*
    - k: Other:_____

- In which region of the United States do you reside?
    - a: Northeast
    - b: Midatlantic
    - c: South
    - d: Midwest
    - e: Mountain
    - f: Southwest
    - g: Pacific Coast

- What is your age group/sex? a: Female b: Male
    - a: under 18
    - b: 19-25
    - c: 26-30
    - d: 31-35
    - e: 36-40
    - f: 41-45
    - g: 46-50
    - h: 51-55
    - i: 56-60
    - j: Over 60

- What is your marital status?
    - a: Married
    - b: Single
    - c: No longer married

- What is your current level of education?
    - a: High school
    - b: College Degree
    - c: Graduate Degree
    - d: Other:_____

- Do you receive the TOPAZ *Romantic Liaisons* newsletter, a quarterly newsletter with the latest information on Topaz books and authors?

    YES   NO

    If not, would you like to?   YES   NO

    Fill in the address where you would like your free gift to be sent:

    Name:_____

    Address:_____

    City:_____Zip Code:_____

    You should receive your free gift in 6 to 8 weeks.
    Please send the completed survey to:

Penguin USA•Mass Market
Dept. TS
375 Hudson St.
New York, NY 10014